Tony was doing a steady 75 mph approaching the intersection. He saw the red lights before he saw the damn fire truck. With his siren blasting, the concentration on the stolen vehicle, and the lights from the two units behind him, it was amazing he could hear anything.

Tony was looking for a way out of the path of the fire truck. Swerving right and giving the unit immediate and hard acceleration might do it. Braking wouldn't make it. If he braked, he'd sure as shit get t-boned.

Tony pressed the accelerator hard. The stolen Toyota's brake lights lit up like a Christmas tree. Tony had two choices, brake, or rear-end the Toyota. Instinct kicked in. Tony braked hard. The unit was specially designed for this sort of situation. The Crown Vic held its traction. The Toyota lurched forward. The driver braked intentionally knowing it would put the fire engine and the police unit in an unavoidable collision path.

It did just that. The fire engine was unable to stop, and Tony was in its path. It caught the rear end of the Crown Vic and twirled it around like a spun nickel.

THE RESERVE

Stuart Cannold

5 Tom Publishing - Sierra Vista, Arizona

THE RESERVE

Stuart Cannold

This is a work of fiction. Names, characters, places, and incidents either are the product of the author's imagination or are used fictitiously. Any resemblance to actual persons, living or dead, names, events, or locales is entirely coincidental.

ISBN# 979-8-9873080-0-4

Edited by Elly Stevens

Book layout & cover design:
Keith Davis
Goose Flats Graphics
Tombstone, Arizona

Published by
5 Tom Publishing
Sierra Vista, Arizona
www.5TomPublishing.com

Published in the U.S.A.

5 Tom Publishing - Sierra Vista, Arizona

DEDICATED TO THE UNIFORM

Somewhere in my Arizona home is a framed picture which tells the story of commitment, loyalty, dedication, passion, courage, perseverance, and selflessness. The picture depicts the image of a uniformed cop, gun at the low ready, walking down a pitch-black alley. The caption reads: "You wouldn't do this for a million bucks. A cop does it for a helluva lot less. A reserve does it for nothing!"

Most reserves do the job for nothing. Maybe they get a uniform allowance. They're lawyers, teachers, plumbers, cops' wives. Some eventually go full time. Many remain reserves throughout their careers.

Years ago, my second field-training officer (God, please rest Loy's soul) said to me, "When the bad guys see you and me side by side, he doesn't look at you and see three digits on your badge, pinpointing the only difference on your uniform, and my two-digit badge. The wacko doesn't know you're a reserve. He'll take us both out, given the chance. Your job is to drop his ass before he drops yours.

A reserve goes through the same training as a full-time police officer. He goes through the Academy. He goes through field training. He puts his pants on the same way a full-timer does, one pant leg at a time. The blood he bleeds is red, just like a trainer's blood. A reserve buddy of mine, who did go full time, got into a shootout his first night out as a reserve. He dropped the perp; didn't kill him but put a round in him. The suspect fired first—and missed.

It's too damn bad he didn't kill the prick! If that last sentence offends you, this book might not be for you.

The very best fifteen years of my "work" life were the years I spent as a reserve police officer. I never met better people in my life than those who wear the uniform, those who train the reserve. My first marriage was shredded basically for two reasons. One, I was rarely home. Two, I was an asshole. I sometimes put in more hours monthly than a full-timer. I loved police work. Take cops off the street and you have no street—you have chaos.

My second wife would go on ride-alongs with me. She observed her first two bodies riding with me. She became a volunteer, a damn good volunteer. She knows of the good I did. She knows some of my fuckups and disappointments. Like most cops' wives, she'd be frightened shitless when the phone rang in the middle of the night and I was at work. That phone call, that knock on the door, is the fear of every cop's spouse. If I had it all to do over again, I'd become a full-time police officer. Those ten-, twelve-, sometimes fourteen-hour shifts, were more exciting than the best blowjob I ever received. (Except, of course, from you, babe. You're the greatest. And I loved the blowjob in the police car! Thanks!!)

Let's wind up this crap so we can get to the reserves story, that is, if you're still reading and/or if you're wearing the uniform. Be it the armed forces or the police, the border patrol, etc., I'll take a bullet for you. You're my hero.

I dedicate *The Reserve* to all who wear the uniform, to all who protect our freedom, to all who put their lives on the line daily for us. Thank you from the bottom of my heart. When you see a police officer, say hello to her or him. Tell the officer you appreciate him. I promise you, he'll never forget it.

I hope you enjoy *The Reserve.* I welcome your feedback. You can reach me at my website: **5tompublishing.com**. Thank you.

God Bless our men and women in uniform.

SPECIAL DEDICATION

Every so often, someone enters your life and leads you down the right path when all appears lost.

Years ago, I purchased a 1957 Ford Thunderbird E-Code, sight unseen. The seller was upfront about the Bird's description. He didn't know what he sold me, and I didn't know what I purchased. About 1490 E-Birds were built by Ford, and approximately, ten percent or 149-plus were three-speed with overdrive. I bought a three-speed with o/d Bird.

Good for me. I didn't have the money to restore her. I had no more garage space. She sat in the backyard waiting for my Restoration Specialist Extraordinaire to find me.

Tommy Youngblood found me. I was at a car show. I was admiring a 50s truck, and I'm not a truck guy. This tall, soft-spoken, friendly guy with a smile walked up to me. "Gorgeous truck," I said. "I wonder who did the body work."

He said, "I did."

I asked, "Who did the paint work?"

"I did."

"Did you also do the woodwork in the truck bed?"

Tommy nodded. "I'm Tommy Youngblood of Youngblood Customs in Tehachapi, California. We do it all. We're a one-stop shop."

After the show, we drove to my home. Tommy checked out the Bird. "She needs more than a total restoration."

I shook my head up and down. "And then some. Money's tight." We worked a deal, pay as you go. It took Tommy and his team two years to restore my Baby Bird. When the work of love was done, she was as perfect as you're going to find. Every nut and bolt were replaced as it should be. The gunmetal grey paint shined like a streetlight after a rainstorm. The red interior was spotless. The engine was better than factory. Wow!

We entered her in Thunder on the Mountain Car Show in Tehachapi, a compilation of 300 hundred cars of every description. She took Best in Class. Then she took Best of Show. We took her to San Diego for its first Concours d'Elegance, and my first Concours, too. She won a Gold Award. She missed top honors, a Gold Medallion, by ½ point. Tommy and team tweaked her. We didn't do the New Jersey Concours nor the Tennessee Concours. We moved to Southern Arizona. The next Concours was in Flagstaff. Tommy, my Restoration Specialist, was at the banquet table when she won another Gold Award. Then we were called to the stage for the Gold Medallion, top honors. My wife saw the tears in my eyes as we accepted the Gold Medallion.

Tommy and team resurrected that Little Bird. Tommy, you ARE my hero. I remember you daily as I look at the awards she won over the years. You are a master of your craft. You are an artist, a perfectionist! Today, my Baby Bird graces a car museum at the Riverside in Laughlin, Nevada.

I said "are" because I know you are now doing restoration work for God. He needed a vehicle restored. When you left us so suddenly on October 15, 2021, you took a big chunk of me with you. I have a strong hunch we will see each other again. You gave me years of joy and you brought an ailing Bird back to health.

Thanks, Tommy Youngblood. Rest in Peace, brother. I dedicate *The Reserve* to you.

ACKNOWLEDGEMENTS

I cannot count the number of people who had a hand in the creation of this book. My beautiful wife Jo encouraged me to take my shot. I did, and I completed what was less of a task than I thought. I actually had fun, although some of the memories will always be painful.

Chief Randy Narramore gave me the opportunity to wear the badge, to sit in front of the black and white, and wrote me a letter underscoring perseverance which hangs on my living room wall. Thank you, Chief.

My second FTO, my friend, my mentor who always had my back, Loy Cleveland you died too damn early, buddy. You're missed. Thank you for hanging in there with me.

Elly Stevens edited this six-year-old manuscript and led me on the path to publication. Elly, a writer of mysteries, and I met online after we read each other's books. Although 2700 miles apart, and although we've never met face to face, we're friends. Thanks for your guidance, Elly.

A great big thank you to Tombstone's Keith Davis of Goose Flats Graphics and Publishing for the cover design of The Reserve, for the page layout, and for building and designing my user-friendly, and attractive website.

This novel would never have come to fruition if it weren't for the men and women who wear the badge. I have never met more courageous, more dedicated, and more caring people than those who wear the uniform. If you haven't walked their streets, if you haven't driven their black and white, you can't know the suffering, the pain, the fear, the memories entranced in their minds forever.

I will never forget my FTO taking me under the yellow crime-scene tape to show me a gangbanger dead behind the wheel of his car.

He had been hit by bullets eleven times. You don't forget that. Nor will I forget opening a backyard gate and immediately focusing on a young teenager, rope around his neck, hanging from a tree. You don't forget those tragedies.

I will never forget the PCP suspect who I damn near shot to death who managed to get my baton. I chose to fight it out, and eventually, he was cuffed and stuffed!

There's a family unit among badge holders that I have never known before and will never again know. Only we know what you think you know.

I am spiritual, not religious. I heard a priest say, "Religion is manmade. Spirituality is God given. I found God in the back of a police car with my hands cuffed behind my back. Yes, I really was one of "those." I lived to drive the black and white. I have an earned doctorate but, by far, the most difficult, the most challenging journey was the destiny to that badge. Today I proudly carry a department retirement badge.

I thank God for this book. I thank God for my journey I thank God for carrying me when I was lost. My loving God sits on my shoulder, and He has a sense of humor. He drives the unit. His badge number is ONE!

And finally, police work today is a far cry from what it was ten years ago. Make no mistake about it, if we didn't have men and women protecting our streets, we would have no streets. You are my heroes. God Bless You!

CONTENTS

Who's Getting Schooled? - 1

Monday, 7:50 a.m.: It's Now or Never - 5

Same Monday, 1:30 p.m.: Grass in Your Class or Secreted Up Your Ass - 11

Wednesday Morning: SAM F - 20

Friday Morning - 22

Spit, Shit, and a SCAR - 24

More Sanity on the Streets Than the Damn School - 34

Screwed But Not Kissed - 46

Money-Making Proposition - 49

Let's Make a Deal, or My Way or the Highway - 53

A Package Deal - 57

Does It Ever Stop? - 67

The Beat Goes On, and On, and On... - 81

More Fun and Games - 83

A Wet Wednesday at Work - 110

Panties or No Panties - 115

You Hit Bottom When You Stop Digging - 117

More About Mick - 121

Whatcha Gonna Do When They come for You? - 125

This Job Ain't for Pussies - 133

Breakfast with Mick - 139

What It's Really About - 145

R and R - 147

You Don't Fail Until Until You Quit Trying - 150

Back in the Saddle - 155

And Now, a Word from My Sponsor - 159

You'll Do What and for How Much? - 165

Dead Drunk - 174

Home Sweet Home - 179

ACLUH8R or ACLULVR - 183

There Is a Way Out - 187

Friday Night at HP - 195

Life's Little Problems - 210

Fighting Fire with Gasoline - 212

A Change of Pace - 227

Yolis for Dinner and, Hopefully, Dessert - 235

Complications - 246

Decisions, Decisions, Fucking Decisions! - 267

More Decisions - 285

Are the HP Reserves in the History Books? Is Yolis History? - 294

Back at the Ranch - Both Ranches - 307

Friday, Fucking Friday - 327

A Man, His Best Friend, and His Woman - 334

Another Ride in a Black-and-White - 338

Lawyer up! - 348

Don't Get Pissed, Get Even! - 355

One Door Closes: Another Door Opens - 371

About the Author - 376

Other Books by the Author - 378

Who's Getting Schooled?

FLACOE is an acronym for the Father Lincoln Anthony Corrections Office of Education. FLACOE, whose main office is in Downey, California, operates schools for minors who are incarcerated for criminal offenses. The schools are public schools, and FLACOE has its own school board. The schools are accredited by the Western Association of Schools and Colleges, WASC.

FLACOE operates twenty facilities for incarcerated minors. Three of those schools are inside the walls of juvenile halls. The remainder are inside "camps." A juvenile hall is analogous to a jail; the camps are (for all intents and purposes) a prison.

If an adult is arrested, that adult is transported to jail, pending the outcome of his case in court. If convicted, he might be sentenced to prison time. The same process is in place for a juvenile. The facilities have walls and fences around them. The Probation camps are "manned" by Probation staff. The FLACOE schools are autonomous—the schools and Probation staff work independently; however, to function at maximum for the sake of the student/wards, Probation and school staff must interact. It is hoped that the interaction will be positive. That isn't always the case.

Each and every FLACOE facility for these kids has air-conditioned classrooms, televisions, cameras, and credentialed teaching staff. Each Probation facility also has a swimming pool for the incarcerated minors. Most of the teachers bust their collective asses in an attempt to educate the incarcerated minors who come to school via Probation staff each day of the week at approximately 8:00 a.m. and leave via Probation staff at approximately 2:40 p.m. daily. Some of the teachers who don't bust their ass for the kids are a problem for school administration, Probation staff, and the kids. This isn't the rule; it's the exception. When a teacher gets "rambunctious," administration is supposed to take control of the ship and steady the course. Too often, administration is too lazy to do the necessary paperwork, or is friends with the offending staff member or both.

When a juvenile is arrested, he/she is transported to a juvenile hall. One of FLACOE's juvenile halls is located in Downey; another, about 30 minutes north of Los Angeles in San Fernando; and one is in downtown L.A.

The most recently built facility, the John F. Kennedy School, is about an hour north of Los Angeles in Lancaster. The facility is the size of three football fields and can house 700 juveniles, from lightweight offenders to heavy hitters. A GTA (grand theft auto) can land a juvenile at JFK for three, six, or nine months. A juvenile convicted of aggravated assault or attempted murder can earn the ward a nine-month sentence.

Most of these kids are repeat offenders and are gang involved. Many are drug and/or alcohol abusers. Make no mistake, although most of these kids have spotty education, they are far from stupid. FLACOE brags about some of their students going on to college and beyond. A couple have returned to FLACOE and to Probation for challenging careers. Unfortunately, most do return to Probation and to FLACOE. They are recidivists.

Tony Farrina grew up on the east coast, Brooklyn, on Flatbush Avenue, when the Brooklyn Dodgers were still losing games at Ebbets Field. The likes of Roy Campanella, Duke Snider, Jackie Robinson, and Gil Hodges were some of Tony's heroes. Tony would have given a big piece of his right arm to play professional baseball. Unfortunately, he never made it past Babe Ruth ball, and, at that, he wasn't very good. His best year he batted 222.

Tony was one of the kids in this facility. Tony never made it to juvenile hall, but he did have an arrest record. He managed to turn his life around and he wanted to do the same for these kids. The major difference was, when these kids were incarcerated, they were "forced" to attend school daily. After a couple of weeks, many showed a spark in their eye. They held their heads higher and could write home that they were matriculating and might even earn a GED or a high school diploma. Then the reality of life stung the juvenile like a wasp. When it was release time, instead of going back to school, they returned to the same gang-infested environment. Most of these kids were screwed.

Tony was out of his house at eighteen. He went to college in New Hampshire, earned his master's at Oakland University in Rochester, Michigan, and taught school in Detroit for two years. In exchange for his teaching skills, the government paid for Tony's credentials and degree.

Making his way west, away from his family, Tony finally landed in southern California in 2016. The truth be known, it was most likely Jack Webb and Dragnet that, like a magnet, pulled Tony west. He also hated the Michigan snow, and southern California had no snow. Tony knew at once he was home.

The tough schools of Detroit were not enough of a challenge for Tony. FLACOE, however, was a natural for him since he had a knack for dealing with tough kids, and FLACOE's kids were really tough. Tony was not so much tough as he was smart, and he truly cared about the kids and about education. He was called "TF" by those who liked him. It was a perfect fit.

Well, almost a perfect fit. Eleven months before, Tony was the acting principal (AP) at a nearby camp. Twice, he had been offered the principal position without an interview. Twice, he told Director Stanton that he was flattered but not interested. Principals worked extremely long hours. APs worked 7:30 to 4:30. Tony liked the shorter hours because it gave him a chance to play at his first true love, police work. Besides that, the principal's salary was only $4500 more than an AP made annually, not figuring the tax bite; it was no contest for Tony. TF was not looking to climb the chain of command; he was happy being an AP.

When Tony turned down the principal slot the second time, he was transferred to the JFK Probation Camp in Lancaster, named after several U.S. presidents. There were six dorms where the boys were housed at night and six corresponding school designations, each named after one of the presidents Lincoln, Washington, Reagan, Roosevelt, Clinton, and Nixon. The Nixon dorm was changed to Obama in 2010.

Tony was informed by the FLACOE director, "The American Civil Liberties Union has taken over the facility and we need a strong administrator to keep staff and students in check."

First, Stanton asked Tony to go voluntarily. When Tony politely said no, Stanton said you're going anyway. Tony, always ready with his sense of humor, said, "In that case, I volunteer."

Monday, 7:50 a.m.: It's Now or Never

Tony looked across the ball field to the camp dorm. The kids were lining up to come to school. Tony shut down his computer and walked past the secretary's desk to the door that led outside. Not all administrators were outside helping to supervise the movement. Tony, however, was all "administration" and kept his eyes on the kids. He took pride in everything he did. If he was shoveling dog shit in his backyard, he did the very best he could do. If he was counseling a kid who got kicked out of class, he gave the very best advice he could give. Tony expected the same of all the staff at the school; unfortunately, that wasn't always the case. If the staff under Tony's watchful eyes were derelict in their duties, Tony sat them down. He believed in progressive discipline, which was a helluva lot easier and a helluva lot cheaper for FLACOE to correct negative action than it was to fire a staff member. It also took hundreds of pages of paperwork and more hours than often necessary. Tony was tenacious. If he had to move for dismissal of staff, he wasn't afraid of it. He knew how to get the paperwork done. It was Downey and the expensive suits that sometimes stalled, or buried the process.

In addition, FLACOE at Downey was publicity shy. If there was a chance the newspapers and/or the news might get wind of an unfavorable story about the staff, Downey would fold and pay off the offending teacher. It beat negative publicity. The suits once paid for a PITA teacher to go to law school rather than fire her. Cheaper, faster, and no publicity.

Tony vehemently disagreed with that philosophy and believed in transparency. He felt that, if one or two staff members who had it coming were dismissed, a message would be sent to the others. Unfortunately, Tony often barked on deaf ears. While he had the reputation for being straight-up honest, a straight-shooter, staff who didn't want to do the job to the best of their ability often didn't like Tony. They didn't call him "TF." They had another name for him—"MF."

Probation marched the kids across the field, one dorm at a time. Each dorm housed approximately 100 juveniles who were dressed in white t-shirts, blue jeans, and tennis shoes in the spring and summer and sweatshirts or windbreakers in the fall and winter. When one group of students entered class, the next group started across the field. The entire process, from initial movement from the dorm to the chair in the classroom, could take twenty to thirty minutes depending on the demeanor of the kids. One fight on the field could cost an hour or two of school.

A slow, steady pace across the field was standard operating procedure because it was not uncommon for the kids to get into physical altercations. Supposedly, there was a ratio of 15 kids per Probation staff. Unfortunately, the ratio ended up being like thirty-plus kids to one Probation staffer. Dangerous, very dangerous, and the kids took every advantage of the lack of staff.

As the last student entered a Lincoln classroom, the Obama kids paraded across the field. As ninety-plus kids closed the gap on the school, Tony winced. Somebody in the group was yelling, "Short assed mother fucker!" Tony tried to identify the offender. Impossible. It appeared from where Tony stood that all the kids' lips were moving with the words, "Short assed mother fucker."

The comment was meant for teacher Roger Rabinowitz, also called "Roger Rabbit" by some of the students. They didn't like Mr. Rabinowitz because he would take it out on the kids, who would heckle the shit out of him any and every chance they got. The more frazzled Roger got, the more the kids laughed. Unfortunately, Roger played right into their games. He'd go off like a firecracker.

Roger stepped away from his classroom door. His arms were waving wildly. He yelled to the Probation staffer, "Take 'em back to the dorm! They're not ready for school. Take them back and settle them down." Roger's suit jacket was blowing in the wind.

The Probation staffer stopped the line in its tracks. The kids were laughing hysterically. They didn't want to go to school anyway. Plus, the culprit couldn't be nailed, and the kids had another notch to punch in their belts.

Tony got on his portable radio. "Brenda," he called to one of the school secretaries. "Can you send the floater to the front of the east office, please?"

"I'm on it, sir."

The floater was a substitute teacher hired for no specific classroom but to be used as needed. This was an "as needed" situation.

Tony talked on the radio as he walked toward Rabinowitz, manning the group of kids who were standing almost motionless on the grass. Roger was pissed. "You wanna fuck around? You're going to pay the price! For every minute you're late for class, we're taking three minutes away from your activity time."

There were muffled chuckles from the line. The kids knew that they could file a grievance with the Probation Director if Roger tried to enforce his threat, but, of course, Roger was bluffing. That chip had long been cashed in. At one time, Probation could be punitive with the kids. No more. At one time, Probation could add "time" to a student's program. Now it took a judge's approval. The probation world was upside down. Most of the country was upside down.

Tony smiled. He spoke softly to the Probation staffer who liked and supported him. They knew Tony would do everything in his power to get the kids into class as expeditiously as possible.

Next, Tony motioned to Roger. "I'm buying coffee. C'mon in my office, Rog."

Tony's office was small, but neat with carpeting and bookshelves. The AP's office was mostly glass. On his desk was a computer, two telephones, a radio charger, and a picture of his current girlfriend and another of his Norwegian Elkhound, Lieutenant.

Roger was shaking his head as he sat down in a wooden chair with a cushion. He added a grin to the head shake. "I can't deal with that behavior. They're not ready for school! They're off the chain!" he protested.

Tony knew better than to interrupt Roger. He let him vent.

"Nobody does anything about the disrespect from these kids. They do it in front of you, in front of me, and in front of Probation. Nobody sees anything. Nobody hears anything. Nobody does anything."

Tony picked up the phone. He punched an inside button. He waited. "Roni, I need a favor. Can you check the east-side cameras? During the movement in front of Lincoln, on the grass a couple of hundred feet from Roger's classroom, some of the kids were mouthing off during the movement. I'd like to know if we can identify any of the kids. There may be just one or possibly more. I'm not certain."

Each classroom had state-of-the-art video and audio. Unfortunately, the "state of the art" of some of the kids was, too. They managed to render several of the cameras inoperable.

You might ask yourself how the kids could do that with supervision in the classroom. The answers were numerous. These kids were masters of deception. They could shield a student who wanted to get to the cameras by getting in front of the teacher so he couldn't see. They needed a few quick seconds to do their damage. The rule was, only one student at a time out of his seat and then only with the teacher's permission. Some of the teachers found it difficult to control many of the kids. If there was a sub in the room, good luck to the sub! After school hours, Probation sometimes used the classroom for activities, guest speakers, meetings with the kids. Sometimes a staffer got distracted with a cell phone conversation. It took a split second for the damage to be accomplished.

Students managed to get into staff purses and steal cell phones, neither of which were allowed in the classroom.

At one time, the facility was co-ed. Whoever had that idea should find another profession. One teacher, a former track coach and a personal friend of Tony's, was helping a student at his desk. He looked up in time to see a female student "finishing off" a male student. Tony knew the deal all too well. He took pictures of the sperm stains and used it in the report to discipline the teacher. The teacher accepted full responsibility. Shortly thereafter, a 16-year-old girl got pregnant. That's when the girls were moved to another facility. It was a Probation staffer who got the girl pregnant! He was terminated, arrested, charged, and convicted. The story made the *Los Angeles Times* and the 6 o'clock news, the 9 o'clock news, and the 11 o'clock news.

"I understand, Rog. I don't like how far left things have gone either, but they have a habit of swinging back toward the middle."

"You see it from an admin's point of view. Being in the classroom is a completely different animal."

Roger was dead on. If the shit hit the fan, Tony could take a breath and think things through. The classroom teacher had to think on the run; and these kids could be monsters. "No argument from me," Tony said as he squeezed the knot in his solid blue tie. It was a nervous habit. "Let's talk about short ass mother fucker."

Before Roger could respond, Tony's in-house phone rang. "Thanks, Roni. I appreciate it." Tony swiveled in his chair. "Nothing on the tape."

Roger smiled. He was cooling. "What do you want me to do?"

"You gotta take the kids. If we can figure out the player, I'll suspend him and call home. We can have a meeting and/or a phone conversation with whosever at home, the culprit, you, Probation, and me. Does that work for you?"

"Do I have a choice?"

"Remember the Pledge of Allegiance? You wanted to suspend a student because he wouldn't stand for the Pledge?"

Rog nodded. "And you politely reminded me that the Court upheld that all the student has to do is remain seated respectfully. As long as he is not disruptive, nothing can be done. What the hell is this world coming to?"

Roger stood up just as Tony's outside line rang. Leaving Tony's office, Roger headed for his class.

The kids weren't in Roger's class fifteen minutes when Tony's phone rang again. Tony knew there was a problem when he saw the phone line light up telling him it was Roger calling. "I've had enough. They won't quit with this short-ass-mother-fucker shit. It's driving me up one wall and down the other. I'm going to walk them around the track a couple of times."

"Did you notify Probation?"

"No, I didn't notify Probation. I've been too busy trying to figure out who the hell is saying it."

Roger was too far gone to reason with him. Tony called Probation and asked that a staffer accompany Rog and the class around the track. He also asked that, when the kids returned to class, a probation officer (PO) sit in the room for a short time. Tony would check in the camera room and see if he could identify the responsible parties.

Same Monday, 1:30 p.m.: Grass in Your Class or Secreted Up Your Ass

His lunch consisted of two cups of coffee and a banana. Tony did take ten minutes, while sipping the first cup of coffee, to access eBay on his computer. Hell, it was supposed to be his "duty-free lunch."

He was into classic cars and owned a 1930 Ford Model A Police Car with machine guns mounted on each window. The cop car wasn't authentic, but it sure looked good and was always a hit at car shows. Inevitably, he would be asked if the machine guns were real. Tony's response was always the same: "Just the one behind the driver's seat!"

Tony received a call from Mrs. Martin in Room 8 who thought she smelled marijuana. Tony walked to the classroom on the pretext of delivering a school transcript to Mrs. Martin. There was no doubt that someone in the room had been smoking the shit. That meant that someone in the room had matches and/or a lighter. Dangerous.

After he returned to his office, Tony notified the Probation Director while Roni checked the cameras. Tony and two probation officers walked back to classroom 8. One of the two POs entered the room and Mrs. Martin stepped outside.

Tony smiled. Mrs. Martin was a seasoned FLACOE teacher with 22 years of service. She had seen most everything in those years of teaching for Corrections. "Any ideas?"

Mrs. Martin was in her fifties, 5' 7" and fit. She wore her black hair short. Today, she had on tennis shoes and brown slacks, appropriate for the setting. "I smelled it from the back of the room, but the joint could have been passed around. You know how that goes."

Again, Tony smiled. She knew her kids. He suggested, "Why don't you grab a cup of coffee? PO Jefferson and I will find out who was smoking."

It wouldn't be difficult to get the kid or kids who were smoking. Finding the shit would be a different situation. The stuff could be secreted anywhere, literally. Since Tony was on the school staff, pat downs or searches were out of his bounds—that was left up to the POs who had police status. Still, Tony had a trick or two in his pocket.

Tony opened the door to Room 8. He motioned to the student closest to the door. He stepped outside without incident. "Had a few puffs?"

The kid shook his head. PO Jefferson looked on.

"Blow on my hand."

The African American student, who looked like a linebacker, shook his head. Tony held up his right hand. The kid blew. "Harder," Tony insisted.

The kid blew harder. Tony held his hand to his nose. Nothing. "Go see Mr. Jefferson." Mr. Jefferson did a quick pat-down through the kid's clothes. Nothing.

Mr. Jefferson got on his radio. He called to another staffer in an empty classroom, "Hawker!"

That PO stuck his head out the door as Tony warned the student, "If you have anything on you, son, give it up now. Mr. Hawker is going to strip search you, and if he finds anything, it's going to go harder on you for lying."

That was a load of crap and the kids knew it. Very little would happen to the ward if he did get caught with the shit. There was so much of it in the facility that the kids could start their own business.

"I ain't got shit." The student walked up to Mr. Hawker then disappeared into the classroom.

Tony called out a second student. He repeated the scenario. Another blank. PO Jefferson did a pat-down. Zilch. The final stop was PO Hawker.

The eighth kid was Tony's first hit. The kid was a skinny Hispanic, 5' 6" and 135 pounds if he had rocks in his pockets. Tony held up his left hand. "Blow."

The student snarled at Tony, "Fuck you."

Jefferson was on the kid like a snake on a mouse. He grabbed the student by his not-so-white t-shirt, lifted him off his feet and put him against the block wall. Jefferson was at least 6' 1" and a good 220 pounds. The Hispanic kid's face looked like white bread. "Apologize to the principal," he demanded.

The kid's feet were off the ground. He stuttered. "I'm sorry, sir. I'm really sorry. I was smokin' but I don't have the weed."

Jefferson let go of the ward. "Blow on Mr. Farrina's hand."

The kid had been smoking. "Who gave you the joint?"

He shook his head. "Can't give him up. I gotta live in the dorm."

"We'll check the cameras."

"Go ahead."

Tony knew the cameras wouldn't give him anything. If Roni had found anything, she would have called him.

Jefferson patted the kid carefully, then sent him to Hawker.

It took another hour to complete the smell test, the pat-down, and the "skin search." When it was over, the team found no matches, no lighter, and no grass. Tony had four positives for smoking. This didn't make Probation any too happy. Probation guidelines mandated that these three kids had to be transported to the hospital to be checked out. A minimum of two POs would be assigned to the transport team. The Camp would be two POs down.

The fact that the team came up empty meant the stash was most likely hidden in the classroom. Tony and a couple of POs would initiate a classroom search.

Monday was maddening to say the least. They spent two hours searching the classroom and found a few contraband pens, some gang letters, a lot of tagging, but no marijuana and no cigarette lighter. That meant either the "cleaning crew" was derelict in their search of the classroom, or the kid(s) smuggled the shit out of the classroom, which really wasn't all that hard to do when you thought about it. There were so many places a student could hide marijuana and a cigarette lighter on himself that a PO may never discover them despite a thorough search.

During another classroom search that Tony had conducted with Probation, Tony found a poem written by one of the young scholars:

Today I think I'll come to class.
I secreted marijuana in my ass.
In my sock is a cigarette lighter.
During math my mind will get brighter.
When you think you caught me smoking,
I'll tell you and the PO you must be joking.
I'll yell, I'll scream, I'll cuss you blind.
I'll tell you you're out of your fucking mind!
Don't pick on me because I'm black.
I know the ACLU is coming back.
'Cause I'm Hispanic you're accusing me.
Check the cameras then you'll see.
I'll bring my contraband to your class.
Even when the POs search my ass.
I'm slick, I'm cool, and I'll break the rule.
I don't need your freakin' school.
So let's continue to play hide and seek.
I don't give a shit; I'm leaving next week!

And the general public thinks these kids aren't too bright. The sad fact is that these kids are damned intelligent, but their focus is in the wrong place. The environment adds to the problems, and a lack of parental supervision is another key factor in the failure of most of these kids. That's not to say they can't overcome these problems; but it's like being in quicksand. Once the sand gets above your knees, it's pretty much over.

Tony finished his report on the marijuana caper at 4:45. He faxed a copy to the regional director, placed a copy on the principal's desk, faxed another copy to the Probation Director, placed one copy in the file of each student who had been caught, and a copy in his own file. If and when the case went to court, Tony had his own report to refresh his memory.

So much for getting out of work on time. But it was about to get later.

One of the ACLU monitors, one of the groups of three assigned to JFK to see that the staff didn't infringe on the "rights" of the juveniles, was an African American man, Cleveland Archer. He was petty and by the book. He would stand on the edge of the grass where he could observe the kids going to school. If they were two minutes late, he would make note. The kids had to have 240 minutes of education per day (4 hours).

Archer was big, meaning he was 6' and probably 260 pounds. His voice was not deep, but his tone was deliberate and exact. He didn't speak until he thought about what he was going to say and then he savored those words. Tony had met very few people who could be intimidating with his voice. Most of those people were attorneys or cops. Archer was neither. He had been a teacher in a Colorado school for high achieving kids. That made little sense to Tony. If you wanted to accomplish change, why place someone on the site to monitor the comings and goings of the facility who had no experience with these kids? Then again, who said the ACLU wanted anything to change?

Just as Tony put on his blue suit jacket, Archer knocked on his door. The door was opened. Tony was tired but he remarked, "Hey, you're here late."

Archer chose his words carefully. "I'm not the only one. Can I come in for a minute?"

Tony wanted out. He wanted to go home and feed Lieutenant. "Of course. Have a seat."

Archer entered. He didn't sit. "I'd like to get a copy of the report on the marijuana incident."

Archer must have thought Tony was stupid. He could have easily obtained a copy from Probation. Tony took his jacket off and hung it on the hook on the back of his door. He uncovered the computer then rebooted it. "Give it a minute to reboot and I'll run you a copy." Then to prove to Cleveland that he wasn't totally ignorant, Tony asked, "What else can I do for you?"

Archer must have been a helluva' poker player. His face didn't crack. "How are you going to handle the boys who got caught? Are you suspending them?"

Tony didn't hesitate. "It's in the report. Each is suspended from school for three full school days." Then Tony added, "At this point."

Archer put his big round ass in an upholstered chair that barely held his weight. "Then there is room to negotiate?"

Tony was tired. He hit CNTRL+P on the computer. You could hear the printer working as it printed out the report. "How about we discuss the situation."

"I'd like to see the kids remain in school. They need their education."

Either Archer hadn't done his homework, or he was playing games. Tony suspected he was playing games, and he wasn't in the mood. He was hungry. Lieutenant probably was, too. "Suspension or not, the kids will be in school. If the suspension stands, the kids will go to SHU School. Same building. Only difference between regular school and Special Housing School is that the SHU classroom has a probation officer in it and a second adult assistant to help the teacher. The kids will get more remediation."

This was beginning to look more and more like a power play. Corrections wanted site administration to play ball with the ACLU so they'd sign off, eventually saying everything that needed to be corrected at JFK was indeed corrected.

Archer looked at Tony, who took five pages out of the printer, stapled them, and handed them to Archer. Tony rubbed his chin. Archer couldn't argue with Tony's explanation. The kids wouldn't be missing school.

He looked at Archer's face. Tony studied it. You could almost hear the fucking rocks in his head banging together.

"I hate to see the kids pulled out of the dorm and sent to SHU."

The SHU, or Special Housing Unit was designed for kids who made bad decisions, who screwed up. SHU was a group of small rooms in a separate building. The rooms were void of everything but a bed and a chair. Each student was assigned his own room. Every twenty minutes or so the kids were let out to watch big screen TV, play ping pong, counsel with a probation officer, or talk with one another. The SHU had a stigma attached to it only because it demonstrated that the offender had been caught by staff breaking a rule. The ward had "lost."

"The fact is the kids were smoking in class. At least one of them had a lighter or matches. This is a locked facility. Shouldn't we be more concerned with how contraband enters the facility?"

Archer tried to stare Tony down as if his face were a weapon. He didn't intimidate Tony—not one damn bit. If the kids were suspended and not coming to school, Archer would have a point. That wasn't the case.

Archer tried to shift in the chair but there was no wiggle room. He wasn't wearing a tie. Instead, he was wearing a white shirt under a tan sweater. He fingered the collar of the shirt. "I understand where you're coming from." Archer stopped to frame his next words. It was a long pause. "Can we not suspend? Can we put them in the substance abuse program and see if that turns the tide?"

Tony inhaled slowly. He held it for a five-count and then slowly let the air out. Tony repeated that action for a three-count. It actually works to calm an individual and clear his head.

Tony knew the three kids. The three were troublemakers. He quickly weighed the pros and cons. If he gave them substance abuse as opposed to suspension, or suspension and substance abuse, he would be building a case if they got caught a second time. It was progressive discipline. If he gave them substance abuse and they learned from it, they might have a lifelong opportunity to stay drug free. Tony would also be doing what Corrections wanted: playing ball with the ACLU, sort of! "Done."

"No suspension?"

"No. Let's try it your way. That'll give the boys and opportunity and a learning experience." Then Tony added, "If it happens again, I'm going to take stronger action."

Archer smiled. "I heard you're a real hard ass. It doesn't play out that way."

Tony smiled, a tired smile. "I tend to be hard on the kids because I care, and I know the value of education." Tony decided to go the distance. "I have an older brother. He has all the brains in the world. He's angry, greedy, and with a few drinks in him, as ugly and violent as they come. He's a high school dropout. A piece of me wanted to emulate him when we were growing up back east. He always had the gorgeous women, money in his pocket, flashy clothes, and the black-on-black 1970 Lincoln Mark. I wanted that. The thing that stopped me was his propensity toward violence. I couldn't hurt people the way he did. I'm talking baseball bats, knives, guns. I couldn't do that. That was one of the reasons I came out here. I wanted to get away from that influence. The major difference between my brother and me is that I managed to get an education. My brother didn't. When I wanted to turn my life around, I had an education to fall back on. Today, my brother has nothing. I've loaned him money for his mortgage payment. He went from a 4200 square-foot home on four-and-a-half acres, to a 1200 square-foot home on a 3500 square-foot lot. He's presently under indictment for two federal conspiracy cases. He's looking at long, hard time..." And then Tony added, "again."

He continued, "I know how valuable education can be. Unfortunately, we have these kids for a short time. They start to turn around and you put them right back in the same environment. It's tough for them; not impossible, but damn difficult. I want them to toe the line but at the same time I want them to reach. I want them to be the very best that they can be.

"We talk about empowering them. But at the same time, they have to accept responsibility for their actions. If you get caught smoking weed in class, there has to be a consequence. In this case, the substance abuse program will work. If it happens again, you and I need to meet again and decide what we do.

"Question. What are we doing about the fact that this stuff is coming in here in quantity?"

Archer nodded his understanding. He scratched his neck. "We're working with Probation on that."

"There are only so many ways that crap can get in here. Staff, school and/or Probation staff, Sunday visiting, and we know parents are getting the shit for the kids, or the Halls when they go for medical."

Archer wasn't giving up anything. He repeated, "We're working on it."

Wednesday Morning: SAM F

Bright and early Wednesday morning Tony arrived at his office. Well, maybe not too bright, but it was still early. He had stayed up late to watch the Dodger game only to be disappointed when they lost to the Mets in extra innings. Jansen couldn't hold the Mets in the bottom of the twelfth. He walked in the winning run.

Tony buzzed Roger Rabinowitz in his classroom. "Morning, short ass mother fucker." Tony waited for laughter, screaming—any reaction.

"Not you, too?"

"C'mon down to my office. I've got something for you."

It was a short walk to Tony's office from Roger's classroom. Roger was in Tony's office inside of four minutes. Roger was smiling. "I know, I know—I'm too sensitive."

"That would piss me off too," Tony said. But I'd show the kids that it didn't bother me, and they'd let go of it." Tony got out of his chair. He handed Roger a blue baseball cap with white lettering.

"What is this?"

"Read it."

Roger seemed to study the lettering. "They call me Sam F.?"

"Sam F. is an acronym for short ass mother fucker. Wear it."

Roger smiled. "The kids won't get it."

"They probably will. But if they need a little help, I'll give it to them. Try it on."

It fit like a tie with a tight knot. Roger shook his head. "You sure you want me to do this?"

"No, but do it anyway. It can't hurt. After the shit they put you through Monday and yesterday, what the hell, it's worth a try."

When the students walked across the field, Roger was standing five feet from his classroom door with his blue suit, white-and-red tie, and the Sam F. baseball cap, for all to see.

It was a Probation staff who first asked what Sam F. stood for.

Tony walked to within a few feet of the staff and said softly, but loudly enough so that a few kids could hear, “Short ass mother F_ _ _ ER.” It wasn’t long before everyone was laughing.

Friday Morning

Tony had stayed up late again, watching the Dodger game again. And again, they lost. The Giants, who were in first place, beat the Dodgers seven to five. Tony was glad he quit gambling.

It was a fifteen-minute drive from Tony's house to JFK School. No freeways involved. No traffic, no construction; an easy ride, and it was the end of the week. Next to Saturday, this was Tony's favorite day. He got to play tonight.

There was a pod or a key room as you were buzzed into the security area of the JFK School. Inside the glassed pod was a probation officer who identified all comers. He recognized Tony immediately and smiled. Tony smiled back. "Welcome to your Friday."

Tony knew the PO. He was aware that the PO worked a three-day shift—three long days of 13 hours. His shift was Thursday, Friday, Saturday. "Your Friday's coming and you get a four-day weekend."

The PO's grin grew to a smile. "True."

"Can you buzz me in? I need to secure my Glock."

The tall, well-built PO, who looked like he spent his four off days at the gym, buzzed Tony into the pod. Tony walked to the rear to a wall of gun lockers. He unlocked locker 13. Tony took his paddle holster and 40 caliber Glock off his right hip. He secured it in the locker, tossed the key a few inches into the air, caught the key, and put it in his suit pants pocket. "See you about 4 o'clock." Tony walked through the Probation offices, across the field, and to the school.

He didn't make it to his office. As Tony walked past the principal's office, he heard the door open. Eddie Peterson was a tall, casually dressed 51-year-old boss to Tony. He was too nice a guy. Discipline of staff was practically nonexistent.

"Tony, I need a minute." Eddie leaned against the door so Tony could enter.

"What's up?"

"Got a call at home last night from Archer."

"Shit," Tony thought. He believed everything went well. He did everything but plant his lips on both sides of Archer's ass. "Now what?"

Eddie laughed. "Do you always think the worst?"

"Yeah. That way I'm not surprised. What's going on?"

"He just wanted to tell me that you handled yesterday's marijuana incident with aplomb."

That was an Archer word. He had to show his vocabulary and his smarts. No doubt a black thing. "Is there an if, and, or a but to this?"

"There you go again, thinking the worst."

"Thanks."

"Well done. There may be hope for you after all."

Tony genuinely liked Eddie as a person. But he should have been a car salesman instead of a principal in a lock-up facility. "I appreciate the attaboy."

"You're welcome." Eddie looked at his watch. "Get to work before your boss climbs all over you."

Tony was looking forward to 4:30. Actually, the boss let everybody escape at 3:30 or so. It was what the boss called "getaway Friday." Tony couldn't wait to get away. He'd fight the freeway traffic, but it would be a hell of a lot worse if he hit the freeway at 4:30 or a quarter to five.

Tony looked at his watch, 2:20. Almost the start of his weekend. If it stayed quiet, all would be fine. Tony was smiling, but not for long.

Spit, Shit, and a SCAR

The inside line interrupted Tony's pleasant thoughts. Richard Tanner was on the other end. Tanner, whose nickname was Dick, really was a dick. Short, solid, with an abusive mouth toward his kids, liked to kick kids out of class more than he liked to teach history. Probation didn't like him, the kids didn't like him, Tony didn't like him, and Tanner's wife didn't like him. They were separated.

"What's up?"

"I'm sending you Soto Washington. He spit in a textbook. I'm suspending him for the rest of today and Monday."

Per the education codes, Tanner had the right to suspend from his class only for acts by students enumerated in the California Education Codes. But teachers could suspend only from their class. Administration could suspend from school.

Corrections was putting more and more pressure on teachers and administrators to not suspend kids. They wanted the offending student "counseled" and returned to class whenever possible. Corrections kept computerized records of who suspended whom, which teachers suspended the most kids, and why.

Forgotten was the fact that teachers were trying to teach and that some of these kids lied like a rug and were downright nasty.

"Send me the writeup." The school day was almost over. Spitting in the book was out of line and an offense for which Tony would suspend. As a matter of fact, Tony knew the kid. Soto Washington was the product of an Hispanic mother and an African American father. Both were gangbangers and drug dealers, and both had done prison time, leaving Soto to be raised by his grandmother until his mom (the first to be released from jail) arrived home. The kid was angry, aggressive and, at times, physically forceful. Tony couldn't blame him.

Most importantly, Tony did not want to get deluged with paperwork at this late hour. He wanted to get on the freeway before the Friday jam caused backup after freakin' backup. As long as Tanner got the suspension report to Tony in the next few minutes, all would be golden. Tony would meet with Soto and would review his findings with Tanner. If Tanner had already left for the weekend, Tony would meet with him prior to school Monday.

Soto entered Tony's office. "Sit down."

Soto was 5' 10." He had the build of a basketball player except for his height. His hair was short, and his teeth were as white as his t-shirt. He looked pissed. He sat in the chair Tony indicated.

"Mr. Tanner said you spit in a textbook." Tony's tone was soft. He looked directly at the 17-year-old. Soto's hands were gripping the sides of the chair.

"Fuck him."

Tony took a breath. He exhaled very slowly. "I repeat. Mr. Tanner said you spit in a book. Why?"

"I don't like history."

"I don't like sitting in my office with you on a Friday afternoon when I should be getting ready to leave for the weekend. Does that mean I can spit on your left shoe?"

The 17-year-old shook his head. "No."

"So why the hell did you spit in the book? Did someone dare you or something?"

"The guy's an asshole. He started yelling at me and calling me stupid because we were reading aloud from the book and when it came to me, I didn't know what page we were on. He called me an idiot."

That sounded like Tanner. "And you said *what*?"

"I told him his dick was as small as his body and that's probably why his wife left him."

Tony didn't dare laugh. He wanted to. He also wanted to hit the freeway. "And then what?"

"Tanner started to walk toward me. I picked the book up so he could see it."

Tony interrupted. "He, meaning Tanner?"

Soto nodded. "I spit in the book."

"And Mr. Tanner sent you to me?"

Soto again shook his head. "Tanner walked over to my desk. He grabbed the book out of my hands. He looked at the spit in the book, and then shoved it in my face."

"He shoved the book in your face?"

"He ground it into my face, making sure the spit got on my face. I wanted to hit the mother fucker and I wanted to cry. I didn't. He kicked me out."

The secretary knocked on Tony's door, excused herself, dropped the suspension report on Tony's desk, and left.

"I want to make sure I have all this, Soto. Mr. Tanner was upset because when it was your turn to read during history lesson, you lost your place. He called you stupid. Is that pretty much correct?"

Soto nodded.

"You told him his penis was as small as the rest of him and that's why his wife left him."

Again, Soto nodded.

"How do you guys know his wife left him?"

"He spends most of the period talking about her and about how he hopes she ain't getting any."

"You spit in the textbook. Mr. Tanner walked over to your desk, grabbed the book out of your hand and shoved it into your face."

Soto nodded.

"Was it a hard cover book like this?" Tony pulled the 12th grade history book off his shelf.

"That's the book."

Before he sat down, Tony looked at Soto's face. It was red. "I need to get a picture of your face." Fuck the freeway. Tony would be lucky if he left work by midnight.

He kept a camera in the bottom of the bookcase. He also had his cell phone. The camera would probably take a better picture. Tony checked his watch. School was out in five minutes.

Tony took three pictures of Soto's face with his cell phone and three more with his camera. He then took a picture of his copy of the textbook with his cell phone and with the camera. Finally, he typed a note explaining what he had done, dated it, and put the time on it. Finally, Tony saved it to the computer.

Tony handed Soto a sheet of lined paper and a pen. "To the best of your recollection, write what went down in Mr. Tanner's class, sign it, and date it."

Tony buzzed the secretary. "Call Tanner, please, and tell him I need to meet with him right after school in my office. Then call Probation and tell them I'm hanging on to Soto Washington for a school conference. Soto is in Obama dorm. Thanks."

Tony told Soto to take a seat outside of his office.

Tanner had to pass Soto before he entered Tony's office. When Soto saw Tanner, his eyes went to the floor. Tanner smirked, then knocked on Tony's door.

"Come on in. Sit down. I read your report and met with Soto, who can't hear us. Before we get started, it's my duty to inform you that you have the right to union representation. I would strongly suggest that."

Tanner was either smiling or smirking. It was hard for Tony to tell. Tanner either was scared or he thought the meeting was a joke.

"Why would I need a union rep?"

"That's your decision, Dick." Tony had to mention that. "Your written suspension report and Soto's description of the occurrence are distant cousins; very distant. Again, you have the right to a union rep. If that be the case, we will continue this conference after you have arranged for a union rep."

Now Tanner was smiling. That was either cockiness or a bluff. Tony didn't see Dick as much of a poker player. "Fine. I'll decline a union rep."

Tony was smarter and more prepared than the average desert duck. He plucked a piece of paper off his desk. Tony handed it to Tanner. "It basically says you have been advised of your right to a union representative, in fact, even encouraged to postpone this meeting and seek a union representative. That understanding the seriousness or possible seriousness of this, you have declined representation."

While Tanner read the cautionary warning, he thought about how nice it would be to wrap Tanner up in a package with a bow tied around it and fire his ass. The guy was as worthless as gasoline in an electric car, whether he did what Soto claimed he did or not. Tony would give long odds that he did.

Tanner looked up at Tony. He held his hands up. "Do you want me to sign it?"

"I want you to get a union rep. If you don't want a union rep, please sign and date it."

Tanner had a pen in the pocket of his creased sport shirt. He used that pen to sign and date the warning letter.

"I'll get you a copy before you leave. Again, I read your report and I spoke with Soto. Tell me in your own words what happened."

"The kids a pain in the ass. We were doing a history lesson on the invasion of Cuba or the attempted invasion. This was important to Kennedy's presidency, and I wanted the kids to be clear on what an asshole Kennedy was."

Kennedy was one of Tony's favorite presidents. Reagan was his favorite.

"We were reading from the text and stopping to discuss." Tanner squirmed a bit in the chair. "You know, direct instruction."

Tanner didn't know direct instruction from a hot iron.

"The kid wasn't even following along. How does a half-breed get ahead in this world if he doesn't get an education?"

"And then...?"

"He spit in the book."

"Did you leave anything out?"

Tanner wrinkled his forehead in thought. "There might have been some name calling."

"Can you be more specific?"

"I think I told him he wasn't too bright."

"Did you tell him he was stupid?"

Tanner held out his hands. "I don't remember."

Tony made a written note on the yellow legal pad on his desk. He'd get the names of all the kids in Tanner's class and ask Probation, over the weekend, to get written, dated, and signed statements from the kids in the class.

"Did Soto say anything to you?"

"He said something about the size of my penis."

Tony decided to have fun. "What did he say about your dick, Dick?"

Tanner rubbed his hands together. He was getting nervous. Tony smiled, waiting for Tanner's answer.

"I couldn't hear him. At that point the class was getting unruly. That's when he spit in the book."

"And then what?"

"I sent him out to you."

"Did you walk to his desk?"

Tanner nodded.

"Is that a 'yes'?"

"Why do I feel like I'm on trial?"

Because you might be, you sorry son of a turd, Tony thought. "I just need to get everything right for the report. You can stop any time you'd like and request a union rep."

Tanner got pissed. "How many times do I have to tell you I don't want a rep. I did walk to Soto's desk. I grabbed the book and looked at it and I saw the spit in that new textbook that the taxpayers pay all that money for. I took the fucking book and I ground it in his face, spit and all. Is that what you wanted to hear? Well, that's what I did, and I'm not sorry. Are you going to suspend that punk or not?"

Tony sighed. How the hell could this guy get a teaching credential?

"Where's this all going?"

The question was fair. Even Tanner deserved a straight answer. Tony looked right at Tanner. "Your class suspension stands. He's out of your class for the balance of today, which is over, and Monday. As far as a school suspension, I'll decide that before I leave today.

Tony continued, "Your actions are reprehensible. What you did to Soto is battery under the California penal code. It's actually 242 of the penal code. In this case, a misdemeanor. It's also possibly child abuse. One way or another, the authorities, the Sheriff, will be notified."

"You gotta be kidding me."

Tanner leaned forward in his chair but stopped short of standing. Tony was ready for him if he did jump up; Tanner was no match for Tony. Tony would have him on the floor before you could say, 'small package.'

"This punk destroys a textbook and I'm the one facing legal action?"

"Tanner, you're a teacher." Tony was being generous. "You set the example. What gives you the right to do what you did to Soto?"

"You ever lose your temper?"

Tanner was going the wrong way up a one-way street. "We're not talking about me."

Tony picked up the phone. He called the dorm. "Is there a PO who is available to meet with Mr. Tanner, Soto, and myself in my office as soon as possible?"

Tanner didn't look too happy.

It was a quarter to four before a PO was available. So much for "set" hours. During the time they waited for the PO, Tony convinced Tanner to apologize to Soto. Tanner did so, grudgingly. Tony sensed that Tanner was more interested in getting this over with so he could start his weekend. He really didn't seem to think he had done anything that serious.

When the PO arrived, Tony called Soto back to the dorm. The PO, Marti Rosenberg, was wearing a grey muscle shirt and black shorts. She entered Tony's office with an apology. "Excuse my dress. I was out the door for a dinner run. They called me back for the meeting."

Tony grew instantly hard. He had a long-distance interest in Marti. Nothing ever grew out of that interest other than a hard-on. "I owe you one. I appreciate you coming up for the meeting. Have a seat. You know Mr. Tanner."

"I know Mr. Tanner," Marti said curtly.

"Good to see you, Ms. Rosenberg." Tanner's eyes were on the muscle shirt that didn't hide too much of Marti's boobs.

"Let's get started. I'm going to recap a 'situation.' Mr. Tanner will chime in if I miss anything or if he feels anything needs to be corrected. Please feel free to stop me at any time if you have any questions. This is serious."

Marti nodded and looked Tony directly in the eyes with a smile as soft as her shoulder-length blonde hair. Tony gave Marti the full version. Tanner sat with his hands in his lap and his mouth shut. "That's it. Questions?"

Marti nodded. She looked at Tanner. "I know, Mr. Tanner, we're far from perfect, but what gives you the right to shove a book, with spit in it, in the kid's face?"

Tanner sat up straight. "The punk spit in the book."

Tony started to speak. Marti beat him to it. "He's a student, not a punk. We expect our kids to screw up. We expect our teachers and POs to set examples."

Tony couldn't have written a better script. Marti was letter on.

She looked at Tony. "Can I assume Soto will be moved to another class?"

"Mr. Tanner is suspending Soto from his class on Monday. Soto will attend all his other classes. Come Tuesday, Soto will be moved."

Marti nodded her approval, crossed and uncrossed her legs.

"I'll send a letter to Soto's parents, outlining the situation. Of course, I will copy the director and Soto's PO." Tony was thinking about the mound of paperwork he had to complete. It was too late to get anything of substance to Downey (the home office). Most of the expensive suits were gone for the weekend. Tony had a choice. He could stay and complete the wad of ink at the office, or meet with Tanner, wrap things up, hit the freeway, and complete the paperwork from home over the weekend. Tony opted to meet with Tanner and then decide, although he was leaning heavily toward completing the tide of typing from home.

Marti left, as did the rest of the school staff except the two custodians. Tanner remained in his seat. Tony looked at him angrily. "You've caused a myriad of problems."

Tanner smirked. "I think you're making way too much of this."

Tony was now beyond anger. He was boiling. He bit down on his back teeth when he was really pissed. Tony was biting hard. "I'm going to file a SCAR tonight. I'm going to drop it off at the Sheriff's office on my way out of here."

"What the hell is a SCAR?"

"Suspected Child Abuse Report."

"Are you serious?"

"As serious as shoving a book with spit in it in a student's face?" Tony took a breath. He calmed himself. "As far as any other charges, that'll be up to the student and the authorities after they investigate the SCAR. Whether or not you are suspended is up to the suits in Downey. I haven't made my decision on a recommendation yet." Actually, Tony had made a decision. He wasn't about to tell Tanner. He wanted to taunt Tanner; fuck up his weekend.

"Unless you have questions, we're done. Have a great weekend," Tony added sarcastically.

When Tanner was gone, Tony located the phone number for the Director's Assistant. Tony called her private cell phone. Paula Burton answered. Tony gave her the rundown.

"Do you have to file the SCAR with the Sheriff? Can't you let Probation handle it in-house?"

Typical FLACOE thinking, Tony concluded. Keep everything under wraps. “Conflict of interest. Look, if the parents smell money, lawsuit money, this thing could get us bad press. If there is a hint, just a taste that we weren’t by the book, we could pay big time—literally and figuratively. My real question is, can I suspend the bastard?”

Paula didn’t hesitate. “No. Absolutely not. I’m going to inform the Director as soon as I hang up. I’ll need your report faxed to me by 10 o’clock Monday morning.”

“You’ll have it. The guy doesn’t belong in the classroom.”

“That’s not your decision and it’s not my decision. Enjoy your weekend.”

More Sanity on the Streets Than the Damn School

Tony's Glock 40 was holstered in a paddle holster that slid neatly and easily into the waist band of his suit pants. The suit jacket concealed the weapon. On his way out of JFK, Tony stopped at the security pod and took his weapon out of the lockbox. He slid it into his waist band, made sure his jacket covered the gun and he was buzzed out the heavy steel security door into the parking lot. Tony walked to his 1998 Corvette Pace Car. His weekend had begun.

He drove the Vette to the gate and leaned out the window to punch four numbers into the key-code activator. The gate opened. Tony drove in, turned to his left, and found a parking space. He was in front of his locker four minutes later.

Tony was 48 when he entered the police academy. It was something he had wanted to do since junior high. His plans were to join the Marines out of high school and, after the Corps, become a cop. It didn't quite happen that way.

All his young life, Tony had problems that followed him into early adulthood. As a matter of fact, Tony's problems followed him from New Jersey to New York, to New Hampshire, to Michigan, and to California. Tony liked alcohol. Specifically, he liked Seagram's, lots and lots of Seagram's. It damn near killed him.

At his locker, he stripped off his business suit and everything else. He took a quick shower, then suited up again, this time in his freshly pressed Hollow Point Police uniform. Tony knew he looked really sharp in uniform. He adjusted his Sam Brown, slid the Glock into its holster, and walked to the bathroom. He stood in front of the full-length mirror and carefully pinned his badge on his chest. Tony was proud of Badge 108, damn proud. He recalled that his ex-wife pinned that badge on him when he was sworn in at the City Council meeting when he was 50. He didn't have the wife anymore, but he had the badge. He'd have it no other way.

His hardest accomplishment to date was earning that badge, the academy at 48, then finding a department to hire him as a Reserve, and then the nine-month probationary period, the Field Training Officers (FTOs) and some of their unnecessary bullshit.

Tony rubbed the gleaming badge with the palm of his right hand. That badge meant the world to him. One of his FTOs, Mickey Cassidy, told Tony he'd either love the department or hate it. Being a cop was either the world or it was nothing. Mickey was 100 percent on the mark. Tony loved it. He couldn't get enough of it. The excitement, the adrenalin, the rush, the danger, the women—it was addicting; almost like Seagram's.

Tony walked up the stairs to the briefing room where he'd ask dispatch to radio Mickey to come 1019 to pick him up. It was 2140 hours.

Tony was all smiles. He was sitting in the passenger seat of the marked black-and-white. His window was down, and the breeze brushed his face. Mickey was driving slowly, as both cops were eyeing the activity on the main street. Once again, life was beautiful.

"22 Adam."

Tony reached for the mic. "22 Adam."

"A 415. 6363 # 6, Rita. No weapons at this time. Father-son dispute. 18 Adam, back 22 Adam."

"10-4. From Florence and Salt Lake."

With light traffic, 22 Adam was on scene in four-and-a-half minutes. Tony put them out. "22 Adam, 97 6363 Rita, # 6."

"Copy, 22 Adam."

As Tony and Mickey were walking toward the building, 18 Adam broke the silence. "We're 2 out."

Tony was a foot or so behind Mickey, as Mickey's stride was longer. Mickey was 41 and stood 6' 1" tall. If you had a six-foot, one-inch pencil, and stood the pencil directly in front of Mickey, you wouldn't see Mickey.

Mickey loved two things. He absolutely loved police work and he loved his wife. There was a story. The two were high school sweethearts, and after high school, Mickey went in the army. When he came back, Tammy was married. Mickey married. Both marriages ended in divorce. The two reunited at their high school reunion, and shortly thereafter, they married.

Tony and Mickey entered the building. It was an old complex, but clean. The building was three stories. Tony spotted the first-floor apartment in the east corner of the foyer. They lowered the volume on their radio as they approached the apartment. They listened. The only sound was a television advertising Camacho's Used Cars.

He looked at Mickey and made a knocking motion to indicate his next move. Mickey nodded. He stepped away from the door. Tony stepped backward, reached out, and knocked. "HP Police." He immediately heard footsteps, then no footsteps, then a lock turning. Finally, the door opened.

A man dressed in solid blue pajamas opened the door. He was in his fifties, tired looking. Tony thought he looked sad. "We got a call of loud noise, possibly an argument?"

The man nodded. He opened the door wider. "C'mon in." The entryway was long and narrow. Mickey observed no other people.

"I was arguing with my son. Conrad is 17. He likes to think he's older."

Mickey asked for the man's ID.

"It's in the bedroom."

"Is there anyone else here?"

The man shook his head. "My son left. He's a good kid. He'll graduate next year and then wants to go in the service. He's seeing an older woman. I don't like her. I'm divorced and I work two jobs to make ends meet. That gives Conrad more space than he needs, in my opinion. Apparently, she was over here earlier today, before I got home from work. She brought beer over. I don't like Conrad drinking. He's too young." The man started walking toward the bedroom. Mickey and Tony followed cautiously. Mickey got on his portable. "We're code 4."

"Copy that. 22 Adam is code four. 18 Adam you can 10-22."

"Copy."

Mickey ran the man's ID.

"How old is the lady Conrad is seeing?"

"Probably damn near 30."

They walked back toward the front door. "Are they having sex?"

The man laughed. "Does Corona sell beer?"

It was Tony's turn to laugh. "Technically..."

"I know. That's what started the argument. I told him she could be arrested because Conrad's a minor. When I told him I was going to call the police, he stormed out of the apartment. I'm calmed down."

Mickey signaled to Tony that the man was clean. "Does Conrad know you called us?"

He nodded. "Yeah. That's when he left."

Tony took a pad from his shirt pocket. "Can I get Conrad's full name and birthdate, please?" Tony ran Conrad for wants and warrants. He, too, was clean.

"Here's my card. If you have any more problems, give us a call. We'll come back and talk with him."

When they were back in the unit, Tony cleared the call. "22 Adam. Talked with Dad. Son had already left the premises. 415 was verbal only. No crime. Dad was advised to call if son returns and causes problems. 10-8."

It remained unusually quiet for a Friday. HP was usually a zoo with all the animal cages unlocked and opened on Friday. The drunks were half smashed and beating on their women. The dealers were out selling their product. The shooters were out robbing and raising hell. The car thieves were stealing cars. But for now, it was like the seventh-inning stretch, a lull in the action. Tony and Mickey enjoyed it.

Mickey was enjoying the quiet so much, he asked Tony if he wanted to drive; that was rare. Do pigeons live in HP? Sure.

Mickey pulled to the curb. They exchanged seats.

"How's things at home?" Mickey asked.

"No complaints. Lieutenant's looking good and Carina's not pressing me; at least not too much." Carina was Tony's latest female friend. And "Lieutenant" (or "LT"), his dog, was named after Lieutenant DeClerq, an HP cop who died young of throat cancer. Tony and the Lieutenant had been good friends.

Between working out, work, the Reserves, and time for himself and LT, there wasn't much time left for romance. Tony always had a difficult time with *balance* in his life. This was one of those times.

"How's things at the Cassidy homestead?"

Mickey smiled that soft, friendly smile. "As great as one can hope for. The only wrinkle is finances. It seems that as fast as I can earn it, Tammy can spend it."

"I'll be your financial planner."

Mickey took his eyes off the road. Mickey looked at Tony with wrinkled eyebrows. "Go."

"I'll save you easily $100 a month."

"Who do I shoot?"

"Whom?"

"Okay, whom?"

"Nope. Quit smoking."

Mickey's eyes went back to the roadway. He chuckled. "That won't happen. But between me and Tammy, we figure we spend at least three a month on smokes."

Tony decided to drive toward what was called the Maywood strip, a few city blocks at the northeast end of HP that was infested with gang punks, drug dealers, guns, and more goddamn guns.

Tony slowly made his way to that area as Mickey cried about his finances. Fortunately, Tony, who had given up smoking when he decided to get into shape for the academy, did not have financial problems. He had a mortgage payment, a few bucks on a couple of credit cards, the Vette payment, and the best food money could buy for LT, which usually included whatever Tony was eating.

Tony turned north on Fremont and east on Telegraph. He was now in the heart of the Maywood Strip. His window was down, as was Mickey's. They could hear all the sounds of the night.

Most of the noise was loud music. There was at least one party per street. Normally, that meant "loud music calls" about midnight. Music calls were dangerous. First, anybody who's tanked is potentially dangerous. Secondly, you never knew who was 417—armed.

The parties were in the backyards. The trick was to get the homeowner to come to the front of the house. No officer wanted to walk through forty or fifty half-smashed assholes. This wasn't Eddie Murphy and *48 Hrs.*

Every so often, some asshole would get gutsy and heave a beer bottle at the responding officers. Then all hell would break loose. All hell meant an airship overhead, possible assistance from an adjacent agency, retreating to don riot gear, and finally kicking ass until peace was restored.

Tony cruised the area for fifteen minutes. He spent most of those fifteen minutes trying to convince Mickey to quit smoking. That was like trying to convince the IRS to give you a break on your delinquent taxes.

Tony headed back to the center of HP. He backtracked. He headed west on Gage. He was a block and a half west of the Gage Bowl when, suddenly, his windshield was covered with glass. "Mother fucker!" he said aloud. *Someone shot at the unit,* he thought, as they had been warned at briefing that gang initiations were taking place. Shoot a cop and you're in.

"Pull to the curb. Now," Mickey snapped.

Tony and Mickey realized at the same moment what actually occurred. There had been no shooting.

Mickey was first out of the unit, going to an Asian woman, now standing on the sidewalk by her car. "Are you okay, ma'am? Do you need medical assistance?"

She shook her head. "No. But look what you did to my car!"

Tony joined Mickey on the sidewalk. "Is anyone else in the car?"

"No. My door...My door is broken. You hit it!"

"Are you sure you don't need medical attention?"

"I'm fine. You didn't hit *me*—you hit *my door.*"

She was maybe 5' 3", 105 pounds.

"Ma'am," Mickey said. "It's illegal to open the driver's door of a vehicle unless it's safe to do so. That's 22517 of the vehicle code." Then he turned to Tony, "Call for a supervisor."

"But you hit my car!" She started to cry. "I'm calling my husband." She pulled a cell phone out of her bag.

Because it's a conflict of interest for HP to take an accident report that involves one of their own, the supervisor had to call a Maywood unit to write a courtesy report.

Mickey told Tony. "Go ahead and start getting her horsepower. I'll write everything up that she'll need. We're going to be tied up with her for a good half-hour, forty-five minutes."

It took only about thirty-five minutes to "mop up" at the accident scene. The Asian lady was cited for 22517 CVC (California Vehicle Code) for opening her door into traffic. She was also billed for the damages. Triple A towed her car. Tony drove back to the Station where they switched units. Mickey followed Tony to the City Yards to drop off the damaged vehicle for repairs.

Pretty efficient for a police department, Mickey thought.

Tony keyed the mic. "22 Adam, show us 10-8 from the Station."

"22 Adam copy."

Another call came in.

"22 Adam, A 459 S. 6161 Alameda. Coverage is the rear door and rear window. 23 Adam back 22 Adam."

Tony translated what dispatch had put out. There was a possible burglary at 6161 Alameda. The alarm that was set off indicated entry may have been gained via the rear door or the rear window. The call was for real. This was no accidental alarm call. His heart rate doubled.

Mickey hung a U-turn. At the same time, he hit his overheads. Several cars stopped hard. Tony remarked, "It's the smoking that's going to kill you, Mick, not the driving. I want to get home tonight."

Mickey cut the overheads but not the speed. "If this is a good 459, it'll be the fourth this month. I'd like to get these clowns."

"23 Adam to 22 Adam. Meet me on 2."

Tony switched the radio to tac 2. "We're on the Maywood strip, stuck at the train crossing. It'll be a couple."

"Copy that," Tony said into the mic. "We'll keep you posted." Tony went back to tac 1 and blacked out the unit. "We're 10-7."

Tony closed the unit door gently. Mickey covered the interior light with his hand. The unit was positioned between the side driveway and the rear of the shop. Their unit, if not completely blocking a car from egress, made it damn difficult to exit the parking lot without taking out the unit.

They walked close to the building, first Mickey, then Tony close behind. They listened. It was quiet. Peyton's Metal and Polishing had been a HP staple. The place had been at the same address for years and was a family-run business passed on from father to sons. One of their products was copper tubing, and copper tubing brought bucks. The fact that the place was in a dark corner of the street made it a likely target. It had been hit half a dozen times during late night and early morning hours.

This was early morning. Mickey hugged the wall and did a quick peak around the side of the building to the rear. He ducked back for cover, then did the same again, this time taking a wider angle. This was called "cutting the pie." Mickey saw nothing out of the ordinary, not even a vehicle.

They were now against the rear wall. It was quiet. When they approached the rear iron-gated door, Mickey stopped. Tony quickly stepped around Mickey to the opposite side of the door. Gently, Tony fingered the handle, and the door gave. It was unlocked. With his flashlight, Tony carefully examined the door and saw pry marks. He pointed to the door. Mickey nodded. Tony raised his flashlight. The white wood door was opened half an inch.

Tony walked backward, not once taking his eyes off the door. He turned down his radio, took out his cell phone and punched dispatch. "We have a pried steel door and an opened inner door. This may be live."

Dispatch: "23 is 30 seconds out. We'll send additional units."

"We need two units, one north of the location and one south. There is no exit on the west side of the building and our unit is blocking the exit from the east side. Give us two more units. One can cover the front on foot and the other can stand pat on Alameda waiting further. Is there an airship available to check the roof?"

"Enroute, sir."

"Copy that. When 23 Adam is 10-7, we'll announce."

Dispatch: "Copy."

Just then 23 Adam walked up to the rear of the building. Mickey whispered to Royce and Lincoln what was going on and what he wanted them to do. Then Mickey stood to the side of the door, leaned in, and pushed gently. "This is the HP Police!" he announced. "The building is surrounded. Put down your weapon and come out with your hands in the air. Come out slowly."

There was a tense silence. Mickey turned to Lincoln. "Give it to them in Spanish."

Lincoln gave the same order in Spanish. More silence. "This is your last chance," Mickey yelled. "Come out with your hands up and do so slowly. The building is surrounded. You can't get away."

Just as Mickey was thinking the perp (or perps) already burglarized the store and made their getaway, he thought he heard what sounded like metal hitting the floor and reverberating. Tony heard it, too.

Tony stepped across the doorway and stood next to Mickey. "Last chance, numb nut, or we send in the dog." Tony took a breath. "Chewy is hungry, so I suggest you get your asses out now."

Mickey looked at him like he was crazy. So did Lincoln and Royce. Mickey whispered, "We don't have a dog anymore." At one time HP had a canine. Unfortunately, he had been killed in a robbery and shootout.

Tony turned to Mickey. "Wanna bet a pack of smokes against breakfast?"

Mickey nodded. "You're on."

Tony carried a Sony pocket recorder. He took it out and pushed the volume to high. "I warned you, asshole. Say hello to Chewy."

Tony let up on the button and the recording sounded like one pissed-off German Shepherd barking up a storm. Except it wasn't a Shepherd; it was a Norwegian Elkhound—Tony's Norwegian Elkhound, "Lieutenant."

"No, no. No dog. No dog, Mr. Police. Keep Chewy on his leash. No Chewy, Mr. Policeman."

"Do you have a weapon? Chewy doesn't like weapons."

"No weapons, Mr. Police. Just me. Just me."

"Put your hands in the air and slowly walk toward the light." Tony didn't turn off the recorder.

"Please put Chewy away. Please. I not give you any trouble. Really, Mr. Police. I'm sorry."

The four officers could see a shadow. "Who's in there with you?"

"No one, Mr. Policeman. Only me. I'm solo. Put Chewy in the car."

"Okay. But if you play games, not only will I turn Chewy loose, but I'll also let his brother Louie out." He turned off the recorder.

A short, small-boned Hispanic man in his forties walked slowly toward Mickey, Tony, Lincoln, and Royce. When he was within eyesight of the four officers, they could see sweat dripping from the man's face. "No Chewy, no Chewy."

"Turn around," Mickey yelled at him. "Put your hands behind your head and interlace your fingers."

As soon as he obeyed orders, Tony stepped forward and grabbed the man by his hands, bending him backward so that he was off balance. If the man so much as flinched, Tony would let go of his grip on the guy and the short Hispanic would fall backward.

Tony grabbed the Hispanic's right wrist and slammed a cuff around his hand none too gently. Then he did the same with the guy's left hand. "You're under arrest for burglary and a host of other charges that will be added later. You have the right to remain silent. If you give up that right, anything you say can and will be used against you in a court of law. You have the right to an attorney. If you cannot afford one, one will be appointed for you free of charge. Do you understand your rights?"

He nodded.

"Do you understand your rights?"

"Yes."

"Somebody, give him his rights in *Espanol.*"

Tony took his time searching the man. He pulled his pant pockets inside out. Tony came up with nothing but lint. Not even ID. "What's your name?"

"My name is..." He hesitated. Tony didn't want to play. He turned toward Royce. "Get Chewy out of the car. They haven't been properly introduced."

"No, no, Mr. Police. My name is Antonio Gonzalez Hernandez Lopez. My birthdate is ..."

Tony knew the man had been through this before. "You don't like dogs?"

He shook his head sheepishly. "I've been bit before."

"A previous arrest?"

"Yes, Mr. Officer."

"For what?"

"Same thing." He made a motion with his head toward the door. "Same place."

"No shit. You got caught once before robbing this place?"

"Si."

"Would you like to meet Chewy?"

"No, no, Mr. Police. Please no. Thank you."

Tony put his hand in his pocket. He pushed the recorder button.

It took the little Hispanic burglar several seconds to grasp what had occurred.

"Fucking cops," he blurted out, without an accent. "Mother fucking cops. You can't do that."

"Somebody put this asshole in the back of our unit before I turn Chewy loose!"

Screwed But Not Kissed

He completed the Tanner report from home and faxed it to the suits in Downey. The report was waiting on his desk when he arrived at work early Monday morning. Attached to the report was a page and a half of notes. Tony read through the notes rapidly, then he read through them a second time more carefully.

He was fuming when he finished. The report had already gone from the area administrator's eyes to a FLACOE attorney and back to the area administrator. That meant that they had taken the incident seriously enough to interrupt someone's weekend or the suits arrived in Downey before dawn cracked. Either way, this incident ranked high on the totem pole.

That wasn't what pissed off Tony. Either the area administrator or the attorney, or both, had decided that Tony would not file charges against Tanner. Both strongly suggested that Tony add a paragraph suggesting—no, mandating—half a dozen anger-management classes and a warning that, if a second similar scenario occurred within this school year, Tanner would face "further disciplinary action." What pure, unadulterated bullshit. *It's no wonder,* Tony thought, *some teachers get away with this kinda crap.*

There was a coffee machine in the lounge, and he really needed the caffeine. When he walked back into his office carrying a cup of hot coffee, he put the coffee on his desk, sat down, loosened his tie, then turned on his computer. His report needed serious editing.

He toyed with his report for about fifteen minutes. When the telephone rang, he ignored it. When his principal called him on the radio, he told him he was busy completing a task for the area administrator.

Tony was telling the truth. Ninety-eight percent of the time he was rock solid honest. Most of the time he was on the side of the person who took the right action at the right time. He was man enough to admit when he screwed up. When someone else fucked up, he took action to correct the wrongdoing. Tanner screwed up. The area administrator was covering up the inappropriate action of Tanner.

Tony couldn't accept the responsibility of not hammering Tanner. Tanner deserved it. The student didn't deserve what Tanner shoved in the kid's face. Unfortunately, Tony had neither Union nor tenure. He was not protected. But neither was he stupid.

Tony picked up the phone. He started to dial the area administrator's number but put the phone down. He booted his computer. When the computer was ready, Tony sent an email to Paula Burton. The text read:

"Richard Tanner acted in a manner that should have criminal repercussions. I have already filed a SCAR with the Lancaster Sheriff. This 'teacher' needs to be removed from the profession permanently."

Tony proofread the email three times. He finally hit the Send button. He accomplished two major objectives: His feelings were captured on paper. Tony's goals were in stone; and there could be no denying that he had attempted to take action. Next, Paula Burton, who had one agenda—to elevate Paula Burton to the highest possible pay scale then retire, could not refute the email. She could twist, bend, and deny a conversation; what was written was forever.

Soon after his arrival at JFK, Paula had asked Tony to attempt to track down sub teachers or teachers who had moved on via retirement or transfer or death. Teachers were responsible for inputting grades into the computer and, because administration hadn't followed up on the grading input, dozens of kids were without grades.

He did his best to track down the errant personnel and was successful in a handful of cases.

When he reported this to Paula, she said, "Give them a FLACOE 'C.'"

Tony responded, "Give me that in writing and it'll be done before you leave for the day."

Angrily, she said, “You'll get nothing in writing from me. I'm directing you to put those grades in.”

That was a violation of the Education Code, not to mention Corrections' policy. If it came back to bite Tony, he could lose his job.

“At the risk of being insubordinate, either I get it in writing, or I won't do it. If you prefer, I can have my attorney call you.”

Paula slammed down the receiver. Fifteen minutes later, the director's assistant called Tony. “If I shoot you a memo, will you put in the grades?”

“Absolutely.” Fifteen minutes after Tony received the memo, he began entering grades.

It was 2:15 when Tony's phone rang. Before he looked at the incoming call number, he guessed it was Paula. His guess was on the mark. Tony picked up the phone.

“It's Paula Burton.”

All Tony said was, “Hello.”

“We need to meet.”

Unless she was in the Lancaster area, it was too late to meet today. “Problem?”

“We'll discuss that in my office.”

Paula's main office was in Downey, approximately 85 miles from the JFK School. “When?”

“How soon can you get here?”

Tony thought, *You gotta be kidding.* This time of day the freeway would be heavy with traffic. The closer he got to Downey, the more traffic he'd hit. Tony thought about lying to her, telling her he had a doctor's appointment, but she'd ask him to get a doctor's note.

When an administrator pissed off a suit, sometimes the offender would be given “freeway therapy;” the individual who pissed off a superior would be transferred to a site so far from home that you'd need a spaceship for on-time arrival. Other times, the offending party would be given multiple school sites to cover as punishment until he relented.

Money-Making Proposition

Tony came on board in February of 1978. He was hired as a teacher and that same year was promoted to assistant principal. Tony's first administrative assignment was at Camp Swellington in Canyon Woods.

The school was tightly run by its director, Walter Minter, who had been with Probation for 33 years. He was easy going and school supportive. He kept the kids in check with positive programs, sports activities, and time off for good behavior and good grades. A student could not get "an early out" unless a teacher signed off.

Tony was a happy man; except for one problem: the kids were in school every other day; that's correct, every other day. One week it was Monday, Wednesday, and Friday; the next week it was Tuesday and Thursday.

The Board of Supervisors added a couple of paragraphs to the California Education Code. Those paragraphs added one hour to the school day of those kids incarcerated. The hour consisted of the teachers showing an entertainment video to the students.

Another paragraph had language that allowed the averaging out of the Average Daily Attendance (ADA) over a twenty-day period, adding the hours the kids were in school so that Corrections could collect state and federal dollars for every student for every day.

Everyone won. Corrections claimed ADA, including federal dollars for the time the kids were and weren't in school. The teachers' union saw to it that the teachers were paid for watching movies for that extra hour. Corrections got fat.

There was a loser. The students. Probably the last chance most of these kids had for an education and Corrections screwed with those kids, most of them minorities—Hispanics and Blacks.

This gave Tony a problem—a major pain in his head and stomach.

What prompted the pain was that Tony, with the Corrections Director, had gotten special dispensation for one particular student to go to school every day so that he could complete an algebra class that he needed for his high school diploma. The student realized that, if he didn't earn his diploma in camp, odds weren't in his favor to complete school "on the outs."

Everything was working like a finely tuned piano when, one day, a probation officer insisted that a "ward" work. Tony asked the PO to take a student who wanted to work. The probation officer told Tony to screw off. When the kid refused to work, the PO handcuffed him and took him to the special housing unit, or SHU. That was the brick the broke the window.

Tony did homework, lots and lots of homework. He read, reread, and re-reread the education codes. He made phone calls. He talked to other school officials. He did "research." Finally, he called the Director.

Jerry Stone told Tony that he didn't want to talk on the phone. He "invited" Tony to his Downey office the next morning.

As Tony recalled, Director Stone started the conversation by telling Tony, "We must pay you too much. That's a nice suit and tie. Damn nice."

That caught Tony by surprise. He wasn't expecting humor. He was expecting threats or worse. "Sit down. Relax. We need to talk."

Tony sat. He was understandably nervous meeting with a real suit, a "honcho."

Stone was 5'10" and slender. He looked like he might be a runner. He had a smooth complexion, brown hair, and was soft spoken. His suit was solid medium blue, his tie was red, and his shoes were shined. "We need to come to a meeting of the minds, here, Tony. Tell me what the problem is, as you see it."

Tony reiterated the situation. Finally, he added, "You approved the program for this student. He was doing fine until the PO got in the way. But the bottom line is that what you are doing, what Corrections is doing, is illegal." Tony was on a roll. "In fact, it approaches federal fraud. These kids need to be in school each and every school day. Just because someone cooked the education code, doesn't make it any less illegal. If these kids were white, would you be doing this? If this was your son or daughter, Mr. Stone, would you allow it?"

Tony took a breath. He watched Mr. Stone's face. The man was smiling. "Suppose I say we are going to continue with business, as usual. What's your next move?"

"I'm going to file suit."

Stone put his palms straight in the air. "No one is going to take your case. I don't know any attorney who will take on the Board of Supervisors."

Tony said one word. "Wrong."

"You have an attorney?"

Tony nodded. "Before we go there, I'm going to be fired, aren't I?"

Stone's smile grew. He shook his head. "Doubtful." It was Stone's turn to pause, take a breath, finger the knot on his tie. "You've got balls, that's for sure. Who's your attorney?"

"The American Civil Liberties Union. I've spent the last six weeks in their office doing research. What's happening here is illegal."

"No one will fire you. They'll be afraid of the ACLU. They may bounce you around Corrections facilities hoping you'll resign. They won't mess with the ACLU."

Something told Tony that Stone was cut from a different cloth. Tony got the distinct impression Stone wanted this done. When Stone next spoke, Tony was convinced Stone wanted it done.

"Are you strong enough emotionally to handle the fight that's coming?"

"Funny, the ACLU attorneys asked me the same question. The answer is yes. I'm tougher emotionally than physically. The Texas Rangers have a saying that goes something like this, 'The little man will always win if he's in the right and keeps on coming.' I'm in the right and most of the time, I don't know the meaning of the word quit."

"One more thing. Can you give me the name of the PO so I can straighten his ass out? I promise you that student will graduate before he leaves camp if he completes the school program you wrote up."

Both men stood up. Both men smiled at each other. Both men shook hands.

Tony wasn't fired, but he was bounced around Corrections. The ACLU went after Corrections on behalf of the kids, and the students attended school five days a week. Corrections was damn lucky the Feds didn't come after them. The teachers lost an extra hour of pay.

Tony was rightfully proud of his fight for these kids, of his victory on their behalf.

There was one shining light in Tony's 85-mile drive from Lancaster to Downey. The longer it took him, the later Paula would be in her office. He almost hoped for traffic. He considered stopping for an early dinner, but he wasn't hungry.

Tony called Carina before he slid behind the wheel of the Vette. "Angel, I gotta go to Downey. Can you go the house and feed LT?"

"Of course, but why do you have to go to Downey so late? Never mind," his girlfriend said. "Don't tell me. For a change, you pissed someone off. Do you have any idea what time you'll be home? I'll have dinner waiting."

She was awesome and not just for putting up with him. She was tall, smart, and thoughtful. She had a good head on her shoulders and also gave good head. What more could a bachelor ask for? "I have no idea how late I'll be. It depends how much Paula's pissed, and it also depends on traffic. I'll call you when I'm leaving Downey."

"Be careful. I love you."

"Love you too, angel. See you later."

Let's Make a Deal, or My Way or the Highway

Traffic was lighter than Tony anticipated. It still took him just under two hours to make the trip. He knocked on Paula's office door at 5:15.

"Come in." She looked up from behind her dark mahogany-stained desk. She had been reading the California Education Codes. She smiled the phony smile that Tony hated. At the same time, she looked at her watch. "You made good time. I guess with your badge you can get away with speeding?"

Maybe she was trying to be funny. It wasn't funny to Tony. "Sit," she said.

Two dark brown, thickly upholstered chairs sat in front of Paula's desk. On the wall behind her desk were pictures of her shaking hands with the mayor, pictures of her with the current FLACOE Director, pictures of her with the current Board of Education, and a picture of Paula receiving her master's degree from USC. Everything was about Paula.

Tony folded his hands in his lap. "I never went over eighty." He didn't smile.

"Let's get down to business. It appears that JFK may be a bit much for you. If that's the case, we have an opening at Hope Center Juvenile Hall."

Hope Center was just off the 5 freeway. As a matter of fact, Tony would have to take the same exit to get to Hope Center that he'd take to Paula's office. That was the threat. Freeway therapy. "What do you want from me?"

Paula looked at Tony. "Sometimes we have to make an end run to score a touchdown. Does that make sense?"

"Look. What Tanner did to that kid is criminal. Tanner is a poster teacher for role model of the year. I did some footwork. This is the fourth or fifth time this son of a bitch did a stunt like this. There isn't a sheet of negative paper in his file. Everyone has covered for him. Now you!"

Paula held up her hand. "Stop! That's more than enough! Would you be more comfortable at Hope Center?"

Once, Tony had a "girlfriend" who worked at Hope Center. They had met at Downey meetings several times, had lunch a few times, and talked on the phone from time to time. He wanted more; she wanted more, but the drive was eighty-plus miles one way. "I don't want to leave JFK," he stated matter-of-factly.

"Then stop being insubordinate."

"I don't see it that way, Paula."

Paula's hands were folded on her desk. She unfolded them and put them in her lap. Tony had taken classes in the academy on interrogation techniques. Her hands in plain sight on the desk, folded, meant she felt like she was in control. Removing them, placing them in her lap where they could not be seen was an indication that she felt she was losing control. One for Tony.

Tony continued. "The SCAR had to be filed. I'm a mandated reporter. My job is at risk if I don't file. Giving it to Probation is a conflict. Probation acts *in loco parentis*, as the parent. It had to be turned into the Sheriff."

"Other administrators give it to Probation."

Tony nodded. Paula's hands were still hidden. *Maybe she was playing with herself.* He tried to picture that. "Other administrators can't get away with doing eighty on the freeway."

Paula brought her hands into sight. She rubbed them together, another sign Tony was getting to her. "Fair enough. I'll give you that one."

Tony had to zero in. "Don't give me "that one." This isn't a game. The law calls for that action." It didn't really, but it was a grey area. Tony was nearing the top of the hill. He kept going. "The way I reasoned it was that the kid's parents could sue the tar out of the deep-pocket county, and may still do that. If we cover up and the newspapers get wind of it, we're in big trouble." Paula liked football. Tony liked baseball. "The parents could win a double header against Corrections."

"Where are you going with this?"

Tony had her. He had turned her 180 degrees. "I'm trying to keep Corrections out of trouble. I'm also trying to bury a teacher, a so-called teacher, who should have been sent to the minors years ago. This clown isn't fit to clean a classroom."

"You're not the jury, Tony. We have a process to deal with...ugh... inept teachers."

"The guy's not inept. He's incompetent. There's a major difference." Tony sat straight up.

"Again, you're not the jury. We'll deal with it."

Tony nodded. The look on his face was sarcastic laced with disgust. "Are we done?"

"Not quite. I want you to write a letter of reprimand for his cite file. Suggest anger-management classes. Remind Mr. Tanner that if another major incident of this magnitude occurs again before the end of this school year, he'll be subject to further disciplinary action. Fax that write-up to my personal fax by Wednesday. I'll review it. If there are corrections to be made, I'll red-pen them and send them back to you for correction. When the letter of reprimand is ready to go, I'll forward it to one of our attorneys to review. I'll make sure I have the letter by Friday.

"You can leave work Friday at lunch. Be in my office by 2 o'clock and will finalize the letter. You can meet with Mr. Tanner on Monday after lunch to put this to bed. And don't forget to remind him that he has the right to union representation."

Tony was laughing to himself. He was also pissed. The letter belonged in his permanent file in Downey; that way, it stayed there for as long as he teaches. The cite file can be "cleaned" at the end of the school year or when he transfers. The wording was too damn general. Meeting on Friday afternoon was Paula's way of punishing Tony. She would have him going back to the fucking Antelope Valley at peak traffic hours. But Tony had the last laugh. She didn't realize Tony worked the HP Police Department Friday night, and HP was only twenty minutes from Downey. *Fuck her and the little pony she rode in on.*

A Package Deal

Before Tony got in his Vette, he called Carina on his cell. “Hi, angel. How goes it?”

“All’s good. LT already ate and I ran around in the backyard with him for a while. We both needed exercise. We’re going to watch the six o’clock news together and then I’ll see if there’s a Scooby movie on for him.”

“Cute. Listen...”

“I know. You don’t want to mess with traffic so you’re gonna go to HP for a couple of hours. Right?”

“Yeah. You good with that?”

“Would it matter? When we got together, I figured you, LT, and HP were a package deal.”

“Is my package a problem?”

“I like your package. As a matter of fact, if you don’t get home too late, maybe I’ll unwrap that package.”

“I won’t be too late. I have to work in the morning and Paula gave me work to do.”

“Be safe, baby. If you shoot anyone, make sure no one’s taping it!”

“Love you, angel. Give LT a kiss for me and a cookie.”

* * *

Tony was in the parking lot of the HP Police Station at 6:15, or 1815 hours. He didn’t stop to grab a bite. He would grab a bite later, while on patrol.

He parked the Vette in the lot, tossed the keys under the seat, and walked to the far end of the lot and down a set of stairs to a silent men’s locker room. Tony opened his locker, stripped, then walked to the shower and turned the knob to hot. It took him thirty minutes to shit, shower, shave, and dress. Now he was ready to go to work, to relax.

Once dressed, he checked himself in the full-length mirror in the bathroom. He looked sharp. His uniform had just come out of the cleaners. His shoes were polished and shined. Badge 108 was polished and gleaming. The only way to tell a full-time officer from a Level 1 Reserve was that a full-timer's badge was double digits. A reserve wore a three-digit badge. There was no 'R' on a reserve's badge; no distinguishing marks on a reserve's uniform.

Tony checked his Glock. It was clean, fully loaded with one chambered. He turned on his radio. It was working. He carried two sets of handcuffs in pouches. Tony was ready.

He walked up a long flight of stairs to the "downstairs briefing room," then to the Watch Commander's Office. Tony knocked.

The WC, Lt. Myles Compose, was reading a report. "TF, what brings you to beautiful downtown HP on a Monday?"

"I couldn't wait till Friday to see you, sir."

"Enter." Lt. Compose smiled but remained behind his desk. "Your partner's off today," he remarked.

"I know, sir. I had a late meeting in our Downey office and didn't want to screw with freeway traffic, so I thought I'd put in some overtime. Is there someone available to ride with?"

"You're looking for time-and-a-half?" The WC was joking. Reserve got zilch, except for a uniform allowance.

"One-and-half times nothing is nothing," Tony said. "At least it was when I went to school."

The Lt. nodded. "Since you're here. Why don't you let dispatch know you're here and you'll be working traffic. Pull a clear unit and tell dispatch you'll be 5TOM."

"No partner?"

"Feel lonely?"

"No sir."

"Can you handle it?"

"Yes, sir."

"Pull mostly traffic. If we have something lightweight in the way of a call, we'll let you handle it. Feel free to back any call you want to. Do you have a book of PD 24s and 25s?" PD 25 were sites for moving traffic violations and 24 were parkers. Either one could get you into a vehicle.

"Yes, sir."

"Then quit standing here and get to work. We don't pay you to stand around and BS with the WC!"

As Tony was just about out the WC's door, he said with a smile, "Be careful out there." Tony nodded.

Miles Avenue was the north-south street that housed HP Police Department. Tony pulled the marked black-and-white out of the Station lot and went south on Miles. As soon as he was on the street, he keyed the mic. "5TOM is 10-8."

Dispatch acknowledged Tony's transmission. "Copy that 5TOM."

Tony's mind was off work. Being a cop demanded all your attention, especially in a tough area like HP.

Tony, a Reserve police officer, found the job even more challenging. Five days a week he was used to one mind set: working as a school assistant principal. Even though the kids were incarcerated for criminal offenses, Tony was a school administrator trying to help these kids get an education. If they didn't get it while they were incarcerated, odds were, they wouldn't get it period. Then, when he put on the uniform, the mindset was one hundred eighty degrees from what he did five days a week.

If Tony hadn't screwed up years ago, he probably would have been a full-time cop. At least he was getting his shot now. And to be cut loose in a tough area—for a reserve to be cut loose in any area—was not common.

Tony liked being out on his own. He could call his own shots. He could drive where he wanted. He wouldn't take any hot calls, but he could back any call that needed assistance. He missed Mickey but Tony was sure they'd be back together after Mickey's days off.

Tony made a right turn heading west on Florence Avenue. The north side of Florence Avenue belonged to HP. The south side belonged to the Los Angeles County Sheriff. Both sides of the street were shopping areas. Tony continued west on Florence.

He was a couple of hundred feet from Rugby Avenue, a northbound one-way street. A dark blue late model Ford made a westbound turn onto Florence from Rugby. The driver was obviously going the wrong way in violation of 21657 of the California Vehicle Code.

Tony closed the distance on the Ford so he could read the plate. He keyed the mic. "5TOM." His first official action on his own.

Dispatch responded. "Go 5TOM."

"I'm going to be 1038 at Florence west of Rugby on 5VSZ678. I'll advise on a back."

"Copy 5TOM."

Tony adjusted his driver's side spotlight so that it reflected off the Ford's rearview mirror effectively, obscuring the driver's vision. She couldn't see Tony. If she could, he'd be blurry. He hit a switch for the right spotlight, beaming it onto the Ford's rear window, cutting off more of the driver's vision. Finally, he activated his high beams.

Tony observed only one person in the Ford. That didn't mean there weren't more occupants.

"5TOM."

"5TOM. Your vehicle comes back no hits to a 2012 Ford Crown Vic. R/O is Sandra Coffey, Woodland Hills. No wants, no warrants."

Slowly, Tony exited his unit. "Copy that. Thanks."

What was the driver doing in HP? Woodland Hills was an upscale, mostly white, residential area 30 miles northwest of HP. You need a few bucks to live in Woodland Hills.

Tony held his flashlight under this left arm, while his right hand was free. He walked slowly to the car. When he reached the driver's side of the car's trunk, he pushed down.

Tony had learned in the academy, and from his three FTOs while in training, that occasionally gangbangers will conceal someone in the trunk. The trunk's occupant would hold the unlocked trunk partially closed. When a cop approached, up went the trunk lid and, BANG, BANG, down went the officer. If the trunk was unlocked, it would now be fully closed by the press of a hand.

Another reason for leaning on the trunk with your hand was that it left fingerprints. If something went down, for example the officer was shot and the driver sped off, once the vehicle was located, the cop's prints was proof positive that he had been on the scene.

Tony stood behind the Ford's post. The driver, the vehicle's lone occupant, had to turn to see him. Tony's eyes scanned the car. He observed no weapons, no obvious contraband. "Ma'am, I need to see your license, registration, and proof of insurance, please."

She was in her mid-twenties. Her white blouse was low cut. Her black skirt was short and had ridden up to her thighs. She didn't bother pulling down her skirt.

Tony took a step forward. He stole a quick glance at her smooth, long legs. Tony liked what he saw.

"The insurance and registration are in the glove compartment. Is it all right to get them?" She paused. "Here's my license."

Just before she reached for the glove compartment, Tony activated the mic on his portable. "5TOM, you can show me code 4."

"Copy that. 5TOM is code 4."

Tony watched her lean across the car to access the glove compartment. She quickly found her papers. "Here you go, officer."

The license belonged to Sandra Coffey as did the Crown Vic and the information supplied to Tony by dispatch. "Do you know why I stopped you?"

She looked up at Tony with a cute smile and bright blue eyes. Her legs opened wider. The skirt was now only a few inches from her crotch. Tony took another half-step forward.

If she was aware that Tony's eyes were between her legs, she gave no hint. "I'm an actress, officer. I just got off the set. I must have made a wrong turn and I got lost. I'm not in a good area so I was trying to get back to the freeway. Was I speeding?"

Tony shook his head. He looked her in the eye. "No. You made a right turn on to this street from Rugby." Tony eyes found his way back to between Sandra's legs. "Rugby's a one-way street northbound. You were going the wrong way."

"I'm sorry." She spread her legs a bit wider. She was wearing pink panties.

If Tony wrote her a citation, he wouldn't write that on the cite.

"I've got an idea. I've got a few autographed pictures on the backseat. Let me give you a couple." She squirmed in the seat, bounced around a bit, and finally ended up with her skirt at her waist exposing her pink panties and her tight little ass. She reached into the backseat and poked around a pile of pictures.

Tony had a clear picture of the outline of her pussy. He was loving it. Tony made a mental note to pull more traffic.

Sandra knew what she was doing. Tony knew what she was doing. Tony didn't like being played like a jukebox. Had she simply asked, "Officer, can you cut me slack this time? I'm sorry. I'll be more careful." Tony probably would have let her go. But now...

She straightened around in the front seat. She handed Tony two autographed pictures.

He'd look at them later but for now he didn't recognize her. "Thanks," Tony said sincerely, "Let me put these on the seat in my unit so they don't get creased." Tony walked back to the unit. He opened the passenger door, set the pictures on the seat, grabbed his cite book off the seat, and started scratching the ticket.

Tony walked back to Sandra's Ford. Her skirt was still hiked up to where Tony could clearly view her gorgeous legs and her pretty pink panties. "Here's your registration and the insurance card, ma'am." He leaned forward. "I cited you for driving the wrong way on a one-way street, section 21657 of the California Vehicle Code. Your court date is printed here. I need one more autograph, please, next to the red X. It's not an admission of guilt. It's a promise to appear."

Sandra looked at him. Her smile turned in to a vicious stare. Either Sandra was one hell of an actress, or she was seriously pissed.

She pulled her skirt down below her knees. She took the pen from Tony's outstretched hand and signed the ticket.

Tony pulled her copy of the ticket from his ticket book and handed it to her. "Please drive carefully in HP, ma'am."

Before she started the Ford, she looked at Tony shaking her head. "If you didn't give me the ticket, I was going to give you my panties, so you'd have something to do when you get off. Want to make a deal?"

Tony started to back away from her car toward the unit. He smiled at her. "I'm not Monty Hall, ma'am. Have a great night. As Tony got back in the car, he thought, *Too bad I'm not Monty Hall.* Her pink panties would have made a great keepsake of his first solo cite.

"5TOM. I'm 10-8 with a PD 24."

"Copy 5TOM."

At 8:30, 2030 hours cop time, Tony decided to call it a night. By the time he changed and got out of the Station, it would be after 2100. He had more than an hour's drive to get back to the Antelope Valley. Tomorrow was a workday, and thanks to Paula, he had additional work to do other than making certain that the school site ran smoothly, and the students and staff behaved.

Tony decided to make one last "pass" around the area between Rita Avenue and Rugby Avenue and then head back to the barn.

Carina was at Tony's house. If she was still awake, "dessert" might be waiting.

Tony drove southbound on Rita Avenue, a one-way street which was lined with low-class apartments and parking lots which often had Toyotas and Hondas stolen out of those lots or stolens that were dumped in those lots. Mickey and Tony had recovered several dumped stolen vehicles on Rita.

He drove slowly, windows down, radio off, checking the eastside and westside parking structures. Everything appeared quiet except for one couple who were making out in a Toyota in the back of one of the lots and a cat that was sleeping on the hood of a beat-up Chevy.

Tony turned right on Florence Avenue. He drove slowly. Florence had light traffic. Several pedestrians were out, either congregated outside closed shops or walking home. It was a quiet Monday night.

On the southside of Florence, which was patrolled by the Sheriffs, Tony observed a Sheriff's black-and-white stopped behind four motorcycles backed in against the curb. The Sheriff was checking license plates. Tony decided to offer assistance. "5TOM."

"Go 5TOM."

"I'll be out to the front of Whiteman's Bar and Grille. Florence east of Pacific on a Sheriff's assist. Will advise."

"Copy 5TOM. Out at Whiteman's Bar, Florence east of Pacific."

Tony made a U-turn. He pulled in behind the Sheriff's vehicle just as four bikers exited the bar, probably the bikers who belonged to the Harleys.

The bikers didn't see Tony nor his vehicle. Their backs were to the Sheriff. Tony exited his unit. He closed the door gently. They still didn't know Tony was on scene.

"Well, well," one of the bikers began. "What have we got here?" He turned to a biker dressed in black vest, dirty jeans, and unpolished boots. "We have a black lone ranger. Now, how about that?" the greaseball continued. His three buddies were loving it.

"Four white boys and one black copper. What do you think about that, Mr. Lone Black Ranger?"

The Sheriff was a big dude. Tony guessed he checked in at 6'1" and better than 200 pounds. The biker idiots were also large, but out of shape from spending too much time drinking beer and riding hogs.

"Look, guys, before you get yourselves into more trouble than you need, let me finish doing my job and we can all go home."

One of the greaseball's buddies stepped up to the plate. "I got a better idea, big boy. Why don't you leave now or call for backup? At the moment, it looks like it's four to one."

Tony announced his presence. "Here's Tonto! Actually, it's four to two which means you're outnumbered."

Greaseball looked puzzled. “Four to two? You’re outnumbered?”

Tony patted his Glock. “Sixteen friends here, plus my ankle holster.” (Tony didn’t carry an ankle holster but he thought about getting one, so that counted.) “The Lone Ranger also has sixteen friends and a second weapon. Get the picture?” Tony observed out of the corner of his eye that the Sheriff was on the radio calling for a backup or two.

Greaseball wasn’t done. He wanted one final swing. “Tonto, aren’t you off the reservation? This is Sheriff territory. You’re trespassing on the wrong turf.”

Tony squared off with grease ball. “I guess you assholes are too busy drinking to read the papers. When the government allowed us to open casinos, they gave us the right of passage. That means we can go anywhere we damn well please. Just like you scumbags.”

Just as the action was about to escalate, three Sheriff’s black-and-whites rolled up to the scene. “What do you know?” the black Sheriff announced. “The cavalry has arrived.”

Grease ball held up his hand. It was dirty. Under his fingernails was grease. “You made your point, Tonto. We’ll ride.”

“Not so fast.” The Sheriff turned to his backup. “Let’s shake them down and FST ’em. If they’re not heavy with heat, they’re probably at least drunk and disorderly.”

Tony had been on the street long enough to know that an asshole was an asshole; add alcohol to the mix and any situation could instantly turn lethal. Hence, when an officer called for backup, backup rolled code and in force.

The black Sheriff walked over to Tony who was about to get into his unit. He extended his hand. Tony shook it. “I’m Ernie Howard.”

“Tony Farrina.”

“I appreciate the back and the support. Without you, things might have escalated in a hurry.”

“I don’t know. You seemed to have everything under control.”

“How long have you been with HP?”

"Two years plus. I'm a reserve."

The Sheriff nodded his head. "They let you drive solo? In this zoo?"

"Actually, up till tonight, I've been with a partner, a full-timer. They cut me loose for the first time tonight."

"You look good out there. You handled yourself real well. I'm going to ask my WC if I can write a commendation to your WC."

Tony smiled. "I appreciate that but really it's not necessary."

"It is necessary and I'm going to do it. Do you have a business card?"

Tony took a HPPD business card out of his pocket and handed it to the Sheriff. "Again, not necessary."

"Again, necessary. Again, thanks."

Tony looked at the unfolding scene behind him. Two of the greaseballs were in handcuffs, two others were mounting their hogs. Tony turned back to the Sheriff. "Be safe, my friend."

"Hey, question before you go. How much do they pay you to do this?"

"I get a uniform allowance every six months."

"No pay?"

"No pay. But I love it."

"Why don't you go full time?"

"I've been offered the opportunity twice. I've got a lot of years in with Corrections and the years aren't transferable. I'd kill my retirement." Then Tony added, "Next life."

"And in my next life, I'll be white."

Does It Ever Stop?

Traffic was light on the northbound 5 freeway at 10:10, 2210 hours. The speedometer in Tony's Vette read 78.

For most of the drive, Tony remained in the center lane. He kept his speed under eighty. He had been stopped a couple of times by the CHP (California Highway Patrol) for speeding, but he had yet to receive a ticket. His badge always convinced the officer to cut him slack. It was embarrassing getting pulled over, so he tried to keep his speed reasonable.

Tony thought about the situation with Tanner and Paula. Maybe he was better off letting it go. On the other hand, letting it go would ensure that Tanner kept his job. He didn't deserve to be a teacher. Unfortunately, in education, there was an invisible shield of protection for the wrongdoers unless the offense was so serious that it couldn't be ignored.

The police had a barricade of sorts that protected those who screwed up. Tony understood it, but he didn't necessarily agree with it.

He had been on 273.5 calls, spousal abuse, when an officer or two would take the suspect out behind the apartment complex and "tune him up." Tony didn't really object to that. The court system was such that if an officer observed bruising, a cut, scratches, etc., the offender had to be taken into custody. Unfortunately, the perp was usually out on bail in less than 24 hours. Then the wife would really get a beating.

If the responding officers roughed up the suspect and warned him that, if they had to come back again, he'd not only go to jail, but he'd be in for a major overhaul, the situation would steady, at least for a few weeks.

Tony was afraid that one day Tanner would go too damn far, or he'd push the wrong kid too far and the student would give Tanner a serious beating. Tony didn't know what else he could do. Corrections didn't want Tony to push it. Maybe he should just soft-pedal it and let the chips fall where they may.

Tony called Carina. He told her not to hold dinner; he would grab a sandwich when he got home.

Tony kept driving and he kept thinking. Before he realized it, he was pulling into his driveway.

Carina was in the custom California king-sized bed and under the clean white sheets when Tony got out of the shower and walked into the bedroom. LT had Tony's place in the bed. He looked at Tony.

"I guess it's going to be a threesome tonight," Tony lamented.

"Doubtful," Carina said with a smile. LT barked. "If you want a threesome, it's going to be two guys and me. Up for that?"

"Doubtful. LT, you're a USC graduate."

Next to the bed was a narrow white wicker nightstand with barely enough room for the phone. It had one drawer with a wicker handle. The wicker handle had a piece of towel wrapped around it.

LT heard Tony say, "USC." His ears stood up as if they had taken too much Viagra. His mouth opened and he wore a big smile. He jumped off the bed and ran around to the nightstand. LT stopped, jumped up, put his front paws on the top of the stand and wrapped his teeth around the drawer handle. He pulled the drawer open. Next, he stood part way up and put his face halfway into the drawer. When he found what he wanted, he ran back around the bed and placed it in Tony's hand. Tail wagging, LT trotted out of the bedroom to the upstairs living room. He jumped on the couch, put his head on the pillow, and went to sleep.

"I'm surprised you didn't train him to put it on you."

"If he were female, I would have." Tony handed Carina the wrapped Trojan. "You can have the honors."

***

There is no such thing as a routine day when you work inside a juvenile facility. It's like saying "routine traffic stop." When a cop thinks he's making a "routine traffic stop," and he neglects his safety, that's the time some Adam Henry, some asshole, is going to pull a gun and send the officer to the morgue.

Tuesday was not routine at JFK. Tony had a report to write. He wanted to touch bases with Tanner to see if his arrogant attitude changed. That was more or less routine. What wasn't routine was the bomb scare phoned into Probation.

It wasn't the first bomb scare threat and it wouldn't be the last. Odds were that some punk who had been released recently wanted vengeance. When human lives were at risk, you didn't play the odds—you took precautions.

So, classrooms were emptied at 920 and the kids were walked, in a line, to the field where they stood. The grass was wet so you couldn't have them sit their asses down. They couldn't go to the dorm because the dorm had to be searched, swept, and declared safe. The same held true for the classrooms and the school offices. Everyone had to be out on the field. No work got done and the kids got a free day or at least they were free for as long as it took to sweep all the buildings. The kids loved it.

The Sheriff would not respond. They said that the staff knew the buildings as well as they did, and, therefore, the staff needed to do the sweep.

At 10:00, Probation had assembled a sweep team. It took three-and-a-half hours to declare all buildings safe and secure. During that time, nobody went potty and nobody went to lunch. Nobody entered the grounds and no one exited the grounds. A count was taken of all staff and all students.

At 1:30, a Probation staffer got on the loudspeaker and announced an all-clear. Probation marched the kids back to the dorm. They took another headcount and gave the kids a head call. Then they took them to lunch.

The school staff hadn't had their lunch break. They had to have one, or the union would go ballistic. At damn near two o'clock, the principal told the teaching staff that they could go to lunch and directly home after lunch. Their school day was over.

Tony called Tanner and asked him if he wanted to meet.

"I'm hungry then I'm going home. I'll meet with you tomorrow during planning period unless you want to get someone to cover my class in the morning," Tanner informed him.

Tony wanted to kick the little bastard's ass all the way down to the San Fernando Valley. Instead, he replied, "I'll see you tomorrow. I'll see about coverage. Have a good lunch." Tony thought he was going to choke on his words. He went to the lounge and poured himself a cup of coffee.

Every Tuesday evening from 5:00 p.m. until everyone left, Pop's Burgers and Fries had a cruise-in at the burger joint's parking lot. The difference between a car show and a cruise-in was that a car show generally judged cars and gave trophies. A cruise-in was just that; you cruised to the venue, parked your car, grabbed coffee and food, then sat around and told lies with the other car owners.

Tony called Carina from his office. "Hi, angel. How's your day?"

"Just another day at the office. How are you doing?"

"SOS with Tanner. We had a bomb scare. Early dismissal. I'm putting the finishing touches on the Tanner paperwork so I can fax it to Paula. Basically, the SOS crap." Tony put the mouse over the printer icon and printed out his report.

"I'm going to get out of here in the next twenty minutes or so. I'm going to run home, feed LT, and hook Mini Me to the Pace Car. How about meeting me at Pop's and I'll let you buy me dinner?"

Tony heard Carina chuckle. "After last night, you've at least earned a cheeseburger. Maybe even fries with it. I don't know where you get all your energy from."

"You inspire me. And yes, I did enjoy last night, very much, very, very much. You have the most talented tongue and mouth in the Valley."

"Only the Valley? I guess I need practice."

"I don't think so. LT did tell me you kept him awake with all your moaning and groaning."

"Cake him!"

For Tony's last birthday, Carina gave him a birthday card that said, "Inside is your favorite four-letter word." When he opened the card, it said, "CAKE."

Carina chastised Tony each and every time he used the word "fuck." That word became an overly used part of Tony's vocabulary and Carina didn't like it, so Tony tried to cool it. Following the receipt of the birthday card, he tried to use the word "cake" instead.

"I'll see you at Pop's. Tell the USC grad I'll try to keep my moaning and groaning down to a low roar next time we have a sleepover."

Tony proofed the report. It didn't much matter. He knew Paula would red-pencil the shit out of the report, even if it didn't need it. She'd nitpick words and punctuation just to piss Tony off and make him do more work. He'd bet his left nut that the report would be in his fax machine first thing in the morning redlined to hell. His final thought before he turned off his computer and locked the office door was, "Cake her!"

There were eleven classic or special-interest cars in Pop's parking lot when Tony rolled in. Among the shiny, expensive, collector cars was a 1957 two-door black Chevy, a 1962 red Corvette with silver coves, a DeLorean, and a 1964 red Impala Super Sport convertible.

Tony's purple and yellow 1998 Corvette Pace Car was an instant hit. The Mini Me, the matching go-cart, was even more of a hit. The custom diamond-plated trailer with purple fenders and yellow wheels made the package a real crowd pleaser.

Tony parked the Vette with the other classics. He exited the car, then popped the hood. Under the hood was a mural designed by Canadian artist Corrado Mallia, who was known worldwide for his creative design work.

Tony had stumbled across Corrado's name at a car show. Another club member had a custom-designed mural done by Corrado under his hood. It was a gorgeous picture of former and late Yankee great Mickey Mantle, complete in Yankee pinstripe uniform, bat in hand, walking up to home plate.

The idea immediately took shape in Tony's mind. Carina was a Scooby-Doo nut. She had Scooby this and Scooby that all over her house.

Corrado sketched out possible likenesses and emailed them to Tony. Four months later, under the hood of Tony's Pace Car, was Scooby-Doo, wearing a HP police uniform complete with a badge that boasted the number 108, Tony's badge number. Next to Scooby the police officer was a bad Scooby being placed in handcuffs by the cop Scooby. In the background was the Pace Car, turned into a HP cop car complete with the license plate HPPD.

The mural was a tribute to one creative artist who took pride in his work, a rarity in today's mostly money-hungry world. Tony was so impressed with the mural that he had it tattooed across his back at a local tattoo parlor.

The Mini Me was a foot longer and a foot wider than your average go-cart. It bragged a 5.5 Briggs and Stratton engine. With Tony behind the wheel, before he ate breakfast, the Mini Me would do forty-five.

Tony took two minutes to say his hellos to fellow car enthusiasts and to check out a couple of the cars he hadn't seen before. He found Carina sitting on Pop's patio. He gave her slow, loving kiss on the lips and sat down. "How was work?"

"Good. Quiet and uneventful. Unlike yours, I'm sure."

Tony shrugged his shoulders. "I'm starved. Let's order."

"Done. I ordered a BBQ chicken salad for both of us and iced tea." Just then a young girl in a black hoop skirt, white blouse, and pink scarf wrapped around her neck roller-skated to the outside table. "Two iced teas. Your dinner will be up shortly."

"Thanks."

"You look pensive. Tell me what's going on." Carina was dressed in dark brown slacks and a beige pullover top. Her long blonde hair was blowing in the Antelope Valley wind.

"I'm bouncing that thing with Tanner around in my head like a pinball. One side of my brain says, bury the bastard; the other side says, play ball with Corrections." Tony took a hit off his iced tea. "What does the counselor think?"

Carina was a drug and alcohol counselor. She liked her profession. She was good at it. She had an above average set of coping skills.

"Are you going to tell me that a guy who can teach his Norwegian Elkhound to open a drawer, fetch a condom, and bring it to him in bed, can't reason out this situation?"

Tony grinned. "That's the other side of my brain."

"I think you're letting someone, maybe two someones, rent space in your head. Raise the rent and tell them to move."

That crap was for the addicts and alkies. "Would you like to translate that into English?"

"Gladly. From what you've told me, Tanner overreacted with a student; he seriously overreacted."

Tony added, "What he did was criminal."

"Okay. But you can't control him, nor can you control what he does. Nor can you control Paula or Corrections. True?"

"I guess."

"All you can do is take the action that is warranted."

"I'll buy that."

"So, it boils down to what action is warranted that you want to take?"

"I want to fire his ass."

"You're not listening. That's an action that is out of your wheelhouse. Only the Corrections Board can hire and fire."

Tony shook his head. "You're right."

"I didn't hear you; the wind was blowing."

"Yeah, I know. You're right."

"Identify the action you want to take, take it, and get on with the game of life."

"How many years of school did that take you? And I already faxed Paula my report. I compromised. It calls for anger-management classes, no more misbehaving the remainder of the year, and the write-up to go in his FLACOE file."

"Do you think you'll get what you want?"

"Only time will tell." The skater in the hoop skirt brought the chicken salads to the table.

"Let's eat."

Between bites, Carina asked, "Is everything else good at the site?"

Tony was still chewing his food. He shook his head. "More or less. I can play ball with Paula and Corrections, or I can take my bat and ball and drive to Downey five days a week in peak traffic hours."

"You'll be transferred?"

"In a heartbeat. Been there, done that, and the Pace Car doesn't need all those miles, not to mention my tired, getting-older body."

Carina smiled. She blushed. "Nothing wrong with that body. Trust me on that."

"It's a bitch. You try to do the right thing for the right reason and something or someone gets in your way. There isn't a doubt in my mind that if these kids were predominantly white, this shit would have stopped a long time ago. It pays for us to keep minorities in check. It gives us better control. These kids probably have their last shot at an education while they're locked up. We're doing them a disservice.

"I'm not saying that even most of these kids would take advantage of an education if we got serious with them. I am saying that some would. I am saying that we're a public school funded by the taxpayers and that I have an obligation to treat any kid the same way I would treat my own. Simply put, that's the rub."

Carina sipped her iced tea. "What happens if you push it? Can they fire you?"

"They could. I am not protected like teachers. I have no union and I serve at the pleasure of the Board. Would they fire me? Probably not, but they could and would run my ass all over Los Angeles County."

Tony took a breath. "I know, put my big boy pants on and make a decision."

"If I were you, counselor, I'd tell you to take a piece of paper, fold it down the middle, list the positives on one side and the negatives on the other. Focus on that and then make an informed decision and go for it."

She inquired, "Why do you think they don't want to deal head-on with Tanner?"

"I don't think, I know. If they go after Tanner, the little jerk will go to the newspapers and all the shit that goes on in FLACOE will leak out. Every so often some of the shit gets out and there is an investigation, such as what is going on now with the ACLU. So, what Corrections does is focus its attention where the ACLU is, and the shit moves to another site.

"Example, maybe the fact that the ACLU has cut down the influx of drugs at the JFK School. It hasn't stopped at the other facilities. How about lack of teaching? How about sex with kids? How about inappropriate actions between staff during school hours?"

Carina put her fork down. She held up her right hand. "Are you telling me that the staff has had sex with kids?"

"Girls' camp—Probation staff arrested at a motel with a girl he took out of camp. A nurse caught screwing a male student. A student getting head in one of my teacher's classrooms."

"You gotta be kidding."

Tony shook his head. "We had a teacher caught with five X-rated tapes that were being shown to kids in his classroom. One was a homosexual prison tape. I was charged with the investigation, even though he wasn't my teacher. They wanted me to do the investigation because of my cop schooling. When Downey approved the paperwork, I called Paula to tell her I was filing felony charges against the teacher. She told me if I did, I would be immediately terminated. The teacher resigned. Zero publicity and he's teaching in another state.

"How about staff having sex at school?"

"You? You gotta be kidding."

Now it was Tony's turn to blush. "I got head in the staff lounge after school. I was having an affair with a Probation secretary."

"Are you serious?"

"Guilty as charged."

"Where you married?"

Tony shook his head. "I know. I know. I was wrong. First time I ever cheated on my wife. If I ever get married again, it won't ever happen again."

"That's bad, Tony. I'm more than a little surprised."

"I know. Spank me."

"If I didn't have to get up so damn early I would. But you'd like it." Carina leaned part way across the table. "I would even make you wear my dirty panties before I took you over my knee, bad, bad boy."

Tony felt a hardness in his slacks. He looked down at his salad and stabbed a piece of BBQ chicken with his fork.

There were several ways to drive to Downey. Tony knew them all. Depending on time of day, Tony guessed which freeway would have the least traffic. It didn't always work out that way. Tony recalled sitting in traffic on the 710 freeway, the result of a jackknifed truck, and listening to the newscaster explain how wide open the 710 was. The guy should have been a proctologist.

Since it was early afternoon, Tony was driving the eastbound 210 to the 2 to the 5, passed Dodger Stadium to the 710, and off on Imperial Highway. He guesstimated that he could make the drive in under an hour and a half, especially because he had Carina with him and could use the diamond lane.

"What made you want to go on a ride-along?" Tony loved the fact that she was interested in his work, that she always listened to his stories and seemed genuinely "moved" by Tony's profession and his avocation. But going on a ride-along surprised Tony.

Carina smiled. "I was watching a rerun of Blue Bloods. It was an episode where an actor goes on a ride-along with Danny to get a feel for what they do for an upcoming role. And I thought, I'd like to see what my guy does. It's okay, isn't it?"

"It's more than okay. I like it." A guy in the number one lane suddenly decided he wanted to get into the number two lane. Without signaling, he cut in front of Tony. Tony hit the brake. "Asshole."

"Isn't that supposed to be 'Adam Henry'?"

"You are watching too much television." If a cop had a guy in the field who was acting like a jerk, the officer might let dispatch know the circumstance so she could roll backup. He couldn't very well get on the air and say the suspect is acting like an asshole. He'd say, "This guy is an Adam Henry."

Tony took his eyes off the light freeway traffic to look at Carina. He turned his eye back to the traffic. "A while back a guy was in court on a traffic cite. During the stop, the clown had been belligerent and basically a real asshole to the officer. Because even a traffic ticket might go to court, and it could be a couple of months before it goes to court, most cops make 'tickler' notes on the station's copy of the cite. I not only do that, but I also make extensive notes in a notebook. Looks great in court and usually freaks out the guy who got the ticket and impresses the hell out of the judge." He paused.

"Anyway, this guy hired himself an attorney who, in court, challenged the cop. The attorney had a copy of the station ticket and said to the cop, 'It says, acting Adam Henry on the ticket. Would you explain to the court what that means?'"

"The attorney knew the answer before he asked the question. Without batting an eye, the officer said, angry and hostile, counselor. The guy was found guilty."

"Cute. Do you write a lot of tickets?"

"I do a lot of stops. It's how you get into cars to find weapons and drugs and drunks."

"Do you profile?"

"When did you become a defense attorney? And what do you consider profiling?"

"Pulling someone over because he looks like a gangbanger. Stopping someone because he's black."

"Let me ask you a question and then I'll answer you honestly. You're a cop. You're working in a marked unit. You observe two cars run a traffic light. You're only going to be able to pull one over. One car is a Ford station wagon with a white family, two young kids and a wife. The other car has three blacks in it, obviously gangbangers. They're smoking and the radio is blasting songs filled with obscenity. Who do you pull over?"

"It's 'whom' and I get your point."

"It's not profiling, babe, it's good police work. If I consistently treat minorities differently than I treat whites, then I have a problem. In my case," Tony smiled. "I hate everybody equally, except you."

"One more question?"

Tony exited the freeway at Imperial Highway and drove east. "That's about all you're going to have time for. Shoot."

"Recently a female officer shot a motorist in the back because he refused commands to stop, walked to his car, and might have been reaching inside. Do you think that was a justified shooting?"

"Great question. I wasn't there. Sometimes cameras don't show the whole picture or the right angle to get an accurate picture of what happened. Here's what I know from watching the video several times, from reading the various accounts, and from hearing the officer contact dispatch to let them know that a shot had been fired.

"First, the guy had already been tased by another officer. The guy's hands were in plain sight with nothing in the hands. He was walking to the car, and it appeared that he was reaching into the car. Several other officers were on scene and there was an airship overhead. I wouldn't have shot. She was obviously stressed. Does that make it a bad shooting? In my opinion, yes. Now supposing he reached into the front seat of his car, grabbed a shotgun, and she fired and missed? You'd have some dead cops on your hands.

"I think she may be found guilty of manslaughter and terminated. It's a different world today. The streets are much more dangerous. Every idiot has a weapon. Most of those idiots have a record.

"Do you know if you get caught carrying a gun and you don't have a prior, it's a misdemeanor. If you have a nightstick in your car, you get stopped and if the officer finds it, you're going down for a felony. That's your NRA at work."

"You're not an NRA member?"

"I told you, you had time for one more question."

"Are you?"

"No, I'm not. And I know you're not."

"You're under oath, officer. Just answer the question."

"Funny. I think the NRA has gone too far. I'm a firm believer in the second amendment and a firm believer in the right to bear arms. But automatic weapons, or weapons that can be tweaked and turn into automatic weapons, are not necessary unless you're fighting a war.

"Do you know how dangerous it is to approach a car you just stopped? If Adam Henry has a weapon in the car and decides he wants to shoot a cop, the best you can hope for is that he's a lousy shot or that the rounds hit your vest." Tony exited the 710 freeway and drove east.

"Do you want to ride with a male or a female officer?"

"Doesn't matter. I can't ride with you and Mickey?"

"I don't think you want to ride in the back of a Crown Vic cop car. Not very comfortable, even without handcuffs."

"You speak from experience, I suppose?"

"Actually, yes. But we don't want to go into that now." Tony rubbed his right shoulder. He strained it lifting weights.

Tony pulled into Corrections' school parking lot. "Do you want to take the car and take a drive? I doubt I'll be more than an hour. There are a couple of fast-food places a block and a half east of here and Stox Coffee Shop a block down on this side of the street."

"I'll take a walk. The exercise will do me good."

Carina could not have been in better shape. She had the body of an 18-year-old and the stamina to match.

"This is a pretty good area but be careful."

"Give me your gun," she kidded.

"Not until I put my vest on." Tony leaned over and kissed her on the lips. Tony exited the car. He walked around the front of the Vette and opened the door for Carina.

"Such a gentleman. I love it."

"East coast manners, ma'am." He gave Carina another quick kiss, turned, and walked toward the entrance.

The Beat Goes On, and On, and On...

Tanner was already in Paula's office. She was behind her desk and Tanner was seated in front of Paula's desk. Neither were smiling.

"Sit down, Tony. Hopefully this won't be prolonged."

It will only be prolonged, if you prolong it, Tony thought.

"I read over your report several times. I thought it would fly as it is but then I noticed a change or two. I discussed it with the attorney, and he agreed with me. I'll let you read it over in a minute but let me give you a summary first. If either of you has a problem with it, speak up. If not, I'll have my secretary make the necessary changes on the computer and we're done for the day. I'm sure we'd all like to start our weekend. And by the way, Mr. Tanner has waived his right to union representation in the spirit of collaboration."

Tony wanted to spit. What a crock of crap.

"Change number one, anger-management classes are a suggestion. Change number two, the write-up will remain in your site file until the end of the school year. If there are no further serious incidents, the write-up will be pulled and shredded. If there is another serious incident, both write-ups will go into Mr. Tanner's permanent file. Change number 3, Mr. Tanner will review his compliance with you monthly and you will record his continued compliance or lack thereof. You will forward me a copy and place a copy in Mr. Tanner's site file."

She should have just rewritten the entire report. Tony wasn't in the mood to push it; he just wanted to get to HP and relax. "Sounds good. Anything else?" There was just a hint of sarcasm in Tony's voice.

Paula smiled. "Mr. Tanner, how does that sound?"

Tanner nodded. "Works for me."

"Tony?"

Tony nodded slowly. He glared at Paula. He sighed. "Terrific."

She handed a copy of the report to Tanner and a copy to Tony.

Tony was in the elevator on the way to the lobby by 3:10. Tanner stayed behind in Paula's office. *Maybe he's licking Paula's ass,* Tony thought.

More Fun and Games

Carina was standing at the passenger door of the Vette. Tony hit the key fob and, after the door unlocked, he opened it for her and she got in. Tony walked around the car to the driver's side.

They were westbound on Imperial Highway on the way back to the freeway. "How'd it go?"

"You would have been real proud of me. I kissed every inch of her ass."

"Better not have. That privilege is only mine. Seriously, how'd it go?"

"Could have been better. Basically, she let him off with a slap on the butt. No paper in his permanent file; no forced anger-management classes."

"Can you let go of that?"

"I'll change the station."

"You're learning." Tony entered the 710 freeway. He could take the 710 to the 5 north and exit Soto Street or he could exit the 710 at Florence and go west to HP. At this time of day, he was probably better off taking Florence.

Tony walked Carina to the watch commander's office. He knocked. Lieutenant Myles Compose was reading a report. He looked up. "Hey, TF. How goes it?"

"Good, sir. I want to introduce you to my girlfriend Carina. She wants to talk to you about becoming an HP cop."

"Are you for real? Nice to meet you, Carina."

"I'm kidding. I called earlier in the week to set up a ride-along. Sgt. Alphonse told me it wouldn't be a problem. Is there someone she can ride with?"

Lieutenant Compose smiled. “I’m sure every male on the force would grab at the opportunity for a ride- along. She can ride with you.”

“I’m Mickey’s partner.”

“That’s not in stone anymore. When it’s appropriate, you’ll be partnered up. Tonight, you have a ride-along.”

Carina looked at Tony and smiled. “Wouldn’t you rather ride with a full-timer?”

“No. I told you I’d rather ride with you.”

“You’ll probably see more action with a full-timer.”

“You see what I have to put up with?” Carina teased, looking at the watch commander.

“Go downstairs and change,” he ordered Tony. “I have paperwork for Carina to fill out. I’ll also get her a vest.”

Tony looked at Carina and smiled as they exited the Station’s lot. She smiled back. Tony was nervous because he was a reserve who had been on his own in a unit only once. He also had a ride-along. Carina was nervous because it was her very first ride-along and she didn’t know what might happen, what to expect.

It was almost dark. “5TOM, show me 10-8.” He turned to Carina. “10-8 means I’m clear for calls. Remember, I’m a reserve. I might get lightweight calls. I can back or assist another officer on any call.”

Carina nodded. “How do I wear this vest? It’s hot and heavy.”

“That sounds sexy. Ever have sex in a police car?”

“No. And, for obvious reasons, I’m not about to ask you the same question.”

Tony laughed. “The answer’s no. But tonight might be the night!”

Tony went westbound on Saturn. “Most of HP is Hispanic. A lot of older people; a lot of retired people; a handful of young Adam Henry gangbangers who want to deal drugs and shoot up the place. Our objectives are to drive around and show a presence, do as much community policing as possible, and see if we can get drugs and guns off the street. Our highest objective is to go home at end of watch in one piece.”

"10-4 Officer Farrina. Copy that."

"That's good. Ever thought about becoming a cop?"

"Not for me. I'm very happy doing what I'm doing, thank you. I'm good at what I do, and I enjoy it."

The car in front of Tony was a red Chevy Monte Carlo. It was occupied twice. At Rugby and Saturn there was a four-way stop. The driver didn't slow down and went through the stop sign.

"We're going to pull these guys over. The driver ran a stop sign. His tags are also eight months expired. Six months or more and the car can be impounded. We want to pull him over in a lighted area for safety. We also want to pull him over on a wider street so we don't back up traffic and it's less dangerous."

Tony picked up the mic. "5TOM a roller."

"Go 5TOM."

"5 ADA 337. It should come back to a Chevy Monte Carlo."

The vehicle went northbound Santa Fe. Tony followed two cars back.

"5TOM, your vehicle comes back no hits to Juan Mendoza Corona, Hope Street, this city. Registration expired February 2016. No RIP."

"Copy that. I'll be 1038 that vehicle northbound Santa Fe at Slauson. I'll advise on a back." Tony looked at Carina. "1038 is the code for pulling traffic or making a stop. RIP is registration in progress." Tony activated his overheads. "When I stop him, you can get out of the unit, but I want you to open the door and stand behind it."

"Got it."

The Monte Carlo pulled over on Santa Fe north of Slauson, just in front of the bus stop. Tony hit the high beams and shined both spotlights at the rear of the car. He exited the unit cautiously and waited until Carina was behind the passenger door before he made his approach. His flashlight was under his left arm. Before he contacted the driver, he unsnapped the thumb grip on his holster.

"Good evening. I stopped you because you ran a stop sign at Rugby and Saturn. Please turn off the engine. I need to see your license, registration, and proof of insurance." Tony's eyes carefully swept the vehicle. "Both of you, please keep your hands where I can see them."

The Hispanic gentleman, who was in his mid-twenties, dressed in black shorts, white t-shirt, and tennis shoes, turned off the ignition, then handed Tony his CDL, his registration, and proof of insurance. Tony checked out the passenger then walked back to the passenger side of the vehicle and stood behind the door with Carina.

"5TOM. CDL check and W 9 on one, please." The CDL was a California driver's license check to confirm that the driver's license was valid, not suspended. The W 9 was a warrants check to see if HP or any other department had a warrant out for his arrest.

From his cover behind the passenger door, Tony watched both occupants of the Monte Carlo. There was no furtive movement. He looked at Carina. She was also staring at the Chevy.

"5TOM, 10-35."

10-35 was police code for I'm going to give you information that the subject does not need to hear. Usually, it meant that there was a warrant for the driver.

"Go with your 10-35."

"Your subject, Juan Mendoza Corona, 6/8/88, has a $50,000 warrant out of Mid Valley, LAPD." No sooner had dispatch voiced those words than a backup unit appeared.

Tony, still standing next to Carina behind the passenger door of the black-and-white, explained what was going on. Sandra Medina, the backup officer, walked up beside them. "Want to pull him out of the vehicle?"

Tony nodded. "We've got two. I'll get the driver out of the car."

Tony walked around the back of the black-and-white. He opened the driver's door and stood behind it. "Driver, I need you to step out of the car, please, and keep your hands where I can see them."

The driver complied.

"Face away from me, driver. Keep your hands in the air. Walk backward toward the sound of my voice."

Again, the driver complied.

Tony "worked" the driver so that he now had him between the two black-and-whites and in front of them. "I need you to drop down to your knees." Tony gave him several seconds. "Now cross your right leg over your left at the ankle. Place your hands on your head and interlock your fingers."

Officer Medina looked at Tony and he nodded. She walked up to the suspect quickly and put her foot under the suspects crossed ankles. If he moved the wrong way, Medina would come up with her foot and the guy would fall forward. Then she handcuffed him, lifted him up by the arm, and walked him back to Tony's unit where he searched him and put him in his unit.

"Passenger, exit the vehicle slowly with your hands in the air. Do not make any sudden movements." There was a time when they'd "dust the passenger off" while he was still in the car. But today, almost everybody had to be considered armed. Since the driver had an outstanding warrant, for officer safety, Tony had every right to pull the passenger out of the vehicle.

Officer Medina and Tony went through the same procedure with the passenger until he was in handcuffs. Medina put the passenger in her unit. He wanted the two separated.

Tony walked over to his unit. He opened the rear door and spoke to the driver. "Step out. Do you have ID?"

While Tony was talking to the driver, Medina was searching the suspect's car.

"It's in my rear pocket. You can get it."

"Do you know why I stopped you?"

"I ran a stop sign and my tags are expired."

Tony examined his California Identification Card. "Do you have a driver's license?"

"It's suspended."

"What for?"

"Failure to appear."

The guy didn't show up for court when he was supposed to.

"What was the original cite for?"

"Running a stop sign."

"What do you have against stop signs?"

The man didn't say anything. He half smiled. "Am I going to jail?"

"We'll see." Tony studied the ID card. He matched the physical description on the card to that of the man standing across from him. "What's your name?"

"Juan Mendoza Corona."

"Birth date?"

"6/8/88."

Tony keyed the mic on his portable. "You can show us code 4." He took his cell out of his pocket and called dispatch. "Would you telephone LAPD, please, at West Valley? Ask them if they'll pick this guy up. If not, I'll cite him out."

Medina cleared the car. She "tossed" it thoroughly and found nothing. She ran the passenger for wants and warrants. The guy was as clean as a baby's new diaper. She took the cuffs off him. "Have a seat on the curb, please. Put your feet straight out and cross them at the ankles. Put your hands, palms down, flat on your knees."

People often got pissed off when the police directed them to do that, but it was for officer safety. The second option would be to put him in the back of the unit but, since the guy was clean, that was a sticky option.

Medina remembered when Tony made a stop on a little guy who had no plates on his car. It was a busy Saturday night and no backup was available. It was 0200 hours. Tony shook the guy down and asked for his ID. The guy said it was in the car.

The guy was white, clean shaven, dressed in slacks and a pullover shirt, and wearing tennis shoes. Tony was going to cuff him and put him in the unit. "Where's your ID?"

"On the front seat of the car."

"Go get it." Tony walked a step behind the guy and to his right. Tony didn't remember seeing anything on the front seat but that didn't mean the wallet wasn't on the seat. Tony often asked himself if he would have cuffed the guy had he been Hispanic.

They were three feet from the guy's car. The guy bolted across the street in front of a moving car. Tony began to follow but stumbled and the car just missed hitting him. The guy got away.

Of course, there was no wallet or any other ID in the car. The car was a stolen out of Florida.

Tony got hell from the watch commander. It was weeks before the taunts from the troops died down.

Tony took the handcuffs off Mendoza. "Here's the deal. LAPD isn't going to come to HP to pick you up. It's a busy night. Consider yourself lucky. I'm going to cite you for driving on a suspended and for the expired tags. I can impound the car for up to 30 days. I won't. Unfortunately, I can't let you take the car because I know the tags are expired by more than six months and the car shouldn't be on the road. If I let you take the car and something happens, the Department can be held liable.

"Here's what I'm willing to do. We're going to play Let's Make a Deal. Lock the car. Either take care of the expired tags at DMV Monday or have somebody tow or flatbed the car out of here." Tony emphasized, "DO NOT DRIVE IT. If you get caught driving it in HP, it's going to be impounded for 30 days. *Comprende*?"

"Yes, sir. I appreciate it."

"Don't drive it, man. When we're gone, don't take it out of here by driving her. If you get caught, I promise you, she's gone for a month, and the fees are ridiculous."

"I won't. I promise."

"Can you get a ride home?"

"I'm going to call a friend."

Carina and Tony got back into the unit. "Show me 10-8 with a PD24. The vehicle is being parked with R/O's permission. It's going to be towed and it's legally parked."

"Copy that, 5TOM."

There was a sandwich shop several hundred yards north of the traffic stop. Tony pulled into the lot and turned the unit around so it was facing the street. He blacked out the lights, but left the engine running.

"Do you want to explain to me what went on? I think I got some of it."

"Sure." Tony watched the street. "The guy we stopped for running a stop sign and for expired tags also had a warrant out for his arrest. It was an LAPD warrant for $50,000 for failure to appear for a suspended-license ticket. I asked dispatch to see if LAPD would come to HP to pick him up. LAPD declined. We are not going to transport him—not on a Friday night. It's too busy. So, we do what we call citing him out in the field. We basically give him another ticket.

"The car was more than six months late on the registration, so the car is impoundable. I cut the guy slack. I told him if he either took care of the fees that are late, or promised to have the vehicle towed, I'd take him at his word and wouldn't impound the car. We're sitting here hiding because I want to see if the guy's word is good."

"Okay, I got that. The black-and-white is hiding so you can see if this guy's going to keep his word." Carina crossed and uncrossed her legs. "Why are you hiding?"

"You lost me."

"A big part of my job, too, is to read people. You're still 'in Downey.'"

Tony smiled. She was good and she knew him well. "You're partly right. My mind is split three ways right now: JFK and Tanner, Downey and Paula, and here. That's what gets cops shot. I have to be one hundred percent here, not anywhere else. That's dangerous as hell when you're wearing a badge and a gun. With all the OIS today, I've got to get that renter out of my head, right?"

"Kenny Rogers said, 'You gotta know when to hold 'em and you gotta know when to fold 'em. And what is OIS?"

"Officer-involved shooting. There has been a rash of them lately."

"Let's go back to Tanner and see if we can put that to sleep. Why is that eating at you?"

"Fair question. I guess it's because I want the kids to have a fair shot at turning their screwed-up lives around and the best way to do it is to get an education. They're forced to attend school at camp, so a teacher who can challenge them intellectually is worth his weight in hundred-dollar bills. A jerk like Tanner is like a counterfeit bill—he's worthless. Not only is Tanner screwing with the kid he assaulted, but he's reaching every other kid who witnessed what happened and any other kids who were told about it. It's like the occasional bad cop—he gives everyone a bad name."

"Are you satisfied that you did everything you could?"

Tony was monitoring the radio. There was a lull in the service calls. Everything was strangely quiet.

Tony raised his eyebrows. "There are other things I can do but, ethically, they're out of bounds. Some are against the law."

"You want to explain that?"

Tony shook his head. "It might incriminate me." He hesitated, choosing his words carefully. "Let's just say sometimes you have to fight a gorilla with a bigger gorilla. Sometimes, instead of holding or folding 'em, you've got to pull the ace from the bottom of the deck."

Carina looked puzzled. "I'm not fresh out of the minor leagues. I work with many of the same population that you work with at the camps and on the streets. I've heard most of it. Are you talking about leaning on the guy?"

"Let's drop it."

Carina wasn't ready to let go. "That could cost you your job."

"Only if I get caught. Someone said there is a thin line between cop and criminal. If I did lean on him, and no way am I saying that's an option, I'd be at the crap table in Vegas when it happened."

"You feel that strongly?"

Tony nodded. "I'm just not sure I want to risk exposure. If Corrections would let me do my job, I have the guy. The Board would have to cut him loose. We're trying to teach these kids that what Tanner did, especially in his position of trust, shouldn't happen."

Carina interjected. "But you're willing to do the same thing to Tanner."

Tony started to respond. He observed a red Monte Carlo driving southbound on Santa Fe. He gave the car a five-second head start, then pulled out of the lot. The unit was blacked out. He immediately picked it up in the number lane. Tony was three cars behind the Chevy. When traffic slowed for a light, Tony read the plate 5VSZ678.

"5TOM, I'm going to be 10-38 on Santa Fe north of Florence on 5VSZ678. I stopped that car a few minutes ago."

After Tony pulled the car over again, he got out, followed by Carina, who stood behind the passenger door. Tony approached the vehicle's driver. Corona wasn't driving. His friend was, while Juan sat in the passenger seat. "Long time no see. How have you been?" Tony greeted the pair.

"I was just taking her home for Juan," the driver, Rafael Tejada, nervously explained.

Juan added, "I thought we had a deal."

"Maybe in Mexico, baby, but not in HP. I gave you a shot. You blew it, baby."

"C'mon man. It's only a mile or so," he pleaded.

"Juan, my friend, I'm disappointed. Give me your license, the registration, and proof of insurance."

"But I'm not driving!" Juan insisted. "Hey, man, don't take the car!"

"Say, '*Adios,* Mr. Monte Carlo.' Say, 'I'll be back for you in 30 days with *mucho dinero.*'" Tony took the license, registration, and insurance papers from the new driver. He repositioned himself next to Carina behind the passenger door.

His backup rolled up and Tony motioned with his head toward the Monte Carlo. "I'm going to impound it and hold it for 30 days. I stopped the driver a few minutes ago."

"I heard the call."

"He's suspended with warrant for FTA. LAPD didn't want to come down south to get his ass, so I cut him slack, cited him out, and let him park the car with a promise to tow or trailer it home or leave it parked until he pays his fees. He promised he would."

"In English or *Espanol?*"

"Chinese for all I care. Since he's no longer driving, I can't take him, but I'm going to cite the driver for 4000 (a) (1) v.c. and impound the car."

Tony radioed dispatch that he was code 4. He requested a 1051, a tow truck.

Officer Dodge volunteered to fill out the CHP 180, the impound form which was basically an inventory of everything that was in the car.

While Dodge filled out the 180, Tony got "Manny and Moe" out of the Monte Carlo. He had them sit on the curb. "You guys know the drill. Comply." Tony searched the Chevy. There was no contraband in the vehicle.

Tony and Dodge waited until HP Tow was on scene and hooked up the Monte Carlo. The driver signed the 180 as did Tony. He handed the driver a copy of the 180. He walked over to Rafael. "I need you to sign here next to the red x. It's not an admission of guilt. It's a promise to appear. Your court date is here. Any questions?"

"It's not my car."

"Whoever is driving is responsible. That's you, *mi amigo*."

"If I don't sign it?"

Tony half turned. "Officer Dodge, how do I say handcuffs in *Espanol*?"

Disgustedly, Rafael sputtered, "Give me the freakin' pen."

Tony handed him his pen. "Don't be pissed at me, asshole. You two clowns broke your promise. I didn't want to impound the car. I like Chebbies. Now it's gotta go to jail, and you guys get to go home and drink brewskis."

"Is there an extra charge for your humor?"

"No, sir. It's all part of the excellent service in HP. You may get a survey card in the mail in the next few days." Tony handed Tejada the ticket. "If you do, the ratings are from 1 to 10. 10 is high. If you give me all tens, the judge will not take 15% off your ticket."

"Is that for real, man?"

"Both of you get out of here. And don't jaywalk."

Tony cruised all areas of HP, giving Carina the two-cent tour. He took her through the 'Maywood Strip,' an area of HP that bordered Maywood. It was a bad area in the northeast corner of the city. There were shootings inside the strip almost every weekend. It was infested with gangs, drugs, and guns.

"Doesn't it scare you driving around these areas at night?" she asked.

Tony smiled broadly. "I love it. I know, it's sick. I guess working with the gang kids for so long, the streets are no big deal. Every once in a while, I run in to a kid I know from camp. I can't get enough of it." Tony eyed several parked cars. He looked at a few kids walking northbound on the sidewalk. Toward the end of the street, he could hear loud music. That would generate a music call later tonight or early in the morning.

"How many of the people you arrest do you think are high or drunk or both?"

"Maybe thirty-five to forty percent. But keep in mind I'm only out here one or two or three days a week. A large part of the arrests made by full-timers are these kids who don't go to school. They burglarize homes to get shit to sell, to steal a few bucks to buy drugs or to steal drugs. It was easier policing the streets when these kids were all supposed to be in school all the time. Now they have tracks. So, some of them are out of school legitimately. It makes the job that much tougher."

"How much of an issue is race?"

"Are you a reporter or a ride-along?" It was a joke. Tony knew Carina was just trying to understand his job.

"It's usually not an issue for me. What pisses me off is that half the criminal population of HP pretend not to speak English. That's dangerous for a cop. If a criminal with a weapon gets a split second on you, it can be all over in a Brooklyn minute.

"I don't see black, white, or brown. Again, maybe that's because I work the facilities. I see criminal. I can give a shitless what color you are. I have a problem with illegals. Illegals shouldn't be in this country. We need to streamline the process for people to come into this country, but they need to be vetted first, and they need to come in here legally."

"What would you do with the people who are here illegally?"

Tony drove out of the Maywood Strip. He headed westbound Gage.

"Send 'em home."

"All of them?"

"Unless there was some compelling reason not to."

"How about those who had kids here who are legal?"

"You mean those illegals who came over here to open the oven and pop out a kid who would be a legal citizen and suck up everything for nothing while our Vets get squat?"

"Wow! We have an issue here. Do you want to tell me how you really feel?"

"I know we have been seeing each other for a while, but there is a side of me you haven't seen."

"Up until now."

"I have a problem with people who break the law."

"What about the spirit of the law and the letter of the law?"

"The spirit of the law tells me if a guy runs a light because he's rushing his pregnant wife to the hospital, I don't stop and cite the guy. I escort him, lights and siren, to the hospital. But when illegals eat up your economy, shoot up our streets, deal drugs or even get a legitimate job and send that money back home across the border, we've got a problem.

"Just last week a woman in San Francisco was robbed, raped, and murdered by an illegal who had been sent back home twice by ICE. Why should illegals get services that our Vets aren't getting? Our Vets risked their lives and, in many cases, sacrificed their lives. They sacrificed their lives for you and for me not for an illegal bastard who comes over here to screw our country.

Tony stopped for a light. He took a deep breath. He looked at Carina and calmed down. "Still want to date me?"

"Now, you're a challenge."

"Why's that?"

Dispatch interrupted their conversation: "22 and 5TOM. A 459 silent, Florence and Salt Lake at the Community Building."

"5TOM copy from Gage and Miles" Tony made a quick U-turn. He drove east on Gage. He drove above the speed limit but without lights or siren. "One of us is saved by dispatch."

Office Yolis was short, dark skinned, and well built. She was one tough cop who knew how to take care of business. She also knew the meaning of the word compassionate. She was behind the wheel of her black-and-white when Tony rolled up behind her.

Tony got out of the unit. He walked up to Yolis who was still in the unit. "Another one of these bullshit calls," Tony said. "Every time we're out here, we get one of these."

Officer Yolis exited her unit. She stood even with Tony's chest. Her eyes moved, not her head. She was about to look up at him. "Let me explain something to you, with all due respect. You are a Reserve, not a full-time officer. That is not going to stop some asshole from putting a round in you. No shitface is going to ask if you're getting paid to chase bullets. No creep is going to ask if you're full time or not.

"Finally, there is no such thing as a routine 459 call. There is no such thing as a routine *anything* call. I know your second FTO instilled that in you because I know your second FTO well and he is thorough.

"This Department has lost one officer in the line of duty. That was Officer Robert H. Keller. He was shot to death October 5, 1967. His killer has never been caught. I know you know that, too, because it's one of the test questions before you get off probation.

"I'm not trying to lecture you. I'm trying to keep you alive."

Tony swallowed hard. Of course, Officer Yolis was correct. She gave a shit about him. Not all officers gave a shit about reserves. Many didn't like reserves. Not so with Tony. He was respected and well liked. He had nothing but respect for full-timers. He knew his place as a reserve. "I'm sorry, ma'am. Of course, you are correct. Thank you, ma'am."

"Enough of that ma'am. One of your FTOs had an expression. He was fond of saying, 'Out here we all step on our dicks once in a while.' I don't because I don't have a dick." She patted Tony on the ass with an open palm. She smiled, looking up at him. "Consider yourself spanked. If you want more, you know where to find it. Go get your ride-along and let's check the perimeter of the building and the park. Keep your eyes open and keep your eyes on your ride-along."

Tony smiled broadly. He could still feel her hand on his butt. She was cute. There was no way she could know he had a submissive side to him. Carina didn't even know...yet.

The threesome walked the accessible perimeter carefully. The front door was locked. Each and every window fronting Florence Avenue was secure. The side windows were locked. None were broken. The three walked to the rear of the park building.

Tony was three feet from the rear door when it suddenly opened. He was reaching for his weapon. Yolis already had her Glock in her right hand. Carina, a step behind Yolis, froze. Tony recognized the female. She worked for Parks and Recreation. She was stunned. In her right hand was a trash bag. She almost dropped it.

Hilda Rosales was 60 years old and frail. She was dressed in jeans, polo shirt, and white tennis shoes. Tony pulled her away from the door. "Who else is inside?"

"No one," She had a slight accent. "Everyone went home at 7 o'clock."

"Is any other door unlocked?"

"No. Just this one. And it was locked until I opened it to throw out some trash."

Tony keyed the mic. "5TOM. We made contact with employee, Hilda Rosales. She states she is the only one in the building. Officer Yolis and I will clear the building."

"Copy that. All units clear the air. Officer Yolis and Farrina are doing a walk-through at Parks and Rec Center."

"Hilda, stay out here with Carina. We're going to make certain no one is inside."

Before they entered, Tony again contacted dispatch. "Where is the coverage?"

"Northeast quad, room 2A. No motions."

"Thanks. Will advise."

Yolis and Tony cleared the building in under ten minutes.

From the time the Parks and Recreation building was cleared, until 2130, HP was abnormally quiet for a Friday night. Tony made a couple of traffic stops but that was it. He and Carina were having an in-depth discussion, basically about Tony's philosophy.

"Why do you think the death penalty is a deterrent?"

"That's not a difficult question. If a perp commits a murder and he's put to death, he's sure as hell isn't going to kill again. That's a definite deterrent." Tony slowed for traffic.

"What about life in prison without the possibility of parole."

"LWOP."

"What?"

"LWOP. Life without parole."

"That sounds like an Italian with bad breath."

"Very funny. No such animal. As long as one attorney occupies this planet, as long as the ACLU breathes air, as long as there are politicians like Brown and Obama, sentences can always be overturned, and new trials granted. Pardons are always a possibility, as are escapes."

"Look at the expense involved in putting someone down."

"You put a sick animal down. Some of these assholes are worse than animals." Carina had Tony wound tighter than a rubber band and Tony knew it. It was too late to turn back.

"The only reason it costs so much to stick a needle in one of these asshole's arms is because of all the appeals he has. People make big money off this shit. Give the convicted one appeal, two at the most. He has a year to get that done and end of story. You'll see crime go down dramatically.

"But as the man in the TV commercial said, 'There's more.' I have a question for you. Suppose you have a teenage daughter. You and your daughter come home from a day at Magic Mountain. You walk into your house and undress to take a shower. Suddenly two armed assholes come out from hiding. They take turns raping you and your daughter. For dessert, they sodomize the two of you. And because one of these guys is high on coke, he brutally beats your daughter to death. He is given life. Every time he comes up for parole, you relive this shit. What you went through isn't enough. You relive it time and time again.

"I had to testify in a child rape case. His stepdad fucked him repeatedly. The kid was nine. The dad finally strangled the kid to death. Every time the case was about to come to trial, the ADA, Assistant District Attorney, had to reorient me about the case to be sure I remembered what I had to remember. I still have nightmares about that child.

"The fucking stepdad is doing 25 to life. He'll get out one day and maybe do it again. Is that right? Put the son of a bitch in the ground and be done with it." Tony made a hard right turn.

"Do you know, there are two of you?"

"I know. I'm a Gemini."

"Seriously."

"Are we having a lover's quarrel?"

"No. We're dating, and dating is when two people get to know each other. You're angry."

"I'm not so much angry as that I'd like to see some things change." Tony thought about it. "I suppose I am angry. I work in a system that makes money off incarcerated minors and doesn't want to do anything to change it. Incarceration is big business. Then I work a situation that is uglier than a toothless witch on a dark Halloween night. This world is upside down and most people are either too blind to see it or they just don't give a shit." Tony made a quick U-turn. He thought, *The four bangers in that car need to be stopped. The car's got a busted driver's-side taillight; PC for me!*

Tony turned to Carina. "Now I suppose you don't want to see me anymore?"

"Did I say that?"

"No, but I can read people, too."

Carina smiled. "I'm just saying you're angry and we don't see eye to eye on all things. Sometimes opposites attract. Besides my panties are soaked." She squirmed in her seat. "Now shut up and pull those bangers over!"

Tony laughed out loud. "Are you aware that dispatch and everyone in or near the dispatch office can hear everything that we say in the unit?"

Carina instantly turned beet red. Then see caught on. "You... you...Adam Henry!" She stuck her middle finger under his nose.

Maybe Carina was joining the team. And maybe he needed a good spanking from Yolis. Tony contacted dispatch. "5TOM roller."

"Go with your roller, 5TOM."

"3 GRH 669." Tony followed the car for several blocks. The driver was within the speed limit. He wasn't weaving. There appeared to be no furtive from within the vehicle.

"5TOM. Your vehicle comes back no hits..."

"Copy that. Thank you." Tony was going to forget about it, then the driver tossed a lit cigarette out the window. Tony immediately activated his overheads. "5TOM, I'll be 10-38 that vehicle, Miles just north of Slauson. I've got four shaved heads on board. If there is a backup available, I'll take one non-emergent."

"Copy that. It may be a few we've got a gang situation on the Maywood Strip."

"Copy."

The red Toyota immediately pulled to the eastside curb. Tony grabbed the mic. He turned to switch to speaker. "Driver, I want you to keep your hands on the steering wheel. Passenger, place your hands on the dash, palms down. In the rear seat, both of you put the palms of your hands against the rear window. Don't anyone make a sudden move." Tony thought about the situation for several seconds. "Stay in the unit."

Slowly, deliberately, Tony exited the black-and-white. He never took his eyes off the vehicle, nor did he take his eyes off the hands in the car. His FTOs and the Academy instructors taught him that it was the hands that would kill you; always watch the hands.

Tony started toward the Toyota with extreme caution. His backup hadn't arrived and something in his gut told him that all was not right with the car or the four bangers in the car. He had yet to clear the black-and-white.

Tony stopped suddenly. He froze in his tracks. He backed up walking around the trunk of the unit to the passenger door. He opened the door and, in a low, firm voice, said to Carina, "Get out." There was no doubt he was giving the orders and the orders were to be followed. "I want you behind the trunk of the unit and I want you crouched down. Do not get up until I tell you to do so. Capiche?"

Carina never said a word, she nodded and did exactly what she was told to do. Tony walked around the unit to the driver's door. He opened it standing behind it, waiting for his backup.

Tony thought about some of the things Carina said when they were driving around HP. She was insightful. Tony was aware he was often two people. He was the educator who wanted to right by all concerned. There was the cop who wanted to enforce the law, sometimes at any cost. Pour a drink or three in Tony and he'd tell you how he could put a gun against the temple of the asshole who recently executed a much-loved Lancaster Sheriff's Sergeant and sleep soundly. Yet, if he heard about someone committing cruelty to an animal, tears would well up in his eyes. Tony had a strong desire to enforce the truth and, to that end, he rationalized that sometimes the ends justified the means.

Tony's back was "21." 21 was a tall, very large Samoan who smoked more cigars on duty than he did police work. The community loved him, other officers tolerated his lack of policework, and the brass were trying to get him to exit the PD, permanently.

Tony knew the gigantic Samoan by the name everyone in HP called him, Toa. It meant brave one or warrior. Toa, if nothing else, when he felt like putting out his cigar and doing policework, was a warrior. A story went around HP from time to time about Toa receiving a 415 fight call. He responded to the call in an apartment complex with two units arriving behind him to back the gigantic Samoan. It seems that two lesbians had gotten into a knock-down, drag-out fight in the apartment. When the three officers arrived on scene, they could hear furniture breaking inside and dykes yelling at each other in language only heard at biker bars.

The front door had a steel security door in front of it. Neither of the officers could get the door unlocked. Just about the time they were about to call for a tow truck to pull it off its hinges, Toa came to the rescue. He grabbed two of the iron bars, put his foot against the side pillar and yanked the door off its hinges. He stepped back and attempted to kick the door in at the lock. His aim was off. His foot went through the wooden door and stuck. He couldn't get it out.

Inside, the female lovers were throwing everything but the bed at each other. The three cops were laughing so hard, Toa's cigar fell to the ground. The question was, would the cops gain entry before the lesbians tired out? It was pretty much a draw. The girls called it a night just at Toa freed his foot. Both ladies were arrested for domestic violence, 273.5 in police parlance.

Now, as Tony's back, Toa asked, "What do we got?" He looked down at Tony who was in the vicinity of six feet tall.

"At this point, a traffic stop. But for safety's sake, let's add suspicious circs. I started to approach but my gut told me to get away. The plates came back clear."

Toa notified dispatch that he was on scene. Tony approached the driver's side of the car cautiously. Toa went to the passenger side. Both cops had their Glocks out, ready, behind their thigh. Both officers had their flashlights under their left arm.

Tony was five feet from the passenger door. "Don't make a move, guys. Keep your hands where we can see them." Then Tony lied. "We have an airship overhead. Every move you make is being recorded."

Tony was at the driver's door and slightly behind the driver who couldn't see much of anything because the spotlights and his high beams were intentionally blinding him. Toa was at the passenger side of the car.

Tony said, "Let me see your driver's license." The kid looked like he was maybe 15.

He shook his head. "I don't have one."

"How old are you?"

"Fifteen."

"Whose car is it?"

"My auntie's."

"What's her name?"

"Aunt Sarah."

"Aunt Sarah what?"

"Aunt Sarah Montrose."

"Where does she live?"

"Compton."

"What's her phone number?"

"I don't know."

Tony was trying to decide if the kid was telling the truth. The jury was still out. The car had come back clean. Tony stood at the car door. He and Toa were cautious. Tony put his flashlight in his back pocket. He called dispatch on his cell. "Can you look up a Sarah Montrose for me out of Compton, please? If there is such an individual, call her and ask her if my 1038 is her vehicle and, if so, if she knows her nephew is driving it. Thanks."

Tony looked at Toa and nodded. "Let's empty the vehicle." Toa nodded, then he said, "We're going to play a game, guys. Here's the name of the game. When I name your position in the seat, you're going to climb out of the car. Make a move that you don't need to make, and I'll squash you like a fucking HP cockroach. Do we understand?"

"Yeah, yeah, yeah," one of the rear passengers said.

Toa looked indignant. "What the hell did you say?"

"I meant yes, sir. Yes, sir."

Tony didn't move. Toa ordered the front seat passenger out of the vehicle. When he was out of the vehicle. Toa not too gently put him against the hood of the car. He handcuffed him. "At this point, you're not under arrest. This is for officer safety. Sit down at the curb. Cross your ankles. Don't say a word and don't move. Clear?"

The juvenile nodded.

Next, Toa did the same with the rear-seat passenger who was also obviously a minor. He handcuffed him and sat him down on the curb. "Hey, partner, slide me a set of cuffs." Tony slid a set of handcuffs across the roof of the car.

"Get out. My side. Keep your hands where I can see them. Slide across the seat."

Three guys were handcuffed, seated at the curb with ankles crossed. Two of the former occupants of the vehicle were juveniles. Toa thought the last one he pulled from the car was over eighteen.

Before Tony ordered the passenger out, he looked at the ignition. It wasn't punched. His cell phone vibrated in his pocket. It was dispatch. "Nobody by the name you gave me out of Compton."

"Copy. Thanks."

"Driver." Tony held his Glock in the air. "See this weapon? Make a move and you'll swallow it. Got it? I'm going home tonight and I'm getting laid. You're not going to fuck that up." Tony took a breath. "One more time, whose car is it?"

"Aunt Sandy's."

"How many Aunties you got?" Tony would put even money down that the car was stolen. You didn't have to punch an ignition to turn some of these cars over. A shaved key would do the trick. "Get your ass out of the car. Keep your hands where I can see them."

Most officers in HP carried two sets of cuffs. This was why. Tony put the juvenile against the hood of the car harder than was necessary. He handcuffed him and patted him down. "You're not under arrest. I'm going to ask you one more time. Lie to me and I'm adding a charge of lying to a police officer. That's a federal felony." Tony was full of shit, but he thought it sounded good. The kid probably didn't know the difference. "Whose car is it?"

"I think it may be in my uncle's name."

Tony was growing annoyed, very annoyed. "Carina, you're good. Come on up for air."

Tony walked the kid to where his three bodies were seated. "Pull up a chair, numb nut." Then he said to Toa, I'm going to get the reg out of the glove compartment, if there is a reg. Then I'll toss the car. Do we have a Victor unit working this evening?"

A Victor unit was a volunteer. They sometimes drove around in marked white vehicles to render assistance at road closures, accidents, to fill out 180s, at checkpoints, and the like. In this case, since the units were busy, a Victor unit for an extra set of eyes wouldn't hurt.

Tony rummaged around the glove box. He found what he was looking for. The R/O was a Roberto Luna out of Compton. He called dispatch.

While he was waiting for dispatch to contact the R/O, Tony tossed the car. Under the front seat was a loaded .357. "Well, well. It looks like the four stooges are 417." 417 was the penal code for a weapon.

Tony walked to the trunk of the black-and-white, cleared the weapon, and locked it in the trunk. Dispatch called. "The car is a stolen out of Compton. The R/O wasn't even aware the car was gone. They got home from shopping a couple of hours ago, parked the car in the street, and went inside."

Tony grabbed the juvenile by the front of his t-shirt. He picked him up off the ground, half dragged, half carried him to the rear of the unit. "What's your name? Don't fuck with me. I've had enough of your shit."

"Daniel Lopez. The car is stolen. The gun is mine."

The kid spoke perfect English.

"Am I under arrest?"

"Not at the moment. Where did you get the gun?"

"I bought it in the hood."

"From whom?"

"Some guy."

Tony had already gotten more from the juvenile than he expected. He didn't figure the kid to roll. He ran the serial number through dispatch. It came back a stolen from a home burglary out of Long Beach a month ago. Everybody in the car was good to go for transport.

It took close to two hours to book the adult, transport the juveniles to Hope Center Juvenile Hall in Downey where they would be housed until adjudication. It took more time to make the parental notification, to book and tag the evidence, and finally, to write the report. While Tony took care of most of the "grunt" work, Toa wrote the report.

If at all possible, and most time it was, reserves did not write reports. The reason was that reserves had a full-time job and if they couldn't make it to court, the case was in danger of being tossed out. Hence, the full-timer did that paperwork. In Tony's case, because he wrote a lot of traffic cites, the judge agreed to hear all of Tony's traffic tickets the same day.

Toa finished his report, put it in the box for the Sergeant to proofread, and went out to the lot to his unit, and to a good cigar.

Tony turned to Carina who was playing on one of the eight computers in the Blue Room. "I'm starving. How about code 7?"

"That's copy," Carina smiled. "Whatever code 7 is."

Yolis was standing behind Tony. He hadn't seen her. "Code 7 is a meal. And not only would I love to join you, but I'm buying."

"I got it," Tony jumped in. "Between my two jobs, I make more than you do. How about Tam's?"

Tam's was a sit-down fast-food place that showed 'love' — cops ate for half price.

"Let me hit the locker room and I'll meet you there in ten."

Yolis, Carina, and Tony sat at a corner booth, Tony and Yolis had their backs against the wall so they could see the entrance, the exit, and all the pedestrian activity, coming and going. Some called it paranoia, but those who wear the badge called it self-preservation. Either way, that was life for a cop.

Yolis looked across the table at Carina. She sat her fork down. "How's the ride-along going?"

"I'm loving it. I thought you guys would have more down time, but it's been pretty busy."

"Give it time. Some days it's absolutely crazy. Some shifts, eating is a dream. It's one call after the other."

"What made you go into police work? Was your dad a cop?"

"I didn't know my dad. No one in my family was in law enforcement. I dated a guy who was an officer in Palm Springs." Yolis looked down at her plate. Then she looked up. "He was shot to death during a traffic stop. I was treated like family by the Department. I decided to pursue it. I went through the Academy and became a Reserve, just like super reserve here." She patted Tony's thigh. Carina couldn't see Yolis' hand. She was very slow in removing her hand. It got a rise out of Tony.

Yolis continued, "I loved it. First time I was asked to go full time, I processed. That was seven years ago. Here we are."

"Any regrets?"

"It's tough on a relationship, especially if you're not part of the team. The hours are crazy. The never knowing what might happen to your partner. It's probably tougher on the partner than on the cop." Yolis looked at Tony raising her eyebrows. "Don't you worry about Tony?"

"Not until tonight."

"What do you do?"

"I'm a drug and alcohol counselor. And I suppose because Tony has a full-time job that isn't law enforcement, the strain on the relationship is not as severe."

Tony took a sip of hot coffee. "The way things are going today, it's almost as dangerous walking into a Starbucks as it is walking up to a car. Did you hear about the asshole who tried to shoot two cops with a semi-automatic weapon in Starbucks up north? The only thing that saved the two black officers was the gun jamming. The shooter was black, too. But if it had been a white cop who tried to arrest a black man, half the city would be up in smoke by now." Tony took a large bite out of his sandwich.

Tony turned up the volume on his portable. It had been quiet for a few minutes. That was unusual. "If I had to do it all over again, I'd be full time. Next life."

Yolis finished her eggs and took a bite out of her wheat toast. "Why didn't you go full time? You don't strike me as the teacher type."

"Well, it's a juvenile facility like Hope Center. And I had a background issue."

"Do tell. I need more coffee anyway."

"I went to college in New Hampshire. I had a bad habit of drinking and driving. One night I had a bit too much to drink and got behind the wheel of my Chevy Super Sport and took off southbound on the 93 toward Boston. It was late at night. The freeway wasn't completed so there were stretches that ran through the towns. I looked in the rearview mirror and way behind me were flashing lights.

"I figured, what the hell could be under the hood of the trooper's car that could outrun my Super Sport?"

Yolis jumped in. "His radio?"

"Never gave it a thought. Five towns later, I'm spread eagle against the hood of his car. One freakin' trooper wearing a Smokey Bear hat. Not five CHP cars and four State cops. Not a helicopter. One trooper. I didn't even get airtime. No channel 9 news. Nothing."

"What did he get you for?"

"Two double-yellow-line violations, speeding 105 in a 25, running a truck off the road, reckless driving, and felony evading. Everything but DUI. I was thrown in jail. In the morning I went before the magistrate, and he showed love. He knocked it down to a misdemeanor, providing I didn't drive for the next 13 months. That kept me out of the force."

"How'd you get in?"

"I met the Chief in the Academy. He took a liking to me. To be honest, there were other police contacts as I was growing up."

"You seem to have come out of it all right." Her hand was back on Tony's thigh. This time a couple of inches higher.

The portable cackled. Two other units had a 415 fight call. "Let's get back to work."

A Wet Wednesday at Work

It was a wet Wednesday at the John F. Kennedy School. For some reason, that science had yet to discover, the rain made the kids antsy. It also had its effect on staff. Since it was a long, uncovered walk to the parking lot, most of the staff stayed on site during lunch. This made for a noisier than usual lunch area. The rain also played havoc with the phones. They didn't go dead but the static sounded like a New York ferry boat foghorn.

The foghorn sounded. Tony put an end to the annoying sound; he hung up the phone.

Principal Patterson was seated behind his desk. His dress was his usual comfortable, casual style of grey slacks, white shirt with throat button open, no tie, and grey sweater. "Sit down. We need to talk." He was shuffling lottery tickets. "Want in?"

Tony knew he didn't call him in the office to discuss lottery tickets. Tony normally didn't buy lottery tickets. "Sure. How much?"

"Twenty bucks."

Tony took out a wad of bills. He always had at least a hundred or so bucks in his pants pocket. He handed his boss a crisp twenty-dollar bill. "I thought Mormons didn't gamble."

"They don't. And it's not gambling. I never win, so it's a donation."

"Give me back my twenty then." Tony reached across the mahogany desk. "I'm kidding. Maybe one of these days you'll hit big, and you'll be able to afford to move to Utah."

"Before we hit those millions, you have a problem."

"Which one today?"

"It's the custodian again. Romeo Johnson is getting worse. Juliette walked into her room after lunch yesterday and Romeo was passed out under her desk. He says he was tightening the screws on the legs of the desk. She said he smelled like the local tavern. We need to do something."

"I talked with him a couple of weeks ago. He told me it was the Listerine people were smelling, which means he's in denial. I spoke with Carina about him, and she said, if he's in denial, there probably isn't much that can be done. Will Juliette put it in writing?"

Eddie shook his head. "She doesn't want to get involved."

"I'll call the union and see if they want to help out. Is that it?"

Peterson nodded. "Paula let me know that you sort of worked with her on the Tanner situation." He stressed the words "sort of."

"I just put that out of my mind. Carina told me to change the station in my head to a tune I liked."

"Get back to work."

Tony left Peterson's office. He was still smiling. Maybe they'd hit the lottery big, and he could retire and work HP full time.

Tony had two teacher evaluations to complete. One was in Donna Germain's classroom, the other in Patricia Orwell's. Donna was a veteran math teacher who had been with Corrections 23 years. She was firm with her students, but fair. Patricia was a history teacher who had transferred to JFK from Hope Center Juvenile Hall. She was a creative teacher who would often dress in the costume of the person or era they were studying. Her kids liked and protected her. If any one student even cursed at her, they'd pay the price that night in the dorm.

It took Tony till noon to do the two classroom observations. It took him another hour to write both evals. He set up appointments to review the observations for Friday.

Tony called the custodian's Union rep. "This is Tony Farrina. Is Frank Plotkin in?"

"Tony, how are you, buddy?"

Frank was a good guy. He was open-minded, tired of Corrections crap, and ready to retire. He had less than a year to go. That made him more open-minded. Frank's office was down the hall from Paula's.

"I'm as good as can be expected. I'm on the right side of the grass and, for now, I'm on the right side of Corrections."

Frank laughed. "Me, too. Hopefully, I can keep it that way until I pull the plug. What can I do for you?"

"Romeo Johnson..."

"You need not say more. His drinking has gotten worse, hasn't it?"

"What do you know about it that you can share?"

"His wife called me. He doesn't come home half the time. She's really worried about him. She wanted to know if we had some kind of program for him."

"And you said..."

"I recommended our EASE Program and told her they'd probably recommend Alcoholics Anonymous. She said the judge mandated AA meetings after his second DUI."

"Did he go?"

"Yeah, but it didn't seem to do any good. They say it's a program for those who want it; not those who need it. Apparently, he doesn't want it."

"I need a cushion. Would you be available to meet; the three of us?"

"Sure. Name it. I'll even call him and set it up. Are we off the record?"

"Your call, Frank. The guy's sick trying to get well, not bad trying to get good. I don't want to crucify him. I want us to help him if we can."

"I like your attitude but don't get your hopes up. After looking at his file and after speaking with his wife, I don't know if he's ready for help. This shit has been going on for several years. I asked around after his wife called me. And I looked in his file. Nobody wanted to step up to the plate before you grabbed a bat. Too many administrators in Corrections don't have the balls they were born with."

Tony couldn't argue with that. There was a lot of laziness among FLACOE administrators and a lot of indifference. The suits loved it when you flew under the radar.

"Friday afternoon good for you? Maybe two o'clock?"

"Why don't we make it about 11 o'clock? That way Johnson can beat the freeway traffic back up to the Antelope Valley."

Tony could reset his evaluation appointments for Thursday. That would work out fine. He wouldn't be expected to go back to work which meant he could get to HP early. There was a god! "Sounds like a date. 11:00 a.m. Friday. Your office?"

"My office. Scotch or vodka?"

"Cute, Frank. We're off the record, so everything is on the table?"

"Yeah. He's on a short rope. The two DUIs factor in here. His absence record is a strike. But like you said, let's see if we can somehow help him. I've got another call. See you Friday at 11."

The meeting with Donna Townsend was the first of the two evaluations Tony had rescheduled. She was short, round, dressed in slacks, loose fitting shirt and tennis shoes. She entered Tony's office with a smile and immediately sat down.

"How are you doing?"

"I'm doing fine."

"You really are." Tony adjusted the knot on his solid blue tie. "I wish I had twelve more like you. You really make a difference for our students. Probation thinks the world of you and that makes my job easier. The kids never seem to give you a problem." Tony watched Donna cross and uncross her legs. She was embarrassed. The good teachers always seem to shy away from praise.

"Let me tell you that I'm not easy on staff. You earn everything you get from me. The bottom line is that you do one helluva job and I certainly appreciate it.

"Everything I read is in your eval." Tony handed it to Donna. "Please read it over. If you have any questions, please ask. When you're satisfied with the eval and after I've answered any questions, please sign it at the bottom. I'll do the same and, by the end of the day, there'll be a copy in your mailbox."

Tony called Carina from his office while he was eating his lunch—a dinner salad with honey mustard dressing. He sipped coffee as he dialed.

"Hey, you," he said when Carina picked up the phone. "Are you free for dinner tonight?"

"Maybe. I have to check my calendar. Of course. For you, I'm always free. Do you want to meet somewhere?"

"Actually, I think I'm going to get out of here on time for a change. I'll run home, shower and change, and come by your place. How's that sound?"

"Sounds good. How should I dress?"

"Why bother getting dressed? I was thinking about Katz, the restaurant over by the Lancaster Performing Arts Theater. We liked that when Steve and Stephanie took us there for our anniversary."

"Good choice. What time are you picking me up?"

"Eighteen hundred." Tony wanted to see If Carina remembered the twenty-four-hour clock.

Panties or No Panties

"Six p.m. it is." Carina did remember. "I'll wear that brown skirt you like with the Corvette shirt. Should I wear panties?" Carina hung up before Tony could answer. He felt a bulge in his grey suit pants.

Katz was a dinner house that served alcohol and catered to the theater and movie crowd and those people who liked to shop the boulevard. Seating was inside in a quiet atmosphere with booths, tables, and outside dining. Prices were not outlandish and the husband and wife who owned and operated the restaurant were warm and friendly. There was never a rush to get you in or out of their eatery.

"How was your day?"

Carina looked rested and relaxed. She reached for the menu. "Quiet. Nothing out of the ordinary. Yours?"

"Quiet, too, for a change. But I need some advice."

"You need advice from me?"

"Go ahead and order first."

"Sounds good. I'm hungry."

They ordered. Tony held Carina's hand across the table. "I mentioned our custodian to you some time ago. The one with the drinking problem."

"Yeah."

"He's gotten worse. I'm meeting with him and the Union rep Friday. He's on his way to being fired if something isn't done to help him. His wife called and spoke with the Union. The guy apparently is very close to being out of control."

"First, if he isn't ready for help, nothing you can say or do will help him. It sounds like he's on a downward spiral. Until he hits his bottom, he'll keep digging. You might suggest AA. I'll give you a copy of the local meetings and a copy of the Alcoholics Anonymous Big Book that you can give him. You can give him my card. Other than that, babe, there ain't a hell of a lot you can do."

"That's what I was afraid of."

"How bad is he?"

"He passed out in the john, and under a teacher's desk when she was at lunch. His story was that he was fixing the loose desk leg. He reeks of booze."

"It's coming out of his body pores."

Tony nodded. "Everybody is complaining that he never even vacuums classrooms anymore. The boss has covered for him."

"That's probably the worst thing you can do."

"So, not much I can do?"

"I can hook him up with another alcoholic who will be glad to take him to a meeting if that's what he wants and if he's ready. Other than that, you can let him know help is available when and if he wants it and you can give him the meeting directory and the Big Book. I'll give them both to you when you take me home."

"Thanks." The food came. "Let's eat." Tony poured cream in his coffee. "By the way, are you wearing panties?"

Carina blushed. "I guess you are just going to have to find out for yourself."

They went back to Carina's apartment. On the bear rug, in front of the electronic fireplace, Tony found out that Carina was not wearing panties.

You Hit Bottom When You Stop Digging

On Friday, Tony arrived at Frank Plotkin's office before Romeo Johnson. Frank got up from behind his desk and shook Tony's hand. "Appreciate what you're doing."

"We haven't done anything yet. And I appreciate what you're attempting to do." This was Tony's first time in Plotkin's office. The minute Plotkin opened his mouth, his words were born in Brooklyn. That was backed up by the pictures on the wall. There was a photo of the Brooklyn Dodgers from the 1950s and others of Campy, Jackie, The Duke, Sandy, Gil, Pee Wee, and the pictures went on. Tony walked over to take a closer look. "That's Jackie stealing home plate on Yogi in the World Series, isn't it?"

"You know your baseball."

"I was a diehard Yankee fan. And Robinson was out at the plate. If they had reviews like they have today, the review would have shown that Yogi made the tag before Robinson touched the plate."

"Arguable. But the fact is, they didn't have reviews and Robby was safe." They laughed.

"Those were the days," Tony said, and he smiled. "I remember playing stickball with a broom handle and a tennis ball. Today's kids don't know what stickball is."

Frank nodded. "That's when baseball was a sport. Today it's all business and money. In the 50s, players would gladly sign autographs. They'd go to Boys Clubs just because they wanted to. Today, you'll pay for an autograph.

"I remember back in Brooklyn, Gil, who also lived in Brooklyn, visited our Temple. He couldn't stop signing autographs. Today, the guys in the clubhouse sign your name.

"Remember when Mickey Mantle signed a contract for $100,000? That was unheard of. That was all the money in the world. Today, your signing bonus Is ten times that." Plotkin frowned. "The times have changed."

There was a knock on the door. Plotkin's secretary escorted Romeo Johnson into the office. Tony shook his hand. The guy didn't look like Johnson. He looked like yesterday's newspaper left out in a rare southern California rainstorm. His hair wasn't combed. His shirt and pants looked like he had slept in them, or they hadn't been ironed in a week. His shoes weren't shined. His face looked like leather and his belt needed more holes. He must have been at least twenty pounds under weight. He smelled.

Plotkin shook his hand. As he was walking back to his desk, Frank said, "Have a seat, gentlemen. Can I get you some coffee or tea?"

"Thanks, no."

Romeo looked down at the carpet. He shook his head. "Can we get on with this meeting?"

Frank looked at Tony. Frank shrugged. "Listen, Romeo, we're here to help you."

"I don't need your help. I spoke with a lawyer, and she told me what I do on my time is my business."

"That's true. But as your Union rep, I want you to know that Mr. Farrina has agreed that everything said here is off the record. I want you to know that your drinking problem is affecting your work environment."

"How's that?"

Tony jumped in. "Romeo, look. I've got a photo of you on the throne in the bathroom at JFK, passed out. I've had a teacher complain that you were asleep or passed out under her desk when she walked into her classroom. You need help."

"And you need to mind your own business! I was fixing her fucking desk so that the freakin' thing wouldn't tip over."

"And what about the picture of you passed out on the john?"

"You had no right to take that picture."

"I never said I took it. I said I have a picture of you. We're not using it for evaluation purposes. As a matter of fact, we're not going to use it at all. We want to help you."

"Why do you give a shit? Nobody else does."

"You're part of the JFK team and we value you. But, and I mean but, we're not going to put up with this crap any longer. Either you get help immediately or, starting Monday, we'll start documenting your behavior."

Frank spoke up. "We've got a program for people who have problems such as yours, Romeo. We'll assist you if you want help. Corrections will not only pay for it, but your salary will be covered as well. Furthermore, no one will know about it unless you tell them, and it won't go into your file."

Romeo scratched a scab on his arm. It was probably the result of alcohol consumption, a lot of alcohol consumption. "I need to think about that."

"As your Union rep, Romeo, I strongly suggest you take the help that's being offered. If not, I can't guarantee that the next time you're in my office, it might not be to keep you from getting fired."

Tony spoke up. "Why don't you give it a shot, Romeo?"

"I told you, I need to think about it."

"I think this meeting is concluded then. I was hoping we could accomplish more. The ball is in your court, Romeo." Frank slid a card across his desk. "Here's my card. If you want that assistance we talked about, call me."

Tony picked up the card and handed it to Romeo. Tony could smell the booze. "I have something in my car for you. When we leave, let's walk downstairs together."

Tony unlocked the passenger door of the Vette. He took the Alcoholics Anonymous Big Book off the seat. "Here's my friend's business card. She's a drug and alcohol counselor. If you want help, you can call her. She'll be happy to talk with you. Here's a list of AA meetings in the Valley. Here's a copy of the Alcoholics Anonymous Book you might want to read. Is there anything I can do to help?"

Romeo started to reach for the book, the business card, and the meeting directory. He stopped, turned sideways, and balled up his fists.

Instantly, Tony dropped everything that was in his hands. He also turned sideways. "Don't even think about it, Romeo. Move another inch and two things are going to happen. I'll bust your jaw and I'll have you arrested for attempted assault." Tony took a step backward. "If you want what I brought you, pick it up; otherwise, get the hell out of here!"

More About Mick

Tony got in the passenger seat of the HPPD unit. Most of the days when he partnered up with Mickey, they split the driving. That was fine with Tony. When Mickey drove, Tony got to take in the sights. The dealers, the bangers, the hookers, and the hard-working people who were just trying to get by in a tough economy.

When Tony drove, Mickey smoked, talked, and lately argued with his wife on his cell. From what Tony was able to gather, Tammy was spending more money that Mickey was earning; and Mickey was working more than his share of overtime.

A year ago, they had purchased a house in Palmdale which Mickey told Tammy they couldn't afford. Tammy promised she'd find a job and go back to work. That had yet to happen. They had missed a couple of mortgage payments. To compound the situation, when Mickey had arrived home a couple of times, there was no Tammy. A canvass of the neighborhood found Tammy shooting pool and drinking with some biker dude. When Tony asked him why Mickey didn't kick the biker's ass, Mickey explained, "Tammy says there's nothing going on, she's just lonely and this gives her something to do. Besides, if I kick his ass, I have to kick hers, too, and that ain't going to happen." Nonetheless, it was obvious it was taking a toll on the marriage.

"So, do you like riding solo or would you rather spend the shift smelling cigarette smoke?" Mickey lit a smoke. "Clear us, college boy, then tell me about your adventures."

"Nothing much to tcll."

"That's not the way I heard it. I hear you and your female partner collared four GTA suspects and you recovered a stolen handgun."

"With backup."

"I would hope so. Good job. Tonight might be too quiet for you."

"In that case, you can drive me back to the Station and I'll take my own unit."

Mickey pulled to the curb. "You can get out here and walk a foot beat."

When Tony first started as a reserve, he was assigned a reserve partner, Bobby Strickland. Together they did walk a foot beat. Strickland couldn't keep his Johnson in his pants and screwed every cute female store clerk on Pacific Boulevard. Not only did he get caught by the WC, but his wife also nailed him.

Strickland was damn lucky. He drew a year suspension and his wife divorced him, but he learned a hard lesson. The divorce cost him his left leg and right nut. He came back after his year and eventually went full time. Today he is a Sergeant and a damn good one. He remarried and doesn't fuck around anymore. A lesson learned.

Mickey pulled back into traffic. "Let's cruise the strip. There were a couple of shootings there last week."

"Works for me."

Mickey's cell rang. It was Tammy. "What's up, babe?" The phone was against his ear, held there by his shoulder. His left hand was out the window holding a cigarette. He was steering with his right knee. Tony gave tickets to people who talked or texted while driving. It was 23123(a) CVC.

"There is no more money in the checking account. I'm dry, broke, nada, nothing. Yeah, really. I'm not the Bank of America. No, I'm not Wells Fargo nor Chase. Goddammit, Tammy, what the fuck do you want from me? You were supposed to go to work. I didn't want the money-pit of a house."

Mickey looked at the phone. "Well, fuck you, bitch." He started to throw the phone out the unit window. Tony grabbed his arm. "That would be littering, partner, and I'd have to cite you."

"She hung up on me."

"I gathered that. You trained me well."

"Don't ever get married...again."

They were on the strip. Mickey cruised slowly. Loud music could be heard from back yards, front yards, and vehicles parked on the street. The majority of the people were still sober, obviously, or the sounds would have included gun shots. Give it time—it was Friday night.

"When is Carina coming out on her next ride-along?"

Tony shrugged. "I don't know. She's pretty busy, but she loved the excitement. She's seeing another side of me when she's out here and I don't know that she liked that."

"Would you like to translate that into an uneducated man's English?"

"I'll try. Up to this point, she's suspected that there was a 'harder,' tougher, follow-the-rules me. She wasn't quite sure. Now she is. I've tried to keep the cop side of me from her. Example: I ran into a situation at work where a kid spit in a textbook. The teacher took the book and rubbed it in the kid's face. These kids may be locked up, but at my school, they're students when they're in school. I got into it with the suits who don't want me filing charges against the teacher. It got a bit overboard. Carina and I discussed it and, reading between the lines, I think she sides with administration.

"The problem with letting it go is that that gives a signal to every other whacked-up teacher that he, or she, can do the same thing and get away with it."

"If a guy takes a swing at me while I'm trying to take him into custody and I knock him on his ass and for grins I kick him in the ribs, do you beef me?" asked Mickey.

"Of course not."

"What's the difference?"

"The difference is the guy took a swing at you. The kid didn't swing at the teacher and the fact is you're comparing football to baseball. The situations are diametrically opposed to one another."

"There you go with those expensive words. Okay, maybe not the best example. The kid spit in the book. What do you do to keep the kids from not spitting in books?"

"Suspend the kid. Bill the parent for the book. Not that they'll pay. If it keeps up, send the kid back to court. There really isn't a hell of a lot you can do."

"So, maybe the teacher got a point across." Mickey made a right turn, driving west, back to the heart of HP.

"I don't agree. The teacher is supposed to be a role model."

"Tony, these kids have been hardcore for years. They've been banging, dealing, shooting, robbing, raping, vandalizing for thirteen, fourteen, fifteen, sixteen, seventeen years. They're not going to stop overnight. Most of these kids are going on to bigger and better things and you and I know that." Mickey paused to watch a homeless man pushing a shopping cart. "I give you credit for what you're trying to do, but if I were you, I wouldn't fuck with the system."

"Wow. I wouldn't expect that from someone who got pissed at me when I told him I asked my ex if she'd be interested in a threesome."

Mickey laughed. "You never did get that wish, did you?"

"As a matter of fact, I did, but not from my ex and her girlfriend."

Mickey's cell rang. He was driving with the phone between his shoulder and his ear. After a minute, he pulled to the curb in front of the Gage Bowl. The area was well lit. "We're on our way. ETA four minutes."

"That wasn't Tammy."

Whatcha Gonna Do When They Come for You?

"That was the Watch Commander," Mickey said after ending his cell call.

"What's up?"

Mickey pulled away from the curb. "Do you know a former inmate at your camp, Eduardo Compos?"

"Of course. Now there's an example of a bad boy who is on the right track. He had a long juvie record. His last bust was an armed robbery of a 711. The cops caught up with him outside the 711 in the parking lot when they were stopping for free coffee. Eduardo's gun jammed and the fight was on. The kid was PCP'd out. It took half of Bell Gardens PD to take him in to custody.

"He was an angry kid when he came to Camp, but he came around. He earned his GED at JFK. His pregnant girlfriend had his baby while he was locked up. He got a job on the outs and started taking classes at Pierce College in Woodland Hills. That's an example of what is possible for these kids."

"How long has he been out?"

"Three weeks. He called me the other day to tell me how well he's doing."

"He's not doing well anymore. Do you know where his girlfriend lives?"

"HP, across from the Station."

"We're going to say hello. He's PCP'd out. He's holding his girlfriend and the baby at gunpoint. He's really whacked out. Detectives have been trying to locate relatives but no go."

"His mom and dad moved when he was locked up. They left no forwarding address and never wrote to him. As far as I know, his girlfriend is the closest thing to a relative he has."

Miles Avenue was blocked off with sawhorses, orange cones, and white Ford Vics manned by volunteers. The only way to get past the "roadblock" was a badge or marked black-and-white. They moved the barrier for Mickey and Tony.

Mickey parked a couple of hundred yards from where the action appeared to be. He tracked down the Lieutenant in charge. Henderson Pence was calmly and quietly giving instructions to HPPD's SWAT team. They were called the STOP Squad, a Special Team of Police. The four men and one woman knelt beside the STOP van that was equipped with everything but a slot machine. Mickey waited till Pence finished his briefing.

"Let's go over here where we have some privacy." Pence was near retirement, after putting in 25 years. He was six foot tall and showing the signs of a tired retiree. His gut hung over his belt. He looked at Tony. "I understand this kid was locked up at your school?" It was a question not a statement.

"Yes, Sir. At the JFK Probation camp."

"The kid's a bad dude."

"He made progress at the school..."

"Never mind that. He has his girlfriend and their baby at gunpoint. I want you to try to talk him down. He's on something, probably PCP."

Tony heard the airship buzzing a circle overhead. He also noticed the news trucks on the wrong side of the barriers. He also observed a man in a cherry picker being hoisted up toward a telephone pole. Pence said, "Forget that. We're going to cut all the streetlights."

Mickey gave Tony a hard look. "You think you can handle that?"

Tony gestured with his hands. "For the girlfriend's sake and for the baby's life, I'd better handle it."

Mickey caught Pence's eye. "Let's do it."

"Your job is to get behind my unit. You're going to get on the phone. I want you to try to talk him into releasing the baby. Whatever you need to say, get him to release the baby. We're going to take this slow and one step at a time. I'll be coaching you. The STOP team will be available if you need them."

Tony looked back at the team. He observed three men and one female STOP officers. He knew them all. He walked to the Lieutenant's SUV. The LT handed Tony the cell phone.

"Just hit the button. We've got a dedicated line in."

Tony hesitated for a split second, no more. "Eduardo, this is Tony Farrina from the JFK School. Do you remember me?"

There was silence. "I know you can hear me. Say something." There was more silence. Tony looked at the LT, then at Mickey. "C'mon, Eduardo, give me some respect here." Tony remembered a class he had taken for training on talking a potential suicide down. The point the instructor stressed was that you want to let the subject know that he is not alone; that you'll stand by him through the entire situation and even after it ends.

"Listen, Eduardo, at least let me speak with your girlfriend. I want to know that everyone is okay." Tony inhaled. He exhaled slowly. He watched Mickey light a cigarette. The Lieutenant was offering encouragement. "You're doing fine. Don't stop."

"Listen, Eduardo. Do you remember how we worked together at JFK? You earned your GED and made a helluva start at turning things around. Right now, this is just a hiccup, just a stone in the road, a nail in the tire. There is nothing we can't fix. We'll walk through it together. I'll be with you all the way; I promise. You've come too far to fuck it up now."

Pence put his hand on Tony's shoulder. He nodded his encouragement.

"Let me speak with your girlfriend." He couldn't remember her name. "You don't want this for your baby. You want to do the right thing."

Tony heard hard breathing on the other end of the line. "It's over, Mr. Farrina. I had it and I screwed up. It's not your fault. It's my fault. I was doing good. I lost my job and couldn't feed the baby. I..."

"Eduardo, that's behind you. We can fix that later. We'll find a job for you. Now, I need you to let the baby go."

"I can't do that."

"Will you let your girlfriend go?"

"I can't do that either. We're all gonna go together."

"Don't say that, Eduardo. The three of you have your whole lives ahead of you." Tony put his hand to his forehead. He was sweating. "I'm telling you, we can work this out."

"She's done with me and she's taking the baby with her. It's over."

Tony raised his voice. He was growing as desperate as Eduardo was sounding. "Don't say that. Nothing is in stone."

The LT was on another phone. Out of the corner of his eye, Tony observed the LT nod. Tony watched Pence raise his hand to his throat and make a slashing motion, telling Tony to stop talking. "Get him to come to the window so that he can see you and you can see him. Maybe that'll be more personal."

Tony nodded. The sweat was dripping down on his uniform. "Eduardo, I need you to trust me. Can you do that?"

"I trust you, Mr. Farrina. You're one of the few people I do trust."

"Good. I want you to bring the baby and your girlfriend to the window. I want to see that they're both okay. Will you do that for me?"

"They are okay...for now."

"I'll make you a deal. Bring them both to the window and I'll send in a pizza and some food for the baby. Deal?"

"I don't want food. I want this to end."

"The baby must be hungry. Let me send some food in for the baby."

"I want to be left alone. I want to spend the last few minutes remembering how close I came to..."

“C’mon, Eduardo, knock that shit off. You’ll turn this thing around and you’ll be right back where you were when you left JFK. Trust me on that.”

“If I bring them to the window so you can see they’re okay, will you let me alone?”

“Absolutely. That’s a promise. My word to you, Eduardo. Prove to me they’re okay and I’ll back off. I promise.”

The streetlights were still on. The man in the cherry picker had taken no action. Mickey was on his third cigarette. Four STOP team members were across the street: one behind a tree in front of the house, one in the back of the house under cover of a shed; another was on the southside of the house behind a neighbor’s car; and the fourth STOP team member was on the northside of the house attempting to peer into a side window. She could see nothing but black.

“C’mon, Eduardo. Let me see that they’re okay. You promised.”

Tony first observed a curtain moving. He froze. Next, he observed Eduardo’s girlfriend. Tony remembered Gigi’s name. He couldn’t remember the baby’s name, but he saw the baby in Eduardo’s right hand. He could see Eduardo holding the baby in one hand over his right shoulder. The gun, in his left hand, was pointing toward the ground.

“Awesome, Eduardo. That’s ...”

Tony watched the gun fall out of Eduardo’s hand. He observed Eduardo fall slowly to the floor. He witnessed Gigi grab the baby before Eduardo hit the floor.

The head shot that killed Eduardo came from the fifth member of the STOP Squad in the cherry picker. Everything was a blur. Tony didn’t feel the Lieutenant’s hand on his shoulder. He didn’t feel Mickey’s hand on his other shoulder. The next conscious memory Tony had was sitting in the Blue Room, sipping coffee.

It was 0300 hours when Tony pulled the Vette into the driveway next to Carina’s red Ford Mustang. Normally, he’d pull the Corvette into the garage. Not this morning.

LT greeted Tony at the door, barking and wagging his tail. Tony got down on one knee and hugged LT. Not far behind LT was Carina. She gave Tony a warm hug. "I saw bits and pieces of what happened on the news. I thought you might want some company. I hope you don't mind."

Tony gave Carina a soft kiss on the lips. "No. I'm glad you're here. Thanks." He walked to the kitchen. Tony opened a cupboard door and grabbed a bottle of Seagram's. "Want a drink?"

"No thanks. I've got a cup of coffee on the table. I thought you might like a sandwich and coffee." She sat down at the table.

"Maybe after a bit." Tony poured two fingers of Seagram's in a glass. He sipped it. "What a bitch." He sipped some more Seagram's. "I had no idea they were going to use me like that." Tony sat at the table across from Carina.

"From what I saw on TV, he didn't leave them much of a choice." Carina sipped her coffee.

"They could have told me. They used me."

"What would you have done had they told you?"

Tony was silent. He shook his head. He couldn't get the picture of Eduardo's head exploding in front of him. He finished the Seagram's then poured himself more. He started to drink it when his cell phone rang. "Hello."

"Tony, it's Yolis. How are you doing?"

"Hey, you're a nice surprise." He lifted the glass and swallowed hard. "I'm not going to bullshit you. It hurts. I set that kid up."

"It was him or the baby, Tony. It had to be. The guy was PCP'd out. He didn't know shit from brown shoe polish. There was no room here for guessing. You saved the baby's life and the girlfriend's life. No two ways about it."

Maybe it was the Seagram's, but that made Tony feel a little better. "Are you still at work?"

"Yeah. They held me over. A lot of the team is tied up with reports, booking evidence, notification, guarding the scene, talking with the press—the usual shit. But I'm young. I can handle it. Listen, I got a call up on the strip. I have to go. If it's okay, I'll check in with you later."

"That would be great. I appreciate it. Really. Be safe." He hung up the phone.

Tony sat at the table, across from Carina. "He was doing so well. It's a shame it had to end that way for him."

"The baby and mom are safe."

"I wish I knew what happened."

"He used—that's what happened. The only cure for an addict or alcoholic is complete abstinence."

Tony wanted to tell her to shut the fuck up, but she meant well. She didn't understand. He worked with Eduardo at JFK. He was one of those kids, one of those rare kids who was turning it around. And then he went back to the same environment. The gangbanging environment. The drug environment. What real chance did he have?

Tony finished his drink. He poured another.

"How's Mickey?"

"He's up to his ass in quicksand. His wife is driving him to the poorhouse. He's working more overtime than he should just to stay afloat. She may be running around on him. I bought him a pack of smokes today because he's broke, and then this.

"We talked on the way home. He told me basically the same thing you did. It still hurts. I thought that kid was going to be a rare success story. Mother fucker!" Tony yelled, frightening LT who got up, ran to the table, and stood by Tony. He was going to protect his master.

Tony rubbed at the stubble on his face. "How about we call it a night?" It was four in the morning.

"You sure you don't want to talk?"

"Maybe in the morning." He held up his glass. "I'm going to finish this, pour me one more, and hit the bed. You going to join me?"

Tony woke up to the blaring of the telephone which was on the nightstand next to the bed. It sounded like a fire alarm. His head hurt, he was hungry, and his mouth was dry. Carina had taken a shower and was getting dressed.

Tony picked up the phone. He listened. “No goddammit, I don’t want solar energy. I thought you guys weren’t allowed to call before 9 a.m.!” He slammed down the receiver.

“How do you feel?” Carina asked.

“I don’t. Not yet. I’m still asleep.”

Lieutenant jumped on the bed. He put his head on Tony’s chest. *He loves me unconditionally,* Tony thought as he held him tight against him. “You’re my hero, LT.” Then, to Carina, “You’re working today?”

“All day. It’s my monthly Saturday. Twelve hours. I’ll check in with you during the day. Are you working?”

“Of course. It’ll probably be good for me.” The phone rang again. “Son of a bitch.” He reached over LT’s head to grab the phone. “Mickey, what’s going on?”

“I checked in with the WC. They want me to take three days off because of the shooting. They don’t want to see your face until next Friday.”

“Fuck that. I want to work.”

“Fuck that. You’re not. It’s SOP following a shooting.”

“I didn’t do the shooting.”

“Nonetheless, you were involved. Next Friday. I’ve got to go. I promised Tammy I’d take her to breakfast.”

Tony hung up. “I guess I’m not working.” He looked at Carina. “I’m off till next Friday.”

“What are you going to do?”

“I think I’ll go to the range.”

Carina left for work and Tony got into the shower, alone.

This Job Ain't for Pussies

Tony was drying off when the phone rang for third time. It was Yolis. "Hey, big guy. How are you?"

"Better than a cavity, I suppose. It's nice to hear from you."

"I thought I'd check in on you."

"I can't work. They gave me a couple of days off. That sucks big time."

"You shouldn't be working. A couple of days off after...after the incident will do you good. What are you up to?"

"Is this a therapy call?"

There was a hesitation on the other end of the line followed by, "Fuck you, asshole. Just because someone gives a shit about you, that doesn't make it therapy." She slammed the phone down.

Tony shook his head. He was angry; angry with himself. He punched a couple of buttons on his phone and Yolis' phone rang. He was about to hang up when she picked up. "I accept your apology. Your move."

"I am sorry. The...ugh...situation was difficult for me."

"Understandable. This isn't a sympathy call. Actually, it's like a I-want-to-get-into-your-pants call."

Tony laughed. He had heard that Yolis was a laugh a minute, with personality and a sharp tongue, that she spoke her mind and it didn't matter whether it was some punk on the street or the Chief.

Rumor had it that some Hispanic banger with a knife attempted to rob her when she was off duty and in soft clothes. The guy, speaking in Spanish, told her to hand over her money. She acted scared shitless. She said she had just come from the bank and had eight hundred dollars in her purse. (She later told police that, when she told the guy she had that much cash, she swore she observed a swelling in the front of his jeans.) She unsnapped her purse, and pulled out her service Glock and deadpan said, “Do you want to hear this bullet in Spanish or English?”

The guy looked terrified. He turned and started to run. A witness said she was smiling as she took dead aim at the fleeing felon who still had the knife in his right hand. She put one 40 caliber from the Glock in his right ass cheek and another in his left. Then she calmly walked up to him, bent down, and handcuffed him.

“I am sorry, Yolis. Last night was difficult to swallow.”

“It’s not for you to swallow. You did what you were ordered to do. If you ask me, and since you didn’t, I’m going to tell you anyway. Those actions saved a baby’s life and probably that of the mother, too. In this business, sometimes things can get real ugly. If you can’t handle that, move on.”

“You get right to the point, don’t you?”

“You want me to coat it with a rubber-fucking flashlight? That’s why so many cops eat their guns. They can’t handle it and they turn to booze. They get shit-faced, and they can’t think straight. They put the gun in their mouth and squeeze off a round. If that’s where your head is, you may as well accept it now and move on. This job ain’t for pussies!”

Tony didn’t believe he heard Yolis just say that.

“Let’s change the fucking subject.”

“Go for it.”

“I was thinking about going to the range. Want to come with me?”

“Which range?”

“The Oaktree in Newhall.”

“Want some company?”

“That’s a drive-and-a-half for you.”

“I make good time. I have a badge.”

And a tight ass, Tony thought. If the badge didn’t do the trick, that ass would always get you out of a ticket. “Are you going to teach me how to shoot?”

"Do you need lessons?"

"Not shooting lessons."

"Give me the address to the range and I'll punch it in my GPS. After the range, you buy lunch. Date?"

"Date."

Tony knew he had time to kill. Yolis had a longer drive then he did. He curled up on the couch downstairs with LT. "You know what, buddy, sometimes life can be a bitch. Sometimes humans can be ugly. They can be mean, cruel, and a pain in the ass. But not you. You love me no matter what. You love everyone unless they threaten me."

Tony looked up over the fireplace. There was a Jim Warren painting that Tony bought on a cruise. It was ALL DOGS GO TO HEAVEN. "I love you, buddy. You really are the Lieutenant and I'm so glad you're here. I hope you're as happy to be here as I am to have you here. We've survived a lot together."

***

Tony waited for Yolis in the parking lot, and he didn't have long to wait. He recognized her black Mustang convertible from the HP parking lot as she was pulling in. Still, he checked out the plate to be sure it was Yolis. The plate read 832 BIT. 832 was the penal code reference for one who had gone through the training to become a police officer. BIT stood for "Bitch In Training." Yolis was a police officer bitch in training. Tony loved the humor.

She parked her Mustang. Tony watched her in his rearview mirror. He drove around the parking lot. She was still in the vehicle when he pulled the Vette directly behind her. He exited the Corvette. When he was at her window, Tony asked, "I need to see your license, registration, and proof of insurance, please. I stopped you because you were exceeding the speed limit in the parking lot."

"Officer, I don't have a license, but would you like to see my handcuffs?" she teased.

"Only if you'd like to see my gun," he quipped.

"What caliber is it?"

“What caliber would you like?”

“About a nine.”

“How about a nine with an extended mag?”

“Isn’t that illegal?”

“Depends.” Tony opened the door. “C’mon, let’s see if you’re as good with your gun as you are with your mouth.”

Yolis smiled. “I guarantee you I’m at the top of my game with both!”

Yolis had her eyes and ears on. So did Tony. The targets were metal. They were at 5 yards, 10 yards, 15 yards, 25 yards, and beyond. Yolis set her duty weapon and a Smith and Wesson 9 on the deck. Both weapons were cleared.

Tony was adjacent to Yolis. Tony had three weapons on the deck. His Glock 27 or baby Glock, a Glock 27, and his new Glock 35, all 40-caliber guns. He smiled at Yolis. “Age before beauty.”

“So, what are you waiting for?”

Tony loaded the new Glock 35. He slammed home the magazine. “Two in the ten ring at 10 yards, then three head shots.” He checked his ears. Tony picked up the Glock, extended his arms, closed his weak eye, inhaled, exhaled, and fired five rounds in rapid succession. The first two shots were center mass, dead on. The head shots were right on target.

Yolis said, “I’ll match it.” She did.

“Nice shooting.”

“I told you I’m good at everything I do and if I’m not, I practice until I get it right.”

“Like a teacher,” Tony said. “If you don’t get it right the first time, he makes you do it over and over again until you do get it right.”

“Let’s try twenty-five yards. Ten rounds, two hands, five and five.”

Tony reloaded the 35. He took a breath and exhaled. He extended his arms and took careful aim. He put one in the ten ring, then one in the center of the head of the silhouette. He repeated that five times.

Yolis smiled. “Not bad for a reserve. Let me show you how a bitch-in-training does it.” She matched Tony shot for shot. “Do you like the nine or the 40 better?”

“I was torn between the nine and the 40. After trying them both, I decided on the forty. The ammo for the 40 is a bit more and the kick is slightly heavier, but I’m more accurate with the 40. Wanna’ try it?”

“Thanks, I’m good. Let’s do some serious shooting.”

They called it a day after three solid hours of shooting. When all was said and done, if they were giving out trophies, Yolis would have won the award. She was more accurate than Tony and a bit faster. But they were both excellent with a weapon.

“How about lunch?”

“Sounds good. Where?”

“I know a place in the Valley which is on your way home and it’s right off the freeway. Follow me.”

Yolis ordered breakfast. Tony ordered a barbeque chicken salad. Before the food came, Yolis asked the obvious. “How tight are you and Carina?”

Tony gave that some thought. He wanted to be honest. To be honest, he had to evaluate their relationship in his own mind. “We’ve been seeing each other for less than a year. I’m not seeing anyone else. I don’t know that she is.” Tony sipped his coffee. “Does that answer your question?”

Yolis shrugged. “Take me out on a date.”

“Is that a question or a statement?” Tony looked around the coffee shop. He wanted to make certain no one else was in earshot. They weren’t.

“Don’t screw with me. I’ve got handcuffs.”

“And you shoot like Annie Oakley. I’d love to.”

“Do you have a first name?”

“Little Bit.”

“Seriously?”

"Seriously. Yolis or Little Bit work fine." Their food came. "Shut up and eat!"

Breakfast with Mick

It was 0900 hours Sunday. Tony was still in his California custom king-sized bed. LT was next to him, his head on the pillow and long, not-so-lean body stretched out. LT was snoring. The phone rang louder than LT's snoring.

Tony reached over and grabbed it. "Did I wake you?" Mickey asked.

"No, but you woke LT. What's up?"

"How about breakfast or brunch?"

"What the hell's going on? I haven't gotten this much attention since I forgot to zip my fly coming out of the bathroom at Dodger Stadium."

"Just looking out for my partner. Besides, Tammy went shopping with my almost maxed out credit card. I'm lonely."

"Give me an hour to shave and shower and feed the LT. Where?"

"Roxy's."

Roxy's was a diner by the freeway. The service was excellent, and the food was tasty and hot. Dress was casual and the place was quiet.

Mickey slid into the booth seat that backed up against the wall; typical of almost every police officer Tony knew. He wanted to keep an eye on everything. When Carina and Tony dined at Roxy's, Tony asked to be seated at the same booth if it wasn't occupied. Carina knew enough to let Tony sit with his back against the wall.

Mickey was dressed in black slacks, pullover blue shirt hanging out of his waist, and tennis shoes. "Give me a straight answer. Man to man. No bullshit. How are you doing?"

If there was anybody Tony could be honest with, it was Mickey. They were close. "I won't kid you. It hurts in several ways." Tony kept talking. "I knew the kid from the JFK School, and he was making progress. I know enough to realize I have no control over that. I can't control what these kids do inside the facility let alone what they do when they get out. Carina likes to talk to me about acceptance. She's constantly telling me to accept what I can't change. I know I can't change the fact that he went back to drugs when he got out.

"What does bother me, what I can't seem to get a handle on, is that the Department used me to get at Eduardo. They used me to kill him." Tony was silent.

The waitress took their order.

"They didn't use you to kill him. They showed you how to do your job." Mickey fidgeted with a napkin. "Before you came on board, I was involved in a shooting on Gage Avenue."

Tony nodded. "I heard bits and pieces of it."

Mickey smoothed out the napkin. He took a pen and drew a diagram then turned the napkin around. "Here. I arrive, and my back up arrives right behind me. We enter the house. The mother and father are in the living room. The forty-year-old son, who was just released from prison, is staying with his mom and dad and younger sister. The place is small. Maybe 1200 square feet, if that. The kitchen doubles for a laundry room. The ex-con is higher than a 747. It's either PCP or cocaine." He noted, "You know how that goes. You're more active than most reserves and you've had more experience than some full-time coppers."

He continued. "My partner and I enter the kitchen. Ex-con is holding his sister around the neck in a chokehold. He's got a kitchen knife against her throat. The point of the knife is digging into the skin. We can observe drops of blood from the knife pressing against her throat.

"I reach for the radio. Ex-con says, 'Touch that radio again and I slash her fucking throat.'" Mickey showed Tony the diagram: "Washer, dryer, refrigerator. Sis and ex-con. Doorless entry."

Tony nodded.

"We have a split second to act. Both of us have our weapons on ex-con. Sister is begging us not to shoot him. She suddenly breaks free. He accidentally drops the knife. We yell to her to get out of the kitchen to run. He reaches for the knife. She tries to get it first. She's too slow. He picks it up and goes to stab her. I hesitate because of the angle. My partner fires three rounds. Round one kills the dryer. Round two kills the washer. Ex-con stabs sister twice. My partner's third round kills the ex-con.

My partner never came back. He's living in Arizona teaching driver training. I had to struggle with the fact that I didn't get off a shot."

Tony pulled the diagram across the table and again examined it. "You did have a bad angle."

"Maybe, but the hesitation caused her to get stabbed twice. I was cleared as, of course, was my partner. The point is you are always going to second-guess what went down at the scene. That's the nature of our work; always has been, always will be. That's just the way it is. You asked to play the game; they just showed you how.

"Let's cut through all the BS. In your case, it's really cut and dry. Two lives were saved. The perp took it in the shorts. Supposing they let you try to talk him down and he killed the baby? Supposing they let you try to talk him down and he killed the baby's momma? Supposing they let you talk him down and he killed the baby and the baby's momma? Supposing they let you try to talk him down and he killed the baby, the baby's momma, and himself? It went down the way it had to go down. You did as you were told. From what I'm hearing, you'll get a commendation. Let fucking go of it."

The waitress brought the food. Mickey said, "Say grace."

"Grace."

They ate.

The waitress came around with a coffee carafe.

"Sure, I'll have more coffee. Cut me off after my third. I'm driving." Tony looked at Mickey. "Let me run another one by you."

"The first one's free. The second one will cost you lunch."

"Done." Tony smiled. "You're a school administrator inside a Probation camp. The teacher catches a kid, the same kid she caught two weeks ago, in the classroom, smoking pot. The kid also has a small amount of grass in a zip-lock baggy and a cigarette lighter. The first time you caught the kid, under pressure, you agreed to put him in a substance-abuse program and not even suspend him. What do you do this time?"

"This sounds like I'm taking a police oral."

"Not funny."

"Deal with it."

"The first thing I want to know is how he got the shit inside a locked facility."

"Good start. But what do you do with the kid?"

"You can't expel him because he's locked up. Is he eighteen?"

"No."

"Can you suspend him?"

"Yup."

"Can you file charges against him?"

"Yup."

"What are you waiting for?"

"We're under the supervision of the ACLU..."

"As is the Sheriff."

"Correct. My superiors are shit scared of the ACLU. Between the ACLU and the suits in Downey, if I suspend or file charges, I get transferred to Downey and that's probably just for openers."

"Are you serious?"

"Like a bullet wound in the chest."

"Damn, they actually told you that?"

"Pretty much in those words."

"Fuck the ACLU. Don't they care about how that shit is getting inside the camp?"

"That's what I said."

"And they said...?"

"Play ball or the rest of the season is in Downey."

"Damn. What about your union?"

"What union? We don't have a union. Teachers do, we don't. I tried to start a union but no soap."

"Did you lawyer up?"

"I talked with several attorneys. I have no case. They haven't done anything yet. Most attorneys are too smart to screw with the ACLU."

"Wow. That's a tough one. You've got two choices. Cave in or fight. If you cave in, you're opening the door for more drugs. If you fight, freeway therapy."

"Do you have any idea how much drugs pour into that place and several of the other camps throughout Corrections? Corrections wants to sweep it under the rug to avoid publicity."

"How many more years till retirement?"

"Too many."

"Retire, take your pension, and join the Department."

"I have too much time in to do that. The regional director had my ass in Downey. She read me the riot act over another situation. But she's put pressure on me for this. They'd love to see me leave because I won't play ball. But now push is coming to shove."

"You have two choices. Fight and bite the bullet, or fold your cards and put up with whatever comes your way." Mickey sipped iced tea. "Do you remember when I was your training officer? One night when the bars let out, we were patrolling Pacific Boulevard and you spot this wetback pissing against the wall?"

"I almost choked him to death."

"I thought you were going to throw him through the store window. You're yelling at him, 'You're not in Mexico, mother fucker!'"

"Yeah, and you would only let me write him a ticket."

"Not me, brother. We used to run the a-holes in for that. But the city council got the bright idea that too many of them were being arrested and cut loose, so they decided to make it an infraction. We end up citing them. They don't give a shit about the cite cause they ain't gonna pay the fine anyway. If they do, it would be in pesos!

So, now you got twice as many pissers out there. Don't deal with it, and you're risking opening the flood gates. Deal with it, and you're closer to HP."

"And I get a bill for that advice?" Tony asked sarcastically.

"Let's try another analogy—I want to earn my lunch. Do you mess with the stock market?"

"Every now and then."

"What was your last play?"

"Sony."

"How much, and what did you pay?"

"I bought over a one-week period at between $17 and $18. As a matter of fact, my broker suggested I not buy because it had just gotten hammered."

"So much the better. But you bought anyway, right?"

"Right."

"Why?"

"Because I had done some Sony homework and felt it would turn around. I figured it might take a year or two, but I didn't need the money, so I figured it could sit there like a bank account."

"Good. You evaluated the upside and the downside, and you made a decision. How'd that work out for you?"

"It's been trading in the low $30 range."

"Excellent. You can be my broker. Do the same homework here, my college-degreed friend. Evaluate the positive and the negative, make a decision, act on it, and let freaking go of it."

"That's basically what Carina said."

"Good minds think alike. Grab the check and leave a decent tip."

What It's Really About

Three years ago, Tony started what he called APEA, Assistant Principal's Essay Award. Three times a year, Tony would offer, out of his own pocket, a $100 gift certificate from Barnes and Noble for the student who wrote the best essay discussing life, change, and success. Tony was the reader and judge of the essays. Some of the essays were moving.

The essay Tony had in front of him was the winner. It read:

> At sixteen, I was again arrested. This time it was for stealing a car, leading police on a chase and possession of a gun. It was my fifth arrest.
>
> I have good parents at home who love me and who have raised three boys, my brothers. My oldest brother was killed in a gang shooting while I was locked up. It broke our hearts.
>
> Until I was arrested this time, it never occurred to me the pain I was causing my parents and the damage I was doing on the streets. I've had plenty of time to think about this at JFK.
>
> My teachers and Mr. Farrina had spent many hours talking to me about my future. Mr. Farrina convinced me that the things I have done are in the past and the best way to make amends to my parents, my brother, and the community is to do the right thing when I get out. Mr. Farrina and my teachers and counselors have helped me earn my high school diploma. When I leave JFK, in six days, eight hours and seventeen minutes, I will have a real high school diploma. More importantly, I will have a positive attitude.

Mr. Farrina taught me that I have to accept responsibility for everything I do. He taught me that if someone pisses me off, it's not because they pissed me off, it's because I allowed them to piss me off. I really am responsible today.

I have enrolled in a junior college and hope to study criminology. One day, I hope to return to JFK as a probation officer and help kids who were once screwed up like me.

Mr. Farrina made me a deal. The deal is, if I stay out of trouble for one year, I can return to JFK as a guest speaker and can speak to the students and staff at an assembly and share my experiences with them. I want nothing more than to do that as today I feel like a new person.

I thank all the school and Probation staff for helping me across a busy street lined with traffic that does not obey laws. Today I'm on the right street, driving by the rules, and paying attention to the road. Today, I am the driver, and it is up to me to navigate the road. Thank you all. I will see you in one year. God Bless.

Written by Ricardo Rodriguez

R and R

It was 0800 hours. Tony was in bed, on his back with his head on the pillow. LT was next to him. "Sometimes I wish the whole world was made up of LTs. You're a good guy, LT, and you don't complicate anyone's life."

The phone rang. "What are you up to?" Tony asked Mickey.

"About the same height I was yesterday. What are you up to?"

"I'm thinking I'm going to spend my last free day at the indoor go-kart track in Burbank. How does that sound?"

"Are you asking me if I want to race cars?"

"If I were asking you, what would you say?"

"Sure. Why not? I've got to get ready."

"I'll come by and get you in about an hour. Work for you?"

"Works for me. See you in a bit." Tony liked speed. He liked to speed on the freeway, and he liked to take the Vette over canyon roads. Since he received his badge, he became more conscious of laws and vehicle codes. It was embarrassing to get pulled over. One of the incidents that kept him from joining a police department full time was the evading arrest law, but that didn't seem to change his driving habits. The badge did. He believed in that badge. He was proud of that badge and Tony didn't want to tarnish it.

"LT, you can stay in bed. I'm going to teach Mickey how to drive a go-kart."

Before Mickey hired on at HP, he drove big rigs for a living. He handled the black-and-white like it was a bicycle. He could weave in and out of traffic like a snake twists its body. He could stop the unit like a catcher's mitt stops a pitcher's 98-mile-an-hour fastball.

They had been in several pursuits together. Mickey drove in all but one. Mickey was batting 100 percent; Tony was batting zero. The single pursuit in which he did the driving, ended in the perp making a getaway over railroad tracks with the arms down and a commuter train roaring toward the carjacker. The fact was that Mickey had a lot more experience on the street than did Tony, which was one of the negatives of being a reserve.

Mickey was a hell of a teacher. Some FTOs wanted to bust your balls; others wanted you to wash out. Mickey had the sense to realize that, one day, Tony might be his backup, may save his life. When Tony had trouble handcuffing a subject, he got pissed at himself. Mickey helped him take the guy into custody but said nothing until they were on their way home. "Putting bracelets on a suspect who doesn't want to wear cuffs is not what you see on TV," Mickey told Tony. There is no easy way to put cuffs on when the subject doesn't want to be handcuffed.

"Tomorrow morning I'll be over at your place, and we'll run a few drills, then you can buy me breakfast at Roxy's. The trick is causing the suspect enough pain that he wants to comply. So, tonight, think about what you might do to accomplish that. You don't want to do major damage, but you want to—you *have to*—get the guy in handcuffs quickly, especially if there's more than one perp involved. Try to get a mental picture of that in your mind's eye. We'll work on it tomorrow.

"I'll leave you with this. One of our officers, who shall remain anonymous, on a traffic stop without a back, had to take a warrant suspect into custody. Adam Henry topped out at 6'1" and 210.5 pounds. She's about 5'3" and 135 soaking wet.

"Adam Henry was not about to go quietly. Several people were watching the show. Not one would help her out. She warned him that she was going to spray him. He laughed. She took out her pepper spray. She shook it up and aimed; but before she could activate it, he kicked it out of her hand. She took her right foot and planted it between his legs. He went down like a Van Nuys whore on the front seat of your car. She had no trouble cuffing him. The growing crowd gave her a hand. Get the picture?"

"Sharp and clear."

The indoor go-kart track was an elongated figure eight. The cars could hit about 45 mph. Mickey was lighter than Tony, so he could get a few more miles per hour out of the car.

They each donned driving glasses and helmet and selected their cars. They strapped in. The "gentlemen started their engines" and the race was on.

Mickey pulled ahead from the gate and let the other vehicles slide by so he could mess with Tony and mess with Tony he did. Mickey eased off the gas so Tony could catch a look at the race car's rear end. Just as Tony thought he had a shot at passing Mickey on his right, Mickey stepped hard on the gas and cut the wheel hard right, very hard right. Tony tasted the guard rail. "Mother fucker."

Mickey was now six car lengths ahead of Tony. Since the sporting thing to do was let him catch up, Mickey again slowed down. He thought Tony learned from his mistake. Mickey was wrong. Again, Tony tried to get by him on the right. Again, Mickey eased off the gas, catching Tony between the rear quarter of the race car and the guard rail. Again, he cut hard right while his foot floored the gas. Tony took an even harder jarring. Mickey thought he might pee his pants.

Tony's middle finger came up. The keeper of the cars motioned Mickey and Tony to knock it off. *After I get even*, Tony thought. He didn't. He wouldn't. He couldn't.

They kept it up for an hour and a half, stopping only for a short coffee break. Tony had a bruised upper right arm. It was the most fun he'd had since...well, it was the most fun he'd had in a long, long time.

You Don't Fail Until You Quit Trying

Wednesday was "graduation" day at the John F. Kennedy School. This meant that seven students who had earned high school diplomas or GED certificates were eligible to walk the stage. Parents and relatives were invited. Unfortunately, graduation did not mean you got to leave the facility. All seven still had time to serve—not much time, but time, nonetheless.

Tony was asked to give a short speech before the certificates were passed out jointly by the Corrections Director and the Probation Director in what was supposed to be a show of unity.

> "Good morning. For those of you who don't know me, I am Tony Farrina, Assistant Principal here at the John F. Kennedy School. For those who do know me, I promise to keep this brief.
>
> (A ripple of laughter.)
>
> "If I were asked to list three key factors leading to a successful life, I would say, education, perseverance, and personality. Education, because without it, it is most difficult to climb the ladder of success. Perseverance, because if you quit, you fail. But you never fail unless you quit trying. I'm going to repeat that because it is so important. You never fail unless you quit trying. Let me give you an example. A friend of mine, a female friend, who had been in jail for numerous DUIs and for passing bad checks, decided she wanted to go back to school and earn her college degree, then go to law school to become an attorney. That's tough to do with an arrest record. She decided that, one class at a time, she'd give it a shot. She got her university degree. She went on to law school. She graduated law school and took the bar exam. When she got the results in the mail, she called me. She told me she didn't pass. I asked, 'You

failed?' She said, 'No, I didn't pass.' I asked, 'What's the difference?' Bev said, 'You don't fail until you quit trying.' That's powerful. I never learned that in school. Bev passed the bar exam on her fifth try. She's practicing law in San Diego today and every so often when she's up in this area, I get her to come up to the girls' camp and talk to them about education and about turning their lives around.

"For those of you who have a personality that pushes people away—and you may or may not know who you are—you have to lighten up. You have to reach out and ask for help no matter how difficult that may be. You have to reach out and offer help, no matter how difficult that may be. You have to smile. You have to stop acting like a gangster because that pushes people away. If you want friends, you have to be a friend.

"I want to wrap this up by going back to education. I have, and this is painfully true, a brother who is four years older than me. We grew up back east and came from good parents. My brother, a high school dropout, became involved in organized crime. A piece of me looked up to him. He had flashy clothes, plenty of money, foxy women, and a 1969 black-on-black Lincoln Continental Mark. He had it all.

"Well, eventually, the hammer falls. And it did. It fell on my brother and his wife. Not too long ago, I boarded a plane and flew back east for the weekend. I got to visit my brother in one penitentiary and his wife in another.

"I want you to hear this loud and clear. I ran three thousand miles to get away from the influence of my brother. I managed to graduate high school, not by much, but I graduated. I went to college. I earned my BA degree, went on to graduate school and earned a master's in Education. In between, I got into trouble—police trouble. I have an arrest record. Truth is, I've been arrested more times than my brother. The difference is, I managed to get an education and had that to fall back on. When I convinced myself that I was done because of my arrest record, Bev showed me otherwise. She convinced me to go to the police academy, one class at a time, and not worry about the results.

"I had not been in trouble in more than twenty years and had proved that I could walk the straight and narrow. In the academy, I met a police chief who lectured me. He took a liking to me. He was, and is the Chief in HPPD where I am one of Chief York's Reserve Police Officers.

"My brother, who is out of jail, is divorced, remarried and out of prison. He has nothing. The money went on attorney fees. The Lincoln was sold. He put on weight in prison and the fancy clothes no longer fit him. The flashy women no longer wanted an ex-con without money. My brother, from time to time, borrows money from me to make his mortgage payment. He always wanted to live in a big house; he got to spend years in that big house.

"To wrap this up, take your pick. Do you want a life of peace and security, or a life where parents, children, and relatives have to visit you in a big house? The choice is yours. You are off on the road—the right road; you're turning your life around. You can take that high school diploma, that GED, and build upon it. Or, when you leave here, you can go back to the gangs, to the banging and to the illegal activity. The choice is yours.

"Not long ago, I cracked open a fortune cookie after dinner in a Chinese restaurant. The fortune read, 'Step aside. You're in your own way!'

"I congratulate each of you. I wish you the best of everything. May your education continue, may you never quit trying, and with your newfound positive personality, may you build success and happiness for you and yours.

"God bless you.

"Let's get on with the ceremony!"

The entire crowd of parents, relatives, and suits stood up. They gave Tony a rousing ovation. They could see that his words came from his heart. They could see how much he cared about the kids. They could see and hear that he valued education, that he valued life.

The certificates were awarded to the graduates who wore blue caps and gowns. Parents and relatives were proud that their once-troubled teens seemed to be turning the corner and heading in the right direction.

Tony made the rounds of the tables during lunch, congratulating the grads and meeting the relatives.

After the keynote speaker, a student, who had once been incarcerated at JFK and was now a probation officer for Corrections, completed his address, the ceremony was concluded. Parents said their goodbyes and headed for the auditorium door. The parents of graduate Deandre Davis stopped to chat with Tony.

Mr. Davis was dressed in brown suit, striped French-cuffed shirt, and a red tie. His shoes were tan, polished, and expensive. He looked at his wife. "Why don't you and Deandre say goodbye at the door? I want to talk with Mr. Farrina for a moment."

Tony smiled.

"First, I want to thank you from the bottom of my heart for all you have done for Deandre. He is a changed man, a graduate, a person with a future. I thank you."

Tony was embarrassed. "I didn't do it, sir. But I thank you. Deandre did it."

"We both know that's a lot of crap." Mr. Davis smiled. "Without the right kind of individual watching over and leading these kids, we know they're lost. This place is a hellhole without people like you."

Now Tony was more embarrassed. "Again, I thank you."

"I don't know how much Deandre has told you about us. Both Mrs. Davis and I are attorneys. As such, I pulled some strings. Next week we have an informal hearing, in chambers, with Deandre's judge. We're trying to get him released earlier so he can begin his semester at Pierce College. Would you attend the hearing and speak in favor of Deandre's early release?"

Tony didn't know what to say. On very rare occasions he had stood up in court in favor of a student's early release from a facility. He could count the times he had done so on one hand. He quickly weighed the pros and cons.

Tony handed Mr. Davis his business card. "I'd be happy to. My email is on the card. Send me all the information, and I will be there."

"How do I thank you?"

"You don't have to. Deandre's success is thanks enough."

Back in the Saddle

On Friday, Tony finally went back to work at HP. The Watch Commander assigned him to ride with Mickey for at least the shift. Tony did so gladly.

Tony drove. Mickey spent the first two hours talking with Tammy and chain-smoking. Tony kept the driver's window down.

"Dammit, Tammy, you can't keep spending money we don't have." He sighed. "I know I'm working a lot of overtime, but I'm trying to keep up with all the money you spend. When we bought the house, you promised you'd go back to work. I'm shouldering more than I can handle. A little help would be awesome."

Tony tapped Mickey on the shoulder. He noticed "something" going on in the city's free parking lot, observing two guys standing, appearing to be a bit tipsy, talking with two girls in an orange 1964 Chevy Super Sport with a black soft-top that was down. One guy was at the passenger side of the car, and one was at the driver's side. The Super Sport was occupied twice. From Tony's distance, the Chevy Impala looked stunning.

Mickey put out the plate. Tony put his lights on. Both Tony and Mickey assessed the situation before making a move. There were several bars in the area, and the guys were probably trying to pick up on the girls. In fact, other than being suspicious and acting a bit tipsy, neither were doing anything wrong. The guys appeared to be in their late twenties, early thirties. The girls, a bit younger. The ladies were attractive from Tony's vantage point. The guys were dressed in slacks, western shirts, boots, and cowboy hats. They were Hispanic.

Mickey nodded. They exited the car at the same time. Tony approached the driver's side of the Impala. The guy flirting with the dark-haired Hispanic girl, who was wearing a low-cut white blouse, either was aware of Tony's presence or he didn't give a damn. Tony took a sideways stance, right side of his body to the rear, keeping his gun well back of the reach of the subject, just in case.

The guy said to his male friend standing at the passenger side of the Chevy, with Mickey within four steps, “What size cup do you guess she’s wearing?” He slurred his speech.

The friend leaned in to the passenger side of the vehicle and looked at the driver’s midsection. He made an ‘I’m-not-sure’ gesture with his hands. “I’d guess a B cup, at best. How about mine?” referring to the second young lady.

“I’m thinking an A cup.”

Tony was about to make a move, but he could see their hands and the girls didn’t seem flustered. He wanted to see how this was going to play out. He inched closer.

The girl in the passenger seat looked over at her girlfriend. “What size athletic cup do you suppose *‘your guy’* wears?”

She put her hands on the steering wheel and lifted herself up. She looked over the door directly at his crotch. “Obviously small, maybe an extra small. How about *your guy*?”

She looked at his face, then his crotch, the back at his face. He was smiling as they made eye contact. “You know, I don’t think he needs a cup at all.”

Both pick-up artists started to walk away. While Mickey stopped his guy, Tony stopped his guy. They ran them both for wants and warrants. They were clean. “Who’s driving?”

“I am.”

Tony shook his head. “No, you’re not.”

“Then I am.”

“No, you’re not. If either of you gets behind the wheel of a car tonight, I’m going to pull you out of the vehicle and the only blowjob you get tonight is the breathalyzer. You both seem like good guys who have had way too much to drink. Go down the street, get yourself some coffee, and hit on the waitresses for a couple of hours. Are we good?”

They took off their black cowboy hats and bowed to Tony and Mickey. *"Gracias, amigo."*

Mickey keyed the mic. "24 Adam. The two male subjects checked okay. They were warned to not get behind the wheel and were SOW's. We're going to make contact with the two in the vehicle." Mickey deliberately didn't say he was going to make contact with the two *females* in the vehicle because that would have brought out almost every male cop on duty, and maybe a female.

"Copy that, 24 Adam."

Tony made his approach to the driver side of the collector Chevy. It looked as nice, maybe nicer, from up close and personal as it did from twenty feet. Mickey stayed back on the passenger side of the car just to make sure there was no hanky-panky.

Tony checked the car, then checked the legs on the passenger; both were impressive.

"Good evening, Officer. Is everything okay?"

Tony nodded. The driver was as attractive as the passenger. "I was going to ask you the same thing. We observed 'Manny and Moe'... ugh...talking with you and wanted to be sure..."

"We appreciate that. And we appreciate both of you." Mickey was now at the passenger door of the Impala. "They weren't dangerous. A little too friendly, but not dangerous."

"Beautiful car. Have you had it long?"

"It was a birthday gift from a boyfriend a couple of years ago."

"Nice birthday gift!"

"Well, when you can't do what's required in one department, you make up for it in other ways. This is how he made up for it."

"Wow." *At least she's honest,* Tony thought. "Then, I take it, you ladies are okay?"

The passenger looked at Mickey. "Hopefully, we're better than okay."

The driver looked at Tony and smiled. "Do you think I look...I mean, do you think the Super Sport looks better covered or topless?"

Tony smiled. He glanced down at his crotch area. At this point, definitely a large cup. The driver smiled. Tony thought she noticed, too. “I’m Marissa. My girlfriend is Tracee.”

“I’m Tony. My shy partner is Mickey. We really should get back to work.”

“Do you guys get a dinner break?”

“Eventually, when it’s quiet in Dodge.”

“Can we buy you dinner when Dodge settles in?”

Tony looked over at Mickey who quickly shook his head. “We thank you for the offer, but we’ll take a raincheck. I haven’t seen this car around HP before. Are you here often?”

“Now that my boyfriend and I parted company, we will be. Are you serious about the raincheck? If you are, I’ll come back and find some traffic law to crush.”

“Sure. Next time. And we’ll buy. Be careful and have a great rest of the evening.”

“You two be safe.” Tony’s hand was resting on the windowsill. Marissa put her hand on top of Tony’s and squeezed. She looked at his waist area. “Is that your nightstick you keep in there?” She pointed toward his crotch.

And Now, a Word from My Sponsor

Tony arrived at his office early for his 7:30 a.m. mid-year evaluation meeting with Paula and his principal Eddie Peterson. He was nervous.

For some reason, eval meetings always caused Tony concern. Nine times out of ten, there was no need for that concern. He did his job, and he did it well. He was far from perfect, but his heart was always in the right place. He held accountable those who needed to be held accountable. He gave praise to those who earned it. He held high expectations for the kids and valued education. This year was a game a bit off the track that Tony was used to traveling. The ACLU added a different dimension. The meeting was in Principal Peterson's office.

There was coffee on the coffee table. Next to the coffee were Danish and sweet rolls. Paula and Eddie were sipping drinks and munching on the goodies. Tony—dressed in a blue suit, white shirt, and a blue tie that depicted a police officer, a badge, a nightstick, and the words, "Protect and Serve"—entered the office. "Good morning." Tony forced a smile. His stomach was churning.

Tony had leveled a shotgun at a robbery suspect. He had taken numerous felons into custody. He had been in several pursuits, either as a passenger or the driver. He damn near shot a PCP suspect who punched him four times, twice in the face. He took that on with the best of them and never had to be transported to the hospital, not once. But this shit shook him up, just a bit.

Paula spoke. "Have some coffee and let's get started. I'm actually here for a meeting with the ACLU monitor, so I thought I'd kill two birds with one stone."

Tony hoped he wasn't the bird to be killed. He poured himself a cup of black coffee and sat next to Paula, across from Peterson's large, mahogany desk.

Paula started the meeting. "Of course, the majority of the input for this evaluation comes from Mr. Peterson. And by the way, his comments are nothing but positive. Among those comments, Eddie states you work long hours; at times, as many as twelve in one day. He states that you, when necessary, come in on weekends to help complete transcripts and to meet with parents who drive up here from L.A. He also told me that you work well with staff; that, when necessary, you do what paperwork is needed to put teachers and other staff you supervise on the straight road for the sake of the kids. He told me you are all about kids and education. He also told me you interact in a most professional manner with Probation staff, that you attend IEP meetings as necessary and that your evals are all up to date."

Tony was getting embarrassed. He was shaming himself for being nervous, the result of projecting the outcome of the meeting. He reached in his pants pocket. He unfolded several bills. He folded three twenties. "Here's the money I promised you." He leaned across the desk handing the money toward Eddie.

Both Paula and Eddie laughed. Tony stuffed the three bills back in his pants pocket. "Thank you for the positive input."

Paula, never one to let things go without having the last word, added, "My turn."

Again, it was nervous time for Tony.

"Mr. Peterson and I had quite a discussion this morning before you arrived. You know how I feel about butting heads with the ACLU and the monitors. It serves no useful purpose. I was going to make note of that in your eval, but Mr. Peterson took up your defense. There is no written directive in this mid-year eval addressing your head-butting with Cleveland Archer. I am going to side with Eddie. I am going to appeal to your sense of teamplay to look past minor occurrences and to do what is best for the team when it comes to the ACLU. Is that a reasonable expectation?"

Tony was big time caught off guard. He looked first at Eddie than at Paula. He folded his arms across his chest because it was damn cold in Mr. P's office, and he was sitting directly under the vent. "Paula, look, I appreciate what you just said. I really do. Mr.

Peterson, I thank you for having faith in me and for acknowledging that I work hard for the sake of the kids. I will do my damnedest to keep the canoe in smooth waters when it comes to the ACLU and the monitors. But..." Tony emphasized the *but.* "When it comes to the welfare of the kids and my staff, how do I let go of something like the marijuana incident?

Please understand, I am not balking at what you said. I am asking for direction."

It was Paula turn to sigh. "Can't you just let go of that? Is it that big a deal?"

"Would you like it if a student was smoking marijuana in a classroom where your child was a student?"

"Why is it you always want to fight?"

"I don't want to fight." Tony was growing seriously frustrated. I want to change what I can change. Grass in the classroom is unacceptable especially when the student has been caught once and was given a pass."

"Would it help any if I told you, in complete confidence, that Mr. Archer and I are meeting today and that is one of the topics on our mutual agenda?"

Paula was a goddamn liar. Tony didn't believe her for a minute; not for a New Jersey millisecond. He shook his head. He looked at Eddie. He was trying to buy time before he responded. Paula was the Hillary Clinton of Corrections. Eighty fucking percent of what came out of her mouth was bullshit. The other twenty percent was for her interests.

Paula looked at her watch. "I have another meeting in here in seven minutes."

Tony nodded. "Okay." His smile was weak. He scratched his chin. He had nicked himself shaving this morning and it itched. "I will do my best. I promise."

"Thank you." Paula handed Tony the two-page typed eval. He read it quickly. "Thank you both." He signed it and gave it back to Paula. She signed it and gave it to Eddie.

"I'll have a copy in your box this afternoon," Eddie told him. He reached across the desk and shook Tony's hand. "Thanks for all your hard work."

Paula gave him a hug. Tony thought she even looked like Hillary. "Thanks. Work with us."

Tony nodded. He turned toward the office door. At that moment, Cleveland Archer entered. He was dressed in a grey three-piece suit, solid grey shirt, and red tie. His black boots shined. You could see your face in them. He walked to the center of the room. First, he gave Paula a hug. Eddie had come out from behind his desk. He shook Eddie's hand and patted him on the back.

Archer started to shake Tony's hand. He suddenly stopped. He stared at Tony's tie. "That tie is inappropriate. It needs to come off."

Neither Paula nor Eddie commented on the tie. Tony was certain they had observed it. "But, sir, I am trying to encourage our students to strive for careers as educators, probation officers, police officers. Who better to turn our inner cities around than some of our kids? Some of our students are light-weight offenders and can make the grade to get into probation work or law enforcement."

"That's not why you're wearing that tie. You're wearing that tie to show kids you can oppress them. I know you're a sworn cop. I also think being a cop, you have no place here. Take that tie off or you are going to start World War III!"

Tony wanted to tell him to shove the tie up his ACLU ass. He wanted to wrap that tie around his neck and pull both ends as tight as he could until the prick quit breathing. "For what it's worth, sir, I have permission from the Probation chief and from Corrections' school director to raise money to build a miniature police academy on our campus. My goal is to get the police to train these kids and to build a curriculum around the physical training and the classroom academics; a small-scale police academy.

"The interaction alone might help the police to understand our inner-city kids and vice versa. It might help each to understand the struggles of the other. It might break down stereotypes. It might break down racial barriers."

"I'm not going to tell you again. Take off that fucking tie and do it now!"

Tony glanced quickly at Paula then at Eddie. Both were poker faced. Both had backed Tony in his quest

To build the miniature academy, both had pledged their support in helping Tony raise money for the project. Both were hypocrites to the max. Tony had run this idea right up the chain of command. He had even discussed it with the kids. No one was against it. No one uttered one word. Tony was left dangling in the fucking desert wind.

He took off the tie.

Things went from bad to "badder" to "baddest" for Tony at JFK. Another teacher complained of smelling alcohol on Romeo Johnson's breath. Another kid was caught smoking marijuana in the classroom, and Tony's police tie, a gift from a Sheriff's sergeant friend, was creased in his suit-jacket pocket.

Carina had taught Tony the Serenity Prayer. She told him when things grew tense at work, or the rare times Tony pissed her off, she repeated the prayer. Tony had been taught in the academy that when things got hairy in the street to take a breath, hold it till the count of five, release slowly and repeat three times. Now he tried both.

It was bad enough that the prick of an ACLU monitor forced him to take off his harmless tie in front of his boss and Paula. Now he had a drunk and a drug problem to deal with. Tony wanted to get on eBay and find an ACLU tie for sale. He wanted to wear it to work in the morning then see if Archer would make him take it off.

It was almost lunch time. He closed his office door and called Carina. She wasn't home or she didn't answer. He didn't leave a message.

Tony called the dorm where the kid who got caught smoking marijuana was housed. "This is Tony in the school office. Is Mike Kahn around?"

"Tony, Mike. What can I do for you?"

"I understand Fabian Webster got caught smoking marijuana in class. I'd like to set up a conference."

"No can do."

"Why not?"

"We had enough of that little prick. He's on his way to the hall as we speak. We're refiling charges on him."

"Is the ACLU letting you do that?"

"Fuck the ACLU. It's done. The kid's got a rap sheet longer than my dick and I've had it with him. If the ACLU wants to push it, I'll pick up the phone and call the *L.A. Times.*"

"Good for you. At least someone here has the balls God gave him. Thanks, Mike. You saved me time and paperwork."

That left Romeo Johnson. Tony made another call. This one was to Union Representative, Frank Plotkin. Tony was two for two. Plotkin was in his office.

"Tell me something good, Tony."

"Romeo is at it again. A teacher complained that she smelled alcohol on his breath. I know that a smell is not conclusive. He'll claim mouthwash. Can I get you to talk with him?"

"I'll call him and get back to you. How far do you want to go?"

"I want him sober and productive at work. One more incident, and I'll start the process to get rid of him. That would mean first putting him on a PIP, a Performance Improvement Plan. I'd rather not go through that bullshit, but if he won't start doing his job, I have no choice."

"Sounds fair, Tony. I've got his cell. Let me holler at him then I'll call you back."

He didn't get a call back from Plotkin. Carina didn't call. HPPD did. They wanted Tony to work a detail after work. He accepted. He always accepted.

Tony left work at 1530 hours. Corrections owed him some time. He was determined to beat the afternoon traffic, and he did.

You'll Do What and for How Much?

At 17:45 hours, Tony was in uniform and in briefing. He sat down next to Yolis who wasn't in uniform. She looked like, and was dressed like a twenty-dollar hooker. Her makeup looked like it was rolled on by a street sweeper. Her mascara was running. Her hair looked like a steam shovel rolled over it. The jeans she was wearing were tighter than a Brooklyn parking space at dinner time. Her nails were longer than a five iron. "What the fuck are you supposed to be?"

Yolis turned to Tony, lifted her eyebrows, smiled, and put her hand on his upper thigh. "Get in my car and I'll show you. But you've got to be generous."

The briefing sergeant walked in. He went directly to the podium. The voices got quiet, real quiet. "Okay, team, let's settle down. We have some extra bodies on tonight. You're probably wondering why?"

A uniform in the back of the room shouted, "Because Ochoa wants to chase skirts instead of perps."

There was instant laughter. It was true. Ochoa had been a copper at HP since the city incorporated. He lived on Viagra. He knew every woman who ever lived in HP. He loved women, and they loved him. He often, after work, spent the night in HP. His wife knew. She either accepted it or didn't give a shit.

"That's funny, Lefkowitz. If you could get it up, you'd probably get a little once in a while. By the way, those callouses on your right hand are from lifting weights, right?"

"No, Sarge, it's from writing reports."

"You wish." The Sergeant slammed his open palm on the podium to get their undivided attention. "Enough. Let's get serious for a minute and a half. We're doing HP pussy parade tonight. We're going to round up the johns."

“What’s Ochoa gonna do for dinner tonight?” somebody else shouted.

“Shut the fuck up and get serious, asshole.” The Sergeant forced his smile to disappear. “Yolis, front and center.”

She drew cat calls and wolf whistles. “Yolis here is our happy hooker. She’ll be wearing a wire.”

“Will she be wearing panties?”

“The pink ones I stole from your locker, dick face.”

The Sergeant spoke. “When briefing breaks, moron,”—his name was actually Morrone—”you and Toast—his name was actually Tostada—stay back. You’re going to be working the detail. Mickey, you and the Italian stallion stay behind. You two are also working the pussy patrol.

“The rest of you, here’s an outline of tonight’s double feature. We’ve got two adjoining rooms at Inn of Happiness on Florence east of Miles. If anyone takes Yolis’ bait, she’ll escort them to room 6. The room is wired for sound and hot with video. We’ll be next door. At Yolis’ signal, we’ll enter through the unlocked adjoining door and hook the john. We’ll escort him down the back stairs where transport will be waiting.

“Morrone and Tostada will be set up east of the motel on Florence. Mickey and the wop will be set up west of the hotel. We’re going to be on tac two for the duration of the operation. The rest of you gutless wonders, it’s SOP. We anticipate closing shop between 0100 and 0330, depending on business.

“Any questions?”

“Yeah, Yolis, how much for a hand job?”

“I think dick face has another pair of dirty panties in his locker. He’ll wrap them around your little clitty and make it hard for you for a five spot.”

“Show’s over. Everyone out and to work. And if you’re not careful out there tonight, you’ll get to wash Blinky’s sticky panties. Hit the streets!”

The pussy police started the operation at 2030 hours. Mickey and Tony were in uniform. They were in an unmarked silver Chevy HHR. Tony was behind the wheel.

Yolis was walking up and down Florence Avenue in front of the hotel. So far, it was quiet.

At 2148 hours, a figure, wearing black slacks, a blue-patterned button-down shirt, black baseball cap, boots, and a grey sport jacket, approached Yolis.

"Hi, pretty lady. How are you?"

Yolis looked the guy up and down and down and up. "What can I do for you?"

"That depends."

Yolis could smell the cologne and the odor of the last cigarette he had smoked. Again, Yolis asked, "What can I do for you?"

"What are you doing out here?"

Yolis was getting annoyed. "I don't have time to play with you. But if you want to play with me..."

The man smiled. "I would love for us to play with each other."

Tony turned to Mickey. "She's good. She's damn good."

"I like that. I think I might like that a lot," Yolis told the man.

The man asked, "How does that happen?"

Yolis looked up at the man, smiled, ran her tongue over her lips. "What did you have in mind?"

"What do you like?"

"I like a lot of things. How about you?"

"I want to taste you. I want to taste all of you."

"That can happen."

He took her hand. "How much will that cost me?"

"It depends on what you want. Tell mama what you want, and we'll work it out. I promise."

"I want to lick you all over. I want to run my tongue between your legs. I want to place you on your stomach and run my tongue from your toes to your ear lobes, stopping every place in between. Does that turn you on?"

The fact is it *was* turning Yolis on. "Seventy-five bucks gets the job done. Do you want to play with mama?"

"I so want to play with mama!" He reached into his pocket.

"No. No. Not here. Not in the middle of the street. You never know when those faggot HP cops might be lurking around. I have a room. Let's go inside. You can pay to lick me every whichway and in every hole when we get upstairs. Mama will take great care of you. Mama promises."

Tony was getting hard hearing Yolis converse with the john. Exactly why he didn't know, but if he and Yolis ever did get together, roleplay would absolutely be in order.

"The attorneys, the judges, and the jury will love listening to this. She is good."

The "clerk" behind the counter at the motel was one of HPPD's finest. Yolis' room was on the ground floor. The adjacent room, of course, was also on the ground floor and both rooms were close to the street so that the two units covering the escape didn't have a long run if the charade went into the tank.

The Sergeant broke in. "Wake up, guys. They're on their way into the room. As soon as the exchange is confirmed, Team A will take the ball and make entry. Sit tight unless there is a flag down, and I'll call that play. Otherwise, remain in your units."

The adjoining room to Yolis' play-for-pay room was now occupied by two people: Yolis and her date.

Only one of those two people was aware that there were eyes and ears in the room.

"What's it going to be?"

"I want to start by licking your tits. Then I want to make my way down to your pussy."

"Stop. You're getting me wet." She smiled. "Money first, honey. Then the entire field is yours to play on."

The not-so-tall john reached in his pocket. He had a thick wad of bills and counted out seventy-five dollars. Yolis stuffed the money in her bra. "Let's get the show on the bed."

That was the signal for the A Team to take down the john. Just as he reached for her blouse, the door adjoining door opened and three of HP's finest entered. The john was startled. Then the picture became clear. "Cunt, you're a cop."

Yolis' grin was wider than the Nile. "That I am. Too bad for you."

Officer Colemann grabbed him, cuffed him, Mirandized him, then started to pat him down. "Is there anything on your person that is going to stick me, injure me, or blow up in my hand?"

He shook his head.

"I'm going to search you for weapons." Colemann started patting down the john. He was searching for a wallet to get his ID by running his hands over the guy's shoulders, then his chest. He stopped suddenly. "Son of a bitch. Get me a female officer."

The team had arrested four johns by 0100 hours. The team was enjoying the show. It was better than *Saturday Night Live.*

Mickey was on his cell with Tammy. Tony was eyeballing Yolis who was walking up and down the street advertising herself. It was a solitary walk.

Tony thought she was hot, even in hooker clothes. She had a soft toughness about her if that made a damn bit of sense. She was sexy, she was intelligent, and she was the epitome of stand-your-ground. She didn't know the meaning of the word back-off.

Tony swatted Mickey on the arm. "Action."

Mickey said to Tammy, "We'll continue this discussion when I get home. Try to be home when I get there." Mickey broke the connection.

A guy about six foot and solid, dressed in a suit and no tie, approached Yolis. "Hey, babe, you're looking good."

He was too close. Yolis took two small steps backward. She mimicked him. "Hey, babe, you're looking good yourself." She stepped half a foot closer to the john. "What's on your mind?"

"You."

"I like the sound of that. Don't stop sweet-talking me, honey."

He looked at the cheap motel. "Is this where you hang your hat?"

"I don't wear a hat; at least not often. To use the past tense—this is where some guy's wearing hats are *hung*."

Tony couldn't believe how fast she was on her feet with the words. She sure as hell deserved a commendation.

"Let's get down to business. Can I do something for you?"

"That depends on how much you want to do something for me."

"And that depends on what you want me to do."

It was the old he-said, she-said. In order to get the solicitation charge to stick and in order to get the DA to file, the john must verbalize a sex act for money.

"I want half and half, maybe more, depending on how good you are. I want a spanking and I want to wear your panties home."

Without batting an eyelash, Yolis asked, "What makes you think I'm wearing panties?"

Tears were streaming down Mickey's eyes, he was laughing so hard. Tony couldn't believe her. She was beyond good. She was unreal.

Mickey looked at Tony. "Jealous?"

Tony was caught off guard. Did Mickey have any idea that Yolis and Tony had been to the range? Nothing had happened but...

"You deserve a spanking. You're a bad boy. You're a very bad boy. The spanking's extra and the panties are expensive. Do some math and give me a number."

The john reached for her hand. Yolis pulled back. "No tickee, no shirtee."

"Seventy-five."

"Double it."

"One fifty for half and half, the spanking and the panties."

"Done. Pay me in the room."

From the adjoining room, Larry Tucker, Autry Savage, and Tolentino Forrester eyed the video. It sure the hell wasn't business as usual. One of their own was in the room putting her life on the line. Whether you believe pay-for-play was a crime or not, Yolis was undercover in a dangerous assignment. Their eyes were glued to the action.

"Put the money on the table and the games can begin."

The john nodded. He walked to the nightstand. Before he took the bills out of his pants pocket, he started to unbutton his shirt. He placed the money on the nightstand. Then he turned to Yolis. "Wanna count it?"

"I trust you. But wasn't it Ronald Reagan who said, 'trust but verify'?"

"Smart girl."

Yolis walked slowly, deliberately, giving the john an eyeful of what he wasn't about to get. She counted the money. "How much did we agree on?"

"$150. Did I miss count?"

"Nope. You're right on."

He turned and walked within inches of Yolis. "Get on your knees, bitch. Unzip my pants."

Swiftly, suddenly, with a thud, the adjoining door swung open. "You get on your knees, asshole. Do it now."

He started to run. Tucker was the fastest of the three. He tackled the john without mercy. Then Forrester was on top of the suspect. The handcuffs were on the john in less time than it takes to switch on a light.

Forrester patted him down. "Roll over on your butt. Now stand up, asshole."

Yolis walked over to him. "For what it's worth, I am wearing panties."

The john sighed and looked down at the brown carpet. He began sobbing uncontrollably.

"It's not all that bad. Are you afraid your wife is going to find out?"

His sobs slowed. "I'm divorced."

"Warrant?"

"Clean. No rap sheet."

"What did you say?" Everyone in the room froze.

The john began sobbing again. "I'm...I'm...a cop."

If a robin shed a feather in that motel room, you would have heard it hit the floor. For a full thirty seconds, there was silence. Eerie, stunned, sick silence.

The honor of being senior officer in this operation went to Autry Savage. He would have taken a demotion rather than accept the task at hand. "Sit the fuck down." That command was followed by, "What's your name?"

"Paul. Paul Sanders." The sobs were softer.

"What department?"

"California City."

"Where the fuck is California City?"

"About two hours north of Los Angeles in Kern County. It's a very small city department."

"What brings you to HP?"

"A year ago, I made an application for HP. I...I remembered they had a lot of hookers running around. Look, it's not like I make a habit of this."

"Shut the fuck up. Where are your badge and your weapon?"

"In my car."

"Where's your car?"

"Around the corner."

"Forrester," Autry commanded. "Take Sanders to his car. Check his ID and bring his weapon up here. Match his ID to his registration. Do not, I repeat, do not run his registration or his ID."

"Copy that."

When Sanders and Forrester were out of the room, the remaining crew laughed nervously, except for Autry. "Mother fucker, nothing's funny here. The guy's a pervert."

Yolis was the first to speak in Sanders' defense. "C'mon, sir. This is the oldest profession on the books. If it were outdated, we wouldn't be here today. It's only a freakin' misdemeanor."

"And what am I supposed to do? Give him a box of rubbers and tell him to practice safe sex? If I let him go and this gets out, we're all in major trouble."

Tucker said, "Point well taken, Yolis. It's a misdemeanor and we have discretion in a misdemeanor."

"Yeah," Autry said dryly. "If the press finds out we let him walk, Trump's press will be a bunt single compared to the home run the press will score."

"I don't think anyone here will phone it in, sir." Yolis was smiling. "I won't, that's for damn certain."

Tucker turned to Yolis. "Can he wear your undies home?"

"Not a chance. When he comes back, ask him if he wants to wear yours."

"Enough," yelled Autry Savage. "Look, this isn't goddamn *Blue Bloods* and I'm sure the shit not Tom fucking Selleck. We've got a decision to make, and I suggest the sooner we make it the better for all.

I recommend we kick him free with a stern warning to stay the fuck in Kern County and pay any woman he wants for their Kern County panties; and that, if he comes back into L.A. County, more specifically HP, we'll sic Yolis on him again."

The vote was unanimous.

Dead Drunk

Trying to shift the life-and-death games of police work to the juvenile shit that went on in the Probation facility was a major accomplishment for Tony when he could execute that goal. The kids did get into trouble, but it was minor compared to the seriousness of the criminal activity that played out in the streets, sometimes a matter of life and death.

Such was not the case on this sunny, mild Wednesday afternoon. Tony's cell rang. He was hoping it was Yolis. It wasn't. It was Union Rep Frank Plotkin. "I've got good news and I've got bad news for you. Which do you want first?"

Tony laughed nervously. "Give me the good news."

"You don't have to worry about firing Romeo Johnson."

Tony nodded into the phone. "That is good news. Did he quit?"

"Cops found him last night in a motel on Sierra Highway in Lancaster. He was dead from an apparent overdose of drugs mixed with alcohol. They'll do an autopsy, and we'll know more in a couple of weeks."

"Jesus Christ. I can't believe that." Tony thought about Johnson's family. "Any word from his wife?"

"No. I'll send out a memo when we know about the services. In the meantime, you can send out an email to your staff stating that Romeo was found dead this morning and that we'll send out further details as soon as we get them, including specifics about the services."

Tony hung up. His head wouldn't stop telling him that he could have done more. He called his principal to relate Plotkin's call. "I'm going to take an early lunch. I need a break."

Carina was free for lunch. They met at Roxy's. Carina arrived first and managed to secure their favorite corner booth. Tony always sat with his back against the wall so he could observe everything—just like a cop.

Carina spoke first. “Pleasant surprise. Judging from the look on your face, you’re not here just because you wanted to see my beautiful face.”

“I always want to see the gorgeous you.”

“Will you voluntarily take a polygraph?”

Tony chuckled. “You know me, that’s for damn sure.”

“It’s fine, Tony.” The waitress arrived at the table. “We’ll have two coffees, please. We’ll be ready to order when you come back.”

“What’s going on?”

“I got a call from Downey about Romeo Johnson. The Sheriff found him dead in a sleazy motel on Sierra Highway.”

Carina didn’t say anything. She watched Tony’s face. She could read the pain. “Now you’re blaming yourself. You’re telling yourself you could have, should have, done more.”

Tony head bobbed up and down. “Something like that.”

“We have an expression. It’s *‘Don’t should on me.’* You can drive yourself absolutely crazy with I should have done this and I should have done that. The fact is you did what you did and Mr. Johnson did what he did. If he wanted to take his life, no matter what you did, it wouldn’t have been enough. The guy was determined to end it. He did. I’ve dealt with countless clients who have either seriously attempted to kill themselves or who had been successful at it. I had to come to terms with the fact that I did the best I could.

“You’re not a mind reader and neither am I. You’re not God and neither am I. Shit happens, my love, and it’s all part of life.”

The waitress brought their coffee. She took their order. When the waitress walked away, Carina continued. “You’re sure as hell not Jewish, so guilt isn’t your middle name. Why do you think you carry the weight of the world on your shoulders?”

Tony responded instantly and defensively. “I don’t carry the world on my shoulders.”

"You could have fooled me."

"I admit I feel like maybe I could have done more..."

"What else could you have done? You couldn't be with the guy 24/7. How'd he do it?"

"Apparently an overdose of booze and drugs. That's preliminary. They'll do an autopsy, of course."

"So, it could have been an accidental overdose?"

Tony nodded. "Could have been."

"Maybe you *are* part Jewish. No way could you have done any more than you did. You know, you have a habit, when we do see each other, of bringing your work home. If you think about it, the stuff that goes on at HP never impacts you like the stuff at JFK. Ever ask yourself why?"

"No." Carina had a valid question. "If I had to guess, I'd say because I know the element I'm working with at HP."

"You've got to learn to accept what you can't change. You can't change people places or things. You can change you, period! You are going to drive yourself to booze or into the funny farm if you don't quit. You're a great guy who is well intentioned. You're also a pain in the ass. Except for when we're in bed, you're like one of my clients."

She was just getting warmed up. Fortunately, the waitress interrupted Carina's dissertation. She brought their food.

He kept clear of any further discussion. He had to get back to work after lunch. Carina said she'd be at Tony's house when he got home. She was going to make dinner and she'd be dessert.

Tony finished up three transcripts and proofread a couple of reports. He also talked to Yolis when she called his cell.

"Just checking up on a fellow officer. How's it going?"

Tony chuckled. "It's going. And you?"

"Good. I'm on the job. I just took down a 417 subject. Traffic stop for running a light. The guy was on probation. I pulled him out, searched the vehicle—one more gun out of the hands of the bad guys."

"Great job. You're quite the cop. You're also quite the actress. I'm going to nominate you for an academy award. By the way, I have a question."

She cut him off. "The answer's yes. I was wearing panties, smart ass. But the first time we go out for real, I won't be wearing any. Does that get you going?"

It did and it was. "I have the right to remain silent."

"When are you working again?"

"Friday. Probably Saturday and Sunday, too. Do you miss me?"

"As a matter of fact, I do."

Tony heard her radio in the background.

"Gotta go. Shots-fired call. Feel free to call me any time; otherwise, I'll see you Friday."

"Be safe."

The last act Tony had to perform prior to leaving work was to make certain everything was in place for tomorrow's school-wide assembly. The assembly was scheduled to be in the gym at 1 o'clock, which meant that the kids would not go to class after lunch and Probation would bring the students directly to the gym from the dorm.

Putting almost all the kids in one place is always dangerous. In the classrooms, a serious attempt is made to keep gang affiliations apart. When the students are brought together for things like a fire drill or an assembly, all kids are within close proximity, making the situation potentially dangerous. Even with additional staff on hand, flare-ups do sometimes occur.

Tony contacted his Probation liaison to remind them of tomorrow's event. He had already touched base with the guest speaker, a former student remanded to JFK after being arrested for his third GTA, possession of drugs, possession for sale, and a weapons charge. The student had turned his life around. He was now a well-known television and screen actor and lately could be seen on commercials.

Tony met the Hispanic Hollywood personality through Carina. When he heard Rodrigo's story, he knew he had to get him to speak to the incarcerated kids. Rodrigo accepted with a smile.

The guy was about 5'9". He was in his early thirties, if that. Rodrigo had long, dark black hair pulled to a ponytail. He looked like he worked out four or five times a day and did not need a weapon to scare the piss out of the average human being. At the dinner table, he was soft spoken, even shy, polite, and friendly. Tony was looking forward to the assembly, as long as there wasn't a riot.

Home Sweet Home

LT greeted Tony at the door with a wagging tail that resembled Yasiel Puig's swing when he missed a change-up. He jumped up to Tony's chest. Tony patted him on the head and gave him a kiss. "Good boy, LT. Keep that up and you'll be promoted to Captain."

"What about me?" Carina walked to the hall from the kitchen. An apron was covering her tan skirt and brown blouse.

"You're already a Captain. If dessert is good, I may promote you to Assistant Chief."

As she kissed Tony, LT barked. He was jealous. "Why not full Chief?"

"You have to work your way up to Chief."

"And I would do that how?"

"First, you have to take your orals."

"And if I pass my...ugh...orals, what's next?"

"A thorough cavity search."

Carina nodded. "Let's go eat. But make sure you save enough room for dessert."

"Did LT eat?"

"Ask him."

"LT, did you eat?" LT looked at Tony and kept wagging his tail.

"Ruff, ruff. Good boy! I've got something for you." Tony kept chew toys and other assorted treats for LT in the laundry room. He fetched a set of thick rubber handcuffs and gave one handcuff to LT, as he held the other cuff. It was a short-lived tug-of-war game. LT won easily. He ran out the garage door and through the doggy door which led to the block-walled backyard.

Tony sat at the kitchen table. Carina brought the food. "Coffee or tea?"

"Iced tea would be great, Hon. Thanks."

She retrieved a pitcher of iced tea from the refrigerator and set it on the table with two glasses. Tony dug into the pot of stew.

"How was your day?"

"Not too bad for a change. Looking forward to the assembly tomorrow."

"You'll really like Rodrigo."

"I know I will. I hope the kids like him. They can sometimes be a tough audience."

"I think he'll do fine. This is great, Hon. Thanks."

"Glad you like it. Have you stopped beating yourself?"

"More or less." He hesitated, shoveled a spoon full of stew into his mouth, washed it down with iced tea, then said, "Sometimes I wish I hadn't screwed things up so I could have been a full-time cop."

"That would be more pressure."

"It's a different type of pressure."

"You've got the option. You told me HP offered you the opportunity."

"Twice. But there's a monetary consideration. I'd be screwing with my retirement."

"What's more important, money or piece of mind?"

Tony looked across the table. He looked into Carina's eyes. "You've got a valid point. One of these days I'll sit down and do some math. I'll see how badly I'd hurt financially if I retired from Corrections."

LT was on the couch in the upstairs living room. He was snoring. Carina and Tony were in the California custom king-size bed. Neither he nor Carina were snoring. Carina's head was on the pillow. She was on her back, eyes closed, sheet pulled up to her neck. Tony was under the sheet and between Carina's legs. "Dessert was never so good."

"Shut up and keep eating. I have plenty of dessert." Her eyes were rolled back in her head. "I think I've finally found a way to get your mind off your problems."

"I'm trying to lose some weight. How many calories are you?"

"I told you to shut up."

Tony laughed. The laugh was muffled. Tony pulled the sheet off Carina. He lifted her feet over his shoulders and buried himself in her shaved sweetness. His tongue was teasing her clit. He ran his middle finger between her ass cheeks and pushed gently.

"Damn, damn, damn, that's good. Don't stop. Don't..."

Tony didn't stop. He buried his tongue deep in her wetness. He loved that taste. His finger slid a bit deeper between her cheeks. His left hand teased her nipples. He wasn't certain who was enjoying it more.

Tony didn't stop until he felt Carina shudder. Then, for good measure, he lifted her legs until her feet were almost pointed toward the ceiling. Then he slid his finger in deeper. He felt her tighten then shake. He knew she was feeling good. That made Tony feel great.

They both relaxed for a few minutes. When she had regained her composure, she said, "My turn for dessert. Roll over, Columbo."

Tony did as he was told. "Do I have the right to remain silent?"

"I sure the hell hope not." Carina worked her way down Tony's chest, to his waist, then to his manhood. He was rock hard. "You could hurt someone with that."

"I'm sure you can do something about that."

Carina licked the extreme tip of his cock. She kissed it. She teased it with her fingers. She licked her way down to the shaft, then back to the head. She licked all around the head, slowly, tenderly.

"I'm loving this dessert. Very few calories too."

"Just make sure you save the best part for where it belongs."

"I promise. I wouldn't have it any other way."

She kept licking, kissing, and sucking. Two fingers squeezed at Tony's nipple. For some reason, a little nipple pain got him harder. She squeezed until she felt him grimace, then she squeezed harder. As if on cue, Tony grew stiffer.

"Roll over, otherwise the check is in the mail."

"I don't think so." She climbed on top of him. Tony dug his legs into the mattress forcing himself deep inside her. She rode him like a wave runner.

"Oh, that's so good."

"It is. It is." She grabbed both nipples and squeezed. Tony smiled. It hurt. It hurt big time. He liked the pain.

"Harder. Squeeze harder."

Carina followed orders well. "Like that?"

"Oh, yes, yes."

"Are you going to come for me?"

"Only if you come with me."

"I'm ready...again. Oh, yes, yes. My god, yes." Carina collapsed on top of Tony.

ACLUH8R or ACLULVR

The JFK School assembly was originally scheduled for the morning. At Probation's request, it was rescheduled for 1 o'clock, after lunch. Probation felt it would be easiest to move the kids from the dorm to the gym after lunch, and then for ninety minutes they'd sit in the gym. At the conclusion of the assembly, Probation would take the kids back to their respective dorms.

Tony, the principal, and a couple of POs stood near the gym doors observing the wards walking across the field in semi-orderly fashion. Cleveland Archer, the ACLU monitor, was in front of one of the classrooms observing, taking notes, and looking for something for which he could "paper" the school and/or Probation.

The kids used to march with their hands behind their back. This kept most of them from throwing gang signs. The ACLU put a stop to that. Then Probation told the wards to put their hands behind their back "diamond fashion." The ACLU stopped that, too. Finally, Probation had one class sit on the asphalt during class movements until the other class was safely in their next classroom; the ACLU stopped that, as well.

Tony had the last laugh, but few people knew it. Tony had gone to the DMV. He had ordered a personalized plate for the Vette. The plate, which the DMV gave Tony, read ACLUH8R, "ACLU Hater."

Tony had the plate a month or two. He received a letter from Sacramento. The letter stated they had received complaints about the plate and wanted the plates returned. The letter gave a telephone number to Tony that he could call if he wanted to discuss it. The letter also informed Tony he was entitled to a meeting with DMV if he wanted to appeal the recall of ACLUH8R.

Tony was surprised that DMV had issued the plate. He was even more surprised that Sacramento let it slip by. But now that he had the plates, he wasn't going down without a fight.

Tony had an attorney friend who did volunteer work for the ACLU and was also a university law professor. Tony's first call was to Troy Henderson.

"Troy, Esquire, how are you?"

"Tony. I couldn't miss that Brooklyn accent anywhere. How are you?"

Tony pictured Troy sitting at his old wooden desk, papers scattered from one end to the other, grading papers with a stern eye toward content and punctuation. "I know you didn't call just to see how I'm doing. What's up?"

"You're right, counselor. I ordered and received from Sacramento a pair of license plates that read Adam Charles Lincoln Union Henry 8 Robert."

There was no hesitation on the other end of the line. "Would you run that by me in layman's English, please?"

"ACLU Hater."

There was a soft chuckle followed by, "I hope you're joshing me."

"Seriously. I've had the plates six or seven weeks and just received a letter from Sacramento that they want the plates back."

"And..."

"I wanna keep them."

"Tony, you're no dummy. You know as well as I do that driving is a privilege. The State can regulate the plates. It's cute, maybe even funny to some. My guess is they're afraid that someone will put a bullet in you, and they'll get sued. I'm also guessing one of my brother's attorneys saw the plate and rounded up a bunch of his lawyer friends and sent DMV a missive."

"I've been pulled over four times by the Sheriff out here in the Antelope Valley since I've had those plates, each time to tell me how much they liked the plates.

One Sheriff pulled me over and there were three of us in my Vette. I knew I was going to get cited. He said he didn't care about that. He stopped me to tell me how much he loved the plate."

"Which tells you what about the mentality of some cops?"

"Seriously, Troy, what can I do?"

"Nothing, man. Send them back the plates."

"I don't go down without a fight. Let me ask you another question. If the plates read Adam Charles Lincoln Union Lincoln Victor Robert or ACLU Lover, do you think we'd be having this conversation?"

"Probably not. But that's what makes this country of ours so great."

The next day, after work, Tony visited the Lancaster Library. He asked a librarian for a book of acronyms. She obliged. Including driving time, it took Tony forty-five minutes to find what he wanted. *Always Causing Legal Unrest,* ACLU was a woman's lib group.

Tony was in business. He went home, called the phone number for Always Causing Legal Unrest and for $25.00 his "wife" was now a member.

Tony called Sacramento the next day. The gentleman on the other end of the line was cordial and friendly. Tony read him the essence of the letter.

"We show a couple of complaints against that license plate. We'd like them back."

Tony played dumb. "I don't understand."

"We've had several complaints. Some people find the plate offensive."

"What's offensive about Always Causing Legal Unrest?"

"Ugh…What?"

"I don't understand."

"Your plate is a slap in the face to the American Civil Liberties Union."

"What the heck is the American Civil Liberties Union? My 'wife' is a card-carrying member of a woman's lib group, Always Causing Legal Unrest. I got the plate to poke fun at my 'wife'. I'll fax you a copy of her ACLU card. Seriously."

Tony had him and Tony knew it.

"Is that true?"

Tony laughed into the phone. Then he pulled the same ploy he tried on Troy. "If the plate read ACLU Lover, would we be having this conversation?"

"Probably not, but let's go back. What does the plate really stand for?"

"The fact is, my 'wife' is a card-carrying member of a woman's lib group, Always Causing Legal Unrest. But I got the plate to piss off American Civil Liberties Union supporters."

"Are you always that honest?"

"I try."

"Our problem is that we're afraid someone is going to put a bullet in you, and we'll be responsible."

"I'll shoot back."

"For what it's worth, I agree with your politics, but I also have a job to do."

"I don't want to bust your horns. It's just too bad some people don't have a sense of humor. This world has enough problems without petty shit like this. And I'll bet you it was some damn liberal attorney who filed the complaint."

"I'll make you a deal. I'll send you back one plate. I'd like to keep the other for my game room."

There was a pause. Then, "I'll make you a better deal. You're being so honest, keep both plates and let's see what happens. Always Causing Legal Unrest sounds like a great group."

He took them off his car but kept the plates. One day he was going to own a police show car and that plate would go on the back of the cop car.

There Is a Way Out

When Tony quit thinking about his ACLU license plates, the kids were all seated on the bleachers in the gym. A probation officer was going over the assembly rules with the boys. Just as he finished, Rodrigo Flores walked to the lectern. Judging from the audience noise, he was immediately recognized.

"I asked that I not be introduced. I wanted to see if you watch enough TV to recognize me. Obviously, you do."

There was a spontaneous round of thunderous applause and not just from the Hispanic kids. Rodrigo was dressed in jeans, buttoned-down black shirt, black boots, and his jet-black ponytail held in placed with a red bandana.

"I'm here today," he began, "because many, many years ago, I was one of you. How many of you have been to or have heard of Camps Mays and Maris in Malibu?" He paused. A couple of dozen hands shot up. "I was at Mays. I got into fights. I got caught smoking, and we're not talking cigarettes. I even got caught stealing money from the principal's pocketbook. I was sent to Maris, next door to Mays, a tougher camp. It did no good. I got into more fights. I was released after serving eighteen months. I came out tougher, harder, and angrier.

"I was on the street less than a year. I got busted driving a stolen car, and I was armed. I was charged with GTA and possession of a firearm. I was sent to Youth Authority. I got into so many fights in YA, mostly defending my turf, that I did three years before they let me go. I was 25.

"By then I had a girlfriend and our baby. I had no way to support any of us, so it was back to my street ways. I managed to stay out of prison for nineteen months. I got busted burglarizing an electronics store. I was sentenced to fifteen years and eventually shipped to Cochran State Prison."

You could have heard a cat purr in the auditorium. All eyes were on Rodrigo. "Now is when this little chat of ours becomes *interactive.* Can anyone tell me what interactive means?"

There were no takers. "Funny, we have the balls to fight, to steal, to shoot up, to shoot, to maim, to kill. We don't have the nuts to raise our hand to answer a question. That's not a putdown—not at all. I was the same exact way. I wouldn't volunteer for shit. But put a gun in my hand, and I was your guy.

"Interactive means you get involved. Somebody, raise their paw and tell me what you think about, late at night, when you put your head on that pillow in the dorm and try to sleep."

No one raised his hand. "Okay, the POs have a bunch of ten-dollar McDonald's gift certificates that I brought along. Raise your hand and share what you think about at night, share honestly, and the gift certificate is yours."

An Hispanic youngster in the middle of the third row raised his hand. "What's your first name?"

"Eduardo." He looked like any other teenager. He was dark-skinned, dressed in jeans, t-shirt, and tennis shoes. His hair was cut short. He was smiling. "I think about all these idiots and wish they would stop yelling so I can fall asleep."

"Okay. What else? Seriously."

"I try to think about why I'm locked up. The last time I got busted, I swore it would be the last time. My mom couldn't stop crying when LAPD came to my house and handcuffed me. When she visits, which isn't that often because she lives in L.A., when it's time to leave, she always cries a lot. It makes me sad."

"What are you going to do about it?"

"I'm not going to do the same things that got me in here the last time."

"How are you *not* going to do the same things that got you busted last time?"

The young man grew serious. He was silent. He shook his head. He was thinking. "I guess I'll quit banging. I'll go to school and won't run the streets."

"Someone said the definition of insanity is doing the same thing over and over again and expecting different results. You have to change.

"You get a McDonald's certificate. Thanks for sharing. Now, I want you all to listen up. I have a question. Three frogs are sitting on a log in the low end of the water. Two of the three frogs make a decision to jump into the water. How many are left?

"Because the acoustics in here are bad, I'm going to repeat that. Three frogs are sitting on a log. Two of the three make a decision to jump in the water. How many frogs are left on that log? The answer is worth a McDonald's certificate.

"In the back. The African American kid who's standing up and looks like he's about to dunk a basketball."

"One, man. That's easy."

"Anyone else?"

Two dozen more kids raised their hand. One yelled, "Same as what he said."

"Give those two young men a certificate, even though they're wrong.

"The answer is three frogs are left on the log. How come?"

No one dared answer. "Because making a decision and actually doing it are two different things. You can lie in your bed all night long with your head on your pillow, swearing you're not going to get arrested again, and you really, really mean it. Then you go back on the street and, before you know it, you're in handcuffs and you're on the bus and you're back to Disney World again.

"It's like the alcoholic who swears he'll never drink again then lands in jail for something he doesn't remember doing because he was drunk. He gets out of lockup and, before he gets home, he gets smashed again.

"You have some hard choices to make. And you have to start making them while you're in here."

A probation officer brought Rodrigo a bottled water. He took a long drink. "Let me tell you what happened to me while I was in the joint.

"A cell mate, who was locked up for attempted murder of a police officer and was doing 25 years to life, started attending AA meetings in prison. After a year of Alcoholics Anonymous meetings, his thinking began to change, and you could hear it and see it in the way he walked and the way he talked. He was more at ease. He didn't want to fight all the time. He began to help other inmates. He helped me without even talking to me. I saw the change in him.

"I want to show you something." Rodrigo opened his shirt then lifted up his white t-shirt. See this?" He pointed to a scar in his upper right chest. "The result of knife fight in a cheap bar. And this." He pointed to another scar. "Another knife fight. Another sleazy bar. And this." There were two round scars just above his left waist. "Compliments of LAPD after I resisted arrest and tried to wrestle a baton away from one of the cops. If you don't recognize them, they're two bullet holes.

"Now catch this. Two years ago, I helped LAPD deliver gifts to needy kids in south L.A.

"So why the change? I started thinking about how comfortable my cellmate seemed to be. And I thought, why the hell am I fighting everything and everybody? It can only end in disaster for me. Actually, it already had. Hell, I was in freakin' prison.

"Then I thought about the streets, the gangs, the cops, my parents, the baby, the lady in my life, and how I was letting them down. But who was I letting down most?"

"Yourself," one of the kids shouted.

Rodrigo turned to a PO, "Give him a McDonald's certificate. Yeah, I was screwing over myself more than anyone."

Another student asked, "Did you go to AA?"

"No. I don't have a problem with alcohol. I can take it or leave it. Like you, my problem was an inside job. It was in my head. My head was turned to K-SHIT."

There was loud laughter. "What did you do?" the same student asked.

"I learned to change the channel."

"How did you do that?"

"Give him a McDonald's. It wasn't easy. It was probably the toughest thing I've ever done. No, not probably. It was the toughest thing I've ever done. I had to give up the streets, the gangbanging, the illegal activity, the hatred for the cops, the self-destructive behavior, pushing people away from me because I was afraid that they'd reject me. I had to get an honest job.

"Now most of this didn't matter because I was locked up, right? Wrong. It did matter. I had to set a plan while I was locked up. I did. I was determined to change my life for the better when I got out. One problem was that I lived in the freakin' ghetto in Pacoima. We couldn't afford to move. But you see, my cellmate also taught me that we have a choice. Just because we couldn't afford to move didn't mean I had to continue running the streets."

Rodrigo pointed to a youngster in the front row. "Get your ass up here." Rodrigo smiled. So did the Hispanic student.

"You look like a sharp guy. Are you?"

"That depends on what you're going to ask me."

Rodrigo smiled wider. He nodded. "I picked the right student." He took a pen out of his pocket. He lifted it high above the podium so most of the audience could see it. He dropped it on the top of the podium. He asked his student, "What happened?"

"It fell. Easy."

"Watch again."

"It fell."

"You're wrong twice. But give him a certificate anyway. Thanks for your help. You can sit down."

Rodrigo waited a few seconds. "Last time." He held up the pen. He allowed the audience time to focus on it. He let go. The pen hit the podium. Rodrigo pointed to a PO. Rodrigo laughed. "For a certificate, what happened to the pen?"

"It fell and hit the podium," the PO said.

"Nope." Rodrigo picked up the pen. "I'm picking it up." He held it high, then let go. "I'm dropping it. The pen cannot pick itself up. It cannot drop by itself. I picked it up. I dropped it. The cops didn't arrest me; I got arrested for engaging in illegal activity.

"If I am going to change me, the first step is accepting responsibility for my activity. If I follow the rules, I'll get into a helluva lot less trouble and I'll sleep better at night. I fucked up the first part of my life. While I was locked up, and with the help of my roommate, I learned to accept that. I decided I was going to accept responsibility for what happened to that pen. I was also going to accept responsibility for everything I did. In other words, I was now going to be responsible for Rodrigo. Think about that. That's a major step. I set some goals while I was incarcerated.

"And by the way." Rodrigo exaggerated a smile. "See these choppers? Pretty, aren't they? I own 'em all. The dentist popped them in. By the time I made it to prison for the last time, I had all my teeth knocked out in fights. The taxpayers paid for these. Thanks, taxpayer! Today, I'm the taxpayer. If you're locked up, and you are, I'm footing part of the bill. So are your loved ones.

"Let's get back to business.

"Like the frogs on the log, I made a decision to change my life. Making a decision, isn't changing anything. Again, like the frogs, I only made the decision, I didn't jump into the water. Hell, I was still locked up.

"Then a strange thing happened. Some of the prison staff noticed that I was trying to change. Then they saw that I was changing. Finally, they observed I had changed. This didn't happen overnight. It happened over a few years.

Then, even a stranger thing happened. I noticed I had changed. I started to feel better about myself. I hadn't gotten into a fight in that lockup in over two years. That was a major freakin' miracle. Even my girlfriend noticed the positive change in me.

"One day, like I'm doing today, a guy who had been locked up in the prison I was doing time in, came to talk with us. The man had served an eight-year sentence for robbery and for pistol-whipping a store owner. It wasn't his first rodeo. It was his last.

The guy had served his time, got out and started doing extra work for the movies. It was usually cash, and it was easy work and he made a few honest bucks. So, he did it for two years. A producer noticed him one day and asked him if he'd be interested in reading for a small part. He said yes.

"If you've ever watched *True Blue,* the cop series, that man was Clay Masters, the show's star. After he spoke to us, several of us approached him. He handed us business cards and told us if we wanted help when we got out, to call him. He added, that from time to time, he comes to the prison to speak; then, after he does his thing, people approach him. He gives them his business card. He encourages them to call him when they get out. They all say they will. He swears no one ever called him.

"I might have been the first to call him when I got out. Don't ask me why. Maybe I felt desperate. Maybe I believed I had nothing to lose. Maybe a combination of both. But for the first time in a very long time, I was able to admit to myself that I needed help, that I couldn't do it alone. So, I called Mr. Masters. I left a message knowing he wouldn't remember me, let alone return my call.

"The next day he called me. After I got over my initial shock, he invited me to meet him for lunch. I did.

We talked. He asked me if I wanted to do extra work. I had nothing to lose. I didn't find excuses for not doing it. I said yes. For fourteen months, I did a little extra work here and there. One day I was offered a small speaking part. Two lines. I jumped at it. A little while later, I earned my SGA, my Screen Actors Guild card. Then Mr. Masters asked me to audition for a major role. I was scared shitless, but I said yes.

I had learned that I only have to do the footwork, the results are out of my hands. So, I did the footwork. The rest is history.

"Today, I have a steady income. I have a beautiful family. I have a great house. My kids are proud of me. My wife doesn't make me sleep on the couch unless I really piss her off. Best of all, I sleep very well at night. Nobody's looking for me and I'm not looking for anyone.

"Today I live life one day at a time. If things don't go my way, I laugh them off. Tomorrow is another day. The only time I go to prison is when I go to speak to men like you. When I'm done, I get to go home.

You don't! Let me repeat that loud and clear: YOU DON'T!

"But, remember the pen. You're responsible for your actions. You can change them anytime you want to change them. You can change that negative channel, but it has to start with you.

"Remember the three frogs. Making a decision is not *doing. Doing* is an action. You have to take that action. Wishing is for chicken-shit people. Action is for men with balls. Decide which is you and enjoy the ride. But if you end up back in places like these, don't blame anyone but yourself!

"Give me a minute to catch my breath and drink a water. Then, by row, if you want to talk, come over to the side and we can chat. I'll give you a business card and let's see how many of you are full of shit and how many of you really want to change.

"Thanks for giving me the opportunity to remember where I came from."

There was thunderous applause. Then there was a standing ovation. Tony never saw such an outpouring of gratitude for a speaker. Tony was digesting several of the edicts set down by Rodrigo.

Friday Night at HP

Tony was out on his own at HP Friday night. Mickey decided to take the night off. He didn't sound too good when he called Tony to tell him he wasn't going to drive to HP with him. Tony worried about Mickey. He worried about his financial situation. He worried about his marriage. He worried about Mickey's constant worrying. On the other hand, Mickey was a big boy. He could take care of himself; or could he?

Right out of the shoot, Tony pulled over a vehicle that had stopped in front of him for a red light. The Oldsmobile had expired license-plate tags, in violation of 4000(A) CVC. Tony asked dispatch to run the plate. It came back expired, giving Tony PC to make the stop.

Tony made the stop east of Miles Avenue on the south side of Florence Avenue. It was a well-lit area; there was heavy foot traffic. Tony was at ease.

Tony walked up to the dark-colored, older Oldsmobile, slowly. He observed one person, the driver, in the vehicle. "Good evening, sir. I'm Officer Farrina with HPPD. I stopped you because your tags are expired. Can I see your license, registration, and proof of insurance, please?"

The man behind the wheel was calm. He was dressed in jeans, a checkered buttoned-down shirt, and loafers. He had a goatee, dark wavy hair, and several tattoos on his neck. "I don't have my license with me. The registration and the insurance are in the glove compartment." He handed Tony a California Identification card. His name was Juan Soto.

"Do you have a driver's license, sir?"

"I'm about to get it."

Tony studied the ID card. The guy was 44 years old, 6'1", and solid at 195 pounds. Tony backed up toward the passenger door of the police unit. He stood behind it. Tony contacted dispatch and requested a license check and a warrant check. Soto came back suspended license. He had no warrants.

"24, you can show me Code 4." Tony walked back to the Oldsmobile. "Sir, I need you to step out of the car. Please keep your hands where I can see them at all times."

Mr. Soto nodded. He kept his hands in plain view as he stepped from the vehicle.

"Please step up on the curb and face away from me." Soto did exactly as he was told. "Place your hands behind your head and interlace your fingers. Spread your legs. I'm going to pat you down for officer safety. Is there anything on your person that might stick me or hurt me?"

Soto shook his head. "No. Just a knife in my back pocket."

Tony grabbed the back of Soto's hands, keeping his fingers interlaced. Tony put his left leg behind the back of Soto's knee. He pulled on his hands. If the guy got "creative," all Tony had to do was pull back, push on the back of Soto's knee with his knee, and Soto would go hard to the pavement.

Tony took the fold-up knife from Soto's back pocket. He put it in his uniform pants pocket. "Anything else I should know about?"

"No."

Tony patted him down. He seemed to be clean. "Mr. Soto, you are not under arrest at this point." Tony felt Soto relax. When he started to relax, Tony reached behind his back. He smoothly grabbed one set of handcuffs and quickly handcuffed Soto's wrists. "You are, at this time, not under arrest," Tony repeated. "This is for officer safety. Have a seat on the curb."

Dispatch called. "24, an update on your 1038. Your subject has no wants, no warrants. He does have priors for two DUIs for attempted 187 and for 20001."

The man had history. Hit and run with injury, attempted murder, driving under the influence. Jack Webb would have called him a real bad actor. "Copy that, dispatch. Thanks."

Within two minutes, another unit pulled up behind Tony. Sergeant Tejeda put himself out with dispatch as Tony's back.

Tony nodded to the Sergeant. "Appreciate it, sir. I want to toss the vehicle. Watch this bad boy for me, sir, please."

"Not a problem. Take your time. I'm betting there's at least dope in the car."

Soto heard the exchange. "I don't do drugs. I drink. I used to drink. I'm sober sixty-three days."

"Am I going to find anything in the car that doesn't belong in the car?"

Soto looked down at the ground. He didn't answer. He kept staring at the pavement. Finally, he spoke. "I have my father's gun under the seat."

Tony didn't hesitate. "Anything else?"

"Ammunition. That's also under the seat."

"Anything else?"

He shook his head. "The gun's not mine."

It didn't matter. He was a convicted felon in possession of a weapon. Another felony. "Is the gun loaded?"

"Locked and loaded."

"If it's your father's, why isn't it locked in the trunk, empty?"

Soto shrugged. Tony walked to the driver's side of the car. He put his head against the carpet. Under the seat was what looked like a .22. Tony carefully slid it out. It was a Phoenix Arms .22. Tony walked it back to his unit, popped the trunk, and cleared the weapon. He locked the weapon in the trunk then went back to Soto's vehicle.

When the search was completed, Tony had the gun, a box of .22 rounds, and a dozen loose rounds in a red-and-orange ski cap turned inside out. On the back seat was a baseball bat. On the floor of the driver's side of the vehicle was a roll of half-spent black masking tape.

Tony walked back to Soto. He asked, "Why the baseball bat?"

Soto didn't hesitate. "I play baseball for HP High."

"Very cute." Tony and the Sergeant grinned. "You're under arrest. We'll talk charges later. I'm going to read you your rights."

"Been there, done that."

"Before you come up to the plate, I'm going to read you your rights anyway. You have the right to remain silent. If you give up that right, anything you say can and will be used against you in a court of law. You have the right to an attorney before questioning. If you can't afford an attorney, one will be appointed for you free of charge. Do you understand those rights as I read them to you?"

"I understand."

"Stand up for me." Tony did a thorough search. He took Soto's wallet out of his pocket. He looked for anything illegal. He found a social security card—an older card. The pillars on the card should be raised. Tony ran his thumb over each pillar. They were flat. Tony suspected the card was a fake, but he wasn't well versed in fraudulent documents.

"Sarge, can I see you a moment? Sit down, Soto."

They walked several yards from the suspect. Tony showed Tejeda the card. "I know less about fraudulent docs than you," he said. "When you get back to the Station, run it by Silverstrein. That Jew knows more about phony documents than the Pope knows about Catholics."

Tony walked back to where Soto was seated on the curb. "Where did you buy the phony card?"

Unlike what you often see on television, once a subject is Mirandized, you need not ask him if he wants to talk with you or if he wants as lawyer. All you need to do is read him his rights. Once he says he understand his rights as they were read to him, he's good to go. If he talks to you, it's implied that he understood his rights and he's speaking to you because he wants to.

"Pacific Boulevard. We all get them there."

"Who did you buy it from?" Tony asked.

"Strike one."

"You should have been a comic. Bad comics don't go to jail. The card's a phony?"

"As phony as a jailhouse lawyer."

At least the guy had a sense of humor. Tony looked at Sergeant Tejada. He wasn't about to ask the sergeant to transport his prisoner. "I'm going to call for a unit to transport. I've still gotta do the 180 and toss the car one final time, then wait for HP Tow."

"I'll transport and book him for you. We're busy. I don't want to tie up another unit."

"Thanks, sir. I appreciate it."

"Not a problem, Farrina. For what we pay you, that's the least I can do." He helped Soto up, then escorted him to the backseat of his unit. "Nice work, Tony."

Tony wrote the CHP 180 form. He called dispatch to call HP Tow to pick up the car. He put a thirty-day hold on the vehicle. Forty-five minutes later Tony was back at HPPD booking evidence. It was too busy to write the report, so that would have to be put off until the streets of HP quieted; probably early morning.

"Show me 10-8," Tony said into the mic as he drove west on Florence from Miles. He stopped for a light. He punched Carina's number into his cell. It rang four times before the machine answered. "Just checking in," Tony said. "If you get a chance, give me a shout."

Just as the light changed, a white Ford truck going eastbound Florence, passed Tony. "Son of a bitch." Tony said aloud, "He's gotta be doing seventy-five!"

Tony activated his overheads and hit the siren to clear traffic. People in California sometimes don't understand that when you see flashing red lights or hear a siren, you pull to the right and stop. Three cars impeded Tony's U-turn. "Mother fucker, move, goddammit!"

He tried to eyeball the truck which was continuing eastbound Florence. He finally completed the U. He could barely make out the taillights of the truck.

He grabbed the radio. "24. I'm eastbound Florence, crossing Santa Fe. I'm attempting to catch up to a truck also eastbound Florence probably crossing Miles. I have no further at this time."

Tony's lights flashed and his siren wailed. He could see the truck. He was gaining. As long as the truck continued eastbound Florence, Tony had a shot at catching him. If he made a southbound or a northbound turn, Tony was fucked. Even if he caught the guy after he turned off, there was no way to testify that this was the same truck after he lost sight of it.

Maybe I'll get lucky, and the guy will go straight, he thought. Tony wasn't lucky. The guy made a southbound turn. With the traffic in front of him, Tony wasn't even sure where the guy turned. "24, I lost him. He went southbound probably at Cross Avenue. I'm going to cruise the area."

Tony's area-search was fruitless. He observed one vehicle that seemed to match, parked in a nightclub parking lot. He pulled up alongside the white truck. Tony exited his police car. The truck cab was empty. Tony felt the hood, but it was cool. He got back in the unit. "24, show me 10-8. Unable to locate."

Tony cruised HP for another hour. He was just about to head for the barn to write his report when he observed a dark-colored Chevy run a red light. Tony was on it like flies on fresh food at an outdoor BBQ.

"24, I'm Florence, east of Santa Fe. Show me 1038 on 7 Lincoln Mary Henry 714. I'll advise on a back."

There was one occupant in the vehicle. She looked to be about 25, attractive, well dressed and on her cell phone.

"You need to hang up, please, and show me your license, registration, and proof of insurance."

"Is there a problem, Officer?"

The car looked like it just came off the showroom floor. It was spotless. It looked to be a 60's Impala. He repeated, "Hang up the phone, please, and show me your license, reg, and insurance."

Tony took a closer look. She was Caucasian, wearing blue slacks, white blouse, and a gold chain hanging outside the blouse. She was definitely attractive.

"Did I do something wrong?"

"You ran a red light. You were talking on your cell phone. Both are vehicle code violations."

"At this hour of the morning does anyone really give a shit?"

Just what Tony needed at this hour of the morning. "Yeah, I do," he said dryly. "License, registration, and proof of insurance, please."

She handed Tony her license. Her name was Ginger.

"The insurance and the registration are in the glove compartment," Ginger informed him.

"Get them for me, please." Tony eyed her carefully as she rummaged through the glove box.

Tony walked back to the unit with the necessary paperwork in hand. He ran her. She came back clean. She lived in the Antelope Valley, not far from Tony. "24, I'm code 4."

"Copy 24. You're code 4."

Tony walked back to the Chevy. "Nice car. What are you doing all the way down here?"

She looked at him and smiled. "If I told you, you wouldn't believe me."

"Try me."

"Are you going to give me a ticket?"

"Well, you ran a light and you're talking on your cell. Do you think you should get a ticket?"

"I'm working."

Tony did not like the sound of that. "Working? Working at what?"

Tony's face gave him away. "No, I'm not working at *that*. I'm a private investigator. I've been sitting on some asshole who is running around on his wife. We're trying to build a case so she can get him for big bucks. He's screwing every bimbo in southern California."

“Are you for real?”

“Like a stroke, Officer. My ID is under the seat. Can I get it?”

“VERY, very slowly. If you come out from under the seat with anything but your ID, I'm a damn good shot.” Tony slowly slid his Glock out of the holster. He hid the Glock behind his leg. He watched closely.

She came out from under the seat with a badge holder and held it out for him. Tony examined it. “You're a licensed investigator.”

“Good job, Sherlock. You would make your academy instructor proud.”

“Does comedy come with the ID?”

“Nope. I had to earn that separately.” She put the ID under the seat. Ginger scrawled her phone number on the back of the card. She handed it to Tony. It read, “Ginger Does It All, and Then Some.”

Tony put the card in his shirt pocket.

“Well, do I get a get-out-of-jail-free card?”

Tony reached into his pocket. It so happened that he carried several get-out-of-jail-free cards in his shirt pocket, just for fun. He handed one to Ginger. “Don't push your luck.”

“Let me push it a bit farther. I'm going to be here for another hour or so. Any chance I can buy you breakfast?”

Tony looked at Ginger then looked at his watch. I've got to go back to the Station to write a report. Let me see what time I get finished.”

“Thank you...”

“It's Tony.”

“Thank you, Tony.”

Tony pulled the Crown Vic into the Station lot. “Show me 1019, please. I'll be report writing.” Tony parked the unit, gathered what he needed to write the report, and headed for the Blue Room. Several officers were busy at the computers doing “paper.”

Tony gathered the evidence he had recovered from suspect Soto and from Soto's vehicle. He walked across the parking lot to the annex. Tony grabbed an evidence sheet from the draw. He carefully listed each piece of evidence on the sheet. Tony carefully booked the evidence individually realizing that if it went to trial, opening each piece of evidence individually would have more impact on the jury. After he booked the evidence, he gathered everything, walked into the adjoining room, and placed the evidence in the locker. He then went back to the room where he booked the evidence and entered the locker number that held the evidence in the logbook.

Tony walked back to the Blue Room. He located an available computer. He spread his notes on the tabletop, set up the computer, and thought for a moment. The one thing he disliked about police work was report writing. Tony sure the hell wasn't a report writer; never was, never would be. He did not even like filling out an application. Tony marveled at writers who could write hundreds of thousands of words creating a novel or a work of nonfiction. As the expression went, "it was beyond his pay grade"—well beyond his pay grade.

Tony opened an application. He filled in the blanks for the reporting number and for the arrest. Then he started to create the narrative.

DR # 08-04676

Hollow Point Police Department
Arrest Report
12021 (A) P.C. / 472 P.C.

Suspect: Soto, Juan

Address: 14141 Lacey Lane, Apt. 3A, Bellflower, Ca. 90706

Data: M/H/601/195/Blk/Brn/DOB:06/08/72

Vehicle: 2005 Chevy/Impala/CA-LP 4GHH491

R/O: Soto, Miguel

Same address as S/Juan Soto

On the above date and time, I was on patrol, assigned to traffic enforcement, in a marked black-and-white police unit in the vicinity of Florence Avenue and Stafford Street. I observed a black Chevy, California license 4GHH491, eastbound Florence Avenue east of

Pacific Boulevard. I observed the tags to have expired June 2016. I contacted dispatch to run the license plate. The records check confirmed the license plates had expired June 2016, in violation of 4000 (A) V.C., unregistered vehicle.

I effected a traffic stop on Florence Avenue east of Stafford Avenue. I contacted the driver, who identified himself as Juan Soto. I asked S/Soto for his driver's license. S/Soto stated, "I don't have my license with me." I asked S/Soto if he has a driver's license. S/Soto stated, "I am about to get it." S/Soto further stated he had a California identification card, which he handed to me.

I contacted dispatch and requested a California license check on S/Soto. The license check confirmed that S/Soto was 14601 (A) V.C., suspended license.

I asked S/Soto to step out of the vehicle and to step up on the curb, S/Soto was cooperative. I asked S/Soto to put his hands behind his head. I asked S/Soto if he had any weapons on his person. S/Soto stated he had a knife in his rear pants pocket. I took the knife, which was later booked into evidence under this DR, a "Boguszewski" three-inch locking fixed black blade knife, from S/Soto's pocket. I then informed S/Soto that he was not under arrest, but for officer safety, I was going to handcuff him. I handcuffed S/Soto and completed the pat-down search, finding no other weapons.

I asked S/Soto if he had any weapons in the Chevy. S/Soto stated he had a loaded handgun under the driver's seat.

I checked the area under the driver's seat. I found a red/orange watch cap. Inside the watch cap, I found a loaded .22, Phoenix Arms handgun, serial # 41511116. Also in the watch cap, I found sixteen .22 long rifle rounds and a box of Remington .22 High Velocity rim fire cartridges, containing fifteen rounds. I also located a loaded magazine under the driver's seat. The watch cap, the .22 rounds, the box of Remington cartridges, the gun, and the magazines were booked into evidence under this DR. Also located on the rear floor of the Chevy were a metal baseball bat and a partial roll of black masking tape.

I searched S/Soto's wallet. I found what I thought might be a counterfeit social security card.

I called dispatch for an officer to assist. Sgt. Tejeda, 7579, responded to assist.

I contacted dispatch and ran a warrants check on S/Soto. The record's check confirmed S/Soto had no warrants, but he had the following prior felony convictions: 273.5 P.C., spousal abuse; 4/4/2001, Case #SB34587; 23152 (A) felony drunk driving, 11/13/2001, Case #SB78780; 11590 HS-Registration as a controlled substance offender, 01/16/2003, Case #4003144.

I asked S/Soto why he had the gun under the vehicle's driver's seat. S/Soto stated he was taking the gun to Western Auto for his father. I contacted dispatch to run the serial numbers on the gun. A record's check confirmed the gun did belong to S/Soto's father.

My attempt to talk to S/Soto's father by phone was unsuccessful. S/Soto's father, Miguel Soto, telephone # 555-458-9334, spoke no English. No officer at the scene of the traffic stop spoke fluent Spanish.

Sergeant Tejada transported S/Soto to HPPD and booked S/Soto for 12021 (A) P.C., convicted felon in possession of a firearm.

I issued S/Soto HPPD Cite # 21314, for 14601, V.C., driving on a suspended license. I also issued S/Soto HPPD Cite #21314, for 4000 (A) V.C., unregistered vehicle. I impounded the vehicle S/Soto was driving per 22651 (H) V.C.

At HPPD jail, I contacted S/Soto and again advised S/Soto of his Miranda Rights. S/Soto stated he understood his rights and he agreed to talk with me. I asked him why he had the gun under the seat of the vehicle. S/Soto stated he was taking the gun to Western Auto for his father because his father said sometimes the gun doesn't fire.

At HPPD, I contacted Officer Silverstrein, 8790, an expert in forged documents. Officer Silverstrein confirmed the social security card taken from S/Soto's wallet in the field was counterfeit.

I again contacted S/Soto in the HPPD jail. I again explained to S/Soto his Miranda Rights. S/Soto stated he understood his rights and he agreed to talk with me. I then asked S/Soto to tell me about the social security card. S/Soto stated, "I know it's phony. I need it to work." I asked S/Soto where he had purchased the counterfeit social security card. S/Soto stated, "You know. On Pacific Boulevard. We all get them there." He could not or would not give me the name of the person or persons from whom he purchased he counterfeit social security card.

The counterfeit social security card was photocopied. The counterfeit card was booked into evidence under this DR.

An additional charge of 472 P.C. was added to S/Soto's charge of 12021 (A) P.C.

***

It was close to 0400 hours when Tony slid under the wheel of his Vette. He was tired but was feeling good. The felony arrest and taking the gun off the street made it a great night. He wanted to call Mickey to see what and how he was doing, but it was too early. He also wanted to call Carina, but it was also too early for that.

Tony headed north on Miles which eventually, with one left turn, would get him onto the northbound 5 freeway in the direction of the Antelope Valley. Without traffic and without accidents to slow him down, averaging a speed of seventy-five, he'd be in his driveway by 0515, give or take.

Tony thought about Rodrigo, his former student and guest speaker at JFK. He couldn't get the dropped pen out of his head. It was symbolic to Tony, very symbolic. Tony liked it. He was responsible for everything he did; no excuses. Couple that pen exercise with what Carina had related to him about the Serenity Prayer, and he had a new vision. Tony could accept most of what he couldn't change. He sure as hell had no problems changing or at least trying to change that which he thought needed changing. His problem was knowing the difference. He turned on KNX, all-news radio. He drove fifteen miles above the speed limit in the middle lane.

Tony realized he worked two jobs that could be very negative on a person mentally and emotionally. At the juvenile facility, he mostly saw the kids at their worst. On the street, no question, he saw mostly the dregs of society. Carina tried to tell him that in not so many words. She was right.

What Rodrigo had said made an impact on Tony. Rodrigo had stated, in slightly different words, what Carina had been trying to tell him for most of the time they had been dating. Tony didn't realize, until recently, that his working environment had been taking a toll on him.

Shortly after coming on the force, a well-liked HP officer, who had been involved in a justified shooting, put a Glock in his mouth and squeezed the trigger. Rumor had it that the officer's actions were a result of a marriage that was falling apart; undoubtedly that was, at least, partially the result of his job, his financial situation, and the shooting. In Tony's mind, the officer found a permanent solution to a temporary problem.

Tony wasn't in that category. He was, however, feeling the effects of his jobs. According to what he had heard from Carina and Rodrigo, he was capable of changing that, and *only he* was capable of changing that. Maybe Mickey would sit down with him during the week and they could talk it out.

Tony was drained. He was tired, but it was a good tired. Police work gave him a satisfaction that nothing else gave him, almost nothing else. His ex-wife got pissed off at him one day when he was getting ready for Mickey to pick him up and she shouted, "Only two things give you a hard on. Getting into that damn Pace Car and getting into that uniform. It's a damn shame that getting into me doesn't get you hard anymore.

She was right. She was nineteen years younger than Tony. She was stunning when they married. Five-foot-seven-and-a-half inches tall, long flowing blonde hair, a body as tight as a miser, and tits firmer than a fucking brick. Marriage and life were great for a couple of years. Then the roof fell in a shingle at a time.

She started to put on weight. She decided she didn't want to work anymore. She enrolled in college and was doing well. Between Tony's two jobs, they rarely saw each other except on occasions when Mickey and Tony would set something up for dinner.

They tried marriage counseling. The female counselor, much to Tony's surprise, put Marla's weight gain on Tony. In different words, she told Tony he was pushing Marla away by rarely being home. Tony's answer was she needs to develop interests of her own. The counselor countered with, "That's not what marriage is all about."

She continued, telling Tony marriage was a partnership between two people. The only partnership Tony knew was in a police unit. Mickey was his partner. His very life sometimes depended on Mickey's actions and vice versa. Until recently, Tony didn't realize what the hell the counselor was talking about.

The counselor, of course, was dead on. At the time, Tony either couldn't or wouldn't see it. Carina had talked with Tony about a balance in life. That was what the marriage counselor was trying to get Tony to see. He was blind.

It didn't much matter. Tony came home from work, from HP, early one morning after working a graveyard shift, as he normally did, and Marla was gone. She had hoped that would snap Tony to attention. It had the opposite effect. After seven years of marriage, he was enjoying his new freedom.

Marla wasn't. She wasn't ready to call an end to their marriage; she wanted Tony back. When he gently tried to tell Marla he wanted a divorce, she went for the jugular. She hired a hard-hitting attorney, who Tony ended up paying for, along with the other ninety-eight-thousand dollars in alimony, retirement, and TSA monies. If nothing else, Tony learned a new word from all the ugliness: prenup!

Tony turned the corner onto Almador Court. He half expected to see Carina's red Toyota in his driveway. It wasn't. Well, at least LT would be at the door wagging his tail waiting for him. He was.

There was a doggy door in the garage that led to the third-of-an-acre backyard. Tony left the door that led from the house to the garage propped open. LT had 24 hour access to the yard.

LT ran to Tony. He jumped up on him, LT's head coming to Tony's chin. Tony put his arms around him. "Good boy, LT. You're my buddy. Yes, you are. You must be starving. I'm hungry, too."

There was special diet food for LT. LT wasn't overweight, but Tony wanted nothing but the best for him. This morning, it would be a couple of hamburger patties for LT and two for Tony. Tony started a cup of coffee in the Keurig while he nuked the burger patties for himself and LT.

While Tony ate, he gave more thought to what was going on at his paid job. He had mixed feelings. Tony hadn't gotten into education because he wanted to; it was a forced choice. He was going to sit down with Mickey to discuss options. Mickey would be able to put out "feelers" to see if HP would pick him up full time. Tony thought they would. He was well liked and did his job and then some. His annual evals, less than good at first, had progressed over the years to where they were today, excellent.

LT finished his burgers, and dripped water all over the kitchen floor as he slurped it from his personalized bowl. Tony sipped coffee and chewed the patty. He smiled. Life was good.

Life's Little Problems

Mickey and Tony stopped at a Denny's off the 14 freeway to grab a bite and to talk. Tony planned to chat with Mickey about the remote possibility of "retiring" from Corrections and going full time at HP.

The conversation didn't start out that way.

Mickey was sucking raspberry iced tea through a straw. He stopped. "Partner, I don't have to tell you, I've been having my problems lately. A couple of weeks ago, Tammy and I almost decided to call it quits. Instead, we sat down and discussed what we each wanted to have happen.

"We don't want to split. We need to straighten out our financial situation, which will take some of the pressure and stress off. We need to start seeing one another more often. My crazy hours and all the overtime I'm working at HP don't help worth a shit. It's a catch-twenty-two. If I work overtime to make the mortgage, Tammy and I don't see much of each other, and she ends up playing pool at the bar with her friend. If I don't work the overtime, they'll foreclose on the house.

"We found an answer. I went online and searched cop jobs. I found one that fits our needs. I have a friend who's a Lieutenant in Clearwater, Florida. Bottom line, we're moving to Florida in two months. I'm going to get on with Clearwater and Tammy's going to train to do dispatch. Problem solved."

Tony put his coffee on the table. He wasn't expecting this. "That's one helluva major decision."

"Someone once told me that it's sometimes better to make a wrong decision than no decision at all. I talked with the Chief. If things don't work out in Florida, I'm welcome back. Hell, if things do work out in Florida, you may want to come on down."

Tony decided there wasn't enough time to start his discussion, besides, Mickey had addressed part of the problem without even knowing there was a problem. Actually, what Mickey said and what Rodrigo said and even what Carina had told him weren't all that different. The decision was his to make. Tony was the captain of his ship.

Fighting Fire with Gasoline

Briefing started promptly at 1800 hours. The briefing Sergeant was Amy Susan Sorentino. Her initials were A.S.S., and she had one tight, stunning, rounded ass, and she knew it. She had fun with it. She didn't flaunt it. She didn't (most of the time) tease you with it. She did show it off. Her uniform was cut tighter than it had to be. For that matter, so was her uniform shirt. Her breasts were as ample as was her ass. Tony would have given up his Vette Pace Car for a look at her bare ass. Well...maybe not the Pace Car.

It was humorous when Sergeant Amy, as she was called, or Sergeant ASS when she wasn't in earshot, was the briefing Sarge, everyone was on time. No one drifted into the meeting room. If someone checked, Tony would bet that absenteeism was lower on the days Amy was at bat.

She stood behind the podium, all five foot eight inches of her. Her voice was surprisingly low. Her jet-black hair was in a ponytail. Every time she turned sideways, Tony could see the panty lines through the tight uniform. He couldn't help but wonder if that helped her become Sergeant.

"Okay, team, let's get started. Day watch was quiet except for the usual stolen vehicles: we had five of them. On your way out, grab a hot-car list off the table. Bring home one of the babies during your tour and I'll buy you dinner."

She looked directly at Officer Banks who was the department flirt, a very married-with-kids department flirt. "I didn't say I'd take you to dinner on Bank of America. I said I'd pay for your dinner. Not that you'd find a pregnant horse in a barn stall, but the offer is open to all.

"We had a smash-and-attempted-grab at Miller's Jewelry Store on Pacific and Gage. The only thing the perp got was a huge gash on his right arm from breaking the window. Pack and Mortinson followed the blood trail where they arrested him after the doctor put sixteen stitches in his arm. He'll make the Hall of Shame."

Somebody yelled out, "Is he going to take the Sergeant's test?"

"No, but he said he'd help you study. The only arrest of consequence was the peeper. He was caught when the crate he was standing on to peer into a first-floor window gave way. He fell off the crate, slammed his head against a tree, and was knocked unconscious. The homeowner heard the commotion, called 911, and the gang unit, who happened to be code 5-ing the area, took him into custody.

"Does anyone have anything for the good of the Department?" Pause. "Okay, hit the street. Be careful and remember, we want you to go home in one piece in the morning. Be safe."

As the troops stood up, Sergeant added, "Oh, one last thing. Yolis, Mickey, Tony, front and center, please."

The threesome looked at each other. Each shrugged. "Let's go to my office."

Tony trailed the pack because he wanted to check out more of the Sergeant's ass. He enjoyed every step.

Her office, which was shared by all the briefing Sergeants, boasted a large, but older, mahogany desk, a cushioned black swivel chair, a scanner, a portable radio, and a computer. On the wall opposite the desk was a Sony 48-inch television.

"Have a seat." The chairs were bridge chairs, but Mickey didn't care. It beat standing. They sat.

"I need you three for a special assignment and I need you in soft clothes. There is probably nothing to this, but I want to be certain. Here's the deal.

"About a year ago we popped a couple of drug dealers in a major haul. We confiscated big bucks and three quarters of a million dollars in coke. We nailed two major players. Both made bail. One fled. God may know where he is, but we don't. Raul Lopez Valdez is due in court Monday. He's being watched closely and will be hard-pressed to make it out of Dodge.

"We have one major witness who is key to the prosecution's case. We thought, and think, we have her in a safe place. I want to be certain. We thought we were cute in keeping her local. I still think we are. But the bottom line is, if she isn't in court Monday morning, the scumbucket walks.

"We tried to make telephone contact, but there's no answer. We've left coded messages to no avail. Here's what I need you to do. I want Yolis and Tony to go the apartment. See if you hear anything inside. If not, we're going to stage a phony accident. You'll go to the door and claim you hit her car and want to exchange information. Not the best of plans but dumb enough to be believed.

"Once you're sure she's okay, your work is done. Mickey will sit in the car, just in case. You'll grab an unmarked unit."

"Our 'wit' is Hispanic. You and Yolis can play husband and wife."

Without a blink of an eye, Tony asked, "Does that include conjugal visits?"

Yolis' rapid response was, "If you play your cards right."

Mickey asked, "Wouldn't it be more realistic if we had an Hispanic husband, too?"

The Sergeant said, "Tony's Italian. That's a Mexican with a job. He'll work." She shifted positions in her chair. "Let's go back to business." She handed each of the three a folder. "In here is a very sketchy outline of the case. Basically, it's all you need to know for the night. Peruse it. When you're done, discuss how you're going to handle verifying that our witness is in the apartment and ready for Monday morning. When I return, we'll put all this together.

Yolis and Tony, or Mr. and Mrs. Farrina, for at least tonight, were in street clothes." Tony opened the passenger door of the unmarked blue Ford Fusion for Yolis. "Mrs. Farrina, are you in?"

"I might ask you the same question."

Tony slammed the door then walked around to the front of the Ford. He got in, started the car, then smiled as he looked at Yolis. "This might be the start of a beautiful relationship," he joked.

"It could be." Yolis wasn't smiling.

Mickey was behind the wheel of a faded 80s silver Olds Cutlass that looked like it had seen better days. He exited the parking lot ahead of Tony and Yolis.

Yolis turned toward Tony who was driving. "Alone at last." She smiled, invitingly.

Tony countered, "Work before pleasure."

"There will come a time..."

"Who's to say? What will be, will be." Tony slowed for a stop sign, looked both ways and proceeded without stopping.

"You just blew a stop sign. Bad cop."

"I slowed."

"You didn't stop."

"I slowed."

"You didn't stop."

"No difference."

"Some time ago, one of our more brazen officers, who had the temperament of a starving junkyard dog, stopped a guy for rolling a stop. The guy argued with the officer that he slowed, looked all ways, and continued. Beefy boy in blue wasn't buying that and exercised his right to display absolutely no community spirit. They kept arguing back and forth, voices accelerating until you could hear both of them in South Gate. The guy insisted he slowed and that was fine. The cop wasn't having it.

"Finally, pissed off to the hilt, the cop dragged the driver out of his shiny Caddy, threw him to the ground, took out his straight stick, and started pounding the poor bastard. Finally, shit-for-brains lifted the stick over his head and stopped. He looked down at the poor bastard, who was every whichway trying to cover himself from the beating.

"Our officer, desperate to complete his teaching lesson for the day, asked his traffic stop with night stick above his shoulder ready to again strike, 'Would you like me to stop or slow down?'"

Tony looked at Yolis. He didn't say one word for several seconds. "Very cute." Tony made a right turn. He drove two blocks and made another right turn. He drove on and made another right. Yolis sat in silence.

Tony slowly approached the same stop sign. He stopped. He said, "left, right, left. Three seconds. Complete stop." Tony smiled. So did Yolis.

"You're crazy."

"Are your panties wet now?"

Yolis reached over the center hump. With her left hand, she grabbed Tony's crotch. She squeezed lovingly. "Are yours?"

Mickey called Yolis and Tony on his cell. He was in place, parked north of the four-story apartment building on the west side of the street. Tony parked on the south end of the street about five feet from a fire hydrant.

They started the charade as they walked along the sidewalk to the apartment building. Tony said, "Can't you leave anything or anybody alone? You've got to start shit wherever you go."

Yolis said something in Spanish. Tony had two years of Spanish in high school. He earned two C's. He didn't understand a word Yolis said.

They kept walking. Tony raised his voice. "You can be a pure pain in the ass sometimes! I don't know what the hell your problem is, and I don't give a shit!"

They climbed a couple of steps to the complex door. Someone was coming out, so they didn't have to buzz their way in.

They continued their argument. Yolis kept shouting in Spanish. Tony kept yelling back. The apartment they wanted was 2B, on the second floor. They walked up the stairs. Tony didn't like elevators any more than he liked airplanes. Elevators made him claustrophobic. Airplanes bothered him because if they broke down, there was no place to go but down.

Tony also had a fear of heights. As a kid back east, heights never bothered him. He had no recollection of falling from a tree or any other high place.

Yolis interrupted his thoughts as they reached the second-floor landing. This time she yelled at him in English. "Who was that whore I saw you with?"

"Your mother," Tony spat back. "Do you have any other questions?"

An apartment door opened. A woman looked out then slammed the door. A second door opened. A man, clad in a black muscle shirt with a Corona in his hand, stepped into the hall. "Take it outside."

Tony looked at him. "I'll give you this broad for a week for one of those Coronas."

Without blinking, Yolis stepped within inches of Tony. She backhanded him across the face. "You can shove that clitty you call a cock into the neck of that Corona. It'll fit with room to spare."

"If your snatch were that tight, I wouldn't need your mother."

Mr. Corona went back into his apartment. He slammed the door so hard, the floor seemed to shake.

Suddenly the door to 2B swung open. Tony eyed a small Hispanic man, maybe 25, wearing blue jeans, tennis shoes, and a dark blue muscle shirt. He stood between the door and the hallway, which meant the inside chain had to be off.

He didn't see any sign of their target. Worse than that, Tony didn't know if she was in the apartment. He had a split-second to make a decision. He could articulate in court a half-assed argument for forcing his way inside. Depending on the judge, he might be successful.

Yolis continued to act like the damaged girlfriend. In plain English, she yelled, "Asshole!"

As if this was the cue, Tony shouldered the door and the young Hispanic with enough force to send him reeling back into the apartment. He fell to the floor with a thud. Yolis was on him like a Republican on an illegal alien. She cuffed him. When he attempted to get up, she kicked him. "Did Simon say you could move?"

Yolis searched him. She grabbed his crotch. "No weapons there, you pussy."

"Where's Sabrina Morales?"

He smiled then he spat on the floor. Yolis kicked him harder. "Answer the man, you cockroach, or the next time I smash your fingers."

He spat again. Yolis stepped on his right hand. She leaned forward. Tony watched the guy's face. Pain turned to agony as Yolis kept increasing the pressure on his hand and fingers. Tony could only hope they had the right guy.

Yolis heard a noise in the closet. She looked at Tony. "Stay with him," he told her.

Tony quickly walked to the closet. Glock at the ready, Tony slowly opened the door. A woman, with what looked like a red bandana tied around her mouth and a belt tied around her arms, sat on the closet floor.

Tony holstered his weapon. He untied the bandana then undid the belt. "You are..."

She didn't know who Tony was, but she sensed he was a good guy. "Sabrina Morales. They have my daughter."

Tony helped her to her feet. She clung to his arm. Tony guessed she might have been 40 years old, maybe a bit younger. She was dark skinned with black hair and brown eyes. She was dressed in slacks and a white blouse. She looked tired and a bit worn, but she was still pretty.

"Where is your daughter?"

They took her. Late yesterday, he and another man forced their way in here. They grabbed Tanya. They said if I testified Monday, I'd never see Tanya again. They said they'd see to it that she was in constant pain and that those who caused the pain would enjoy themselves." Tears streamed down Sabrina's face.

"Let me understand. Yesterday, this animal and another man forced their way in here. They took your daughter, who is how old?"

"Fourteen."

"They left this guy here and threatened your daughter if you testified Monday. Did I get it all?"

She wiped her tears with the back of her hand. “Yes. And you two are the police?”

Yolis said something to her in Spanish. She smiled.

Tony took a deep breath. “We’ll do absolutely everything we can to bring Tanya home safe and sound.”

Tony reached for his cell phone. He called the Station. He walked into the kitchen before he started talking. “It hit the fan, Sarge.” He went on to explain.

“I’m going to leave Yolis here with her permission and yours, of course. We are going to need another officer to respond, preferably a female. Mickey and I are going to try to talk ‘no nuts’ into being reasonable. We need to find out the whereabouts of Sabrina’s daughter. These guys are animals.”

“Do you have a plan?”

“No. But I need you to trust me. I know I’m only a reserve, but from my vantage point, that can work to my advantage.”

“Want to explain?”

“Not really. Will you trust me?”

“I can’t hear you. We have a bad connection.”

Tony called Mickey. Their conversation was brief but to the point. Tony updated him. He gave Mickey an ETA.

Tony walked back to the living room. The asshole was still on the floor with Yolis standing over him. “He’s Conrad Lupe Gonzales. I ran him. He’s got a jacket longer than your arm and mine put together. Most of them involving violence.”

Tony shook his head. “We’ll get along real well. You’ll stay here. There’ll be another officer here momentarily. Mickey and I are going to take Gonzo for a drive. It’ll be a short ride if he cooperates. If he doesn’t, well...there are many potholes in HP.”

“I want my lawyer.”

“We’ll get you your attorney. We don’t want to step on your rights.”

Yolis kicked him. “Get up.” She grabbed Gonzales under his left arm and yanked. He stood straight up. Tony grabbed him. “You’re all mine now.”

Yolis walked over to Sabrina. “It’s going to be fine. My partner is going to take care of business. He’s a good man.” She looked at Tony and smiled. Tony grinned back.

They walked down the street to where Mickey was parked. He opened the back door. “Get in, asshole.” Tony walked around the back of the unmarked car. He got in the back seat next to Gonzales.

“Officer Cassidy, meet Conrad Gonzales. Eventually, we’re going to charge him with kidnapping, assault, battery, attempted murder, bribing a witness, threatening a witness, conspiracy and...”

Gonzales interrupted. “You cops think you’re so fucking smart. But let me tell you something. If I don’t call in to my partner every fucking hour, that little cunt is stale pussy. Got my point?”

“Mickey, drive over to the 60 entrance. The south side. There’s a basin there. Let’s go sightseeing.”

The car moved away from the curb. Gonzales laughed. “You can’t scare me. I don’t frighten, pig.”

“When’s the last time you called in?”

“Fuck you.”

“I’m man enough, asshole, if you’re woman enough. I’m near enough if you’re queer enough. I’m only going to tell you this once, you’re fucking with the wrong cop. She’s coming home in one piece or they’ll never find the pieces of your body. I’ll send your ugly, fucking head back to your mother in a douche bag.”

Tony realized Yolis had confiscated Gonzales cell phone. But it didn’t much matter.

“What time is it, pig?”

Tony told him. “Twenty minutes for my call. Let me tell you what’s going to happen to that sweet pussy if I don’t make that call. My partner will make her suck his cock. Just before he comes, he’ll pull it out of her mouth, turn her around, bend her over, and fuck her up the ass. Just before he comes, he’ll pull out of her ass and make her suck him clean.”

Tony wanted to shut him up. He wanted to break his face. But he didn't want to show marks; not just yet. "You really don't want to do this. I promise you, you don't."

He laughed. "Yes, I do. But I'll make you a deal. Let me out of the car and we'll only fuck her once each. Deal?"

"You're a sick, sorry son of a bitch. And you really don't know who you're screwing with." Tony looked at his watch. Sixteen minutes if asshole was telling the truth.

"I bet she gives a great blowjob. Probably better than your mother."

Tony stared at him. The guy was one of the sickest psychos he had ever met. Between the facility and the PD, Tony had met some real whack jobs. "Let's get off your mother's asshole. I just got off yours. Give me the number. I'll dial, you talk."

The car bumped several times. Tony knew the car was jumping the curb which meant they were almost at the wash. He had thirteen minutes. "Enough. You're up to your ugly face in charges. Make the call and that's one less charge."

"Suck my dick and we'll call it even."

Mickey had remained silent the entire drive. He looked over his shoulder to the back seat. "My partner's more fucked up then you can imagine. Do what he asks, and I promise you won't regret it."

"Who the fuck are you?"

"I'm going to be your second worst enemy if you don't make the call. That's my promise." Mickey stopped the car. They were at the bottom of the basin. It was darker than hell.

"Last chance," Tony said. "For once in your miserable life, do the right thing."

"Kiss both sides of my ass, cop, then kiss me down the middle."

"That's it. Mickey, why don't you go have a smoke. I'm pitching the next couple of innings. You can warm up in the bullpen."

"Can't I watch?"

"This time, I think it would be better if I handled business on my own. They can't take away my pension."

Mickey got out of the car. Tony got out. He walked around the back of the vehicle. "Last chance, jerk-off. You've got..." Tony looked at his watch, "...eleven minutes."

Tony pulled Gonzales out of the unmarked car. "Go grab your smoke. I'll call you when we're done here."

Gonzales scowled, "In that case, you might want to give up cigarettes. We're done here."

Tony slammed him against the car as Mickey turned away and started walking. He stopped, didn't turn around, lit his cigarette, and disappeared into the basin darkness.

"I'm through playing. I want two things and I want them now. I want you to make that call. I want to know where the girl is being held."

"And I want a million-dollar winning lottery ticket, pig."

Tony nodded. "Okay. If that's the way you want it."

"What I want is my attorney."

"You'll get your attorney."

"I want him now. I know my rights."

"You don't know jack shit. But I think you're about to meet him. Last chance." Tony looked at his watch. If Gonzales was telling the truth, the hour would be up in seven minutes. "What's it gonna be?"

"I want my lawyer. Can you say lawyer, cop?"

Tony didn't say a word. He grabbed Gonzales who was no taller than 5'9". He spun him around like a doll, forcing him against the car. Tony ran a second set of cuffs through the rear door handle of the unmarked car. He again spun Gonzales around. He hooked the second set of cuffs to the cuffs binding Gonzales' hands. Gonzales was now wearing two sets of cuffs. He was securely cuffed to the car. For the first time, Tony observed fear in Gonzales' brown eyes. "Still want to play?"

"I told you, I want my lawyer."

"Make the call first." Tony looked at his watch again. Five-and-a-half minutes.

"Fuck you."

"I think I see your attorney. He's part of a law firm. The firm is Boot, Boot, and Boot. Paul Boot, the father and his two sons, Raul and Saul. How many Boots are you going to need?"

Gonzales looked at Tony as if he was crazy. At this very moment, Tony was probably insane. He was focused on only one goal—getting Tanya home safe.

"Paul Boot, meet your new client, Conrad Lupe Gonzales." Tony wore steel-toe boots. He dug his left foot into the soft dirt. Swiftly, he buried the steel toe of his right boot between Gonzalez' legs. It was a home run in any major league ballpark.

Everything that wasn't anchored down in Gonzales stomach came up. He had spit and puke all over his shirt. Tears streamed down his cheeks.

Mr. Gonzales, I'd like you to meet Paul Boot's son, Raul. Raul Boot, meet Conrad Lupe Gonzales." Tony dug his right foot into the soft earth. Just as Gonzales seemed to be recovering from Tony's solid hit, Tony came up with his left steel-toe boot. Again, he scored a solid hit. Again, everything left in Gonzales' stomach found a new home. The guy was in agony. Tony was enjoying it. Maybe he was fucked up, after all. But Tony had an innocent life to save. He was going to do whatever was necessary to bring her back to her mother in one piece. Tony looked at his watch. Three minutes, fifteen seconds.

Gonzales was regaining a bit of composure. His face showed agony. He remained standing only because he was handcuffed to the door handle. "Are we done playing games or do you need to meet the other family member?"

Gonzales tried to lick some of the puke off his lips and chin. "Give me the phone."

"Fuck you, punk. Give me the number."

Gonzales gave the number up. Tony dialed and put it close to Gonzales mouth. "Screw around and you're a dead wetback. I swear it."

Gonzales said into the phone, *"Viva Mexico.* I'll call back in one hour."

Tony sighed. Part one was over. "Well done. I think you still need to meet the rest of your defense team. Saul Boot, I'd like to introduce you to Conrad Gonzales. Mr. G, meet the final member of your defense team, Saul Boot." Tony hit home with his right boot.

He called the Sergeant. "I need you to get me an address for this phone number. Sabrina's daughter should be at this address. If not, I need to know right away. If she is, I also need to know that asap."

"Copy that."

"Is everything code 4?"

Tony looked at Gonzales. "Is everything code 4, *mi amigo?"*

"My suspect in custody says everything is code 4. We'll know soon. Keep me posted, Sarge."

"Fuck you, cop."

Tony sniffed the air. "Wake up not-so-speedy Gonzales. Wake up and smell yourself." Tony again sniffed. "You stink." Tony uncuffed Gonzales from the car's door handle. He secured the cuffs around his wrists and led him to the unmarked unit. "Get your Mexican ass in the American car, asshole. I'm going to make you one final promise. If one hair on the girl's head is harmed, you'll never make it back to the Station. *Comprende,* wetback?"

"Up yours."

"Let me read you your rights." Tony did. "Do you understand each of those rights as I read them to you?"

"Yeah, yeah, yeah."

Gonzales was coming back to life. "You're going to pay for what you did, pig. You're going to pay, big time. I'll have your job. I'll sue the city. I'll sue you."

Mickey stepped out of the shadows. "What have we got?"

"The Sergeant is putting together a team to extricate Tanya. We're waiting for the results. Border crosser in the car here is threatening me with loss of my job. Do you think they might yank my pension?"

Mickey laughed. Tony got paid a uniform allowance twice annually. That was it. He chased bullets for free. Factor in the gas, the wear and tear on his car, the food, etc., it cost Tony money to be a Reserve for the City of HP.

"I got a flash for Mr. Stink-you-very-much." Tony leaned on the opened car door. He stared at Gonzales. "Let me explain the facts of life to you, shit-for-brains. If you so much as think about filing a complaint, if you even think about it, I'm putting word out on the street that you rolled over like a $5.00 Mexican whore. Got that, asshole? Try me. Your life expectancy will be less than Saddam Hussein's and he's already dead."

He turned to Mickey. "Do me a favor, Mickey. Snap some pictures of our guest here. Get good shots of his face. Then let's pull him out of the car and take a few full-body poses. Proof positive that our Mexican friend was treated well by HP's finest."

They waited patiently for the results of the raid. It was nerve-racking, to say the least. Mickey smoked cigarette after cigarette. Tony paced. Neither could stray far from the unmarked unit. It had no cage in it. Gonzales had to be eyeballed.

"Remember the guy they called 'White Bread?' I think Peter Pelmier was his actual name." Tony was at the open car door. "He threatened a suit against our fine city."

"I remember him. The little dude with the tattoo of Mickey Mouse on his neck."

"That's the guy. He swore he'd own the city when he got out. Trouble is, he never got out. True story, Gonzo. They found the rat hanging from the top of a jail cell door. He wrapped one pant leg of his jailhouse coveralls around his neck; the other around the cell bar." Tony hung his tongue out of the side of his mouth. "That was it. Game over. Autopsy report said it was suicide. There's one cell at HPPD that has no camera. Guess what cell 'White Bread' was housed in, Gonzo baby? The moral of that story is, you mess with bull, you get the horns."

Mickey lit another cigarette. Tony began pacing again. It was 2245 hours. It was taking longer than Tony thought it should take. He walked back to the car. He opened the door and leaned in. "If you gave me the wrong fucking number, you're a dead Mexican. I hope you understand that. You'll never see booking, never!"

Tony called Yolis. "Hey. Are you still at Sabrina's?"

She was.

"How's she doing?"

"We're waiting, too."

Yolis asked how he found out where the hideout house was.

"I can't go into that over the phone. I'm not even sure I got the right address. Let's just say our friend was cooperative. His legal team threatened to give him the boot if he didn't come clean."

Then he added, "After this shit is over, how about you take me out for a drink?"

"Are you asking me out?" Yolis was surprised.

"I'm asking you to have a drink with me after we get back to the barn and call it a night."

"I gotta think about that." Yolis laughed. "I thought you'd never ask."

A Change of Pace

Mickey put out his cigarette. "I can only hope Florida will be as much fun as HP." Tony didn't know if Mickey was being sarcastic. "I'm going to miss it. I'm going miss you, too, partner. We have some great times out here."

Tony shook his head. "A long time ago, shortly after I first started here, you told me I'd either hate this job or I'd love it. You were right. I love it. I absolutely love it. Next life, I'm going to be a full-time cop and you're going to be my partner." Then Tony added, as Mickey lit another cigarette, "You won't smoke either."

"This life is difficult enough. You want me to look ahead to a second life?"

"Just saying, partner."

"How are things between you and Carina?"

"Good." Tony added more softly, "I guess."

"You guess?"

"I haven't talked with her in a couple of days. I called and left a couple of messages. She called and left one message. We just haven't touched base."

"Do you realize if the two of you get serious and tie the knot, she can be Mrs. Carina Farrina?"

"That's like if Tuesday Weld had married Frederick March the 3rd, she'd be Tuesday March the 3rd." Tony smiled. "Your turn."

Mickey took a step toward Tony. He kicked the back door of the unit closed so Gonzales couldn't hear them. He lit a cigarette. "Seriously, what are you going to do about him?"

"Meaning what?"

"You didn't get the information out of him by going down on him. There's gotta be damage somewhere."

“Do you see any bruises or marks? Do you hear him complaining?”

“I know a cop who shoved a broken-off broom handle up a perp’s ass to get a confession.”

“I think I remember that. A Haitian guy and a New York cop?”

“That’s the one.”

“I also remember the cop somehow got caught.”

“Yup. And the Haitian is very rich today.”

“I know there is a point to all this.”

Mickey blew smoke toward the heavens. “Just a learning curve, my friend.”

“If it were your daughter being held hostage and being threatened with every gross sexual act known to man, would you have a problem using a bit of ingenuity?”

“When you graduate college, you get to call it ingenuity? I call it friendly persuasion. But the attorney is going to call it excessive force.”

“It’s not going to get that far.”

“Are you sure?”

“I’m sure enough. And if it does, as Robert Kennedy said, we’ll cross that bridge when we come to it. Besides, as I said before, what would you want a cop to do if it was your daughter?”

“Not arguing that. I want to know that you covered your ass.”

“My ass is covered. I’m not Haitian.”

“I heard. You’re Italian. A Mexican with a job.”

“So, when are you guys planning on moving?”

“We are looking at anywhere from three to five months. We’re going to fly down, for a long weekend or two or three, rent a car, get the lay of the land, and see where we want to live that isn’t too far from work. Housing is more affordable and there’s no state tax.”

“Just humidity and alligators.”

“And here it’s wind and earthquakes. Sometimes life is a compromise. You have to do what seems best at the time.”

"I understand. Desert your partner in his time of need."

"You seem to be doing pretty okay for yourself. You're out on your own when you want to be. If anybody deserted anyone, partner, you left me to fend for myself."

"How's Tammy on the move?"

"She's the one who brought it up. I think it's a great idea. A new start, new friends, new job, new opportunities. Hell, even a pay raise. I'm sure they have a reserve program."

"Hell, if I ever walked away from Corrections, I'd shoot for full time."

Tony heard a noise from the unmarked car. He looked. Gonzales was tapping his head on the window.

Tony walked over. He opened the door. "You finally found something positive you can use your Mexican head for."

"I gotta piss."

"So, piss. I'm not going to hold it for you. Mickey, the guy's got to piss. Wanna hold it for him?"

"I don't think so, thweetie. You hold it for him."

"He can't find it without a magnifying glass and a tweezer."

"Listen you, assholes, I really gotta piss."

"That sounds like a personal problem." Tony looked at Mickey. "Whatdaya think?"

"Sounds like a personal problem to me, too."

"Put the handcuffs in front of me and I'll go behind the tree."

"Those handcuffs are staying right where they are."

"Then pull down my fly."

"Pull down your own fly."

"I can't with my hands cuffed behind my back."

"Here we go. Mickey, we're back to square one. Personal problem."

"I swear I'm going to piss my pants."

"They're your pants." Mickey walked over to the car.

"You guys are enjoying this, aren't you?"

Tony spoke first. "I'm enjoying the shit out of it. You can do what you did to an innocent teenage girl, get a sick thrill out of what might be done to her, but you can't take pissing yourself."

Mickey said, "Live with it."

Tony's cell phone vibrated in his pocket. He immediately looked at Mickey. Hopefully, this was the call they were waiting for. Hopefully, the Sergeant was going to tell Tony they extricated the girl successfully. Hopefully.

That wasn't the case. It was Carina.

"Hey, you're no easy person to reach."

"I can say the same."

"How's everything going?"

"Busy. You?"

"Same."

"Listen, I'm in the middle of a situation..."

"I won't keep you. I hate to ask but I need a favor. I have to go out of town overnight...a business thing. Can you make a quick stop at the apartment and check on the cat? Check her milk bowl. She'll have plenty of food."

"Sure. Glad to." That wasn't true. Tony liked kittens but he wasn't a cat person. The few times Tony spent a full night at Carina's, her cat thought he was her personal toy to play with. "I don't know what time it'll be, but I'll get it done."

"I appreciate it. I'll call you when I get back."

"Take care and don't work too hard."

"You be safe."

Tony checked on his prisoner. The front of his pants was soaked. "You pissed your pants...and my car. You're more trouble than you're fuckin' worth!" Tony looked at Mickey. "I've got plans for this prick. Major league plans." Tony was intentionally talking loud enough so Gonzales could hear him. "He may not see HP today."

Tony's phone vibrated again. He grabbed it out of his shirt pocket. It was the Sergeant. "We got her. She's a little bruised, a little battered, and emotionally a wreck, but she's alive and on her way to the hospital. We took Valdez into custody without incident. He whined like a baby girl when we cuffed him."

"I have mixed emotions about that. But I really need him alive. I need two approvals from you. First, tell Valdez his good body Gonzo rolled on him like a freaking steam shovel. Second, I need to kick Gonzales loose, at least for now. Let's say our apartment entry was unlawful, so he walks, for now."

"Do I want to know what's behind this?"

"No. I need you to trust me. You sent us to do a job; we accomplished that job. Rules had to be bent to get Tanya home alive. That's all I can say about that. As far as Gonzales is concerned, I need leverage. Kicking him loose is my leverage." Tony could picture the Sergeant's face. It wasn't a pretty picture. But she had a reputation for letting her officers play as rough as they had to. She always had their backs unless they seriously crossed the line in the sand.

"This coming from a reserve."

"The best damn reserve you ever had."

"So why not come onboard full time?"

"That could happen, if you'll have me."

"I won't have you, but I'd like to have you on my HP team."

"Funny. Let's see what happens. Will you underwrite my requests?"

"You've got it."

"Thanks, Sarge. You're more appreciated by your team than you realize."

"Great job, Tony. And you're right." She stopped talking.

"Right about what?"

The Sergeant hung up.

The heart of Gonzales' gang turf was Florence and Salt Lake Avenues, but instead of dropping him off there, Tony continued to the Station. He parked in the no parking zone in front of the Station and got out of the unmarked unit. Mickey got out and opened the rear door. "Get out, scumbag."

Gonzales slid across the seat. Mickey helped him out then slammed him against the car. He took the handcuffs off him but held him tight. The three of them walked to the front of the police station. A uniformed cadet met them at the entrance to HPPD. In his right hand was a cell phone. Mickey turned Gonzales around so that he was facing the street. He put his arm around him as if they were best of friends. Tony was on the opposite side of Gonzo and had his right hand on his shoulder and was smiling broadly. The cadet snapped five pictures.

"Thanks, man. Send those to my email and my cell, please."

The cadet nodded. "You got it, sir."

Tony looked at Gonzales. "Make any noise, punk, and I'll plaster these photos on every billboard in HP, after I send them to your gang buddies and to Valdez. Your life won't be worth your pissed panties, pussy. Get back in the car."

Tony drove to Green Tree Park. In front of dozens of people, some of whom Tony knew were friends of Gonzo's, Tony stopped the car. He got out and made a show of opening the door for Gonzales. Then loudly Tony said, "Thanks for breakfast, buddy. And as far as the information you gave us, if it's usable, you're home free." Then he whispered to Gonzo, "If you get arrested in this damn city again, these pictures will be all over the front page of the paper." Then, loudly, "Give our best to your family. See you soon."

Tony stopped by Carina's place to check on the cat. From there he went home, showered, then changed clothes. He was anxious to meet Yolis for a drink. Tony liked her.

Unless you're a cop, most people don't understand the relationship among police officers. It's like a private community. Carina once said to Tony, the only time I see you really smile is when you're around other cops.

They share the same bond. They see what most people never see. More often than not, they hide their true emotions and don't want wives and family to see the inner turmoil they're constantly fighting because of all the bad shit they see on the street daily.

A cop enters a coffee shop and immediately scans the room. He knows all the exits and entrances. The cop sits in a place in a restaurant where he can see as much as possible, just in case. He'll sit down and adjust his weapon, just in case.

Today's world is different; and not for the better. Laws are lenient and there are whackos out there, foreign and domestic, who want to take out as many Americans as they can. It seemed to Tony that half the Country was armed.

Tony taught Carina that, after shopping, to look under her car as she was walking to it. To check the inside of the car before she got in it. To hit the key fob to unlock the car just before she arrived so she could quickly enter the car; and then lock it. Hell, even when Tony entered his car from a parking lot, he never put on his seatbelt until he was out of the lot.

The average citizen never thinks of these things. Today, one has to, sometimes for survival's sake. If a guy is wearing his shirt hanging over his waist, Tony is immediately checking for bulges. It could be a gun.

One day, Tony was outside his bank waiting in line at the outside ATM. He noticed a guy, in slacks and shirt hanging over his pants, walking near and around the ATM. Tony went into the bank where the Chase people liked him, and he knew some of them by name. He approached one of the bank employees he recognized. "Hey, you got a guy pacing around by your outside ATM. He's about 6', well put together, wearing grey slacks, blue shirt hanging over his pants, and a bulge, that could be a gun, under that shirt. I'm just trying to be cautious."

The bank official took Tony over to a corner. "You cops are never off duty, are you?"

"Never."

"He's undercover security."

Tony thought, *He needs lessons in undercover.*

The point is, the guy didn't have to be working for the bank and might have been casing the place. He might have been waiting for the right time to walk in and shoot up the bank. Cops are always restless and always looking for the worst. It's a professional habit, and Tony would have it no other way.

Yolis for Dinner and, Hopefully, Dessert

Yolis' blue BMW convertible pulled into Scotland Yard's parking lot and Tony noticed it right away. Scotland Yard was a dinner house and bar in Woodland Hills, a distance equal in miles between Yolis' house and Tony's place in the Antelope Valley.

When Tony wanted to impress a date or wanted a tasty meal or a quiet upscale bar to sit and chat, SY's was the place.

Tony walked in, nodded to the host taking names for dinner. He gave Tommy his name then entered the bar area. The lights were down, but it wasn't dark; yet it wasn't so light that you needed sunglasses. There was ambience. Most of the crowd was middle-aged, dressed in jackets and slacks, even suit and tie. The women were dressed casually. The band was playing 50s music, some Sinatra and some Dean Martin.

Tony found Yolis seated in the far corner of the bar. He walked over, smiled, took her hand, kissed it, then sat close enough to her so that he was almost brushing up against her.

Yolis wore a black skirt with a slit up the side that didn't stop. Her blouse was white with the initial Y above the left breast. She wore a tiny badge necklace that hung just below her shoulder line. "Is this business or pleasure?"

"It's my pleasure." Tony rested his hand on Yolis' thigh.

"Are we on the list for dinner?"

"Yup. Hungry?"

"Starved."

"A little business before pleasure?"

"Shoot."

"How did you get Gonzales to give up his godfather?"

Tony smirked. "The less you know about that the better. Let it suffice to say that his legal team, Boot, Boot and Boot, recommended he be cooperative."

"I don't think I want to know any more." She put her hand on top of Tony's. "I've been waiting for this night for a while. I've watched you for some time now. I like the way you walk."

Tony wondered if she was speaking literally or figuratively. "Tell me about Yolis."

"Not much to tell."

"Tell me anyway."

"I was born in L.A. and grew up in Bell. My father worked for Farmer John. My mother worked at a dry cleaner. I have a brother four years older than me. Somehow, I kept away from the gang influence and did pretty good in school. My mom and dad taught me respect for the police. At sixteen I became a cadet in Bell. After high school I worked security. When I was old enough, I applied to Bell PD. They sent me to the Academy. I had a tough time with some of the physical stuff, but I never gave up. My parents supported me and other guys in the class helped me. Getting over the wall was difficult. I didn't have the upper-body strength. A couple of the guys took me under their wing. The long and the short of it is, I graduated the Academy. The waiting list at Bell was long. HP was hiring. I went through their process.

"I thought the Academy was tough. The nine months it took to get through all the police hiring tests is a bear. After each test, you wait for the result to see if you move on. I don't have to tell you. The hiring process is the same for you as it is for me. But, we're here."

"We're here because we're not all there."

"Speak for yourself. I'm as sane as I'm going to get."

"Do you want to move up the Department chain?" Tony motioned to the waitress and ordered drinks.

"Probably eventually. Depending..."

"Depending on what?"

"Oh...things change. I want to meet the right guy. I'd like to keep my job, but I'd also like to settle down and start a family. Does that make sense?"

"Perfect sense."

"And you?"

"Someday."

"Someday, what?"

"Someday, I'd like to settle down, too, and have kids."

"You've been married?"

"Once. You?"

Yolis shook her head. "What happened to your first marriage?'

"We drifted apart." Tony took his hand away from Yolis' thigh. "She doesn't care too much for cops. I was rarely home. It worked fine while we were living together. It even worked for the first two or three years. After that it became a disaster. It's a miracle neither one of us got arrested for domestic violence. She got even with me. She took me for a lot of money. I now know the meaning of the prenuptial."

"You sound bitter."

Tony shook his head. "I'm not bitter. I'm wiser. She came into the marriage a high-school dropout. She left the marriage one class away from her BA. I paid for most of that. The house was mine before we married. She never paid a dime toward the mortgage. Yet, I got hammered. I understand she was pissed but the divorce laws in California need a tune-up." The waitress brought the drinks.

Tony lifted his glass. "A toast."

Yolis lifted her glass. "A toast."

"Here's to the good guys, the bad guys, and what's between our thighs."

"I'll drink to that."

The band was playing "I Did It My Way." The girl behind the mic was singing up a storm. Tony liked it. It brought back memories. "You said you have an older brother. What does he do?"

"He's in New York. He works for the school district. He's married and has two boys, and he loves to ski. So, New York is the place for him. I hate the cold."

"Are your parents still around?"

Yolis nodded. "Dad is happily retired. Mom works now and then to get away from Dad. They have a small condo in Sun Village. They love it. They'll be celebrating their fiftieth wedding anniversary this year."

"How about your folks?"

"Dad was a civil lawyer. Mom worked parttime in the jewelry business. God rest their souls, they've both passed on. My Dad and I had a rough time when I was growing up. He was a flaming liberal who supported the ACLU. He donated money to help support the many attempts to do away with the death penalty. On the other hand, I am a firm believer in capital punishment. I think the ACLU needs to disappear and I believe we have too many people who get away with bending the law until they break it. I'm not racist but today, if you're a minority, you get more for free than most." Tony was on a roll. He couldn't stop if he wanted to. "If you're in this country illegally, you're not undocumented, you're illegal. I'll grant you, we need to streamline the process for getting into this country legally, but first you have to be vetted."

Tony ordered another round of drinks. He was sure Yolis would not share his views.

"So, if I'm illegal, I need to go back to Mexico."

"If you're in the United States illegally, you need to go back where you came from and come here legally. You broke the law to come into this country. What about all the people who waited in line to get here legally?"

"I was born in this country. My parents came here legally from Mexico. I agree with you. No argument here. The problem is what do you do with the children of illegals?"

"That would be the parents' call. They can go back across the border with the parents or stay with a relative or, if they're eighteen, they're on their own."

Yolis finished her drink. "How did you end up in education? I don't see you as a teacher."

"Good question." Tony laughed and took a sip of his drink. "I was on stakeout one night and I heard an ad on the radio for a program called Teacher Corps. They were looking for non-teachers, people who had graduated college in a field other than education. They would pay your salary and pay for your master's degree if you signed a contract to teach in the inner-city for two years. You were given a choice of five inner cities.

"Understand, I liked working as an operative. The hours were crazy and most of the work was done on the weekends which killed my social life. The pay was awesome. I saved money because I had no time to spend it. Then I realized there was no future in it. So, I checked out Teacher Corps. Of the five cities offered, the only one I hadn't been to was Detroit. I signed a two-year contract.

"Detroit is a crazy place. Unbelievable nightlife and cold as hell in the winter. The place was as dirty as the Bowery in New York. If you drove across the river to Canada, you could eat off the street.

"I taught some pretty difficult junior high and high school kids. As a matter of fact, no one wanted the kids I taught. It was like *Welcome Back, Kotter*. I had an ability to reach these kids and enjoyed it.

"The government paid for my master's degree at Oakland University which was then part of Michigan State. So, it was a win-win.

"Leaving was tough. I almost stayed. I wanted a warmer climate, so I figured if I tried California, and didn't like it, I could come back to Detroit. If I didn't try it, I'd always wonder.

"The kids and I had built a hell of a rapport. On my last day, I was walking around the classroom in the morning and noticed that, in some of the desks, the kids had water pistols. I knew what was going to happen at the end of the day. At lunch, I drove over to Sears and bought me two water pistols, big water pistols, like 357 Magnum water pistols.

"Sure as shit, at three o'clock, when the bell rang, all hell broke loose. Out of the desks came the kids' pistols. Out of my jacket came my pistols. They drowned me with those pistols. I drowned a couple of them.

"I had water in my pistols. Want to guess what they had in theirs?"

Yolis was smiling broadly. "I'm afraid to ask."

"Perfume, perfume, and more perfume. They said, go home and explain that smell to your girlfriend."

"It sounds like they really liked you."

"It was mutual. We all gained from it. Plus, I now had a career opportunity. So, I moved 'west young man.' I got a teaching job and eventually met a man who worked for FLACOE. He turned me on to Probation camp schools and the rest is history."

The waitress came to them in the bar area. "Your table's ready." She escorted them to the dining room. They sat down next to each other. Yolis took a sip of her drink. "Can I propose another toast?"

Tony lifted his glass. "Please."

"To those who serve and protect. And to two special people who serve and protect. To us."

"I think my ice melted." They touched glasses. "To us."

"To us," Yolis repeated. "Does it ever get to you working with incarcerated kids and then working at HP? You see a lot of negative."

"I try my best to balance it with positive, but it doesn't always work."

"What do you do for relaxation?"

"I belong to the Vette club. We have activities."

"Such as?"

"We cruise-in the Vettes to places like the Reagan Museum, the Peterson Museum, The Fire House in San Pedro, the Indoor Kart Track in Burbank. We go to Vegas, Laughlin, the river when it's warm. We do volunteer things for the kids.

"Last year a group flew to New York and went on a cruise ship to New England. We're pretty active."

"I haven't heard much about you."

"Last question."

Tony knew what was coming. He hit the black circle on the target.

"What's the story with you and Carina?"

"We're dating."

"Is it more than dating?"

"I'm here with you, aren't I?"

"You're evading the question."

"We've been seeing each other for over a year. I'm not seeing anyone else and I'm sure she isn't. However, she is getting a bit uncomfortable with my being away so much. She hasn't said anything, but I can sense it."

They ordered. "What are your career plans?" he asked.

"One day I want to be a police chief."

"Are you serious?"

"As serious as that goddamned smirk on your handsome face. You got something against a female police chief?"

"Not at all. I'm impressed. HP?"

"I doubt that will ever happen. HP is so damn sexist, I surprised they have toilets in the ladies' room. How about you?"

"For now, Carina has taught me to take it one day at a time, to live in the now. Right now, this minute, I'm damn content. I have great food, great drink, and I have awesome company."

"And if you play your cards right, you might have me. If you'll excuse me, I need to go to the little girls' room to powder my nose."

Tony thought about his predicament, if you could call it that. He was "seeing" Carina, but he sat with Yolis. Tony considered himself an honest guy. He didn't like to "play" with people's feelings. He and Carina had never discussed their "situation." But there seemed to be an understanding that neither was dating anyone else. Carina had keys to Tony's house and Tony had a key to Carina's place. Sometimes life could be complicated.

Rodrigo's "pen" exercise jumped into Tony's head. He had to accept responsibility for his actions, plain and simple. This situation didn't just happen; he allowed it to happen or wanted it to happen or both. Obviously, he wanted it to happen.

He remembered the Serenity Prayer Carina had repeated for him several times: "God, grant me the serenity to accept the things I cannot change. The courage to change the things I can; and the wisdom to know the difference."

This wasn't a difficult situation if you applied that prayer. He could change it. But doing so would involve hurting someone. There was an old expression that Tony and his high school buddies used to banter about. "A stiff cock has no conscience." But Tony wasn't a teenager anymore; he was an adult. If he could make split decisions with a gun in his hand, he could certainly make this right.

Yolis came back from the ladies' room. "You're still here," she said, as she sat down. "That's a good sign."

"You're not getting rid of me that easily."

"Who said anything about getting rid of you? I may keep you around for a while."

"So, I got the third degree. Now it's my turn. Are you seeing anyone?"

"You get right to the point." Yolis put her hand on Tony's thigh. She started counting with her other hand.

When she got to five, she stopped. "Nope. Just you."

"How come?"

"Between work and college—I'm taking classes to advance in my pay grade—I don't have time. Besides, nobody's really caught my interest."

Tony nodded. "I'm surprised. I would think guys would be chasing you all over L.A. to get a date with you."

"A couple of guys at HP have hit on me but I don't really want to play where I work. I guess you're the exception to the rule." She squeezed Tony's hand. Tony liked the warmth of her grip. "Many guys are threatened by the fact that I'm a police officer, a female cop at that. It frightens them off."

"I can understand that."

"And as you said, if you're not in the profession, it's difficult to live with. So, here we are."

"Here we are." Tony smiled. He was very comfortable. He liked the company. "An ex-husband?"

"Nope. No ex. No current. Hopefully, a future hubby. I guess we'll see."

"You and Mickey are pretty tight?"

"We're close friends. We live within a few miles of each other and often commute together. He was one of my FTOs and we hit it off. Why?"

"This is just between you and me. If you say one word, you'll never see what's inside my panties. Okay?"

"That's an offer I can't turn down."

"Mickey protects me. For some reason, he thinks I need a big brother. Occasionally, when I've gotten the itch to mess with one of my colleagues, Mickey has discouraged it. With you, it was the opposite. I swear if you say anything, you're dead meat."

"I won't say a word. I promise."

"You do know that he's leaving HP?"

"I know. I'll miss him. But it may be the best thing for him and Tammy."

"He also misses riding with you."

"Yeah. I miss riding with him, too. But I like being out on my own. I like calling my own shots."

Yolis took a sip of her drink. "You're easy to talk to. I'm enjoying myself."

"I'm enjoying myself, too. You're more fun than a felony arrest."

"You're a riot."

Tony looked down at the slit in Yolis' skirt. "If that slit went any higher, I'd have to arrest you for very decent exposure."

"As long as you handcuffed me and searched me for weapons, Officer, be my guest."

"There is either a dominant or a submissive side to you. Which is it?"

"A couple more drinks might ply that out of me."

"How about you?"

Tony felt his tongue loosening. "As a matter of fact, I'm..."

The waiter brought the food. "Saved by the food. To be continued." Tony kept stealing glances at what was inside that slit.

They ate in silence, save for the occasional remark about police work and a story Tony told on himself. "I was riding with Mickey, my second FTO. We got a silent alarm call at a condo up behind the high school east of Miles Avenue. Mickey and a back had the front door. I was told to take the back door.

"It was late in the afternoon but still daylight. You know how most alarm calls are false alarms. Well, I'm the new kid on the block and I'm trying to do everything by the book. All of a sudden, this guy in a suit and tie comes running out the back door. I've got him dead bang. I prone his ass out, suit and all, on the pavement.

"I get on the radio and tell the world I've got one at gun point to the rear of the condo. Half of HPPD roll out.

"It turns out the condo was owned by one of our esteemed councilmen. For some unknown reason when he saw the police approaching, he got scared and ran out the back door.

"When we 'dusted him off,' he was cool about it. As a matter of fact, he thanked me for doing my job so well."

"He's lucky you didn't shoot him." Yolis went back to her steak.

"That reminds me of an even funnier story. I'm sitting on the couch downstairs in my house late one afternoon. I've got the TV on. Next to the couch is a window that faces my neighbor's bedroom deck. As I'm watching the TV, out of the corner of my eye I observe a white male, about 40, climbing one of the poles. He makes it to the top of the pole and onto the deck.

"My neighbor is a veterinarian and I know he's at work, but his wife and young son are at home. I grab my Glock and run over to their house. I knock on the door. When the kid comes to the door, I grab him to pull him out of harm's way. I tell him to call his mother. He does. She comes to the door.

"I tell her that someone climbed up to her deck and entered her bedroom and is still in the house. After some stammering, she explains it was a friend of her son's—they were 'playing hide and seek.'

"They were playing 'hide my baton.'"

"You're full of stories. Where the hell do you live?"

"Actually, I live in a great area on the west side of Palmdale and have a very nice house. Even after my ex got finished fracturing me financially, the payments on the house are less than some people pay for rent."

"I'd love to see your place."

Tony took a bit of his veal parmigiana. He ignored what was a statement.

They finished dinner, passed on dessert, and had coffee. Yolis turned to Tony. "How about a nightcap at my place?"

Complications

It was a warm sunny day—hardly a cloud in the desert sky—that Monday morning when Tony drove to his office. That was about to change.

Tony, sporting a new blue double-breasted suit, a new French-cuffed white shirt, and a solid red tie that said Corvette on it, stood just outside the administration building as Probation delivered the kids to school. Tony watched the line of students carefully. He was looking for anything out of the ordinary. He didn't want the kids going into a classroom with any unfinished business that could spill over into the class. It was quiet.

It was quiet until one of the kids eyeballed Tony. The line was going in one direction and the kid's eyes in another. Suddenly the student said, "Hey, I know you... You're not a principal, you're a cop."

Tony motioned the kid over to where he stood. The student complied. Tony didn't recognize him. He turned the kid around so that they were both facing away from the oncoming lines.

"You're not a principal; you're a cop. You arrested me."

"Where?"

"HP. Hollow Point. You don't remember?"

Tony shook his head. The kid was about five-eight, thin build, jet-black hair, brown eyes, Hispanic.

"You had your wife with you. I was driving the stolen Toyota. Those other two fools were with me." He turned and pointed to two kids in another line. "I had the .357 under the seat."

It all came back to Tony. He had a temporary office worker from the school with him. He pulled the car over on a traffic violation. The plates came back clean. The woman who owned the car didn't realize it had been stolen. Fortunately, instinct kicked in. Tony called for backup. When backup arrived, he made the approach. Three juveniles and an adult were taken into custody without incident. Another gun was off the street. The gun was also stolen.

Tony looked at the student. “Actually, you’re wrong twice. I’m an assistant principal, and it’s ‘police officer’ to you. If you quit stealing cars and quit carrying guns, stolen guns, you won’t end up in places like this.”

Tony smiled. “Put that behind you and do the very best you can while you’re here and earn school credits and you can turn a negative into a positive. I’m here to help.”

“I almost believe that. And you’re a cop.”

Tony let it go. “Get back in line, sir.”

Tony looked up at the clear desert sky. He could see the shining sun rising. It was going to be a good day.

A man once said, ‘It never rains in southern California.’ That man is full of shit. It was about to pour. And even though that was a figurative rain, it was going to damn near drown Tony.

The first chance of rain came at about noon in the form of the ringing of Tony’s cell. On the other end of the line was Carina. “Hey stranger. What’s happening?”

“Not much. You tell me.”

“Not much here either. Got back in town late Sunday night.”

“How did everything go?”

There was a brief hesitation. “Everything went well. How about an early dinner tonight? My treat.”

That sounded ominous. Was there anyway she could know about Yolis? Tony doubted that. Maybe they offered her a promotion and she wanted to celebrate. Maybe she brought Tony back a nice gift and wanted to give it to him over dinner. In that case, it would be nice if he had something to give Carina.

JFK was unusually quiet. This was a blessing. It gave Tony a chance to meet with some students and check on their progress. Tony called it maintenance.

There were a couple of high-level meetings in Eddie's office which Tony was not privy to. At one point, he observed Paula, Cleveland Archer, and another male he didn't recognize enter Eddie's office. That was nothing out of the ordinary. In the north end of Corrections, JFK seemed to be the rallying point.

Tony closed up shop early. He was home playing with LT before four-thirty. He fed LT, gave him a cookie, hugged him, then went upstairs got undressed and took a shower. He didn't shave. A five o'clock shadow looked manly, at least in Tony's opinion. Besides, if he shaved, he wouldn't have time to stop at the florist and get Carina flowers.

As he was drying himself off, he thought about Yolis. Then he thought about Carina. Then he thought about Yolis. Tony was glad he didn't take Yolis up on her invitation for a nightcap. That wouldn't have been fair play. Tony had a decision to make. After all, he was responsible for his actions.

Tony got behind the wheel of his gorgeous Corvette Pace Car. He started the engine. He listened to its throaty roar. Tony smiled. He had no idea there were clouds overhead and they were about to open up and drench him.

He drove to the florist and purchased a flower arrangement, one that he thought Carina would like and one that would look good as a centerpiece on her dining room table. From the florist he drove to Roxy's. He looked around the parking lot. Carina was already there.

Tony parked the Vette in a "safe" parking space. He grabbed the flowers off the seat then walked the short distance to the entrance. He looked around and spotted Carina seated in the last booth so that Tony could sit with his back against the wall. There was nothing behind him and he had an unobstructed view of the restaurant.

Before he sat down, he gave Carina a kiss on the cheek. "Here." He handed her the floral arrangement. "A welcome-home gift."

She smiled. "Thanks, Tony. Unnecessary, but thank you."

He sat down across from Carina. There was a cup of coffee in front of him and a menu.

"I ordered you coffee. Is that okay?"

"Fine, thanks. We have some catching up to do."

Carina nodded. "This is awkward. Before we order, let me get this out of the way."

Tony had seen this look on suspects before. Usually, the look gave away a sinister something that was to follow.

"My business trip this weekend wasn't all business, Tony. I met someone. You're away so much, I felt lonely. He has time for me." She was looking down at the tabletop. "It's not that I don't want to see you anymore. I want to be free to date others. Does that make sense?"

Tony hesitated. He swallowed. His pride was hurt. The fact that she either lied to him or mislead him, hurt. He had played fair; Carina hadn't. "I understand completely." That was a true statement. Tony didn't like the situation one bit, but he understood.

He picked up the menu. "Let's order."

The storm hadn't even started. That was a sprinkle compared to what was to come.

Carina ordered a salad. Tony ordered a steak sandwich. He was in the mood to bite down hard on something to get the bad taste out of his mouth. He didn't like what had happened—what was happening.

There wasn't a whole helluva lot he could do about it.

Carina stopped forking the salad into her mouth. She reached into her purse. Tony watched her. He supposed she was looking for a tissue. She wasn't. She handed Tony his house key. Tony hesitated only for a split second. He took it.

He fished in his pocket for her apartment key. He took the key off his Corvette keyring and handed it to her. She avoided eye contact when she reached for the key. It was a very awkward moment.

***

There were more, what appeared to be, high-level meetings of the brass and suits at JFK Thursday and Friday. There was talk about what the meetings might be all about, but it was all FLACOE rumor.

Tony made a few phone calls trying to get to the bottom of what the meetings might be about, to no avail. It didn't matter because he was sure it had nothing to do with him. He was wrong. Dead wrong. It had everything to do with him.

The torrential downpour continued. Friday night was clear and calm when Tony pulled into the HP Police Department parking lot. Considering Carina had chopped off his balls, he was in a pleasant mood. He no longer had to make a decision. He was free and clear to pursue Yolis.

Tony carefully backed the Vette into a parking space. He grabbed his gear and walked the parking lot to the steps that led downstairs to the men's locker room.

Mickey wasn't in the locker room. Tony hadn't seen Mickey's car in the lot, but he hadn't looked for it. He wondered if he took the night off.

Tony showered, changed into his uniform then walked up the front stairs to the Blue Room. Mickey was on the computer. Tony walked over and put his hand on his friend's shoulder. Mickey was finishing a report.

He looked over his shoulder and nodded. Mickey saved his work and immediately shut down the computer. "Let's go outside and talk."

Tony didn't like the sound of that one freaking bit. They walked out to the parking lot. "Bad news," Mickey said, not mincing words. "Two of our reserves got busted in a prostitution sting in Pomona early this morning. Kingsley and Battling. The big guns are trying to keep it out of the papers and off the TV. You know that won't happen.

"The problem that it creates is that the City Council has been trying to do away with the reserve program for several years now. This may give them the ammo they need."

"Mother fuckers! How fucking stupid can those assholes get?"

Mickey glared at Tony. "Look at who's living in a glass fucking house before you start heaving rocks, my friend. I'm not saying that what they did is justified, not by a long shot. I am saying we're all human. Examine your record before you prosecute a fellow reserve."

Mickey was right. Tony knew exactly what he was referring to. Mickey was three hundred percent correct. "You're right. Of course, you're right. I suppose we'll hear about it at briefing?"

"We'll soon see." They walked up the carpeted stairs to the detective bureau offices then into the briefing room.

Tony's mind was on the reserves who got busted screwing prostitutes. More accurately, his mind was on the impact it might have on the reserve unit. Tony was deep in thought when Yolis walked in and sat down, right next to Tony.

Somebody said it's always darkest before the dawn, Tony thought. A ray of sunshine was about to appear in the form of Yolis' right hand which she placed on Tony's inner thigh and squeezed. She leaned over and whispered into Tony's ear, "It's either you this weekend or my vibrating dildo."

Tony covered his mouth to keep from laughing. He had an answer for Yolis. He turned to respond, but the Sergeant beat Tony to it. "Okay, girls and boys, let's settle down. We have some serious shit to cover, not to mention the crimes committed during the day watch.

"Let's start with two of our reserves getting nailed for plucking prostitutes in Pomona. They got caught up in a sting and they're on camera. Both are suspended and will undoubtedly be fired. Whether or not something can be done to avoid prosecution remains to be seen, although in my opinion, and under the freedom of information act, it's going to be impossible to keep it out of the newspapers. Aside from the major damage and major embarrassment to the Department, both these reserves have families and there is probably irreparable damage done to the families.

"The lesson here is before you go out to pay-for-play, make certain that your dessert in not listed in the police menu."

From the very rear of the room came, "Tony, did you copy that? Leave the he/shes on the Boulevard for the Sergeant. He doesn't like competition."

"That's very funny, pencil dick. See me after briefing. We're doing our own sting tonight. I need you to dress as a queer to attract the dykes. Excuse me, you're already dressed."

The Sergeant smiled. "Here's the possible impact. As is well known to the troops, some of you don't like our reserve population. The City Council, for sure, doesn't like them. This could be the key that unlocks the door to escort them out the door permanently. We'll have to see about that.

"Are there any questions about that?" Silence.

"Okay, let's move on to the day's crimes. We had the usual stolen vehicles. Pick up a copy of the hot sheet off the table on your way out. We had an armed robbery of the Sub Shop at Pacific and Calderon. If you guys want to continue to get your subs at half price, we're looking for a male Hispanic, approximately 20 to 25, five-eight, thin build, with a tattoo of an angel on the right side of his neck. He was wearing a black hoodie and grey sweatpants. He was last seen riding northbound Pacific Boulevard on the east side of the street on a twenty-inch bicycle, blue in color.

"The only other thing from earlier that's noteworthy was a shooting in Maywood. Two gangbangers exited a dark-colored Chevy and both opened fire on the vic who was walking northbound 42nd street on the east side of the street. When officers arrived on scene, the vic, Oscar Villalobos, was DRT (Dead Right There). The suspects, both described as male Hispanics in their twenties, average build, about 5' 8" tall, wearing ski masks with eye slits.

"Of course, nobody saw shit. So, what we've got here is two for one. One less gang punk to litter our fine HP streets and two shooters. We can expect retaliation."

In the middle of the room an officer yelled out, "Sarge, I'm trying to take copious notes. Can you spell retaliation?"

"Hernandez, after briefing, will you meet me in the parking lot? My battery is dead. I was thinking if I attach the battery cables to your nipples, maybe the unit will start." There was a smattering of laughter.

"Okay. If there are no questions, hit the streets. Tony, you're riding with Mickey tonight. I want you to make sure Mickey stays away from those hookers."

Yolis waited till all the cops were just about outside the briefing room door. She leaned over. "You don't need hookers, big boy; you've got me. I'm free. She grabbed Tony between the legs and squeezed. Damn, is that you or your baton?"

Mickey let Tony drive. That meant one of two things, maybe both. Mickey was either planning on spending a lot of time talking with Tammy on the phone or he was tired. Maybe both. "Any comments on your buddies getting fucked for the screwing they didn't get?"

"Stupidity. But like you said, I'm not the one to call anyone names." Tony wasn't about to talk freely inside the unit. It had absolutely nothing to do with trusting Mickey—he trusted Mickey completely. But it wouldn't be the first time the boys who pulled the strings bugged a police unit.

"I can only hope it doesn't affect what HP does with its reserves. I could be out of HP."

"You'd get picked up at any other department that has reserves. Some even pay."

"I have an allegiance to HP. It was city of HP and the Chief who picked me up. I like it here."

"You like Yolis."

Tony tried to show no reaction. "I like it here."

"Speaking of Yolis..."

"I wasn't speaking of Yolis."

And then came another deluge. "That asshole just ran that stop sign. He didn't roll through it, he ran it!" Tony flipped a U-turn. He was on the car like IRS on your unpaid taxes. Mickey put out the plate.

"22 Adam, your plate comes back a stolen out of Hollenbeck. A 2008 Toyota Corolla 4-door. Your location?"

"We're westbound Saturn crossing Rugby. The vehicle appears to be occupied one time. Speed is 35, traffic is moderate."

"Copy that 22 Adam." Several units were in position to back. The rule was to not light the suspect vehicle up unless two units were behind the suspect vehicle. Preferably, they wanted the vehicle in a lighted area with light traffic. The subject could be armed. He could have just committed a felony, or it could be a kid who stole the vehicle for a joy ride or to impress his date.

"22 Adam, your location?"

Mickey put it out. Tony was three cars behind the stolen. Judging from the way the suspect was driving, he wasn't aware 5-oh was on him.

Tony saw a second unit pull in behind him, then a third. Tony could light him any time. He hit his overheads, then the siren.

The Toyota immediately swerved into the oncoming traffic lane, narrowly missing an eastbound vehicle that swerved right and braked hard to avoid the stolen.

"Son of a bitch," Tony muttered. "This guy is seriously fucked up." Tony stayed with him.

He went southbound on Santa Fe, increasing his speed to sixty-five, then seventy. Mickey put out the location. 23 Adam, one of the secondary units, blew a tire. He was out of the pursuit.

The Toyota again crossed the roadway into oncoming traffic, forcing the northbound vehicle to the shoulder of the road. The guy was begging for an accident.

Tony stayed within three car lengths, focusing on traffic, speed, and pedestrians. He had no time to be nervous; not so with Mickey. Mickey was used to driving in pursuits, not being the passenger. His eyes were darting all over the place.

Mickey updated the location. "We're southbound Santa Fe, just north of Florence. Can you get an airship up?"

"Negative 22 Adam. We have activity in Southgate. 26 Adam will assist."

"Copy that." The Toyota made a tire-screeching left turn on Florence, heading back to the center of HP. Tony's hands were heavy from squeezing the steering wheel.

The Toyota picked up speed. He was now in excess of seventy-five. Florence was four lanes wide, two westbound and two eastbound. The lanes were wide. It was early evening and traffic was lighter than normal.

Tony knew the WC was monitoring the pursuit. If at any time he thought it was too dangerous to continue the chase, he could call it off. Tony didn't want it to end that way. He wanted it to end with the perp in handcuffs in the back of his black-and-white.

Suddenly, the Toyota veered to his right then back to his left. The tires smoked as the Toyota now headed westbound Florence. Tony slowed, made his U, and followed three car lengths behind the stolen.

Two secondary units followed closely behind Tony.

Mickey, mic in his right hand, yelled so that he could be heard above the wailing sirens, "Close it up just a bit. Maybe half-a-car length."

Tony goosed the gas pedal. He closed the distance by a few yards. The guy's speed increased. Tony observed something fly out of the driver's window that appeared to be wrapped in a clear plastic bag. Mickey also observed it. He put it out over the radio so another unit could retrieve it.

"Speed now seventy-five to eighty. We're westbound Florence approaching Santa Fe." The guy was staying in HP. Maybe he knew the area. Maybe he was looking for a place to bail.

He made a hard northbound turn at Santa Fe. His tires squealed in protest. Tony fishtailed as he followed the Toyota. The guy was pushing eighty-five. The streets were flying by faster than Mickey could put out their location.

"22 Adam. Airship should be 10-8 in five."

"That's a copy."

Tony's eyes darted in every possible direction trying to see anything that might cause him a problem. Traffic continued to be light.

If the guy kept going north, he'd run into the freeway, then the CHP would take over. HP did not have spike strips and Tony wasn't PIT certified. The guy was hauling ass, much too fast for a PIT. Tony kept a two, two-and-a-half car distance.

At the next intersection, in Vernon, the light was red. The guy never touched his brakes. Nothing was coming. He cleared the intersection. Out of the corner of Tony's eye, he observed a figure on a bicycle off to his right. The guy had the green light but there was no way he couldn't hear Tony's siren.

Mickey observed that the old guy on the bike was wearing headphones. There was light traffic heading southbound. Tony could only hope he got through the intersection before the guy on the bike reached the intersection. It was too late to brake. He'd skid into the intersection and take out the bike and its rider. Tony had the skill and the presence of mind to take the one evasive action that could ward off a tragedy. He put the pedal to the floor. The Crown Vic roared through the intersection, missing the bicycle and its rider by inches.

Tony was exhausted. Mickey was sweating. He sighed, smiled, wiped sweat from his face then said, "You pulled that one out of your ass."

"EVOC training at his best." EVOC was also called Pursuit School. Expert drivers taught officers the art of chasing a vehicle. At the end of the day-long course, you got to chase the instructor through a mock town. Tony had been to Pursuit School twice. Both times he was able to stay with the instructor. At 53, Tony's reaction time and skills were slower than that of a 23-year-old. For his age, Tony was at the top of his game.

The Toyota, and the guy behind the wheel, were also at the top of their game. He continued northbound on Soto Street, which is the continuation of Miles Avenue. He was still doing a steady seventy-five.

Mickey observed it first. A split-second later Tony observed it off to his right and closing fast. He saw the red lights before he saw the damn fire truck. With his siren blasting, the concentration on the stolen, and the lights from the two units behind him, it was amazing that he could hear anything.

Tony's first thought was that the fire engine was going to take out the Toyota. Then he realized the Toyota would clear the intersection. Tony and the Crown Vic might not.

Tony was looking for a way out of the path of the freakin' fire truck. Swerving right and giving the unit immediate and hard acceleration might do it. Braking wouldn't make it. If he braked, he'd sure as shit get t-boned.

Tony pressed the accelerator hard. The Toyota's brake lights lit up like a Christmas tree. Tony had two choices, brake, or rear-end the Toyota. Instinct kicked in. Tony braked hard. The unit was specially designed for this sort of situation. The Crown Vic held its traction. The Toyota lurched forward. The driver braked intentionally knowing it would put the fire engine and the police unit in an unavoidable collision path.

It did just that. The fire engine was unable to stop, and Tony was in its path. It caught the rear end of the Crown Vic and twirled it around like a spun nickel.

Tony's high-speed driving skills kicked in. He held the steering wheel lightly, letting the car do a 360. He backed off the gas gently, then ever so gingerly braked. The car came to a stop parallel to the curb. It didn't roll. Both he and Mickey had their seatbelts securely fastened. Tony had a couple of knee bruises. Mickey's shoulder was bruised.

The fire truck had very minor damage. The driver suffered a sprained neck. One of the firemen cut his knee. That was it. The worst injuries were about to come when the newspapers had a field day with the story, not to mention the crap Tony was going to get from team HP. He couldn't wait.

Even though Tony's skillful driving was able to keep the car from a secondary impact, the damage was done. Tony was DNF—Did Not Finish the pursuit.

Four people were admitted to the hospital. No one was seriously injured, but three of the four were detained overnight for observation. Two of the three were Mickey and Tony.

It was still raining and there was another storm on the horizon.

When Tony got to the hospital, he found a television in the emergency room. He had a cute, obliging nurse change the station to channel 9. Sure enough, the pursuit was still going on. The jerk was on the northbound 5 just south of the 118. The California Highway Patrol was in pursuit. Half the CHP was behind with an airship overhead.

Traffic was light. The 5 was as open as a racetrack. The driver held the speedometer at a steady eighty-five.

Tony shook his head. He was pissed at himself. The same nurse who changed the channel for him, nudged Tony. "It's time to get you inside. We need to check you out." She couldn't have been more than 5'1", maybe 115 pounds. She was built on top and narrow around the waist. The accident and the sour end to the pursuit hadn't taken a toll on Tony's dick. As he moved forward, she apparently noticed. She blushed. To change the subject, she said, "Right this way, officer."

"Call me Tony. Can we get a TV in here? I've gotta see the end of this pursuit."

"Only if you promise not to give me a ticket if you ever pull me over."

"Done."

She called to an orderly. Two minutes later Tony was watching the Toyota casually heading north on the 14 freeway toward the Antelope Valley.

"I'm going to go over your bumps and bruises. The doctor will be in shortly."

Tony half heard what she said. He was listening to the news crew in the helicopter above the 14 freeway making sense of what was happening. There was speculation that the CHP would use a spike strip. There was speculation that they wouldn't attempt a PIT because speed was too fast. At this point, Tony wanted to see a sniper in a helicopter put a round in the rear tire of the Toyota. That was on his Christmas list, but Santa had better gifts to deliver.

Tony felt the nurse's hands on each side of his right thigh. "Do you feel any pain?"

"It's excruciating. But not the thigh. Actually, that feels good."

She blushed again. "By the way, my name's Suzie. They call me Little Suzie. Nurse Little Suzie."

"They call me DNF, did not finish the pursuit. I was the primary unit in the pursuit. I had the meeting with the fire engine in Vernon."

Cute Little Suzie squeezed the inside of Tony's thigh. Fortunately, or unfortunately, for one or both, Tony's erection relaxed. "I know about the pursuit and the accident. You're famous. You're all over the news."

Tony guessed a more appropriate word would be 'infamous.' His eyes were still glued to the television. Tony heard from the helicopter, "He appears to be slowing down. He's waving his hand out the window. He's at a crawl. The CHP is stopping the light traffic behind them. He's stopped. I think, folks, this pursuit has come to an end. My best guess would be he's run out of fuel."

The CHP chasing the stolen lined up behind the Toyota. One of the Highway Patrol Officers started barking orders to the driver. He obeyed.

He exited the car, picked up his shirt, did a 360 to show the officer he wasn't armed. He followed orders to prone himself out on the freeway, facing away from officers with arms outstretched. Next, another officer approached, put one knee in the small of his back and handcuffed him. Finally, he was searched and put in the back of a CHP unit.

Tony had to admit the end was smooth and seamless. Triple A with a gun had accomplished what Tony failed to complete.

The doctor came in. He examined Mickey and Tony and basically gave them both a clean bill of health, save for a few cuts, bruises, and bumps. He then made the mistake of putting Mickey and Tony in the same semi-private room.

The first thing Tony did from his bed was hit the remote. It was news time.

"We have late-breaking news from Vernon where a HP police unit did battle with a Vernon fire engine during a pursuit that ended on the 14 freeway south of Acton. It is a surprise to nobody that the Ford Crown Victoria police car, driven by Reserve Police Officer Tony Farrina lost the battle. Fortunately, nobody suffered serious injuries. A fireman and Farrina and his partner are being held overnight at a local hospital for observation.

"More from the scene from Clark Christiansen..."

Tony winced. It was bad enough that two HP reserves got busted in a hooker sting. Now, he smacks up a unit. If ever there was fodder for the City Council to call it quits for their reserve program, this was all they needed.

Christiansen: "We're at the corner of Frederick and Lansing where Tony Farrina managed to collide with a fire engine, lights and siren screaming. How one cannot see a fire engine coming...well...I guess things happen. Fortunately, the CHP swung into action and pursued a Toyota, stolen out of Hollenbeck, onto the 14 freeway where the Toyota slowed to a stop after running out of fuel.

I guess this begs the question what do you get when a Crown Vic police unit and a Crown fire engine collide? You get a 'Crowned Vic.' Back to you guys in the studio."

Tony turned off the television.

"Why'd you turn it off? I'm sure the talk shows are going to have fun with that during their monologue."

Tony tossed a pillow at Mickey. The pillow fell on the floor. "You can't throw any better than you can drive."

"Thanks for the support, *partner.*"

"If it's any consolation, when they investigate the accident, I'll plead temporary insanity. I was the idiot who let you drive."

The fun and games were interrupted by the appearance of Yolis. She had an envelope in her hand. She walked to Tony's bed, squeezed his hand, kissed him on top of his head then handed him the card. "I'm afraid."

"You should be."

He opened the card. It read, "Accidents don't happen, they're caused. Get well soon." Yolis signed it, "Your new driving instructor."

Inside the card was a smaller envelope. Tony opened it. It contained two tickets (which Yolis had designed) for EVOC Training.

"You really know how to kick a guy when he's down."

"Sure. It gives you incentive to get up." She looked at Mickey. "How are you feeling?"

"My pride is hurt more than my body. I thought I trained him better than that."

Yolis said, "I'm sure age is a factor. At his age, it's amazing he can still climb behind the wheel of a unit."

"You guys can stop any time you'd like."

They did stop. Tammy walked in. "Am I missing the party?" She walked over to Mickey. She kissed him on the mouth. "And women can't drive, huh?"

"Don't look at me. I wasn't driving."

"I will look at you. You were the trainer. How come your partner got all the glory? I haven't heard much about you."

"Stick around. I'm sorry to say I'm sure there's more to come. A whole lot more."

Yolis was in uniform. "I'd like to stay and really make fun of you two, but I've got a special detail tonight."

Tony took the bait. "And that would be what?"

"I'm doing traffic enforcement with a special eye out for fire trucks driving westbound and police units traveling north. My assignment is to stop the fire engines who have the right of way so the police black-and-white can run the red signal.

"See you soon." Yolis was out the door before Tony could grab the remote to throw at her.

Exactly seven minutes later, Carina came in. She stood at the side of the bed. "How are you two?"

"We're fine," Mickey said. "The only thing that's really damaged is our pride."

She walked to the bed, bent down, then kissed Tony on the cheek. "You okay?"

"Like the man said, pride's damaged; other than that, nothing serious. We'll be out of here tomorrow. The only reason we're even here overnight is so that they can use us as target practice."

"Speaking of target practice, a couple of uniformed officers are waiting to see you. One of them has a present for you."

"I don't think I want it. How are you?"

Carina, dressed in brown slacks and white pullover sweater said, "Okay. Sad, but okay."

Tony thought that could mean a dozen different things. She could be sad because their relationship was over. She could be sad because maybe she thought she made the wrong decision. She could be sad...

Two uniform officers entered the room. Sean Mendelsohn was a motor officer. He carried a brown paper bag in one hand. With him, was Don Stewart, a detective. He was dressed in a light blue suit. He was empty handed.

"Nice of you guys to drop by," Mickey said.

"Don't go there so fast. They're not here to pay their respects."

Everyone in the room laughed, except Tony.

"C'mon," the motor officer snapped. We're a family in HP. We came bearing gifts." He held up the brown paper bag. We want to check on your wellbeing."

"Do you have a warrant?"

"Got something better than that," the six-foot motor officer said. "Right Don?"

The detective, who stood six three and stood as skinny as a brand-new No. 2 pencil, grinned. "Show him, Sean. Show him how the HP family cares about his health and welfare."

Sean walked to the bed table. He slid it to the foot of the bed. "C'mon team, gather around."

Tony slid two pillows under his head so he could watch the show.

"In here we have a Crown fire engine." He set a toy fire truck on the table. "Here is a Ford Crown Victoria police unit." He set a toy car on the table so they were perpendicular to one another. He reached into the bag. "Here is a traffic light." He set that down at what was supposed to be the street corner. "You'll notice the northbound light is red and the westbound light is green. Try to comprehend that red means stop, green means go."

Sean was poker-faced. Everyone else was enjoying the demonstration, even Mickey. Tony looked sad.

"Oh yeah," Don piped up. "Almost forgot." He reached into his suit jacket pocket. "This is a Highway Patrol car." He placed it on the table in front of the fire engine and police unit that were now locked in an accident embrace. "Here is a Toyota, in fact, a stolen Toyota. I stole it from my kid's toy chest." He placed the Toyota in front of the CHP unit.

"What we want to take away from this lesson is how the CHP handled a pursuit without crashing. We also want to learn how they take the suspect into custody without damage to a state vehicle. To make sure you have time to digest the lesson, we're going to leave the vehicles in place, so you can study the situation and maybe quiz each other during the night if you get bored. I just need the stolen Toyota returned." Without another word, two of HP's finest exited the room.

An hour and a half later, after everyone but the two injured parties had departed the hospital room, Tony's cell rang. He was sitting up playing with the fire engine and the police car. "You got more abuse for me?"

Yolis laughed. "No, babe. I want to make it up to you. I thought I'd drop by when I'm EOW, maybe an hour or so. I'll grab some drinks and you can pull the curtain on Mickey. Maybe we can see how hurt your…um…'ego' really is."

Tony smiled. "I just massaged my ego. It's in good shape."

"Gotta go. I got a 211 call. See you later."

"Be careful. My ego and I will be waiting."

Yolis never made it back to the hospital. A gang shooting on the Maywood Strip put a dead end to her images of teasing Tony in his hospital bed, or on it, depending on their privacy. In the morning, Tony and Mickey were wheeled out of the hospital to cloudy skies with more rain anticipated.

Tony spent the quickest five minutes of his life in the downstairs locker room at the Station. He had taken enough ribbing at the hospital. The television stations were still broadcasting his monumental fuck-up. The local newspaper ran a front-page article featuring the Crown fire truck t-boning the Crown Vic with the headline, "Reserved for the Inexperienced!"

The front-page newspaper story pissed Tony off more than Carina's admission of an adventurous weekend. It was almost a certainty that the Department would have to fight the City Council hard and fast or lose their cadre of reserves. It was raining again.

Tony drove from the Station north to the 5 freeway. He listened to 50s music on the all-oldies station as he drove. Traffic was moderate for a Sunday afternoon.

Mickey had decided to hang at the Station. Tony was sure that wasn't an accident. The brass most likely wanted to discuss the pursuit with Mickey. On top of the insult Tony already dealt himself by his faulty driving, Mickey might get his hand slapped. Mickey was the senior officer in the unit with a reserve officer. Maybe the reserve officer should not have been driving. That was a decision the suits would make. Tony just did not want injury added to insult. Mickey wasn't at fault. Tony was the lone ranger in this case. He just hoped the decisionmakers saw it that way.

The fact that Mickey was leaving HP for Florida, if they knew about that, might play into their decision on whether or not to paper Mickey. He was more than well liked in the Department and in the community. He had served with distinction for twelve years. He would have been promoted twice had he taken the tests. Mickey preferred the streets to occupying a desk and pushing paper. Tony was going to miss him.

Tony could hear LT's barking from the driveway. Lieutenant knew the sound of the Vette engine. LT was all over Tony when he unlocked the house door. "You missed me, LT. I missed you, too." Tony walked to LT's cookie jar. The jar was one of Tony's Christmas presents last year for LT. The inscription read, "LT's Personal Property. Keep Your Paws Off!"

LT jumped up, placed his paws on Tony's shoulders, licked him, then gently took the cookie out of Tony's mouth. It was great to be home.

Tony was walking upstairs when his phone rang. It was Yolis. "Sorry I couldn't make a hospital visit. Duty called."

"What the hell was it?"

"Several bangers decided the Maywood Strip was Dodge City. They decided to shoot it out. When the dust settled, three gangbangers died, and nobody saw shit."

"That's par for the course. Great for home values."

"I had all sorts of kinky ideas for that hospital bed."

"All talk and no action. I've heard how you are," Tony joked.

"Trust me, babe, you don't want to start with me. You're still news."

Tony knew when to shut up—sometimes. This was one of those times. "This is going to be a discussion at the next City Council meeting, I'm sure. It isn't bad enough that two of our guys got caught in a hooker sting, I had to get into it with a fire truck. The City Council wants to do away with the Reserve. This might hammer the nail in the coffin."

"I don't want to pop your balloon and don't go asking me questions, but I've got a friend on the Council. According to my friend, they were going to kill the reserves a couple of months ago. They voted to do a bit more investigation and then go from there. I'd guess they don't have to do any more investigation.

"Why don't you come full time?"

"My retirement is not transferable. I'd take a beating on my retirement."

"Take your FLACOE retirement and start another retirement with HP."

Tony thought about Yolis' comment. "That's something to think about. Either that, or I hit the lottery and don't have to worry about working."

"Or find a rich woman to support you."

"Are you rich?"

"I don't want to support you, so what difference does it make?"

"Cute."

"Do you know the only word in the English language that starts with and F and ends in a UCK, other than your favorite word?"

Tony shook his head into the phone. "I haven't the faintest idea."

"Firetruck."

"That's funny. I think it's two words. How about I call you tomorrow?"

"That's sounds good. Listen, Tony. I know you're taking a lot of shit over the incident. And I know I'm giving you a pile of that shit. But for what it's worth, babe, I feel for you, and I'm in your corner. Anything I can do, I'm there for you. All you need do is pick up the phone. Sometimes that phone feels like a thousand pounds. It really isn't that heavy."

"I appreciate that." Tony hesitated. "I like it when you call me, babe." He was smiling. His first real smile in a while.

"I'll talk with you tomorrow, babe. Sleep well. Dream about me. But keep it dry. Save the best for me."

Decisions, Decisions, Fucking Decisions!

Monday was a school holiday. That usually meant an extra day for Tony to work HP. This Monday was different. He needed a day away from the pressure and punking of the "incident," as some at the Station were calling it. Even if he wanted to work, he was informed that he needed to take the week off.

It was unusual that Tony hadn't heard from Mickey. He'd call him later, in the early afternoon. He was certain, because of the accident, Mickey was told to take a couple of days off, too. Tony was more interested in knowing if Mickey had heard anything more about the possible dissolution of the reserve program.

Tony walked downstairs with LT. It was breakfast time for both of them. LT got a mix of top-notch dry dog food and warmed wet food. Tony called it a diet fit for a Lieutenant. Tony's breakfast consisted of gourmet coffee and whatever was in the refrigerator. In this case, a ham and cheese sandwich.

It was ten o'clock when Tony got LT's leash out of the closet. LT new what that meant! He walked to the front door and sat on the carpet which Tony had purchased for LT because he liked to lie in front of that door. Whether he was protecting the house or liked the cool air by the door, Tony wanted LT to be comfortable. LT's tail was wagging faster than a flag flapping in the Chicago wind.

"Yes, buddy, we're going to the park. If you're a good boy, we'll get ice cream afterwards."

Tony put LT on the leash and opened the door. LT sat down, waiting for Tony to lock the door. Then they walked to the Vette together which Tony left in the driveway. That's how far out of touch Tony was after the "incident." The Vette was always garaged.

He and LT walked to the passenger side of the Pace Car. When Tony opened the door, LT jumped up onto the passenger seat. "In, big guy?" Tony shut the door.

Sergeant Steve Owens Park was named after a slain Lancaster Sheriff's Deputy. The Sheriff was "executed" by a home-invasion thug who was determined not to go back to prison. Somehow, the three-time loser managed to get the drop on Deputy Owen. He shot the Deputy in the shoulder. When the Deputy fell to the ground, the creep stood over him and pumped three more rounds into the Sheriff, including one round to his face. Unfortunately, the bastard was pinned down within an hour and taken into custody alive. Such was the life, and death, of a police officer. God rest Sergeant Owen's soul.

Tony drove the Corvette slowly over the speedbumps. The parking lot wasn't crowded. Most Antelope Valley residents were at work.

A couple of young women looked at the purple and yellow Pace Car and smiled, admiring the rare vehicle. Sometimes the smile carried over to Tony. With LT in the car, the vehicle became more than a babe magnet; it was instant ass, if Tony wanted it. He didn't. In his high school days, Tony was a player. In his college days, Tony was still a player. When he was married, he made the mistake of running around occasionally. Now that he was in his 50s, he wanted one woman in his life. Tony sensed it was only a matter of time.

He parked the Vette in a corner parking place so it wouldn't get dinged. He reached in the back for LT's blue Frisbee®, then he walked to the passenger door and opened it for his Lieutenant.

The northeast corner of the park was set aside for dogs that were trained to be off leash. Tony and LT trotted over to that area. LT ran past the entrance as Tony threw the blue Frisbee into the air. LT fielded it like Yasiel Puig then ran it back to Tony where he dropped the Frisbee at Tony's feet. Tony rubbed his head. "Good boy, LT, good boy."

Tony picked up the Frisbee. Before he could throw it, Lieutenant took off running. His gait was that of a thoroughbred. Tony leaned back and heaved the toy high into the air. LT watched it over his shoulder as he ran. Several people were standing on the sidelines watching. They were amazed.

One man yelled, "The Giants can sure the hell use him!"

LT caught up to the Frisbee. On the run, he watched the blue sphere come down softly. He caught it in his mouth, took a few steps forward, turned, then ran back to Tony. He dropped it at Tony's feet. Several people, including Tony, applauded.

Tony reached in his pocket. He gave LT a cookie before he again threw the toy. LT chased the Frisbee down, caught it cleanly in his mouth and ran it back to Tony. This time, after picking it up, Tony ran with it, stopped, threw it behind him and watched LT. He stopped running forward, turned, ran faster looking over his shoulder and caught up to the Frisbee. He was a bit out of breath as he ran it back to Tony who picked it up. "Last throw, LT. I think we're both tired." Tony made the throw an easy one. LT took about twenty steps, caught it, returned it, and sat at Tony's feet.

LT was huffing and puffing. Tony's shoulder was starting to bother him. "It's time for ice cream, LT. You earned it. I've got some water in the Vette." LT looked up at Tony as if he understood every word. He probably did. They walked back to the Pace Car, side by side.

Across the street from Sergeant Steve Owens Park is a strip mall. There is a small ice cream shop in that mall named after the brothers who own and work the shop. The brothers are Martin and Lewis Stripleton. The ice cream shop is called Martin and Lewis Ice Cream.

Tony pulled the flashy Vette to the front of the shop where he parked. Leaving the windows halfway down, he exited the car, telling the excited LT he'd be right back. Tony came back to the car with a chocolate cone for himself and a double scoop of vanilla ice cream, in a dish, for LT. He set the dish on the walkway, got LT out of the Vette, and they ate ice cream together. Tony's mind was off the "incident" for a few hours.

***

The five-day weather forecast for Tony's end of Corrections indicated clear skies with temperatures ranging from the mid-fifties to the high-seventies. In Tony's world, there were back-to-back downpours in his immediate future.

When Vince Scully, the very best of the best, was still at the mic for the Los Angeles Dodgers, he would often say, "Deuces are wild," when the batter had a two-ball, two-strike count on him, with two outs and two men on base. Well, on this fine, clear, warm southern California spring day, it was *TUES*day, so Vin, you can add that to your deuces.

It was a Tuesday. Dodger fan Tony, who had been to Ebbets Field as a kid growing up in Brooklyn, was a Vince Scully fan. Today, however, was not going to be a day about Vinnie or a day about the Dodgers. Today was going to be all about Tony.

When this Tuesday was in the history books, it became one of the most infamous days in Tony's life. If Tony was a writer, and if Tony was writing a book about today, the chapter would be headed AMBUSHED! As Tony backed the Vette out of the garage onto the concrete driveway, he had no idea, as he drove north toward JFK, toward work, that the Indians were gathering behind the cover of the mountains and their mission was his scalp.

The kids came to school in orderly fashion. There were no fights, no skirmishes, no yelling, no cursing. It was as if the sound suddenly went dead on your big screen—picture only. Tony liked that. He smiled. Maybe there was hope, after all, for some of these street-smart kids. Maybe if their energies could be channeled in the proper direction, there would be hope. Tony couldn't give up on them, especially since most everyone else had called it a day.

Tony's radio suddenly changed channels to K-SHIT. He flashed on Carina—probably a dead issue. He flashed on the HP reserve program—probably soon to be in the history books. He flashed on Yolis. He smiled again as he walked back into his office looking up at the sunny southern California skies.

The third item on Tony's Tuesday morning agenda was to call a student, James Holister Brown, into his office. Holister was a star third baseman for his high school team. His nickname was Hoover, not because he attended Hoover High. Brown caught his nickname after the vacuum cleaner. Every ball that came close to third base, Brown sucked up.

Unfortunately, Brown liked to also suck up the green. The green that said, "In God We Trust," on the back. The bigger the bill, the more of it Brown sucked it up. For a kid with the smarts Brown had in his brain, his thinking sometimes short circuited.

The vacuum was making big bucks. He was a high school senior, and he was a star hot-corner scooper-upper, possibly with a major league future. Unfortunately, the scoreboard flashed E-5 when his principal noted Brown's flashy suits, his gold jewelry, his diamond earpiece, and his Caddy convertible. Shortly after administration caught his action, so did LAPD. The boys in blue paid homage to DEA. Like the major league scout who came to check out Brown at several games, DEA set up shop in Brown's Compton backyard.

Like the scout, they liked what they observed. They liked Brown's action so much, DEA set up surveillance on the young, flashy, overactive high school senior who had a shotgun arm and could gun a runner down throwing from third to first on the dead run. Unfortunately, Brown's arm was not the only gun he carried. DEA made note of this on their scorecard.

The last ground ball Brown scooped up was on opening day of the CIF high school baseball conference. The next object scooped up was Brown. When they took Brown to their downtown dugout, he was charged with possession of numerous drugs, possession for sale, conspiracy to launder money, possession of a firearm, and DUI. For giggles, they arrested his adult girlfriend who happened to be in his black Escalade when Brown racked up his final score. She was charged with contributing to the delinquency of a minor.

Coaching Brown was his very high-priced mouthpiece, who coincidently also graduated Hoover High but instead of dealing drugs, dealt himself a hand at Pepperdine followed by a great deal at Loyola Law School where he graduated with honors. He stood pat, culminating his winning streak with a first-time pass of the bar and an invitation at a full partnership with a very well-known law firm in Beverly Hills, an accomplishment equivalent to hitting 300, with 30 home runs and 30 stolen bases in your rookie year.

So, we had one Compton success story as a mouthpiece for a Compton failure who, unlike his attorney, appeared hell-bent on self-destruction.

If there was one positive in this laugher of a ballgame, it was that Brown was a minor. Mr. Mouthpiece pulled strings to see to it that his client was not tried as an adult.

The two made quite a pair. Brown was instructed on dress code. He was drilled and practiced on how to walk into the courtroom, how to look at the jury, how to address the judge, and how to sit in the courtroom. His dress was sharp, always in suit and tie. His demeanor soft spoken, even shy. The only jewelry observable was that worn by counsel, Owens Williamson Nathaniel, whose suits were custom-tailored, his French-cuffed shirts carried his initials, and his own black Cadillac Escalade carried the personalized license plate: OWN LAW, the OWN, of course, being his initials.

Showmanship brought clients to the firm. Clients translated into dollars for representation. Nathaniel, Esq., was convinced that more than one jury acquitted his client because of his stature in many communities. To that end, OWN drove and owned a second Cadillac Escalade, this one dove white. It carried the personalized license plate: LAWYR UP.

Brown thought the world of his attorney, and was convinced that his money and OWN's shucking and bullshitting would win him the ballgame.

Unfortunately for Brown, even the very best of them stumble and fall. This was one of those games. When the line score was in the books, it read Brown, a maximum of three years at JFK with the possibility of adult prison at the age of 18, depending on his behavior at the juvenile facility. Thanks to OWN's skill, his ability to "work" the judge and his skin color, there was the possibility of a reduced sentence based on certain factors. Factor 1: A clean school record while incarcerated. Factor 2: A clean probation record while incarcerated. Factor 3: Earning his high school diploma while at JFK.

All three factors were easily obtainable for Brown. JFK had an interschool baseball team. He was actually recruited by the Probation honchos to play for JFK. The facility never had a winning year; this could be their first. If it happened, there was a movie deal in the making. The working title was *Error at Third Base*. Two of the backers were OWN's law firm and Brown's juvenile judge. Oh, the inner circle of Corrections.

Tony called Brown into his office. The "kid" stood 5'11" tall. His complexion was smooth. He wore his black hair short. His classy dress was temporarily off the table, as standard dress for JFK is t-shirt, blue jeans, and tennis shoes. Brown was in compliance.

"Come on in and grab a chair. Your monthly school court report is due next week. So, let's take a few minutes to go over things." Tony pointed to his computer screen. "Teacher input is up to date. Per your teachers, academics are fine. You have a B in math and a B in history. Everything else is an A. Congrats, you're looking good. Behavior is reported to be excellent. I see another great report." He paused.

"In general, how are things?"

"No complaints. I'm accepting the fact that I did what I did and now I'm paying the price. I've learned not to make the same mistakes when I get out. How are my credits?"

Most of the kids at JFK were sorry they got caught. But they would never tell an adult that. Hopefully, Brown was telling it like it is. "You need another 50 credits and you're gold. You've already passed the necessary exams, so, by the end of fall semester, you should be a high school graduate. One advantage to being here is that we have school during the summer which gives you one extra semester."

"I'm going to be here after I graduate? What will I be doing school-wise?"

"You can take computer college classes. We'll see when you get closer to graduation. Who knows, when your judge sees all your glowing reports, maybe he'll cut you slack. Any other questions?"

"Nope. Next week we play Mays. That's a big game for us. I want us ready for that game."

Tony scooped a framed picture off his desk. It was a picture that he was proud of but one that also brought back memories, some good, some not so good. "Recognize the person in the wheelchair?"

Brown shook his head. "I recognize the guy in the sharkskin suit."

Tony smiled. "The guy next to me is Roy Campanella. Campy was a catcher for the Dodgers back in Brooklyn where I grew up. They played at a Stadium called Ebbets Field. Every so often, my dad or grandfather would get game tickets and to Ebbets Field we'd go. Campy, who was half-black and half-Italian, was my idol. In 1958, in January, Campy was driving home from his business, skidded on a patch of ice, and rolled his car. He ended up paralyzed, never to play baseball again. For a long time, he wanted to die. Spirituality changed his mind. He went on to write a book called *It's Good to Be Alive*. He became a coach for the Dodgers when they moved out to California, coaching from his chair.

"I moved out here. I wrote the Dodgers a letter and asked if Campy would make a guest appearance at Mays/Maris where I was the assistant principal. They said for $500 he would. That was back in 1978. Corrections was too cheap to pay the $500, so I said I would.

"Campy came out and spent half the day at Mays and the other half at Maris. The picture was taken at Mays. The kids loved Campy. Of course, so did I. It was a dream and a half.

"When I tried to pay Campy, he refused to take my money. I wrote an article about his visit, which was published in an education magazine called *THRUST for Educational Leadership*.

"My grandfather, the one who used to take me to Ebbets Field when he could get tickets, would fly out to visit me every summer. I'd get tickets and we'd go to Dodger Stadium. I made a copy of the article and showed it to a Dodger usher. He took my grandfather and me upstairs to where Campy coached. I handed him a copy of the article and thanked him again for coming to the camp. We talked about Brooklyn and the Dodgers for a while. What a thrill!

"My wife, ex-wife, made a Dodger blue wall in our upstairs hallway. It's filled with pictures and memorabilia from the Brooklyn days to California. It brings back a lot of memories. Memories money just can't buy."

"Wow."

Tony looked at his watch. It was later than he thought. Brown needed to get back to class. "Listen, if there is anything I can do for you, you know where to find me. Good luck against Maris next week. I'm going to try to make that game. So, if you hear some nut screaming at you, it's me.

"Now, you'd better get back to class before your teacher hangs me up like a bad curveball." Tony stood up. He extended his hand to Brown.

Brown extended his hand before he was completely out of his chair. He lost his balance, stumbled, caught his left ankle behind the chair leg and went to the carpeted floor.

Tony reached down. "Are you alright?"

"I'm fine. Clumsy, but fine."

Brown stood up. He didn't realize that, when he fell, cellophane-wrapped marijuana fell out of his sock. Tony grabbed it. "Have a seat." Tony took a sniff. It sure the hell didn't smell like Carina's worn panties.

"It's not mine."

"Sit the fuck down." The cop in Tony kicked in. This disappointment in Tony kicked in. The pissed off in Tony kicked in.

"What's not yours?"

"The...the thing you found."

"You mean the bag with oregano in it?"

"What's oregano?"

"What's not yours is oregano." Tony stood over Brown. "Are those your tennies?"

Brown nodded up and down.

"Your socks?"

"Yeah."

"Your jeans and your belt?"

"Yeah."

"Amazing. Everything on you is yours except what was in your sock."

"Not mine. I was holding it for someone."

"Who?"

Brown shook his head from side to side. "We had special visits yesterday. One of the guys got a special delivery. It's his."

"Whose?"

"I can't tell you. I have to live in that fucking dorm."

Tony sat down. "Probably not for long."

"What do you mean?"

"I have to turn in a report to the judge. Unless the judge smokes oregano, I don't think he's going to be thrilled with this."

"You can't do that to me!"

Tony picked up a pen. He dropped it on his desk. "Remember Rodrigo—the assembly? The pen doesn't fall. I dropped it. I'm responsible. It's about time you accepted accountability for your shit. You had a deal, a great deal. You have a contract. You broke it."

"But that shit's not mine."'

"Dumbo, if you hand me a stolen gun and I put it in my waistband, when the cops find it, do I go to jail?"

"Probably."

"Yes, I go to jail, Sherlock. It's called 417 of the penal code. If it's on your person, it's yours. Furthermore, don't put it on me. You did it to yourself. And for what it's worth, I do think it's yours. You're either selling it or buying favors with it."

"Fuck you. Can I leave?"

"No, you can't leave." Tony picked up the phone. He dialed the dorm. "Is Wolfe Simmons around?" Tony held the phone to his ear while eyeballing Brown.

"Wolfe. Tony. How goes it? I need you to come up to my office if you can. I have your boy Brown here. I was gathering information for his court report when a cellophane bag fell out of his sock. It wasn't filled with chocolate." They hung up.

Brown remarked, "I thought you were a decent guy."

"I thought you were a decent student with a decent head on your shoulders. Your turn."

"This isn't funny."

"I'm not laughing. But I'm going home tonight."

"What does that mean?"

"It means if you want to quit ending up in places like this, you gotta play by the rules. The definition of insanity is doing the same freakin' thing over and over again and expecting different results. You keep doing the same shit. You keep getting the same results."

"Cut me some slack. I'll never screw up in here again. Word."

"You're a day late and a dollar short. I cut my last slack yesterday."

"Don't do that, man. They'll come down on me hard."

"You should have thought of that sooner. Whose shit is it?"

"The fucking man in the moon. Do what you gotta do." Brown looked at the carpet. "It's my shit."

"Who brought it in?"

Brown looked at Tony, then out the window. His PO was walking across the grass to Tony's office. "I got it... If I tell you, will you let me off?"

"This isn't *Let's Make a Deal*; who brought it to you?"

"I got it from a PO. We have a deal. The weed for me striking out the first time at bat against Maris. He bet large that I'll go down swinging first at bat. I don't strike out but I'm going to this time."

“Not that I believe you, but who’s the PO?”

“Cut me slack?”

“I told you—no deals.”

“You can get the same action. You can make three month’s pay, all tax free, on one at bat. I’ll even tell you who’ll take your bet.”

“You know you’re a conniving little shit. You just struck out and you haven’t even gotten to the plate.”

Wolfe Simmons opened Tony’s office door. They shook hands. Wolfe sat down. Wolfe was 6’, 200 pounds of muscle, friendly and likeable. He was also Brown’s PO. He was also going to be at the ballgame. Tony had some thinking to do. He didn’t have much time to do it.

“Your boy here got caught with the goods. He’s going down and I’m guessing it’s going to be a hard tackle.”

Wolfe looked at Brown. “What happened?”

“He’ll tell you.”

“I’m asking you. What happened? And don’t make me ask you again.”

“I had a little bit of weed.”

“A little bit?” Tony took the cellophane bag out of his desk drawer. He held it up. “Just a smidgeon.” He tossed it on the top of the desk. Tony took a picture of the weed with his cell phone. “I’ll attach the picture to the court report.”

Wolfe asked, “Where’d you get the weed?”

“I found it.”

“Don’t fuck with me. Where’d you get it?”

Either they were double-teaming Tony or Wolfe wasn’t the guilty PO.

“All I’ll tell you is I got it yesterday.”

“Visiting?”

“I told you. I got it yesterday. Nobody wants to cut me slack so I’m not talking.”

Wolfe asked Tony, "Is he suspended?"

"Three days. I'd recommend SHU so he can go to school and continue to accumulate credits."

"Okay."

"You'll have the report before lunch. I'll fax you a copy along with a copy of his court report."

Wolfe and Tony shook hands. Brown didn't shake with either man.

The first item on Tony's oregano agenda was testing it. Normally, that would be an activity left up to Probation. Tony had a drug kit and had training in drug identification, so he did the simple test. Tony was shocked. It didn't come back as oregano.

He decided to forego lunch. He wasn't hungry. He wanted to hammer out the report and the kid's evaluation for the court and get all that shit behind him. He got on his computer.

Tony finished the first draft, poured himself a cup of coffee and took a break. The break was short lived. Appearing in his doorway was Cleveland Archer. Apparently bad news traveled faster than a Clayton Kershaw fastball.

"We need to talk."

Fuck you, Tony thought. "What you mean is you need to talk. I need to listen."

"Can we get your principal in here?"

"Anything you have to say, you can say to me. Come on in." Tony's voice was not very inviting. "Do you want coffee?"

"No. What's going on with Brown?"

"He got caught with marijuana stuffed in his sock."

"How did you happen to find the marijuana?"

Tony wanted to say, *This isn't a mother-fucking courtroom and you aren't a goddamn judge.* "It fell out of his sock."

"You're sure it's marijuana?"

As sure as I am that you're a liberal mother fucker who's as stupid as a baseball that's just been fouled off. "I tested it. It's grass."

"*You* tested it?"

Tony sipped hot, vanilla nut coffee. He was beyond annoyed. "Nothing says that I can't test it."

Archer crossed then uncrossed his legs. "I understand you have to turn in a regular court report?"

Tony nodded. "Correct."

"Are you going to burn the kid?"

That was the third strike. "I don't think I heard you. Did you just ask me if I'm going to 'burn' Brown?"

"I did."

"Let me explain something to you." Tony's temperature was rising at an alarming rate. "You, my friend, are not an attorney. You are an overpaid monitor who sneaks up on people and takes notes and then twists those notes to fit his liberal existence. I am enforcing an order of the court by preparing the periodic evaluations attesting to James Brown's academic and behavior history here at JFK. 'Burn' the kid, my ass. I'm completing an anecdotal record of his performance both academically and behaviorally. To do anything less, to do anything less than accurate, could place me in contempt of court. It could cost me my job and my badge." Tony deliberately turned away from Archer, who loosened his red tie. "Your move."

"I think we need to look at the entire picture. This child could well end up in an adult facility because of your 'anecdotal evidence.'"

"This almost-adult could end up in prison because he chose to fracture the fucking law and violate FLACOE policy. I'll go back to what I said to you a long time ago. Why aren't we more interested in how that shit enters JFK?"

Archer decided to back out of the batter's box and take a breath. "If I asked you to cut the kid a break, would you?"

Tony didn't hesitate. "Not on your life. You're asking me to do everything I hold close on the line for someone who intentionally violated the law."

Archer shook his head. He squinted. He drew a deep breath, a very deep breath. "I know you and I don't see eye-to-eye on these kids and how we treat them. I understand that. This kid's life could well depend on this one situation, this one mistake."

Tony thought of that fucking pen falling. "When does this kid start to accept responsibility for his actions? There have to be consequences for CONTINUED negative behavior. If I drive at eighty-five on the freeway and continually get pulled over and the cop continues to give me a break, I'm going to continue to do eighty-five on that damn freeway. On the other hand, if I get a couple of tickets and my insurance goes up, up, and up, and I eventually have my license suspended, I may learn to drive like a sane person and in the long run, save someone's life." Tony held up his hands. "Does that make any kind of sense?"

"This is not about a damn driver's license. This is about a kid's future going up in smoke. It may seriously be his last chance in life."

"He keeps playing with matches, he's going to eventually start a major fire. Only he has the hose to douse the flames."

"I want you to turn a blind eye to his situation."

"Tell that to his judge."

"I'm telling it to you. You do not, I repeat, you do not want to force my hand."

Tony wanted to tell him to get the fuck out of his office in the worst way. Instead, he stared at him the way he and LT would sometime stare at each other playfully. Tony wiped his lips with his hands. "Are you threatening me, Cleveland?"

Archer came back without hesitation. "Let me remind you, you serve at the pleasure of the Board of Education."

"Let me remind *you,* I have an order from a presiding judge. If you're asking me who I'd rather have fuck me in the ass, the Board or the judge, the answer is neither. If I'm not going to bend over for either of them, why the fuck do you think I'll take it up the ass for you?"

Archer rubbed his hands together. "I can usually get through to most people. I understand you think you're standing on correct convictions. In this case, you're not. You're going to do major harm to Brown and to yourself. How about you think about it for an hour, and I'll come back?"

Tony could have both reports done in an hour. His answer wasn't about to change. If, in the court report, he failed to mention the grass, he could be held accountable for an 'error of omission.' He could be held in contempt. More importantly, his badge could be on the line. Archer was so far off base that he could be picked off. The only thing backing him was that Corrections and the Board of Supervisors didn't want to fuck with the ACLU. Actually, neither did Tony, but Archer had backed him against the wall. Tony fought back hard, fast, and dirty when cornered. It was called survival.

"My answer won't change in an hour. But suit yourself. I know an education reporter for the *Los Angeles Times;* I may give him a call." Tony actually did know the *Times'* education reporter. Whether or not he wanted to take on the ACLU, the Corrections Board, and the Supervisors was another question.

"Are you threatening me?"

"I'm enlightening you. JFK is a place for education, for reform, and for growth. I think in the last half an hour, we both got a piece of all three." Tony turned his back on Archer. He started stroking the computer keyboard. Over his shoulder, Tony said, "See you an hour." What he didn't say aloud was, *you asshole.*

Tony not only had both reports completed before Archer returned to his office, but he had time to attach a picture of the "oregano" to both reports. He also had time to fax a copy of both reports to Probation and to fax both reports to the requesting judge of the juvenile court, and then copy Paula and Eddie via email. All this before Cleveland Archer made a second appearance at Tony's office door.

Tony was sipping a second cup of vanilla nut coffee when his phone rang. It was Paula. "I received an urgent call from Cleveland Archer a few minutes ago. Do you want to tell me what's going on?"

Tony didn't answer right away. He wanted to piss Paula off more than he wanted to think about his answer. He decided to fire a fastball. "One of our finest got nailed with enough marijuana stuffed in his sock to get everyone in his dorm higher than Charlie Sheen and one of his hooker friends. Archer wants me to bury the situation. I told him that I am under a court directive to send in a regular court report, and an additional report highlighting any out-of-the-ordinary action. In the middle of last month, I sent in a report noting student Brown's academic excellence for the semester. Archer wants me to let this go. I can't. The court would have my cute little ass."

"Is there any way you can...ugh...'modify' the report? Cleveland seems to think the kid's future depends on this situation."

"Archer is grandstanding, Paula. He made it a pissing contest. I'm locked in. Do you really want me to screw with the court?"

"Can you call the court and request to speak with the judge verbally?"

Tony smiled. "Too late. The paper's already in the mail. (Actually, it was already faxed and emailed). As a matter of fact, if you check your email, you have a copy of both reports."

He wanted to ask Paula if Archer was doing her or if she was blowing him or both. They were both too fucking cozy.

"You already sent the judge the paperwork?"

Tony was now enjoying this. "And a picture of the marijuana in Brown's possession."

"Why didn't you talk with me before you did that?"

Tony reminded Paula, "I don't ask your permission before I send the judge a positive on Brown. I didn't see any reason to do so."

"You're causing problems, Tony. Major problems. We're trying to do everything we can to get the ACLU to sign off on the memorandum and leave. This may well protract the situation."

"Where are the kids in the standing, Paula? If they know we covered for one, which has been done in the past, they know they can get away with it. Isn't it about time we cracked down at the source?"

There was silence on the other end of the phone. That was a plus because Tony was trying to decide whether or not to tell Paula about Brown's accusation of a PO dealing him the grass.

Paula's tone changed. "I guess what's done is done. But understand, there will be serious repercussions."

Tony didn't want to threaten Paula with the *L.A. Times* education reporter. Tony's best guess was that Archer had already been there and done that.

"Where's the Brown boy now?"

"He's on a three-day school suspension. I met with Brown and his PO. I'm guessing they took him to SHU so he can attend school and not miss out on his credits." Then Tony added, "If he isn't too high to concentrate on his academics."

"Damn, damn, damn, Tony! You keep starting fires and I keep putting them out."

Tony wanted to tell her what he really thought. If she'd play the game by the rules, if she'd stop locking all the skeletons in the closet, maybe JFK could really make progress. Until you dealt with teachers who showed porn to kids, teachers who pushed books into kids' faces, staff who handed out drugs, nothing was going to change; in fact, it would mushroom, and it was, and the mushrooms were poisonous. If you backed your teachers when kids threatened them, jerked off in front of them, threw things at them in class, teachers might be able to teach. Until then, the classroom would continue to be as crazy as the mass teen fights in the many Malls across the country. Without classroom discipline, teachers cannot teach; maximum education cannot take place.

Tony couldn't help himself. His mouth opened and out it came. "If we're done here, I have another fire I have to start."

Archer never did come back to Tony's office. Tony's best guess was that Cleveland Archer received a phone call from Paula who told him that Tony had filed his reports. End of story. Except it wasn't. The battle had just begun (only Tony did not know it) and the real war was in the wind.

More Decisions

After school, Tony called Mickey who had a scheduled day off. "How about I buy dinner tonight? I need to talk to you. Will Tammy give you a pass tonight?"

"I'm sure she'd love to get out of cooking dinner. She's packing and planning, so that works out well. Where and when?"

"How about Lenny's in the Mall? It's quiet in there. We can talk."

"Six work?"

"Six is fine."

"Is this about Carina?"

"No. That is what it is. Somebody said, if you love someone, set them free. If they come back, then it was meant to be. If they don't, move on. Or something like that."

"Do you love her?"

"I guess. But I think that relationship is doomed because of my police work, which may be doomed because of a couple of male sluts and a reserve who can't drive for shit."

"So, what's this all about?"

"We'll talk about it at Lenny's. I need an ear and some advice."

"See you at six."

Tony was naked and just about to hop into the shower when the phone rang. He almost didn't answer it. It was Yolis. "How's the sexiest cop in southern California?"

"Only southern California? What about the rest of the state?"

Tony was laughing. "What's up, beautiful?"

"Just checking up on you."

"You caught me at a great time. I was just about to get into the shower."

“Hey, there’s a water shortage. How about I join you?”

“Babe, if you were here, I’d gladly take you up on that. Do your handcuffs rust in water?”

Yolis was laughing. “Not if I dry them off when I take them off. How are you doing, for real?”

“It feels like the whole world is coming down on my head. If it’s not one thing, it’s another. Mickey and I are going to meet for dinner. I needed someone to talk to. I seriously need a sounding board. I got myself in a ‘situation’ at work.”

“You mean Corrections?”

“Yeah. I went against the wishes of the ACLU who have taken over the facility, and I think things are about to get ugly. Next day off, if you’ll spend the day with me, we can talk about it.”

“I’d love to spend the day with you. How about the night?”

“That’ll work. Listen, sweet pea, let me jump in the shower so I’m not late to meet Mickey.”

“Think about me while you’re soaping up. And then think about how unlucky you are that it’s not my hand soaping you up. You could have me and the bar of soap instead of Nurse Little Suzie and her four sisters.”

Tony was again laughing. Yolis was damn good therapy.

“Thank you, babe. Just hearing your voice is soothing, seriously.”

“I know. All the guys I arrest in HP tell me that, babe. Behave yourself. And watch what you get on that soap.”

Mickey was seated at a rear booth with his back against the wall when Tony walked in. Mickey was on his cell. “My son just walked in. See you later, angel.” Mickey put the cell phone back in his pocket as Tony slid into the seat across from Mickey.

“Tammy says hello.”

“Thanks, Dad.” Tony was still thinking about Yolis and the comment about the soap. He was careful not to leave any telltale signs on it.

The waitress brought two menus. “Can I get you gentlemen something to drink?”

They both ordered coffee. Tony added, "I'll have an ice water with the coffee, please."

When the waitress left, Mickey asked, "What's up?"

"I need a sounding board. I think I got my ass in a bind at work and with the ACLU." Tony related what had happened.

"Bringing that shit into the facility is a crime. It's actually a wobbler. It could go down as a misdemeanor or a felony."

"I know that. But aside from the fact that it's a crime, the kids have a right to an education and the teachers have a right to teach. This shit has been coming into the facility for longer than women have been allowed to vote. Corrections covers it up, and it's not the only bullshit Corrections sweeps under the carpet. This was the bullet that blew out the tire. I can't...I won't deal with it anymore. So, I did what I did." Tony couldn't stop talking. It was finally all coming out. "If a PO is bringing this shit into the facility, he needs to be buried."

The waitress brought their drinks, then she took their order.

"Is your job on the line?"

"I don't know that they'd actually have the balls to fire me. If they did that, there's nothing stopping me from going to the newspapers which I already threatened to do. It's more likely they'll threaten me with 'freeway therapy'; move me as far away from my house as they can. Make me hit the freeways at commuter travel times where it could take me two hours to get to work and another two to get home, not to mention the gas and the wear and tear on my Vette."

Mickey, who was listening intently, shook his head. "What's done is done. You filed your reports. That's a done deal. The remaining question is how do you land on your feet? You don't have a union, do you?"

"No. Do you know a good attorney?" Tony sipped his coffee.

"A couple but not in your field. You probably need an education attorney, someone who specializes in educational law. But for now, nothing has happened."

"Yet." Carina taught Tony to always put yet at the end of a sentence and that Y-E-T stood for You're eligible, too. "What about hostile work environment? If I go after them and they come back at me, then I would think it's retaliation."

"That you'd have to run by an attorney. I have a suggestion. For example, the first thing you want to do is contact an attorney and see where you stand. Then you'll have a better idea of what course of action you have, if any."

Mickey was right on. "Like one step at a time?"

"You're a fast learner," Mickey kidded. "Sometimes God works in strange and mysterious ways. Maybe he's trying to tell you something."

"When did you get so spiritual?"

"Always have been. You've just been too busy busting criminals—and trying to decide if you want Carina permanently or you want to move on to Yolis—to notice. Nothing, my well-educated friend, happens in God's world by mistake. Nothing."

"The only thing I have to worry about is a damn job."

"I got that covered for you, too, buddy."

"How's that work?"

"You don't realize how well thought of you are at HP. They'll pick you up full time in a heartbeat. So, my second suggestion is that you get HR on the phone in the morning and see how much you get if you retire."

"I'm too young to retire. Besides, after my driving exhibition, do you think they'd take me?"

"Shit happens. They'll slap your hand and send you to EVOC again. Or, they may let Yolis teach you how to drive."

"And the horse you rode in on."

"Ye of little faith. In the Department, we can buy time. Does Corrections work the same way?"

Tony nodded. He hadn't thought of that. He would only need a couple of years. "I have over a year of sick time accumulated. I'd only have to buy back two years and I think CALSTRS would finance that."

"See that? I'm solving all your problems and I haven't billed you yet."

"Yes, you have. I'm buying dinner."

"But, if you call right now, I'll throw in a two-for-one bonus," Mickey joked. "Move to Florida with Tammy and me."

Tony had not given that a thought. He looked at Mickey. "Could you get me in a department?"

"Probably. But if you're seriously interested, I'll make a couple of calls in the next few days."

Tony was feeling better already. "I've got options. I thought I was doing the dead-man's float in the ocean. You brought me back to shore."

"We look out for one another. Think about it." Mickey suddenly looked serious. "Are you and Carina history?"

Tony shrugged. "I guess. What happened, happened suddenly. I wasn't expecting it. I guess she met someone else. I think the real problem is that I was rarely home. I think police work scares her. Being a cop, even a reserve, is tough for most women to handle. I can't say I blame them."

Mickey threw his hands in the air. "You didn't answer my question. Are you guys done?"

"I suppose. I'll call her and we'll talk."

"First things first," Mickey suggested. "Call the Corrections Office in the morning and I'll see if I can get ahold of an attorney who can help. I'm off tomorrow anyway."

"I'll take tomorrow off. I don't like doing that, but..."

"I wouldn't do that. Bad idea. After what went on, I wouldn't push my luck. You can do what you need to do from work. No sense stirring up more shit."

"I suppose you're right."

"Don't suppose. Of course, I'm right."

The waitress brought their food.

"Shut up and eat!"

On the short drive home, Tony thought about Mickey's suggestions. He was right on. Tony had to focus on one situation at a time. He couldn't do anything about the attorney until he heard back from Mickey. He couldn't do anything about the Corrections situation until he called Human Resources in the morning. He could call Carina to clarify that situation.

Tony parked the Pace Car in the garage. He walked into the house to a very happy LT, who jumped up on Tony. "My hero," Tony said. "I missed you, buddy." Tony walked over to a jar labeled LT and extracted one of Lieutenant's cookies. LT ran over to Tony and sat by his side. Tony put the very edge of the cookie between his lips and knelt down. Gently, LT took the cookie from Tony's lips. "Good boy. Good boy."

Tony went upstairs to his library which doubled as his computer room. It boasted a wall-to-ceiling bookcase that held many of his college and university books and some of his police memorabilia. He sat down at the computer table. He picked up his cell phone and called Carina.

Tony doubted he'd get an answer. She was probably out. Tony was wrong. She picked up on the third ring. "How are you? It's Tony."

"I know who it is. I'm good. How about you?"

"Weathering all the bullshit. But I've got wide shoulders. I manage to land on my feet." Tony had to ask. "Got a few minutes to talk?"

"I'm alone, if that's what you mean. And yes, I'll always have time for you."

"This is awkward for me." LT walked into the library and sat down next to Tony. He put his left arm around LT's neck. "I guess I'm curious about what happened to us."

"I know. And I'm sorry for the way it happened. I don't think you and I have a future. You're away from home more than you're home. The police work frightens me, Tony. Cops are getting killed every week, sometimes every day. When you go to work, it scares me. I went on a ride-along thinking that might help. It made it worse. Do you know how dangerous your job is?"

"I love it."

"I see that. I saw it in your eyes and your face when I rode with you. I think you love police work more than you love..." Carina didn't finish the sentence.

"I understand. I really do. I just want you to know that I'll always be here for you."

"And me for you. Promise you'll keep in touch, and I'll do the same."

The call was short and sweet and nowhere near as painful as Tony thought it might be. After he hung up, Tony looked at his watch. He turned to LT. "Let's go watch *Cops*." Tony grabbed the remote and turned on the television. He sat down on the couch and LT jumped up next to Tony. They were just in time to hear, *"Whatcha gonna do when they come for you...?"*

***

It was Wednesday, and unusually hot and dry in the Antelope Valley. It was a minimum school day as it was every Wednesday for FLACOE Education Students. The kids were out of school at noon. Following lunch, the teachers either had meetings, used the time to do lesson plans or grade papers, or they snuck out early. Tony used the time to call Human Resources. He was packing up to get out of Dodge when his cell phone rang. The Dragnet ringtone told Tony it was Mickey. "You have the right to remain silent," Tony said into the phone before Mickey could say a word.

"I want my lawyer."

"So do I."

"I'll show you mine, if you show me yours."

"Go."

"I got the names of three attorneys who are waiting to talk to you. I don't want to send them through your school email, so I sent them to your home email. Did you have a chance to call HR?"

Tony swiveled in his chair. He looked out his office window at the hot desert sun. "I sure did. It's better than I thought. I can buy two years and retire. I won't get what I'd get if I hung in to 65 but, if I cash in now and take a full-time police position, I'll be in damn good shape. I might even be able to buy you and Tammy dinner when you come back to L.A. to visit."

"And if you move to Florida, your pension isn't taxed. No state tax in sunny Florida."

"Just fucking hurricanes, swampland, and freakin' alligators. Did the attorneys have anything positive to say?"

"The fact that they want to talk with you is positive. It can't hurt to run it past them. They call it a freebee. Anything new on your end?"

Tony turned off his computer. "Scary quiet, like the calm before the rampage."

"I gotta get off the phone. I've got to shower, shave, and hit the freeway. Duty calls. If all's quiet in the city, I'll give you a call from patrol."

Tony stood up and walked to the door. "Thanks, Mickey, as always. Even though you rarely hear it from me, I appreciate the hell out of you and all you do for me."

"Don't get mushy on me. Save that for Yolis. She's waiting. Bye."

When Tony arrived home, he and LT went out to the block-walled backyard. They played catch with a tennis ball for half an hour. Tony would throw the ball off the back wall and LT would go nuts trying to play the ball off the wall. He looked a little like Matt Kemp trying to play the carom off the Dodge Stadium wall before he was traded. The only difference was that LT had a better sense of where the ball would land once in hopped off the wall.

"Damn, LT, you're good. Now that you've worked up an appetite, how about dinner?"

LT knew the word dinner. His tail started moving back and forth like a crack addict's hands, anxiously awaiting his overdue fix. After dinner they curled up together on the couch in front of the big screen, to watch two reruns of *Two and a Half Men*. It wasn't LT's favorite show. He fell asleep with his head in Tony's lap and snored loudly enough that Tony had to turn up the sound. Tony fell asleep in the middle of the second episode.

At work, on his lunch hour, Tony called the first of the three attorneys who were on the list that Mickey had given him, Ray Bestuss, a Beverly Hills attorney. They had quite a chat. The upshot was, in the opinion of the attorney, that Tony's civil rights might (and the key word was might) be violated if they terminated him. There were several mitigating factors. The attorney did not see a nexus between Tony's assistant principal position and his reserve police officer work at HPPD.

The attorney also told Tony that since his FLACOE evaluations were excellent, they would have to come up with a solid reason for punching Tony's ticket. Finally, the attorney suggested that, if they did threaten to fire Tony, for a fee, the attorney would make a phone call to Corrections on Tony's behalf.

Tony liked what the attorney had to say. He liked the fact that the lawyer was willing to move ahead. He felt better after that phone call, which was good, because the other two attorneys felt Tony's case was iffy at best, that basically Tony was an at-will employee, and the Corrections Board had a right to let him go because they 'lost faith in his ability to perform.' In Tony's mind, that was bullshit. Both those attorneys, at least the way Tony read it, were at least non-committal until Tony mentioned ACLU. Then the tone changed. In Tony's mind, it was more likely that the bastards were afraid to tangle with the freakin' American Civil Liberties Union.

At least he had one lawyer who might be willing to take a crack at his case and shake up Corrections. Tony punched in 'Ray Bestuss' on the computer.

Are the HP Reserves in the History Books? Is Yolis History?

Tony called Mickey from his house. "Hey, what's up?"

"I'm on my way to work. What's going on with you?"

"I spoke with all three attorneys. It sounds like two of the three are afraid of the ACLU. That's my assessment. The Beverly Hills lawyer, Ray Bestuss, is willing to talk to Corrections on my behalf, for a fee. That's a positive. Have you heard anything about the reserves?"

"Nothing definite. Rumor has it that the reserves will soon be history in HP. I haven't seen Tuesday night's City Council agenda and I doubt it would be on the agenda this soon; but if they're going to kill you guys, it will be up to the Council."

"I've made calls to a couple of other departments. I could probably get in elsewhere. At this point, and after getting sage advice from my sometimes partner, my options would be to join another department's reserves, go full time, or quit playing cop altogether."

"Sounds like college boy is finally studying."

"I've been studying hard, and I've been listening to my instructor. I scratched off quit copping. I don't want to give it up."

"Good. That leaves you to find another department that will pick you up as a reserve or go full time."

"School police is looking but that wouldn't give me the adrenalin rush I need." Tony laughed at his own comment.

"Have you talked this over with Yolis?"

Tony looked at the phone with a questioning glance. "What's with you and Yolis? You keep bringing her up?"

"I think the two of you make a cute couple."

"Seriously?"

"Seriously."

"I got other concerns right now."

"Who said Yolis is a concern? Not only is she quite a cop, but she's also a sweetheart with morals, principles, and an eye on the future. She's a helluva catch." Mickey paused. "I'm pulling into the Station lot. I'll call you later."

Shortly after Tony got home, he changed into sweats. He and LT got into the Vette, and Tony drove to Sgt. Steve Owens Park where they went for a jog on the track. LT outlasted him. No surprise to Tony. No surprise to the Lieutenant.

When they got home, he fed LT and jumped in the shower. The phone rang while he was drying himself off with a large, soft, blue beach towel. "Mickey, don't you ever work?"

Mickey chuckled. "I am working but I had to call you. I'm in the parking lot on Rita south of Saturn. The lot on the west side of the street. A citizen found your boy Gonzo. He's no longer a wit against you. They found him hanging from a tree. Guess what was in his mouth?"

"It sure wasn't pussy."

"They cut his dick off and stuffed in his mouth; a warning to other gangbangers—don't rat a brother out."

"I guess you lucked out."

"Fuck him. If I'm supposed to feel sorry for the little wetback prick, uh...former wetback prick, I don't. He had it coming. I won't have nightmares over that one. The community is a helluva lot safer with Gonzo off the streets," Tony swallowed. "Do me a favor. Did they cut him down yet?"

"Nope. The coroner may make it by midnight if we're lucky."

"Great. Get me a picture. A full-body picture if you can. I want to frame it and put it in my living room."

"You never stop amazing me. How can one guy, as educated as you are, be as fucked up as you are?"

"Ask God."

"Hang on. God's here and she wants to talk to you."

"This is God, Tony. Don't screw with me."

"Cute. Are you keeping your good eye on Mickey?"

Yolis said, "I'm keeping both eyes on you. I'm off Thursday. I'm driving out your way and I'm taking you to dinner. Find a place, and if we need reservations, make them. I'm bringing my toothbrush and I won't be wearing panties. Do you understand those rights as I read them to you?"

"Yes, God. Or is it 'Goddess'?"

"Whichever you prefer."

"I prefer Goddess."

"Then I'll bring my pink handcuffs." That was followed quickly by, "Gotta go. The suits are here. Thursday, reservations. Underwear, for you, is optional; so is Viagra."

Tony sat at his desk pounding the computer keyboard writing a letter of recommendation for one of his top-notch substitute teachers who was applying for a full-time teaching position with FLACOE. It was nerve-rackingly quiet at JFK. Tony was waiting for the other bookend to fall off the desk. Archer, Paula, the director—someone—was sure as hell going to reach out to him and slap him up the side of his head. It had to happen. It was as sure as sunshine in the summer in the desert.

But there were still more storms on the horizon. Mother Nature, Corrections and its players, and the City of Hollow Point and its suits were not finished raining on Tony's parade.

Tony smiled. With his head turned to K-SHIT, with the pressure coming down all around him, with the possibility of being out of work, Tony was still smiling. The smile was broad. It started when he awoke at 0530 hours.

Following his workout, feeding LT, and playing briefly with him, taking a shower and shaving, Tony put on a freshly pressed blue suit, a monogrammed white-on-white French-cuffed shirt, a blue-and-white tie with a picture of Donald Duck on it, then smiled as he looked at himself in the bathroom mirror. Not bad for someone who was fighting the world. Maybe Carina's advice and maybe Mickey's spirituality had gotten into Tony's head.

That was part of it. Possibly a big chunk of it. He was learning to deal with his situation one problem at a time, doing the footwork, and letting go of the results. The results were not his business. He couldn't control how others handled what might or might not come down.

The biggest factor in Tony's attitude, he was certain, was Yolis. He was like a dog waiting for the cellophane to be peeled off the bone he was about to chomp on. He wanted to spend time with Yolis, time away from HP—just the two of them.

Tony thought about her crack about Viagra. Tony did have a bottle. The container held twenty 100 milligram pills. He could stay hard for hours with one of those pills. When he and Carina really felt like a marathon love-making session, he would pop one of those babies and off they'd go. There wasn't a room in the house that wouldn't have their love-making seal of approval on it. Maybe he'd pop a blue pill, maybe.

It was Thursday evening and Tony was already seated at a booth in the rear of Charlie's Steak House, in Acton, about 12 miles from his house. He was sipping a 7 and 7, enjoying the soft country music, and eyeballing the customers. Surprisingly, his mind was not tuned to K-SHIT. It was tuned to K-YOLIS.

The more Tony thought about his options, the better he liked them. Maybe it was time to move on. He had lived in California for over thirty years. He built a decent retirement, made it through the police academy, attended universities in California, and... He realized that if he moved out of California, he and Yolis would be history. Hell, he didn't even know her first name, but that was about to change. She had promised Tony that when they spent their first night together, she would tell him.

He had no control over what action, if any, Corrections would take. Tony did what he felt was the right thing to do. That's what mattered most.

He eyed Yolis as she walked toward the table. She was dressed in white blouse that hugged her chest, black slacks, and black boots. Beaming, she slid into the seat next to Tony, handing him something wrapped in colorful giftwrap, but not boxed.

"A little something for your collection."

"Is it safe to open here?"

Yolis placed her hand on Tony's thigh. He could feel the heat her hand generated through his suit pants. She looked around. "Sure."

Tony felt the package. It was soft. "It's not boxed."

"That comes later."

He shrugged, then tore into the wrap. It was a pair of Yolis' black-lace panties. He laughed.

"The ones I wore all day today thinking about you, about us. They're probably still damp."

Tony felt himself blushing. His face was hot. He rubbed his red tie. He guessed his face was almost as red as the tie. "You're crazy."

"You ain't seen nothing yet."

Tony put the black panties in his side pocket. He wanted to sniff the scent, Yolis' scent, but that would be a bit obvious in the restaurant. "How about a drink?"

"What are you drinking?"

"Seagram's and 7."

"I'll have the same."

The waiter walked over. Tony ordered a drink for Yolis and another for himself. Before the waiter left, he placed a green candle in the middle of the table and lit it.

"It's hot enough in here," Tony said, "without starting a fire."

"I'm hoping to get it hotter."

"How's HP?"

"It's still there. It hasn't changed. But the reserve program may change soon from what I'm hearing. But nothing for sure yet."

"What will you do if they dump the reserve program?"

"Mickey and I discussed that. I do have a couple of options. If HP will have me, I could call it quits with Corrections and go full time. I could find another department that is looking for reserves. I could move to Florida with Mickey and his wife and join his department. As my coach, he tells me to take it slow and easy and one step at a time. That's sage advice."

"Do you own your home?"

"I make payments. The bank owns it. But I'm an owner not a renter, if that's what you mean."

"You'd have to sell the house before you could move?" That was a question.

"I could rent it. The rent would more than cover the mortgage. That would give me an investment property. I'd have to get a property manager to keep an eye on things. Again, one step at a time."

The waiter brought their drinks. Yolis picked up her glass. "To change."

They clinked glasses. "I'll drink to that."

After dinner, they drove to the mall and walked around window shopping and holding hands trying to walk off dinner. An hour later they were in their cars. Yolis followed Tony to his house. She pulled her BMW next to his Vette in the driveway.

"We're in a good area but let me open the garage. You can pull in next to me."

"No automatic garage-door opener?"

"I hate those damn things. They have a habit of breaking. Besides, sometimes that's all the exercise I get that day. Let me run in the house and open the garage."

LT met Tony at the door. He gave him a quick rub, closed the door that led from the house to the garage, and opened the garage door. Tony pulled the Pace Car in first, then guided Yolis and her black BMW next to the Vette. He helped her out of the door.

"Aren't we the gentleman!"

"Actually, I didn't want to scratch the Vette when you opened the door."

"That's one. I'm keeping score. You will pay for that." She looked around the garage. "I like that. 'Pace Car Parking Only.'"

The sign hung on the beam in front of his car. "You need to get one that reads 'BMW Parking Only,'" she added.

Tony hesitated, grinned, then said, "That depends on how good you are. And remember, you promised to tell me your first name."

"That depends on how good you are."

He took her hand. "We've got company."

"Who?"

"Lieutenant."

Yolis looked puzzled. Tony led her to the door. LT was standing just inside the door and startled Yolis. "Yolis, meet LT. Lieutenant, meet Yolis. You'll know her by her first name in the morning."

LT sat. Yolis bent down. "He's gorgeous."

"Say hello properly, LT."

LT held out his paw. Yolis took it and shook it. "He has better manners than you."

"I know. He trained me. But he's a faster learner."

"You're going to get hair all over you so there are lint rollers all over the house. They work very well."

"What kind of dog is he?"

"A Norwegian Elkhound. They're born and bred in Brooklyn." Tony led Yolis to the couch in the downstairs living room.

"Seriously."

"I'm kidding. They're from Norway. They're hunting dogs."

"They hunt New Yorkers?"

"Actually, Moose and Elk. We have a couple of crows who like to screw with LT when he's out playing in the backyard. They dive-bomb him and he goes crazy chasing them. He has access to the backyard through a doggie door. I was eating breakfast one morning while he was out in the back. All of a sudden, he came charging into the house, jumped on the couch, and placed a crow on the couch for his proud papa."

"He killed the crow?"

"I don't know how the hell he caught it, but he did. What they do is shake it and it snaps their neck. The other crow was long gone." As they were seated on the couch, LT was lying between their feet. "Can I get you a drink?"

"Half."

"What do you want?"

"7 and 7 would be great."

Tony made their drinks, handing one to Yolis, and giving LT a cookie. He pulled the cocktail table close to them, threw coasters on the table, and sat next to Yolis. After he put his drink down, he reached in his suit jacket pocket and pulled out Yolis' black panties. He dangled them in front of her. Then he buried his nose in the crotch and inhaled. "Wow. I never smelled cop underwear before! I love it."

Yolis was redder than a traffic light. "You're one sick puppy, you know that."

"I'm a sick puppy? Who gave me her sexy, black, lacy, hard-on-making, wet panties?"

Tony held up his glass. "I think we're a match. Here's to sick puppies." They tapped glasses. She took a sip. Tony took a sip. LT barked, his tail wagging. "He likes you."

"Let's take this party upstairs." Tony stood up. He extended his hand to Yolis. "LT, you stay down here, please."

LT looked at Tony. His tail was wagging but his brown eyes looked sad. "I know you want to watch but not on the first date. I'll make it up to you tomorrow. We'll watch porn."

"How the hell did you pass a department psych?"

"Two department psychs."

"Two?"

"I took the written, then was singled out to take the one-on-one oral."

"In other words, they almost found out that you're crazy?"

They walked up the carpeted stairs.

"Almost."

"Bathroom"

"There are two. One around the corner and one here in the master bedroom. Take your pick."

Yolis started to walk out of the bedroom. "Why don't you use my panties to get yourself hard? I'll be back before my panties are any wetter." She sipped her half-empty 7 and 7 then walked to the bathroom. Tony began to undress.

Yolis came back from the bathroom. She was wearing the prettiest tan west of Florida. Tony was wearing only his tighty-whities.

"Put your head on the pillow. Face me and relax. I've dreamed of this moment for long, long time. I've had a thing for you for a long, long time." She looked at his crotch and pulled down his pants. "It looks like you've had a thing for me for a long, long time."

Tony blushed. She had already gotten him rock hard, sans Viagra. He put his hands behind his head. Yolis climbed on the bed and straddled Tony. Tony started to move his hands.

"Don't move. Keep your hands behind your head and don't move," she ordered. "This is my show for now. You'll have your time when I tell you. Clear?"

"Yes, Officer. Perfectly clear."

Yolis kissed each side of his face lightly. She tongued first his left ear then his right. Slowly, she moved down to Tony's chest. He wasn't hairy, neither was he smooth. She stopped to nibble on each nipple.

"Damn." Tony squirmed.

"You have the right to remain silent." She bit gently, teasingly on first one nipple, then the other. She was driving Tony crazy. She loved it. Tony was on a pink cloud.

She tongued his midsection, working her way slowly down to his belly button. Tony grew harder. Yolis smiled, feeling his erection on her left arm. "I thought you left your nightstick in the unit?"

She worked her way lower. Her right hand reached up squeezing Tony's left nipple then rubbing the nipple with thumb and finger. Her mouth found Tony's manhood. She kissed it. Her left hand worked its way under Tony's butt. Her talented tongue licked Tony's raging hard-on. Up and down the shaft, top, bottom, sides. She worked ninety percent of it into her mouth and halfway down her throat. Tony was going absolutely crazy.

"When I get finished with you, there won't be a woman around you'll want more than me. You can take that before a judge!"

Her thumb and finger applied more pressure to Tony's nipple. Her left hand played with Tony's ass until her finger found the opening she was looking for. "Few men will admit they like this," she whispered working just the tip of one long finger into his hole. "Most men love it."

She worked that finger around his anus opening while she licked and sucked his engorged dick. She licked it like it was a lollipop and she was a child determined not to let one lick go to waste.

Just when Tony thought he couldn't hold back any longer, Yolis stopped. She smiled, laughed slowly, and slid down to his toes. "One little piggy..." She sucked one toe then the other until she had sucked all ten. She noticed Tony's rock-hard penis had lost some of its stiffness. "Rollover, big boy. I have to search you for contraband."

Tony obeyed gladly. His face was in the pillow.

She started at the very top of his head and tongued her way down to his feet, slowly, teasingly, excitingly. When Tony couldn't take any more, he rolled over and sat up. "My turn. On your stomach."

Yolis was as naked as Alaska is cold in the winter. She obeyed without hesitation.

Tony kissed the sides of her neck then worked his way down her back. He stopped to tease each ass cheek with his mouth and tongue, running his tongue in between the cleavage.

"Oh, that is so unfair, but it feels so, so good."

Tony reached a hand under and between her legs. He felt Yolis' wetness, her warmth, her womanhood. He felt her convulse. He slid a finger inside her but not deep. He slowly, gently, slid it out. He tasted it. He loved the scent, the taste, the joy she was feeling as he teased and caressed her.

Finally, he rolled Yolis over. He licked her toes then worked his way up between her thighs. He tasted her; she was delicious. He didn't know how much more he could take. He wondered how much she could take.

His mouth met hers. His lips tasted hers. His tongue danced with hers. It was fire and passion. He had never made love with a woman before with so much passion, so much energy, so much feeling.

He mounted. Slowly, he slid inside her. The two of them were one. She was warm, wet, wild. Her fingernails raked his back. His toes played with her toes. He was now deep inside her. She was tight. It was beyond belief. She was right. He probably never would want another woman after this experience. It wasn't sex; it was so much more.

Tony squeezed her nipples. She smiled. Her brown eyes were glazed. He wrapped his hand around hers. He went deeper until his body was in the air. He couldn't go any deeper. "I'm going to come."

"I already did. Twice. The third time's the charm."

"Jesus!" Tony yelled, as he could hold back no longer. "Jesus!"

"I'm coming with you. I am. I am." Her whole body shook. He held her tight. When he caught his breath and had some control over his senses again, Tony said, "You're an animal. A gorgeous, loving animal."

"And you're a stud; my handsome, loving stud. I think we make great partners."

Tony was still gasping for breath. He rolled over, pulling her close, very close. "You're amazing."

"I'd promote you to captain, if I could."

"LT wouldn't like that. He's the boss in this house." Tony kissed Yolis on the mouth. "And now I get to know your first name."

They fell asleep in each other's arms before Yolis could reveal her first name. It didn't matter; he didn't care any more about the name.

He didn't care anymore that Carina had screwed around on him. Finally, there was a ray of sunshine poking its head through the clouds.

The sunshine would not last long.

Yolis awoke first. Tony awoke when she kissed him. "Hey, babe, how do you feel?"

"Like a cop who just took a bank robber into custody. I feel great," he said.

"Me, too." She took Tony's hand and held it between her breasts. "It's Yolanda."

Tony tried to clear his head. "I'm confused."

"Good sex does that to you, huh?"

"It wasn't good sex; it was dynamite sex! If I said it was the best I ever had, you'd think I was full of it."

"No, I wouldn't. I'm all that and a Glock with an extended mag. I know that." Yolis smiled.

"So, what's with Yolanda?"

"You wanted to know my first name. It's Yolanda."

"Yeah, I got that. But why hide it?"

"Yolanda Yolis. Think about that for a minute."

Tony thought about it. "You drained my brain."

"I knew I drained something, but I didn't think that it was your brain. What are the first two letters of my first name?"

"Y-O."

"The first two letters of my last name?"

"Y-O."

"Yo Yo. I went through school being called Yo Yo. I hated the hell out of it. So, I went by Yolis when I got older. I'm a female in a male-dominated profession. I take enough shit. Can you imagine if the guys got a hold of my first name?"

"I see your point." Tony grinned. "Yo-yos aren't the only thing that goes up and down." Tony grabbed Yolanda's hand and put it between his legs, then on his rising manhood. "Play with that for a while. See how many times you can make it go up and down."

Tony was awake before daylight. Yolanda was still asleep, sound asleep. He left a note, threw on clothes, backed the Vette out of the garage and headed to his first of two stops. The second stop was Starbucks.

Yolis was still asleep when Tony got back to the house. He walked up the stairs quietly, but not quietly enough. "Hey, welcome to the world of the living."

"Where'd you go?"

"Thought you might like Starbucks."

"Damn. Not only is he dynamite in bed, but he also gets me coffee in the morning. You just might be a keeper."

"I'd better be. Here. This will wake you up." Tony handed her the coffee. "And a little something to remember me by." Tony handed her a gift-wrapped box.

She put down the coffee. "If what's in this box is what I think it is, smart ass, you better never again trust your little pee-pee in my big mouth."

"Open it. I've got to shower and shave. Some of us have to work for a living."

Back at the Ranch—Both Ranches

Friday was the day Tony was certain the shit was going to hit the fan at JFK. Then, to make matters worse, the department might make a decision on the reserve program. Tony had a lot to think about. His head, however, was turned to K-YoYo. He could still feel Yolis on every part of his body. It felt like the gentle warmth of the sun was shining on each and every inch of him.

Every time the phone rang, Tony was sure he was going to be called into Eddie's office to discuss his future with Corrections, or lack of future. It didn't happen. Friday was one of the quietest days at JFK that Tony experienced in months. He was able to catch up on student meetings, on teacher and ancillary evaluations, on emails and phone calls. It was a quiet day. He even managed to find time to send flowers to Yolanda.

Tony headed to HP at 1605 hours. He was on the 14 freeway southbound just south of the 10th Street West exit when he glanced up in his rearview mirror. The familiar lights of the California Highway Patrol car behind him were beckoning Tony to pull the Vette over. He pulled to the shoulder, rolled down his window, and kept his hands on the steering wheel.

He watched the officer's approach in his rearview mirror. The guy was young, tall, trim, and neat looking in his tan uniform. He was all business when he approached Tony's window. "License, registration, and proof of insurance, please." He had his right hand on his gun.

Tony did not remove his hands from the steering wheel. He had been on the cop end of the stop thousands of times. He knew what to do and what not to do. "I'm a reserve police officer and I'm legally armed. I have a loaded Glock on my right hip and my ID in my inner-right suit-jacket pocket."

“Slowly, with your left hand, take out your ID. Keep your right hand on the wheel.” The CHP officer stepped back several inches and his grip tightened on his weapon. Approaching in the background, Tony observed another CHP car. Standard operating procedure when a gun is involved.

Tony, slowly, took his ID out of his suit-jacket pocket. He held it in his left hand, keeping his right hand on the steering wheel. The cop was cool; Tony was cool. Hopefully, he would be cool enough not to cite Tony who had absolutely no idea what speed he was doing. His mind was on Yolis.

“Take your license out and show it to me. Do you have any idea what speed you were doing?”

The second unit was pulling up behind the officer who initiated the stop. “No, sir. I don’t. I apologize. I was on my way home from work at the juvenile Probation camp on Stevens Boulevard and Lynn Court to HP for my shift. My mind was elsewhere. Again, sir, I apologize.”

He examined Tony’s license. “It must be nice to drive a bad-ass Corvette like this and, because you have a badge, you think you can break the traffic laws. Is that how it works?”

“Sir, no sir.” Tony observed a second CHP officer approaching.

“I love you guys. You get a few bucks ahead, you buy a nice car, you get some statutes, and you think the law doesn’t apply to you. Get the hell out of the car, NOW!”

Tony’s fuse was lit. It was burning down quickly.

“Keep your hands where I can see them. One furtive move and you’re toast.” Then he said with a smile, “See, I can use big words, too. I can’t spell ‘furtive,’ but I can say it.”

Tony thought he was probably taught the word in the CHP academy. Then he thought the guy was nuts. He got out of the Vette. Then he looked at the second officer.

Tony shook his head. “Fuck both of you. Do you smell that? You scared the shit out of me.”

The three stood on the shoulder laughing so hard there were tears streaming down Tony's face. The second CHP officer was Leonard Skipper. On his off days, he was a substitute teacher at JFK. He and Tony were friends.

"I spotted your Vette when you got on the freeway at Avenue I. I called Ron over here on my cell and told him to pull your ass over. Got you!! How's it going?"

"Same shit, different day. Some rough patches but nothing I can't handle. How about you?" Tony shook hands with Ron.

"Same old, same old." Then he turned to Ron. "This is the guy I told you about who went through the academy at 48. He was sworn in as a level-one reserve at 50. He's a good guy. Write him for seventy-four in a sixty-five. We'll cut him some slack."

"If either of you clowns ever drive through HP, I swear you'd better watch your rearview." Then as he got back in the car, Tony said, "One *FURTIVE* move and you're done." They high-fived each other and Tony was again on his way to HP.

Briefing was all but over. It was, for all purposes, over but briefing Sergeant Delgardo had yet to say, "Hit the streets, gentlemen and ladies, and watch your backs. We want you back here safely at end of shift."

Delgardo stepped away from the podium. "One last item. Two units are in the shop—one for a blown head gasket, another for a b/o radio. And I want to compliment all of you for not busting Farrina's chops about busting up an innocent unit. The result of that is that Farrina will be riding with Mickey tonight. Two reasons for that. We're short units as unit 198 is in the body shop for resurrection, and two, maybe Mickey can teach his former trainee how to fucking drive. With that, I have a suggestion. If you find yourself on the same street as Farrina, and he's driving, turn the fuck around even if you're on a one-way street!

"Now, get the hell out of here. First felony bust tonight gets breakfast on me. And don't go busting some poor bastard bum pushing a shopping cart and call it grand larceny. Be safe."

Tony was not a fan of the briefing Sergeant. Delgardo was fat, old, ugly, and did not like reserves. Which meant, if things went as Tony expected, soon Delgardo would just be fat, old, and ugly. Delgardo could go suck on his nightstick as far as Tony was concerned. He thought of the positive. He thought of Yolanda.

The skies over Hollow Point were dark and clear. There were stars in the sky. In Tony's forecast was rain with a few minutes of heavy downpour, but Tony had no idea.

Tony cleared the car while Mickey watched, talked about Tammy, Florida, and a new beginning. "I'm nervous about it but at the same time, I'm excited. I'm not one for change, but a big piece of me is looking forward to it."

"Did you get your Florida alligator hunting license yet?" Tony razzed.

Mickey blew a white cloud of cigarette smoke toward the HP sky. "No. Did you get your California driver's license yet?"

"Ooh! That stung. I'm going to turn the unit sheet into the WC. Finish that smoke 'cause you know there's no smoking in the unit. And I wouldn't want the smoke to obscure my vision." Tony started to walk toward the Station.

"Don't worry about your vision. I'm driving. I don't want you embarrassing me again."

Their first call was an anonymous call to dispatch. The caller stated she thought she had observed two young men climbing through a basement window of her neighbor's house. She also stated the neighbors were away on vacation and no one should be in the house. Dispatch added that the caller sounded HBD (has been drinking).

Mickey made a U-turn. He headed to the call. There were no units to back.

"We need to hire more officers. Seventy sworn officers don't cut it any more out here. These streets are too active," Tony said.

"True. But for now, I want you to watch how I drive. Between here and the call, I won't hit anything."

"You should have been a stand-up comedian. You're not rolling code, chasing some asshole."

Mickey was laughing. "Just messing with you, partner. It could have happened to any one of us." Then quickly he added, "But it happened to you."

Mickey turned off his lights. He rolled to a stop two houses south of the possible burglary. "Put us out, partner."

Tony keyed the mic. He put them out at the address dispatch had given them. Mickey and Tony had flashlights in their hand as they walked quietly to the house that might be occupied by two burglars. They walked around to the south side of the house. No windows, including basement windows, appeared out of the ordinary. The rear of the house checked secure. They came around to the back of the house on the north side. The three basement windows all checked secure. The first-floor windows were secure. The upstairs windows looked secure.

Tony got on his portable. "22 Adam," he whispered. "We checked the accessible perimeter. All appears secure. We're going to check the front door."

"Copy that, 22 Adam. Further from the original caller is that there is a front-door key in the flowerpot to the right of the front door."

"Copy." Mickey and Tony kept their flashlights pointed at the ground as they climbed cement steps to the porch. The flowerpot was observable and accessible. Tony felt inside the pot and immediately found the key.

Tony looked at Mickey. There was probable cause to enter the house. In one respect, he wished he had taken the time to find the neighbor who had contacted dispatch. However, if the burglars were, indeed, in the house, the time spent tracking down the neighbor might give them time to get away.

Mickey put his ear to the door. He heard nothing. He peered in the curtained window. He saw zip. Mickey looked at Tony and shook his head. No backup covering the back of the house. No dog. No airship. No shit. They had to do what they had to do. "22 Adam. We're entering the premises."

Mickey nodded to Tony. As gently as he could, Tony slid the key in the lock. He turned the key gingerly. He turned the door handle, and the door opened soundlessly.

Mickey nodded to Tony again. Mickey, Glock drawn at the low ready, entered the house. Tony was on Mickey's right, one step behind him. Mickey observed nothing amiss. Tony shined his light to his right. Everything appeared to be in place.

They took three more steps. Absolute quiet. Mickey shrugged. Tony shrugged back. Mickey heard the noise first. It sounded like footsteps upstairs and directly overhead.

Tony pointed to the steps. Immediately, Mickey shook his head. He pulled Tony toward the kitchen and out of sight in case the burglars, if they were burglars and not some damn cat, came down the stairs.

When they were in the kitchen and safely tucked away on either side of the kitchen entryway, Mickey said loudly, "All's quiet here. Guess the neighbor had one too many brewskis. Let's get the hell out of here. We've got three more calls stacked up."

Mickey slammed the kitchen door hard. They waited. Thirty seconds went by. Mickey raised his eyebrows. Tony motioned a 'what gives' sign with his hands.

Then they heard footsteps on the stairs. Then voices. "I told you cops are dumber than the handcuffs they carry. I told you we'd never get caught. We got a few thousand in jewelry and cops who are so stupid they'll kick themselves if they ever figure out that they were in the house the same time we were. Dumber than handcuffs."

They waited until they were halfway between the front door and the stairs, in no man's land. Mickey and Tony turned their flashlights on at the same instant. They had guns drawn, pointed, aimed and ready to put finger to trigger, if necessary. It was Mickey who spoke first. "This is your handcuffs speaking. If I don't see your hands, you're dead meat." One of the two Hispanic males dropped a shopping bag to the floor. "Don't shoot, man! Don't shoot! We're not carrying. Don't goddamn shoot."

"Get your asses on the floor. Face away from us. Keep your arms out to your side. Cross your legs at the ankle. Move, and I'll put a round in what little brain you have left, you dumb shits." They couldn't have been more than 20, but they were adults.

Mickey covered Tony who holstered his weapon. He cuffed one then searched him. He cuffed suspect two then searched him. They're both clean. Tony keyed the mic. "22 Adam. We have two in custody for 459. We're code 4 and will be 1015 with two in a few."

Several things crossed Tony's mind—booking and jailing their arrestees, booking the evidence, and writing the report. Finally, he thought about Yo Yo.

"Partner," he said to Mickey. "Let's get some pictures upstairs and of the heist. You want to babysit, or you want to play photographer?"

Mickey looked at the perps. "Which one of us is dumber than handcuffs?"

"Both of you," the taller of the two spat at Tony. "You just got lucky."

"I've got the better cell, partner," Mickey commented. "I'll snap the pix. Besides, I won't hit anything walking up the stairs."

A suspect does not have to receive his Miranda warning unless he is under ARREST and going to be questioned. They were under arrest, but Tony wasn't asking questions. He was hoping for a spontaneous confession. It didn't come, not immediately.

"How about you help us up? This hurts."

Tony didn't say shit.

"It's not like we killed someone," the shorter of the two said. "So, we robbed a house. Big deal. It isn't the first house we robbed, and it won't be the last. He should see the shit we have at our apartment!"

The taller of the two said, "Shut up, man. Shut the fuck up!"

"They can't use any of that! We haven't been Mirandized, or whatever it is. They can't use it in court."

Tony was deadpan. It wasn't easy to keep from laughing. Mickey came bounding down the stairs. "I had a Kodak moment and got some good shots."

"Let's get a couple more of 'Manny and Moe' on the floor with the loot nearby."

After Mickey snapped more pictures, they helped the two up. Tony searched them again when they were standing. He couldn't help himself. "We may be dumber than handcuffs, but you two are dumber than a box of rocks." He couldn't wait to tell Mickey. He couldn't wait to tell Yolis.

Tony put the two geniuses in the back of the black-and-white and securely seat-belted the two perps. While Tony was taking care of business, Mickey called dispatch. He then slid behind the wheel of the Crown Vic.

"How about a quick stop at Sam's on the way in for a cup of joe? I'm buying," Mickey suggested.

"If you're buying, I'm drinking coffee. But..." Tony was concerned about the two prisoners.

"I need some caffeine. It's a long night and I'm already tired. Besides, dispatch asked me to grab her a ham sandwich and an iced tea."

It took Mickey six minutes to get to Sam's. He parked the patrol unit in front of the large front window so that he and Tony could easily observe the unit and the two prisoners.

They walked inside. "Talk to me." He was curious about what Mickey was up to.

"Nobody's questioned them. If they want to talk between themselves, that's fine. We can enjoy a cup of coffee while they talk themselves into a confession."

"But you can't hear a word they're saying. Are you planning on reading their lips?"

"There's a recorder under the seat. I switched it on before we got out." The courts have held that there is no expectation to privacy in the back of a police car. Anything they say that incriminates them is ours and can be used in court to convict them. "How do you take your coffee?"

They were watching the unit and Manny and Moe from their seats. The coffee was fresh, hot, and tasted good. "So, what's the latest at JFK?"

Tony shook his head from side to side. "I haven't heard a thing. I thought by now the other shoe would fall. I guess not. Corrections' wheels turn slowly. I'll probably hear about HP and the reserves before I hear about Corrections. Are you guys packing yet?"

"Tammy's on top of that like a K-9 on a car filled with drugs. The only bad part about her doing the packing is that anything she thinks is old and I don't need, ends up in the trash."

"Have you hired a mover?"

"We're going to see how much we actually have when all is said and packed. If we can, it would be a helluva lot cheaper to rent a couple of U-Hauls and do the job ourselves. I figure if worse comes to worst, we can rent a third U-Haul and you and Yolis can drive her down."

Tony sipped coffee. He looked at Mickey. Tony's eyes told the story. "Do you miss anything?"

"I try not to. One of my goals when we move to Florida is to shoot for my detective shield. So, I'm using you and Yolis for practice."

"Got it." Tony looked outside. Their prisoners were talking away. "We should get these idiots to the Station so we can book 'em and get back to work. It's not like we have a flood of units working the streets."

"Good point." Mickey finished his coffee. He walked over to the counter and retrieved the dispatcher's order. "Let's do it, partner."

Mickey left the recorder, a gift from a detective friend, running. It was voice activated.

"You didn't get us anything? Not even donuts?" the tall one asked.

"Don't you ever quit?" Tony half turned. He looked at the two prisoners' screen. "You'll get your donut in state prison the first time you bend down in the shower to pick up the soap. And your donut already has a hole in it."

It was a short ride from Sam's to the Station. Mickey parked the car smoothly between the white lines. While Tony escorted S-1 to the booking cell, Mickey sat in the car with the other prisoner. When Tony was finished, Mickey led S-2 to the booking area. When they finished booking the perps, they went back to the unit to listen to the recorder.

"You, asshole. I told you we'd get caught. We should have quit while we were ahead. Quinto said he'd give us between thirty-five and forty grand for that jewelry. But you had to go just one more time."

"You worried for nothing. These idiots never Mirandized us. They can't use anything against us. And now they're stupid enough to leave us in the car together to get our stories straight. It's no wonder there's so much unsolved crime. You got cops who are too stupid to do anything but drink coffee and eat donuts."

Mickey glanced at Tony. "I know, partner, he must be talking about you, not me."

"If you wrote these two into a movie script, you'd have to take it out. Nobody would believe that people in real life can be dumber than handcuffs!"

They booked the stolen jewelry into evidence, plus the two flashlights the perps carried and two illegal knives. They also booked two screwdrivers, the secret tape recording, and the pictures taken at the crime scene. Their report would have to wait until calls quieted down or until after shift. Tony and Mickey went back to the unit, back to the streets, back to work.

Their first call was via cell. Dispatch contacted Tony regarding a loud music call. In other words, someone was partying and undoubtedly a neighbor complained. It was still kind of early, 2105 hours. But time didn't matter. If you felt you were being disturbed, you could call the Station at high noon and an officer would be dispatched to check it out.

Apparently, the owner of the home was a friend of the assistant chief. This call from dispatch was a friendly caveat. She didn't put it out over the air because calls are recorded. *Nuff said,* Tony thought.

Tony looked at Mickey who was behind the wheel. “The 415 call, the owner is friendly with the Assistant Chief of Police. I wonder if he’s there.”

Mickey made a left then a quick right. “We’ll find out soon enough. Not that it makes much difference. A disturbance is a disturbance.”

“True. Did you read about the male lifer in a northern California prison who just had ‘reassignment surgery’ on the taxpayer’s dime? What the hell is this world coming to? The asshole is in jail for life. What the hell difference does it make? We have vets who can’t get a freakin’ doctor’s appointment to treat a real medical emergency, and he becomes a she and we pay for it. I think I’ll write that off my taxes.”

Mickey made a final turn and could hear the music blasting from the corner. He drove to the middle of the street and stopped. The street was lined with cars. The party was in the backyard. “Put us out, partner.”

Tony said, “Show us 97.”

“Copy 97.”

Mickey and Tony walked to the chain-link fence surrounding the front of the house. They tried to get someone’s attention, but that was a dead end. They opened the chain-link gate and entered. They didn’t want to go into the backyard. That could be dangerous.

Tony shined his light into the yard. He caught someone’s eye. They, in turn, talked to someone else who in turn talked to a third party. Finally, a middle-aged man, dressed in freshly pressed tan slacks and checkered sport shirt approached. He had a beer in one hand and a cigarette in his mouth. His hands were in plain sight. “Good evening, gentlemen.” Mickey nodded. “I know you’re working but can I get you something to drink or something to eat?”

Tony was hungry. “Thanks, but no thanks.”

Mickey contacted dispatch. He let dispatch know that they were making contact. “Are you the owner of the house?”

“Yup. Actually, the bank is for another twenty-seven-and-a-half years. But yes, it’s my house and I’m responsible for the loud music.”

"Can I see some ID, please?"

He reached in his pocket. He took his driver's license out of his wallet. "Here you go."

Tony jotted down the man's horsepower. His name was Gomez. "A neighbor called us, sir. We would not be here if someone hadn't called. You either need to invite the neighbor who complained to the party, and we do not know who that was, or you need to lower the music. If we are called back, you are risking a major fine and we might confiscate the equipment. My suggestion is you tone down the music. I could hear it from the Maywood Strip."

Mr. Gomez laughed. "Thanks, guys. I'll turn it down. Have a good one."

"Enjoy your evening, sir. Thanks for your understanding."

On the way back to the unit, Tony contacted dispatch, "Contacted homeowner Gomez. Advised, complied. 10-8."

"I need to call Tammy," Mickey said. "Go ahead and drive. But if you hit anything, anything, even a damn ghetto pigeon, I'm taking your license and buying you a trike with training wheels."

"Will it have a seat in the back for you?"

Mickey didn't answer. He already had Tammy on the line.

Except for two loud music calls, it was quiet on the streets of Hollow Point, which was surprising for a Friday night. Mickey spent the better part of an hour speaking with Tammy on the phone and smoking cigarettes. Tony drove around the four-square-mile city thinking about Yolanda and making damn certain he didn't hit anything.

On the northeast corner of Gage Avenue and Santa Fe Avenue, was Mom and Pop Grocery that also sold liquor. The store closed at 2300 hundred hours. It was 2242 hours. Tony was driving west on Gage Avenue and stopped for a stop sign. He was going to turn south but changed his mind and turned north.

"22 Adam, a panic alarm at..." Tony never heard the rest of the transmission. As he made the turn, he observed a man running across the street. The man was wearing dark clothing and a black baseball cap. In his right hand was what Tony thought to be a gun.

Without say goodbye, Mickey put the cellphone in his pocket. “The guy’s got a gun!” Mickey yelled just as the guy stopped in his tracks and pointed the weapon at the windshield of the police unit.

“Get down, Mickey! Get down!” If Tony swerved right, the guy would get off at least a round. If he swerved left, the guy would still get off a round. He wasn’t more than ninety feet from the armed man, who had just knocked over the Mom and Pop Grocery and had put two rounds in the old man who did exactly what the armed 211 suspect directed him to do. The suspect shot him anyway.

Tony had one viable option and only one. “Stay down, Mickey.” The guy took dead aim. Tony slouched low in his seat and put the pedal to the floor. The guy got off a round which went into the air before the push bars of the Crown Victoria slammed into him. The gun fell to the street and skidded across the road. The guy went up in the air, over the hood of the car, over the roof of the car, and way over the trunk of the car. He came to a stop against a tree on the east side of the street.

Mickey was on the suspect before three squad cars skidded to a stop behind their unit. Mickey bent over him. The suspect was swollen, bleeding, and his tennis shoes were in the street. His shirt and pants were torn. He looked like he had just been hit by a car.

Tony ran across the street. He carefully picked up the gun, a 9mm Glock. He walked it over to the trunk of the unit, opened the trunk and cleared the weapon. He locked the gun in the trunk then walked over to Mickey and the perp. The suspect was semiconscious.

Mickey turned away from the 211 suspect just as three officers approached. Mickey looked at Tony. “I thought I told you not to hit anything.” Mickey laughed. The laughter was out of relief. The laughter was for the fact that they were still alive. If you weren’t a cop, you wouldn’t understand.

Mickey shook his head. “Before the shit hits every fan within a couple of hundred miles of HP, you need to swallow and digest something. If you didn't do what you did, chances are we'd be dead now. Chew on that. You saved our lives. Nice work." Mickey wanted to slap Tony on the back. Too many people were standing around.

The EMTs arrived. Three ambulances were on scene, including one at the grocery store. The fire department arrived. An airship was overhead. So much for the quiet night in Hollow Point.

The remaining hours of the evening and the early hours of the morning were spent under the yellow tape of the crime scene, measuring distance traveled, trajectory of the suspect's body, marking shell casings, interviewing witnesses, interviewing Mickey and Tony, looking for more witnesses, and checking recordings from various store cameras.

Pop Granada-Lopez, the owner of Mom and Pop Grocery, was in critical condition with two bullet holes in his body. The suspect, identified as Cruz Almada Portello, was in a different hospital, also in critical condition.

There was more media on the scene than Mickey or Tony had observed in one place since watching the Academy Awards on television. As far as Tony was concerned, the future of the reserves was cemented in stone. The reserves could be pronounced dead!

Tony was numb and the more experienced Mickey was well aware of Tony's condition. Mickey had seen other officers who were forced to use their weapon up close and personal and the effect it had on the officer. The suits had already hustled Tony to the Station.

Mickey ran the suspect on a computer in another police unit at the scene. The scumbag had a long history of criminal activity, including assault with a deadly weapon, domestic abuse, possession of drugs, and weapons possession. One of HP's finest.

Mickey asked one of the on-scene detectives if he could help. "Your best help would be with your partner at the Station. Depending on what we come up with, this can be dicey." The detective started to walk away. He stopped. He turned back to Mickey. "I shouldn't be saying this so early in the investigation but, from preliminary results, your partner did the only thing possible. You guys could be on your way to the morgue right now if he didn't take out the asshole with the unit. You can tell Tony for me, in my eyes, he's a hero, no matter how these cards fall."

Mickey went to the Station. They had Tony in a room by himself. No one, at this point, was allowed into that room. Tony was calm, at least on the outside. He ran the situation through his mind's eye a few dozen times. He could come up with no other solution. He did what had to be done. He was the one in the arena who had to make the split-second decision. He made the call. It was the right call.

Once again, Tony and Mickey made the news. He probably set a record for an HP reserve. He got more ink then the freakin' HP Mayor.

The morning *Los Angeles Post* was the first major newspaper to show interest in Tony's story. The liberal newspaper titled the story, "To Reserve or Not To Reserve." Then, staff reporter Herman Goldman went on to write,

"Late last night, Tony Farrina, the very same reserve police officer for the city of Hollow Point who last week broke more traffic laws chasing the vehicle he SHOULD NOT have been pursuing and ended up in a major traffic collision with a fire truck, took out a suspect with his police unit. Yes, you heard it right, and you heard it here. Farrina, who should have been terminated for his shenanigans during the pursuit, lived to embarrass HP once more.

"Farrina, with his full-time police partner, Mickey Cassidy, sitting next to him, took out a suspect who had just robbed a grocery store. Instead of a taser or a nightstick, RESERVE Ofc. Farrina used his police unit to slam into the suspect, sending him hundreds of feet over the police vehicle and onto the sidewalk.

"A call to the hospital advised us, that if the suspect survives, he may be paralyzed for the rest of his life.

"A RESERVE cop? A police car as a weapon? Do I need to say more?"

Tony read the article and wanted to puke. He read the article over and over. He wanted to puke again and again.

Several of Tony's FLACOE colleagues read the article. A couple of them asked him questions. One or two of the questions were even intelligent. It was the staff who talked behind Tony's back that pissed him off. Tony was well aware that the suits, the Probation department, and the ACLU had read about Tony's deed on the streets of HP. Tony figured this was sealing his FLACOE fate.

Yolanda and Tony met for dinner Tuesday. There was no 'dessert.' Yolis had to work. Mickey had coffee with Tony twice between Saturday morning and Tuesday, and they talked about Tony's actions. Mickey continued to assure Tony that, under the circumstances, there was no other course of action. That helped some. Tony had nothing but respect for Mickey.

The department insisted Tony meet with their shrink. He did so gladly. Tony had respect for doctors and the work they did, be it physical or mental or a combination of the two. The meeting with the head doctor held no surprises. Unlike the ACLU, the doctor was genuinely interested in Tony's wellbeing.

"Have you stopped running it over and over in your head?" the man in the blue three-piece suit asked from behind his desk.

"No." Tony shook his head. "But the frequency is decreasing. I know I had no choice. I'd probably be having a more difficult time had I not reacted as I did and one of us got hurt." Tony rubbed at the stubble on his cheeks. "He made the call. I didn't. My choices were clear. My reaction was measured. It was the only course of action left to me." Tony continued to rub at the two-day-old stubble.

The doctor had a neatly trimmed goatee. He was fortyish and friendly, and smiled throughout the session. "Let me give you my impression. At this point in time, what you are feeling is..." The doctor carefully chose his words. "...is as it should be. You're still wrestling a bit with what you had to do. Note, please, that I said, 'what you had to do.' I read the Sergeant's follow-up report. I concur. You had no choice. Your actions seem correct for that particular set of circumstances. The first incident, the unfortunate collision with the fire engine, leaves questions. But from what we've discussed, you're at ease with that. So, my conclusion for you, and the written conclusion that I will forward to the powers that be at HP, is that you are fit to return to duty at week's end." He paused.

"Do you have any questions for me?"

Tony nodded. "Is there a timeframe when I might let go of this?"

The doctor played with his facial hair. It was obvious he was searching for an answer. "Unfortunately, no. Each individual swallows and digests food at a different rate. This is similar. You are still in the chewing stages, but the pieces are getting smaller. You have demonstrated to me that you've accepted what you had to do for what it was: a necessary reaction to the situation you did not, and I stress, you did *not* create."

Tony understood. The doctor held his hand out and Tony reached across the desk to shake it. His phone rang. "Excuse me." He turned sideways. "I see. Thank you."

The doctor was 'worrying' his goatee when he addressed Tony. "Your Department called. Cruz Portello took a turn for the worse. He died in the hospital two hours ago."

Tony was instructed to remain off duty for another week. He was unhappy about that but had no choice. He and Yo Yo met for a quick lunch Wednesday afternoon in the San Fernando Valley, more or less halfway between HP and the Antelope Valley.

They met at the Friend's Restaurant just off the 5 freeway. She came bearing gifts. "You look good." She was wearing tight blue jeans and a white frilly blouse that accentuated her ample breasts. She was carrying a newspaper.

"I thought you might like this." She sat down on the opposite side of the table from Tony. She handed him the newspaper. Before Tony could open the paper, she said, "I miss you lots, babe. I can't imagine what you're going through but know that I'm here for you, Tony. What you did was exactly what had to be done. That asshole sealed his own fate. He pointed the gun. You saved Mickey's life and your life. If you let the guy take you out, I'd have to kill you again. Keep this in mind when the shit starts rolling around in your head: "I need you. You go nowhere until I let you go. Understood?"

Tony smiled and looked into those beautiful dark eyes. His eyes wandered a little lower. "Yes, Mistress."

"You got that right." She took his hand, squeezed it, caressed his fingers, then held his hand in hers. "Your hand's cold."

"My heart's warm."

She took his other hand in hers. "That better?"

"Better, but not best."

"Open the paper. The editorial page."

Tony opened the *Hollow Point Press Telegram* to page eight. The locals wanted a piece of Tony's ass. Bill Williamson's editorial read,

"Most of our readers know I have had many problems with the HPPD. A few nights ago, one of our reserve officers, Tony Farrina, who happens to be a school administrator, took out an armed suspect with his police unit. In light of this occurrence, the press has been, to say the least, unkind to an officer who chases bullets for free.

"Like any other sworn officer, Farrina attended the academy and then went through the grueling process, generally six months to a year of testing to get hired by HPPD. Then he went through another year of training with three Field Training Officers. He was one out of approximately 100 to make the grade.

"Unlike several of the stories you read in various newspapers, unlike some of what you may have seen on television news, my story is encased in facts. I did my homework. I watched store videos. I interviewed individuals who were at the scene. I spoke with police officers, some of whom were at the scene. No names will be revealed. But rest assured, the facts are accurate.

"Tony and his partner Mickey Cassidy were on patrol when Tony turned a corner just as a call of an armed robbery was put out by HPPD dispatch. The call was still incomplete when Farrina turned north onto Santa Fe from Gage Avenue. As he completed the turn, a gangbanger with a long criminal history and an illegal gun in his possession was fleeing the scene of a robbery at the Mom and Pop Grocery. Before leaving the grocery store with the night's cash, Portello viciously pumped two rounds into Pop. (Pop is fighting for his life in a local hospital.)

"Portello was running toward his vehicle and in the middle of Santa Fe when Farrina completed his turn. There was less than 90 feet between the punk and the cruiser. Count those feet. Ninety feet.

"Portello leveled his weapon at the unit's windshield. Farrina, thinking more about his partner than himself, yelled to Cassidy to 'get down.' Farrina had no way to get out of the sight of that weapon. Portello left Farrina no choice.

"Reserve Officer Tony Farrina did what had to be done to save the life of his partner and his own life. But let's take this one step beyond. Had Farrina attempted to swerve to the right or to swerve to the left, had Farrina attempted to brake, at which case the windshield would certainly have been shattered by bullets, the attempted murderer would have gotten away, and more lives would have been put at risk. Tony Farrina did not put this situation in motion. Tony Farrina put an end to this situation. He had no other choice. Let me repeat this: Officer Tony Farrina had no choice.

"Those of you who follow my column know I call it when I see it, as I see it. I have had my problems with some of the actions of some of the officers of HPPD. Not so in this case. Reserve Officer Tony Farrina has my full support in this case. As a matter of fact, Officer Farrina has my backing for an unconventional finish, yet a job well done.

"Finally, as of this writing, Cruz Portello is expected to survive so he can face a myriad of charges.

"Do your community a favor. Do Reserve Officer Farrina a favor. Check your facts before you react. Once you have your facts in order, you too will understand that Farrina acted in the best interest of the community he is sworn to protect!"

Tony folded the newspaper. "Keep it. I have a couple of copies at home," Yolis added.

"That's pretty powerful. And coming from a guy who calls the PD every time he thinks they screwed up. I owe him a thank you call."

"That should sure make you feel better."

"It does." The waitress took their order.

The story did make Tony feel better, but he knew that people tend to remember the negative and there was more negative out there than there was positive.

"I'm going to make at least two calls this afternoon. One will be to my attorney to see what he thinks the impact of the notoriety might be on my FLACOE career. The second will be to Bill Williamson at the paper."

"Can you make that three calls? Call me and let me know what your attorney thinks."

"Done."

Tony made the call. He called Williamson to thank him. The guy was friendly and offered Tony the very best of luck with his dilemma. He also promised Tony that his phone call was off the record.

He then called his attorney. Tony was nervous as hell waiting for the lawyer to pick up the phone. "You are legally in the right. But sometimes right doesn't necessarily pull the cart, if you know what I mean. I have to tell you, I think they've got you by the balls. My best guess is that, to keep this out of the courts and out of the newspapers, they'll offer you some sort of deal to leave quietly. If you've major league pissed off the ACLU, they might go for the jugular.

"I would do this: If and when they want to meet with you, tell them you a need a day or two to consult with your counselor. Call me and I will organize a strategy. I might want to be in on the meeting. But I don't want to complicate things. If it looks like they're going to make you an offer to hit the road, then you can handle the meeting on your own and fax me the paperwork before you sign anything. Then again, they may let this go in light of the latest and greatest—the positive press. We'll have to wait and see. As we say in my business, 'the jury is still out on this one.'"

Finally, Tony called Yolanda. He was hoping to catch her in a free moment, but it didn't work out that way. Apparently, she was tied up. He left a message on her voicemail.

Friday, Fucking Friday

On Friday morning it was sunny and warm in the Antelope Valley. Normally, Friday was one of Tony's favorite days. His workweek was over, and it was time for play at HP. This Friday was an exception. Tony was *persona non grata* at the PD. The next time he would see work at the Station would be a week from Friday, unless he took a day off work during the week.

Tony went into work with a smile on his face anyway. He was in control. He thought about Yolanda. Tony smiled, but it was to be a short-lived smile.

Tony set a cup of coffee on his desk. He lit up his computer and started to open his email. His phone rang. It was Eddie Peterson. "Good morning and happy Friday to you, too." Tony greeted.

"Listen," Eddie said. "We're having a meeting at 8:00 in my office. I've arranged coverage for you."

Tony nodded to no one. Here it comes. This had to be it. They were going to fuck with his Friday. Tony caught himself. They couldn't mess with him unless he allowed them to. He was responsible for his actions. "Should I bring my bullet-proof vest?"

"You might need it."

Tony looked at his watch. 7:45. "I'll see you in fifteen." He sipped the coffee and bit his lower lip. He opened his email. There was nothing there of any consequence. He called the secretary. "Do we have any unfilled teacher absences?"

"No sir. As a matter of fact, we have a floater." A "floater" was a term for an extra sub who could cover for teachers who needed to be pulled out of the classroom for one reason or another. Tony nervously looked at his watch. He had enough time to finish his coffee, turn off his computer, go to the men's room, and walk to Eddie's office. Actually, he had time to accomplish one other task.

He slid open his side desk drawer and took out the file folder that contained his annual FLACOE evaluation, which Eddie, with input from Paula, had given Tony six weeks ago. It was signed, sealed, and letter perfect, with the narrative that stated, "Tony was asked to leave Mendenhall to come to the John F. Kennedy School to assist in a reorganization plan that would help the school get back on its feet. Tony has, with his team, excelled as a member and accomplished this goal with aplomb. Thank you for an awesome job, Tony."

Tony put that evaluation in his suit-jacket pocket. He didn't know why he took it with him; it just felt comforting to have there. He walked to Eddie's office.

Tony began to open the door and scan the room before the door was completely open. HP training at its finest. Seated at his desk was Eddie; no surprise. In front of Eddie's desk was Paula; no surprise. Seated at the north corner of Eddie's desk was Cleveland Archer; surprise, surprise.

Archer locked eyes with Eddie. Cleveland was wearing an expensive grey suit with white shirt and blue tie. He held a fixed stare at Tony. Then, he adjusted the knot in his tie. Eddie couldn't help but think Archer was tightening his grip on Tony's neck. Maybe he was.

Tony's eyes didn't move from Archer's. Tony's light brown suit was complemented by a brown shirt and red tie. Tony adjusted the knot on his tie.

Paula broke the silence. "Have a seat, Tony. I think you know everyone here."

Tony nodded. "That I do." He broke the gaze with Archer. He intentionally walked around to the south side of Eddie's desk and moved the chair. Tony positioned himself so that he was directly across from Cleveland and would be looking right at him, if he so chose.

Tony had had time for one other issue before he left his office. At HP, Tony sometimes carried a voice-activated tape recorder. He took it out of his suit-jacket pocket. He held it up. "For the sake of accuracy, I'd like to record this session. That way, if anything comes up later, we have a clean record of this meeting. Any objections?" Tony never ran that by the attorney.

Eddie was the first to speak. "Fine with me. I don't think that should be a problem."

Paula spoke up. "If that makes you more comfortable, have at it. But remember, this is not a 'you against us' meeting. It's a 'make things better' meeting."

Tony looked at Paula. He smiled. She was as full of shit as a carnival porta potty at closing time.

Archer was the last man sitting. "I think recording this session demonstrates a lack of faith in the process. I take it as a personal affront. But since no one else has a problem with it, I'll go with it with one footnote. Each of us is to receive a copy of the tape within 48 hours of the meeting's conclusion."

Tony nodded. It was now time to get on with the hanging. He placed the voice-activated tape recorder on Eddie's desk. Tony could swear he saw Eddie nod and give Tony a hint of a smile as he leaned back in his seat.

Paula heaved a sigh of what Tony thought was a bullshit attempt to show the small group that this meeting was not painless to her. To Tony, it was like the hangman checking the strength of the rope that was about to go around the neck of the horse thief. Only Tony was no horse thief.

"We're here today," Paula began, and Tony thought to himself, *We're here today because we're not all there.* Paula finished the sentence, "to solve a team-building problem; a mission problem."

Eddie spoke. "The bottom line, Tony, is that it is felt," then Eddie added, "by some in this room, that you are at cross-purposes with the needs of the facility."

Tony had heard more bullshit but that was usually when Jerry Brown was addressing the State of California on budget issues or when the City of Hollow Point was addressing sanctuary cities. "Can you be a bit clearer, Eddie, please?"

Archer didn't wait for Eddie to respond. "We're trying to help kids and you want to asphyxiate them. Is that clear enough?"

Tony was thrilled he had the recorder going. He was also glad he had his most recent eval in his jacket pocket. "You're entitled to your opinion. I sure as hell don't see it that way. I believe we all have to be accountable for our own actions; otherwise, we don't show improvement."

"I think what Mr. Archer is saying, is that sometimes you get your police role confused with your professional role at JFK; that causes damage to our kids," Paula stated.

Tony did not want to respond to that. He glared at Archer who had is hands folded in his lap. Tony had a good idea where this was going. They were wording him up to the gallows one damn sentence at a time.

"We are looking to solve this problem and make it a win-win."

Tony hated that expression. There was no such animal. If someone else won, then someone lost; plain and simple.

"We are here to offer you a couple of options. There is an opening at the juvenile hall in Downey. They need an AP."

"Hope Center is damn near ninety miles from my house, one way, in peak traffic time. You gotta be kidding me."

"The second option is retirement." Paula held her hand up. "Before you tell us you don't have the time in to retire, we've investigated that. We'll buy you that time and offer you two more years and cash TSA if you elect to retire. I'll give you the particulars in writing before you leave." Paula took a couple of breaths. "We know you worked hard and made major advancements, but we need to move on, and we need to do so without a timelapse. We'd like an answer within seventy-two hours."

Tony looked at Eddie and raised his eyebrows. He looked at Paula and locked eyes. He then stared at Archer. "I need to talk with my attorney. Assuming I can get in touch with him in your timeframe, I'll have your answer within seventy-two hours." Tony again looked at all three. "I want all here to know that I firmly believe, in most cases,

I acted in the very best interest of all concerned. I'm human and I also make mistakes but giving candy to kids, to anyone, when they screw up, accomplishes nothing. Remember the pen then Rodrigo Flores, our former student dropped during the assembly? Now there's a man who learned about accountability!" Tony swallowed hard but he couldn't get rid of the lump in his throat. "You'll have your answer."

Tony stood. He reached across the desk first shaking hands with Eddie. Then he shook hands with Paula. He walked to Archer and held out his hand. "I would like you to know that I understand what you are trying to accomplish. I just do not agree with it. I hope you can understand what I am trying to do."

They shook hands. Tony retrieved the recorder. He left the room.

Tony walked outside to help supervise the 10 o'clock movement of students from the dorm back to the school following their head-call break. All was quiet.

Now, Tony had something else to think about. Did he want to call it a day with Corrections or did he want to drive to Downey five days a week and then to HP on the weekend. His Vette would love that.

Another possibility would be to sell his house in Palmdale and buy a place closer to his new assignment. The only problem with that would be replacing what he had in Palmdale with three quarters of a million dollars in the Downey area. He didn't have that kind of money.

Tony walked back to his office following the student movement. He closed and locked his door. He called his attorney. Ray Bestuss was in and took the call.

Tony gave him the rundown.

"Congratulations on two fronts. First, you had the smarts to think about what I should have—the recorder. Second, the fact that they are offering you options, and one of those options is a buyout, is an obvious win for you. So, a double congratulations." There was silence for a few seconds. "Any thoughts of which way you might go?"

“There is no way in hell I’m going to make that drive. It would cost me as much in gas as it does for food. If I decide not to fight it, I’ll probably opt for the buyout. That leads me to a question. If I fight it, do I have a chance in hell?”

“You probably have a damn good chance. If I handle it for you, you have better than a damn good chance. But, while you might end up winning the war, and Corrections has a deep, deep pocket, there are many battles before the truce that can take a toll on you financially and emotionally. And this thing could drag on for years.”

Bestuss went on to say, “I’m not cheap. Up until now, no charge. After today, if we fight, I’ll need a retainer. I’d handle the rest on contingency, but I’m going to need money to cover ongoing expenses. We’re probably talking fifty grand out of your pocket before this thing sees settlement.

“My suggestion is, when they give you the written buyout proposal, shoot it to me, and I’ll go over it. No charge. In return, if you stop me in HP for speeding, I get a get-out-of-jail-free card.”

“Done.”

“I’ve got another call. Congrats and let me hear from you.”

“Thanks a million, and keep that heavy foot off the pedal. I’m not working today.”

Tony poured himself a cup of coffee. He sipped the coffee slowly. He didn’t understand it, but he felt sense of relief. He accepted the situation for what it was. The only thing left was negotiating a settlement. He knew he wasn’t willing to make that crazy drive day in and day out. Corrections knew it, too. Paula knew it; Archer knew it. It was what it was.

The ringing of the telephone snapped Tony out of his world of thought. It was Assistant Chief Foxx. “Sorry to bother you at work, Tony, but I wanted you to hear this from me and not the news. The family of Cruz Portello has filed suit against you and the PD. The Department has found you blameless and also found his death was justified, that you had no other alternative. You feared for your life and the life of your partner. As far as the suit goes, experience tells me that the counsel will eventually settle rather than fight it. But that's not 100% at all."

"The suit is against the Department and me?"

"Right."

"I have insurance protection for the reserve association. Do I need to notify them?"

"They've been notified. It would be premature to line up an attorney at this point. Let the wheels turn. You'll be kept in the loop, of course. How do you feel?"

"I'm all right. I suppose the end of the Reserve program is near?" That was a question. Tony didn't expect an answer, but he got one.

"If I were a betting man, and I am, I would bet that the City Council votes to kill the reserve program at its next meeting. That's one bet, Tony, that I'd gladly lose.

"You know how to get in touch with me if you need anything at all. Don't give up until the judge bangs his gavel. Understood?"

"Understood, sir. Thank you."

After work, Tony stopped at Subway and bought himself an Italian hero sandwich and a bag of chips. He wanted nothing more than to eat dinner and sit on the upstairs couch with LT in front of the big screen and watch the Dodgers take on the Cubbies.

Tony did his best thinking when he was relaxed. And he often relaxed watching the Dodgers game, which was the only reason he subscribed to cable.

A Man, His Best Friend, and His Woman

After Tony put his Vette in the garage, he unlocked his door. There to greet him was LT. "I know, buddy. I'm glad to see you, too. Tonight, it's just you and me and the TV. You can pull for the Cubs. I'm betting on the Dodgers and Kershaw. Let's eat."

LT was on the carpet next to the kitchen table, enjoying his feast with a few scraps from leftover human dinners tossed into his food. Tony finished his sub. He sat on the couch enjoying his chips. LT sat on the couch next to Tony. He put his head on Tony's lap, his body stretched out the length of the couch. Tony cursed at the big screen as the Dodgers went down in order. The Cubs' pitcher Travis Wood was on his game. The Cubs bullpen was strong so strong that the only Dodger hit of the game belonged to the redhead Justin Turner. When the top of the ninth was in the history books, it was all over for Dodgers who were shut out two-zip.

The phone rang. It was Yolanda. "Hey, how are you? Do you want some company?"

Soon Yolanda was at his door.

"Sorry, LT. You get the couch tonight. At least for a little while. I've got company." Tony stripped down to his jockeys. He took a quick hot shower, toweled off and walked into the bedroom. His guest had a scented candle lit. It was on the shelf on the top of the custom headboard.

"I don't know who smells better—you or that candle?"

Yolanda grabbed him gently between the legs. "You'd better answer yourself correctly."

Tony laughed. "No question. You beat that candle, hands up or hands down."

"Good answer." She pumped a bit of lotion into her hand, rubbed her hands together, then reached down for Tony's stiffening penis.

She rubbed both hands on either side then rubbed his shaft with one hand and his balls with the other.

"Damn that feels good."

"You're in good hands. Always remember that, babe."

Yolanda was enjoying turning Tony on. She had no trouble doing that. The games went on for an hour and a half. She wore him out. Tony, in turn, returned the favor. His head was on her chest. "I've got some serious decisions to make. Wanna help?"

"I thought you'd never ask. What's up?"

Tony looked between his legs. "Not 'him' anymore. You took care of that."

"Glad I could help. Decision-making time. Talk to me."

Tony brought Yolanda up to date. "As painful as it is, and it is painful, I could be done with Corrections in short order and done with HP."

"Hang in there. As I heard it, you could probably go full time with the Department."

"Maybe yes, maybe no."

"Okay. Assuming you leave Corrections, and that sounds like a sure thing, what would be your first choice?"

"Full time with the Department."

"Good. If the Department doesn't pick you up, second choice?"

"Another Department."

"Where?"

"Whoever is hiring."

"You've got a lot of choices." Yolanda kissed Tony's cheek. "I think the only real problem you have is what to do with me."

"That's not a problem. I think I'll keep you around, if you'll have me."

"Try getting rid of me." She reached between his thighs. "I think the big guy is ready for me."

***

Tony's administrative time off flew by as quickly as a firefly in a windstorm. In those several days off, Yolanda and Tony spent quality time together. Following one of their "quality meetings," Yolanda sat Tony down over a cup of coffee.

"I've been doing a lot a thinking about your situation. I have a strong suggestion."

"Not just a suggestion," Tony offered, "but a 'strong' suggestion?"

"Shut up and listen before I put another Viagra in your coffee." She drank from her coffee cup. "Here," she took a paper out of her pocket, "is a list of the things you have to do and decisions you have to make."

Tony looked at the list. They were numbered. (1) Negotiate a FLACOE deal (or drive to hell and back daily); (2) If HP does away with its reserve program, decide if you want to go full time; (3) If you want to go full time, decide what department(s) you want to apply to; (4) Decide how many times a week you want to spend with Yo Yo, then give her a key to your place.

"This hasn't been signed and notarized."

Yolanda suddenly grabbed Tony's hand, licked his palm, and slammed it so hard on the paper it startled LT who was lying by the kitchen table minding his own business. "It is now."

"Okay. I know this. What's the point?"

"I thought you'd never ask." She put her coffee cup down. She ripped item one off the paper. "Here. Focus on number 1 only. Put the rest of this stuff out of your mind, except for me, of course."

"What is this? Psychology 101?"

"Something like that. If you focus on all these problems, you'll drive yourself nuts. If you focus on one at a time, you'll get them done in short order."

"How come I never learned that in school?"

"Because you were probably too busy flirting with all the pretty girls."

Tony reached up and squeezed her nipple. “Not all, just the ones with ripe tits.”

“I don’t doubt it. Update me on what’s going on with your out-the-door FLACOE deal.”

“My attorney is out of town; he’ll be back tomorrow. The deal is offering me three years’ retirement time, which allows me to retire. It is giving me $50,000 in the form of an annuity, payable over 5 years. From the state, I’ll receive a COLA, a cost-of-living adjustment of 2% every year, not compounded. If I were to take that and get a job with a PD, I’d be in great shape. I could almost keep you.”

“It sounds like you’re well on your way to hog heaven.” She squeezed Tony’s hand. “Here’s the hard part. “Let go of the rest of it. Don’t focus or even think of item two. It’s not here yet. I know that’s easier said than done but do the best you can. It makes life a hell of a lot easier.”

“How did you get so smart?”

“It goes with the big tits.” She finished her coffee. “We’ve got to get ready for work. It’s shower time.”

“How about we save water and shower together? We are in the middle of a drought.”

Another Ride in a Black-and-White

Tony didn't even ask who was driving. He got in the passenger seat. Mickey was on the phone with Tammy as he got behind the wheel of the Crown Vic. "Talk to you later, angel. Gotta keep tabs on my boy next to me. Gotta make sure he doesn't do any more damage. Love you."

"I'm playing you, man; you know that."

Tony looked at his partner. He was going to miss him when he moved to Florida. He was a helluva lot more than a partner; he was a trusted friend. "I know. Don't sweat it. Not that it matters, but try to keep me out of trouble."

Mickey drove north out of the Station lot and west on Gage. "Here's one for you," Tony said. "These two friends pack up their van and head to the mountains and the ski resort. They make it halfway up the mountain when a sudden storm makes the mountain road impassable. They find a secluded farmhouse and approach the door. One of them knocks. Finally, a cute, fairly young lady answers the door. They explain their plight and ask if they may stay the night.

"She explains that her husband died recently, and she is all alone in the house. She suggests, since they're out in the middle of nowhere, that they use the barn. They thank her profusely and promise to be out of the barn at the crack of daylight.

"They're good to their word. The rest of the ski trip is awesome, and they arrive home without further incident. About nine months later, one of the friends gets a letter from the lady's attorney. He reads the letter and takes a couple of minutes to make sense of it.

"He then drives to his buddy's house. He asked his buddy if he remembers their winter excursion. The buddy replies, of course. He asks him if he remembers stopping at the farmhouse. Again, a positive response. He asks if he remembers the barn. Sure, his best friend says. By chance, did you wake up in the middle of the night?

"'Yes,' the buddy replies sheepishly. 'I did.'"

"'Did you happen to go up to the house?'"

"'I did.'"

"'Did you happen to have sex with that nice lady?'"

"His friend nodded, then smiled. 'More than once.'"

"'Did you lie and give her my name instead of yours?'"

"The friend nodded and says, 'I'm sorry about that. She's pregnant, huh?'"

"'No. Actually she died and left me a small fortune.'"

Mickey, who was stopped for a light, laughed. "Pretty funny; pretty funny." He made a left on Pacific Boulevard, drove to Florence Avenue, and drove west. "That guy just tossed an empty cigarette box out his window. Let's pull him over and remind him he's not in Mexico. Call it in."

Tony put the plate out. Mickey lit the guy up. Tony approached the car. Mickey hung back on the passenger side of the car and watched the driver of the green Chevy pickup truck that looked like it came out of Tijuana. "Sir, I need to see your license, registration, and your proof of insurance, please."

The guy was wearing jeans, a white t-shirt, and a cowboy hat. He looked like he just crossed the border or crossed under it.

"Why?"

Tony was feeling good which was good for the driver. Tony snickered. "Because I asked nicely and because you tossed a cigarette box out your window. We call that littering in the States."

"You're serious?"

"As serious as the recent earthquake you had across the border. License, registration, and insurance, please."

He reached in his shirt pocket. He handed Tony his license. "The registration and the insurance papers are in there." He pointed to the glove box.

"Anything in the truck I should be concerned with? Knife, guns, hand grenades?"

"Yeah, I got a grenade up my ass. Do you wanna pull the pin?"

Tony wanted to yank him out of the car. The only two things that stopped him were his two recent infamous incidents. "So, if I pull you out of the truck, you'll explode?"

Grudgingly, he reached into the glove compartment. "Here."

Tony took the license, registration, and insurance papers to the passenger side of the unit. He ran the guy for wants and warrants. He came back cleaner than a freshly laundered police uniform. Mickey was standing next to him. "Write him or warn him?"

"Your call, partner."

"You pulled him over."

"You ran the plate."

Tony smiled. He was having fun; something he hadn't really had in a long time. "I'll give him a pass." He walked out from behind the passenger door and started toward the truck.

Mickey yelled, "Tony, stop! He's got something in his left hand, out the window. It's black."

Tony stepped back behind the unit's door. He drew his Glock. Mickey's was already out, at the low ready. "Sir. Whatever is in your hand, drop it. Do it now."

He held the object up higher. "It's a fucking recorder and I ain't dropping it."

"Cover me from the passenger side. Approach slowly. Watch his damn hand."

Mickey approached from the driver's side. He used the back of the truck for cover. He illuminated the object with his flashlight. It was a recorder. "It's a recorder, Tony. Keep your weapon out. This guy's got a lesson to learn, and I just became his teacher."

Mickey holstered his weapon when he could see both of the guy's hands. He yanked the recorder out of his hand and tossed it on the passenger seat. “Get the fuck out of the truck, moron.” Mickey opened the door watching his hands. “Get out.”

“What’s happening?”

“What’s happening is that you’re an asshole. Do you realize that from where my partner and I are, we can’t tell whether you’re holding a recorder, a camera, a cellphone, or a fucking gun? You could have gotten yourself shot.”

“Or run over by one of your cars.”

Mickey grabbed him by the front of his t-shirt. He half-dragged him to the passenger door, letting go when he was behind the door. “Partner, walk around to the driver’s side of the truck. Get in. Pick something and hold it out the window. It could be anything, his recorder, your Glock, anything.”

Tony hesitated then did as requested.

“Okay, asshole. Tell me what my partner’s holding. Guess right and you’ll get no ticket. What the hell is it?”

Mickey couldn’t see it without lighting it up.

“I don’t know.”

“Neither do I. Get the point? We don’t know what it is, so we assume the worst. You get shot and right away you blame us. Then you sue. It’s all bullshit. Common sense says you do as you’re told, and you can argue your case in front of the judge. “Partner, come on back. Don’t put away what you had in your hand.”

Tony walked backed to the unit. At the low ready was his baby Glock, the Glock 27. He carried it as a backup piece.

“Get the message?” Mickey was cooling off. The guy was getting color back in his face.

“Would it do me any good to apologize?”

Tony handed him his license, insurance papers, and registration. “Go on. Get out of here. Next time don’t throw shit out the window and, if a cop stops you, play nice. We’re only trying to keep you and the rest of the community safe.”

HP was surprisingly quiet the rest of the night. That gave Mickey and Tony a chance to talk about Tony’s future; that is, when Mickey wasn't on the phone with Tammy. Little by little, Mickey and Tammy were firming up their Florida plans. They were excited. "How about code 7? I'm hungry."

"If you're buying, I'm eating."

"If I'm buying, it's Norm's. See if we're clear."

Norm's 'showed love' to the tune of 50 percent off. Tony called the Station on his cell. They were clear code 7. Tony put them out at Norm's.

They parked the unit in the parking lot where they could see it from inside the coffee shop. "Go ahead in. I'll be in in a minute. I want to grab a smoke and make a quick call. Order me a coffee."

Tony walked in and sat down and was immediately met at the table by a cute, young, blue-eyed, blonde waitress who was all smiles. "I love a man in uniform," she said, looking Tony in the eye. Tony was seated in a booth facing the door. Whether she was kidding or not, Tony didn't know. Women loved to tease a cop in uniform. He didn't care. He wasn't interested. He knew exactly what he wanted, and he had Yolanda. Mickey slid in the seat across from Tony.

"The only thing better than a man is uniform is two men in uniform. What can I get you, gentlemen?"

"We're both going to have coffee," Mickey said.

"Make that three coffees."

Yolis sat down next to Tony. She slid close.

Tony didn't put their code 7 or their location out over the radio. He wondered how Yolanda knew where they were. As if on cue, Yolanda smiled at Tony. "Don't strain your brain. It's the detective in me." Then she looked at the waitress, "I know what I'm going to have."

The waitress smiled at Yolis and took her order. Mickey and Tony ordered. Before she turned to walk away, the waitress said, "The only thing better than two men in uniform is two men in uniform and a woman." She left their table.

Immediately, Yolis looked at Tony and Mickey. "You guys bring out the best in people, don't you?" She reached down and squeezed Tony's thigh.

"How goes it?" Mickey asked Yolanda.

"Not as quiet for me as it's been for you and your boy, but it's still been quiet. Are you ready for your big move?"

"I hope we're ready. Tammy's been busy busting her cute little behind to get everything packed and ready. Then, on the other end, she's seeing to it that Florida is ready for us."

"Have you made up your mind on a Department?"

The waitress, whose name according to the name tag near her chest was "Cindy," brought their coffee.

"It's more like, has a department decided on me? Actually, Florida has several departments that are actively seeking cops. I have a family friend who is with the Sheriff's Department in Broward County. He said I should have no problem getting on. That is, as long as my partner doesn't do any more damage while we're in HP."

Tony poured creamer and one sugar in his coffee. Jokingly, he said "There is another option. Move to Florida. No state tax, affordable housing, warm weather all year round. Alligators, hurricanes, and troublesome Cubans instead of illegal Mexicans. What more can one ask for?"

Yolanda piped in. "That is another possibility. We need to be open minded."

"Did I hear 'we'?"

"That's a general 'we,' or whatever you call it. You're the teacher."

Mickey held up two hands. "Hold everything, folks. I think we have a new bidder. Are you saying that you would consider leaving the Department to move to Florida and join a police department in Florida?"

"Your former FTO should be given a detective shield. He's quick, real quick."

Mickey laughed. Tony was trying to sort out all this new information. He had a quizzical look on his face when he turned to Yolanda. "Are you serious? Would you really move to Florida?"

She didn't bat an eyelash. "Would you?"

Cindy brought their eats. As she set their plates on the table, she eyed Yolis. “Wouldn’t a foursome be neat?”

Tony got behind the wheel of the unit after code 7. He cruised the Maywood Strip looking for trouble. He found nothing. “So, would you consider moving to Florida?” Mickey asked.

“My tutors have taught me to take one step at a time. I’m doing that. Right now, I suppose anything and everything is on the table. The first thing I have to do, or I should say the first thing my attorney has to do, is negotiate me a good severance package.”

“When do you expect to know about that?”

“This coming week.”

“Would Yolis go?”

Tony smiled. “You heard that for the first time just as I did. Would I like it? Yes, I’d love it. I don’t know if she’s screwing around or if she’s serious.”

“Are you serious?”

“What the hell is this—the Trump-Clinton debates? Hell, yes, we’re serious. As serious as your cigarette addiction.” Tony pointed to an older red Mustang. “That clown just ran that stop sign. Let’s give him a look.”

Mickey put the location and the plate out, in that order. Tony lit him up. He made the stop under a streetlight on westbound Slauson Avenue. Tony contacted the driver. “I need your license, registration, and insurance, please. You ran the light on 53rd.”

The guy was dressed in slacks and sport shirt. Sitting next to him was a blonde in a short red skirt that almost matched the color of the Mustang. “You’re right. I was talking to my friend.” He indicated the female by pointing to her.

“Is there anything in the car that doesn’t belong in the car? Weapons? Drugs? Bazookas?”

“Nothing. Just us. My license is in my pocket. The registration and insurance card are in the glove compartment. Is it all right to get them?”

"Give me your license first, please." Mickey was now at the passenger door. He was talking with the blonde.

The driver complied. Now you can get me the registration and the insurance. Tony and Mickey both watched carefully as he reached into the glove box. He handed Tony the license and registration.

Everything looked code 4 to Tony. "Are we code 4, partner?"

"Looks good."

Tony contacted dispatch. He put out a code 4. He stepped back to the passenger door of the unit. Mickey was still talking with the blonde. "22 Adam. Advise when you're clear for a L1/Want 9 on one."

"Go ahead 22 Adam."

Tony gave dispatch the information on the driver's license. He waited. 22 Adam. 10-35."

"Go ahead with your 10-35."

"Your subject, Julio Gomez Guerrero Parades, comes back with a fifty-thousand-dollar warrant out of Bellflower for FTA. His license is suspended. I'll roll a second unit."

"Copy that, dispatch. Thank you."

Mickey held his position at the passenger door. He watched Parades carefully. Tony approached the driver's door, slowly, carefully. His hand was on his holstered weapon. "Sir, I need you to step out of the car, please. Please keep your hands where I can see them."

"Can I ask why?"

"Sir, I need you to step out of the car slowly. please. I need you to keep your hands where I can see them, please. I'll explain everything in a minute."

Parades complied. Tony held onto the guy's belt and walked him to the curb. "Please put your hands behind your head and spread your legs. At this time, you are not under arrest." Tony slapped one handcuff on the right wrist and pulled the hand down. He then pulled the left hand down and cuffed Parades left wrist.

"You just said I'm not under arrest."

"You're not. At this point, this is for officer safety." Tony patted him down carefully. He was clean. "Have a seat on the curb, please. Put your feet out in front of you and cross your right ankle over your left."

Mickey had the blonde out of the Mustang. He was checking her ID just as Yolis rolled up to back them. Yolis walked over to Mickey. "Do you want me to pat her down while you run her?"

"Sure. Thanks." Mickey examined her California ID card. "Hang on, Yolis."

Tony looked down at Parades. "You have a warrant out of Bellflower for failure to appear. Do you know anything about that? Your license is suspended."

He nodded. "A couple of months ago I didn't have the money to pay a ticket. So, I didn't go to court. That's what it's gotta be. Am I going to jail?"

"We have a twenty-thousand-dollar threshold. Anything more than that and we arrest. Stand by a minute."

Tony called dispatch. He asked dispatch to contact the Bellflower Sheriff to see if they'd come to HP to pick up Parades, what the warrant was for, and to make certain that it was still a "live" warrant. If the answer was yes, they'd go 10-15 with him. Otherwise, they'd most likely cut him another ticket for the FTA.

Mickey pulled Yolis aside. He showed her the blonde's ID. The picture on the California ID card did not resemble the blonde. The ID said she was Carl Nethers out of Pomona. "What's you real name, ma'am? No games. Honesty goes a long way here."

"Carl Nethers, just like it says."

"Where do you live?"

What he said matched what was on the ID. "Are you a male?"

She nodded. Tony smiled. Yolis laughed. "Are you his girlfriend or did he just pick you up?"

"I'm his girlfriend."

Tony handed Yolis the ID. "Run him for me, would you? I'll pat him down. Anything on you I need to know about before I pat you down?"

Carl shook his head. Carl was cute. Damn hard to tell. "Put your hands behind your head and interlace your fingers, please. Spread your legs," she ordered. He was at least 5'9". He was clean. "Have a seat on the curb next to your friend."

Mickey watched the duo. Yolis and Tony stepped off to the side. "She's clean. No record, no wants, no warrants, no license."

Dispatch called Tony on his cell. The warrant was for FTA on a traffic matter. Bellflower was too busy chasing calls to send a Deputy to pick Parades up at HP. Tony walked over to the couple. He stepped in front of Parades. "Bellflower won't come for you. We'll cite you out in the field. You're driving on a suspended, so we're going to impound your car. We're going to give you another cite for driving on a suspended."

Yolis said, "I'll start the 180."

Mickey said, "I'll write the cites and watch them."

Tony inventoried the Mustang for the 180 Yolis was writing. That left Tony and Mickey with only one report to write for the night—so far.

Parades asked Mickey, "How long are you taking the car for?"

"Probably thirty days. I'll ask my partner."

"Do you have someone who can pick you up?"

"We'll probably take a cab."

Tony finished inventorying the Mustang. He walked over to Yolis' unit. She was completing the CHP 180. "Make a note on the 180, please—the spare in the trunk of the Mustang is flat. Nothing else noteworthy."

"Got it." Yolis smiled. "How about we send them over to Norm's? The waitress said she wanted a foursome."

Tony didn't understand.

Yolis explained. "He/she, the 'stang's driver, and the waitress. That's four!"

Lawyer Up!

It wasn't until noon on Wednesday that . Tony finally got the call he was waiting for. It was from his attorney. "I've got news for you."

The students were back in the dorm and Tony was enjoying a cup of coffee thinking about his girlfriend. Before he responded to the lawyer, he said, "You said news; you didn't say good news or bad news, just news."

Attorney Bestuss laughed. "That's for you to determine, Tony. They're offering you three years' service, which will give you the necessary time and age to retire. That's not going to give you what you'd get if you hung in there for the full term, or close to it, but it's better than an asp in the back of the legs. They upped the buyout to $65,000."

"How about medical? If I retire, I get no medical." Tony had a package in mind. "I want five years, full medical for life, for myself and any family I may have and $100,000 buyout."

"I doubt you'll get it."

"Then they can shove that asp up their collective ass."

"I'll give it a try. You're making me work. I'd better not get a damn traffic ticket the rest of my life."

Yolanda didn't have to work until this evening. Tony called her. He could tell by the sound of her voice that she had been sleeping. "Hey, gorgeous. How's the prettiest cop in California?"

"Awake. Hey, babe. What's hap'nin'?"

"I just got a call from Attorney Bestuss. Corrections offered me a package. I don't like it."

"I like your package. As a matter of fact, I love your package. If you and your package were here right now, I'd unwrap it." There were several seconds of silence. "What's the offer?"

"Three years of time, $65,000 cash payout. I want five years, $100,000, and paid medical for life for me and my family."

"You have no family."

"If you and I keep playing around the way we have been, we may have a family. Anyway, I told the attorney to take a shot for me." Tony scratched at the stubble on his face. He had to shave. "Are you serious about Florida, angel?"

"I'm open. You and I can discuss it. My point is, and I don't know why I'm so open with you, I don't want you in one state and me in another. I want to be with you."

"Me, too. Babe, I've got to get in gear. I have an appointment with a girlfriend who is taken her orals for the Sheriff tomorrow. I promised her I'd practice with her and throw some questions at her. I'll give you a shout after that and before work."

"Sounds good, angel. I love you." Tony was shocked that those three little words actually came out of his mouth. He was even more shocked at Yolanda's response.

"I love you too, babe."

JFK became a strange place to work. Knowing that one way or another Tony was not long for the facility made him sort of a lame duck. Even though only a few of the "suits" were aware of the situation, Tony knew that anything he started, he wouldn't be able to finish. There was frustration for Tony in that. Major-league frustration.

Tony called a couple of students into his office and reviewed their credits toward graduation with them. He talked with a few students who had been kicked out of class. He helped close out student transcripts for counselors who were buried and were trying to give kids their transcripts before they left JFK. Without a properly completed transcript, it was impossible for the incoming school to properly place a student. His probation officer usually gave a student two days to return to a school on the "outs."

During the rest of the week, Tony did little but classroom re-entry conferences, student transcripts, and covering a classroom for a tardy teacher.

There was sun poking through Tony's sky. It was starting to shine a bit brighter. The ringing of the phone did not stop the sun from shining. It was his attorney. "Tony, Ray Bestuss. How are you?"

"I guess that depends on what you have to tell me."

"I think you are in better shape than you realize. Corrections caves in fast and hard; at least in this case. Here's where we're at. $75,000 buyout, 4 years' service time, and life-time medical. Do you want to play hardball and risk pissing Corrections off to the point they take the deal off the table, or do you want me to seal the deal?"

"That's not a bad offer." Tony thought about Paula and Archer. His water started to boil. "Tell them I'll take 90 and 5. If they won't budge, fine, I'll bite the bullet."

"Thirty-eight caliber or .40?"

"Cute. For what you're charging me, I'll bite 'em both. And I won't write you a cite even if you do twice the speed limit."

"They want to close this out as soon as possible, so I should be able to get back to you some time tomorrow. They want this contract enforceable, if we come to agreement, within thirty days. Doable?"

"Doable."

Tony hadn't been off the phone ten minutes when the phone rang. This time it was Assisting Chief Foxx. "Tony, ACOP Foxx. How are you, my friend?"

"I'm okay, sir. How about you?"

"I'm well, Tony. I have good news for you and better news. Which do you want first?"

"I'll take the good news, sir."

"I was just part of a closed-door meeting with the City Council. They voted to keep the Reserve Program intact, for now. They're going to appoint an ad hoc committee to examine the program and make commendations for the positive and make recommendations for its future. That's says to me, they don't want to lose the program. That's the good news."

"That's great news, sir. And the better news?"

"The better news is that the Department wants to invite you to test for a full-time position."

"Wow, sir, I'm flattered. I was not expecting that. As a matter of fact..."

"Let me be rude and cut you off, Tony. We cannot, and will not, bow to reporters nor will we bow to public pressure. As a reserve, you have distinguished yourself. None of us are perfect. With a little driver training, my personal opinion is that you'll make one hell of a full-time police officer. We'd be lucky to have you."

"Thank you, sir. You really have no idea how much that means to me." Tony was already trying to think ahead. He had to reel himself in. "Can I have a few days to think about that? I have a lot going on and I need a few days, sir."

"No problem, Tony. No rush. You're still part of the team. Let me know when you've made a decision. Please let ME know. I'm the one who's going to handle this."

"You got it, sir. You made my year. Thank you, sir."

Tony felt like a balloon about to burst inside. He wanted to call Yolanda. He wanted to call Mickey. He wanted to tell Paula to shove her job. He wanted to tell Archer how much damage he was doing to kids and then he wanted to punch him in his ugly mouth.

Tony thought about the dropped pen, about the Serenity Prayer, and about responsibility and accountability. A lot of people stuck their necks out for Tony. He didn't want to show them disrespect. He had to first focus on what was in front of him. That would be Corrections' offer. If the calls had come in the opposite order, Tony might have made a snap decision. God sometimes works in strange and mysterious ways. But Tony now believed God was sitting on his shoulder and he had one awesome sense of humor.

The next night, as the sun was setting and Tony and Yolanda were sitting on his couch, he turned to her. "I've got some decisions to make, and I'd like your input."

Yolanda smiled. "I'd love to help. What decisions?"

"My attorney called today. Corrections has upped the offer to 5 years, $85,000, and full medical for life, including family. It's as good a deal as I think I'll get. The only other option is to drive to hell and back on the 5 each day and pound the crap out of my Vette."

"It sounds like you already made your decision." Yolis squeezed Tony's hand.

"I'd like your input."

"Before you put Archer on his ass, I think you need to get away from that situation. You can do yourself major damage if you explode just once. From the things you've been telling me, sometimes I think Archer is pushing you so that you will go crazy."

"In other words, you agree that I should take their offer and tell them to shove the job."

"I wouldn't burn my bridges, but I would move on."

"Okay, one down." Tony kissed Yolis on the mouth. LT, who was lying at their feet, barked.

"Jealous, aren't we?" Yolis said to LT. He barked again.

"That leaves the PD."

"I know the City Council, with reservation, gave their nod to the Reserves. I was at the meeting. I was one of several officers who spoke in favor of continuing the program. I don't understand your decision."

"The ACOP called me earlier this week. He offered me an opportunity to put in for full time."

Yolis lit up like the corner liquor store neon sign. "That's awesome! You have nothing stopping you. Take the buyout, then you're free to start another career."

"I couldn't agree more."

"So?"

"What about Florida?"

"What about it?"

"When you were trying to put the make on that waitress in Norm's and the subject of Florida popped up, you said 'we.' I'm not yet a dick but that leads me to believe that you might be interested in a move to Florida."

"Let's understand a couple of things," Yolis smiled. "First, the only one I want to 'make' is you. Second, you are a dick. And I like dick. ONLY dick and only your dick. Now, Officer, are you asking the lady if she would consider moving to Florida with you?"

LT looked up at both Tony and Yolis. "Of course, you're coming with us," Tony assured the Lieutenant. "You're part of this team."

"I'm waiting for an answer."

"Yup. I'm asking if I move to Florida, would you come?"

"I'd love to. But it's not that simple."

"Here's what's simple: If you don't want to go, I'm not going. I want to be where you are."

"I love you, babe."

"I love you too, angel."

At the same time, they looked at LT. "And we love you, too."

After a brief pause, Yolis asked, "How would something like that play out?"

"It's probably easier for me to make the move than for you. My popularity with FLACOE is lower than Mexico's peso. It's either HP for me or Florida. It might be kind of fun to take a shot of Florida. If we don't like it, we can always come back."

"True."

"The cost of living is a hell of a lot cheaper. Housing is affordable. No state tax. A lot of positives. According to Mickey, we should be able to get picked up by a PD."

"*You* should be able to get picked up."

"I checked with Mickey. You'll probably have an easier time than a male. They're looking for women."

"Nice. What would you do with your house?"

"Good question. I could either sell it, lease it, or rent it. Housing prices are going up. I hate to sell it. I could rent or lease it for more than my mortgage. I'd hire a property management firm to handle the property. The hassle is moving all this stuff."

"I have nothing keeping me here." Yolis tucked her legs under her and slid close enough to Tony so that their knees touched. "I'm liking the idea. Do I get to sleep on it?"

"Only if you sleep on me." They got off the couch.

Tony telephoned Paula from work on Wednesday. He said, "I'll take the deal."

"I'm glad for you, Tony. I think, under the circumstances, it's for the best. I want to thank you for everything you've done for the kids, for the school, and for Corrections." She took a breath. "When will be your last day? I'd like to plan a little something."

"Give me a week after the papers are signed."

"That's fine, Tony. In the meantime, please keep it low key. The terms of the agreement are confidential, and I wouldn't say anything to anyone until the Board approves the deal."

"Sure." Tony hung up. He had mixed emotions about leaving, but he had high expectations for a full-time position at either HP or in Florida. He had even higher expectations for Yolanda and him.

Don't Get Pissed, Get Even!

Tony turned on the computer and opened his email. He was concentrating on something else. He had a score to settle in HP. He wanted to do it. It was wrong. Dead wrong. But...

There was a kid who was an HP "shot caller" locked up at JFK. He was the one who made all the decisions for the local gangs. If a drug deal went down, he orchestrated it. If a chop shop opened in HP, it was with his approval, and he took his cut. If it were hands-off someone, he put out the word and that was that. If you wanted someone taken out, you got his approval.

In the middle of first period, Manuel Ortega, "Little Manny," was in Tony's office, comfortably sitting in a leather chair next to the office door.

Tony and Ortega had history. It was the second time he had been doing a "tour" at JFK. He and Tony got along. They seemed to understand each other. "Little Manny" was respectful, cooperative, kept out of trouble, and did reasonably well in school. He was three months shy of his eighteenth birthday when he was busted in Bell on a bullshit charge, supposedly assaulting a cop. He didn't. Tony knew the story.

The kid was on the scene of an armed robbery, but he didn't do what the cops said he did. They wanted Ortega, they lied, they got him. End of story.

Tony wanted something. Little Manny, who was 5'11" and built like a steam roller, could give it to Tony for a price. Tony had to decide whether he wanted to pay the price. Tony thought about a lot of things. He thought about the PD. He thought about Florida. He thought about Mickey. He thought about LT. He thought mostly about Yolanda. He decided to take it one step at a time.

"How goes it, Manuel?"

“Pretty good, sir. Disneyland ain’t all that bad. Considering I’m here on some humbug bullshit, I can pull the time. What’s up?”

“Just wondering how you’re doing?”

“I had a visit from Mom Sunday. You know she lives in HP so it ain’t easy for her to get here. But when she can, she always makes it. I feel bad for her. But it is what it is.”

“I have a question for you, Manny. A few months back, a dog was tied to a railroad track. Do you know what I’m talking about?”

Manny nodded. “There were some very bad feelings over that one. I almost evened that score.”

“Supposing I wanted to even ‘that score.’ Could you help?”

Manny scratched the right side of his neck, which was tatted with HP and a heart next to it. “I could. WIIFM?”

W-I-I-F-M, or ‘what’s in it for me,’ is what the kids asked the POs when the probation officer wanted some information from them. In other words, what do I get in return?

“An early out.”

“Can you really make that happen?”

“Manny, Manny, Manny. How long have we known each other? If a cop can bust your ass on a bogus charge, I can get you an early out.”

“Can I ask how?”

“Not really. Trust me.”

“Exacto, Mr. Farrina. What for what?”

“The guy who tied the dog to the tracks gets the same treatment. The week after that happens, maybe two, you’re outta here. You’re back in HP and you’re taking care of Mom.”

“Word?”

“Word.” They bumped fists. “It needs to happen during the week, and it needs to happen in the next two weeks.”

Manny smiled. “You’re a good man, Charlie Brown.” Manny stood up.

“Right back at you,” Tony told him. He called him back to class.

When Manny was on this way back to class, Tony closed the door and sat at his computer. He had a picture of LT sitting on the couch at home as his computer wallpaper. Tony looked at it. “This one’s for you, LT. This one’s for you, buddy.”

The very second Tony made that ugly deal, he forced another decision. Tony wrestled with this ever since that dog was tied live to the tracks. He couldn’t get the picture out of his head. Working both sides of the street, so to speak, had its advantages. Tony couldn’t accept what had occurred. He had to get word out on the street that certain things were unacceptable. This was one of them. Tony wouldn’t and couldn’t get credit for settling the score. That was fine by him. If it started a minor gang war, so much the better. Less filth to clean up. That’s the way the streets worked and that was something Cleveland Archer and his gang of ACLU attorneys didn’t understand.

Tony’s office phone rang. It was Mrs. Clarke. She wanted to know if Tony had time to see a student about school credits.

“Sure. Send him down, please.”

***

Beginning Friday night, Tony had a busy schedule, and he was excited by it. He was in the locker room at HP, out of the shower and in uniform by 1800 hours. He cleared briefing by 1900 hours. He and Mickey were partnered up, which was outstanding as far as Tony was concerned because there were a few things he wanted to run by Mickey. The extra bonus was that Yolanda was working.

The first hour was quiet. Mickey drove and cruised the Maywood Strip. They performed one traffic stop to inform the driver he had a busted taillight. That was the extent of their enforcement duties for their first hour on the street.

This gave Tony a chance to grill Mickey about Florida. “Do you think I would have a shot at a Florida Department?”

“I can almost guarantee it. And before you ask, so would Yolis. As a matter of fact, she would probably have a better shot than you.

She's damn better looking. Are you two serious about Florida?"

"It's down to Florida or HP. I look at it this way. If I stay here, I'll never know if I would have liked Florida. If we go to Florida, and we don't like it, or it doesn't work out, we can always come back. The thing is that Yolanda and I want to be together. And, if we were that far apart, partner, I'd miss you."

"The hell you would. You just want someone to keep you out of trouble." Mickey drove away from the Strip and went west on Gage. "I don't know if you're aware, but the Florida police car you'd be driving for the first year has training wheels."

Tony nodded. "And your Glock shoots blanks."

"Let's head back to the barn. I have to use the head." Mickey drove another mile and a half then turned south on Miles Avenue. He was almost at the Station when Tony spotted two occupants driving southbound in a beat-up Chevy pickup truck. Both brake lights were out.

"Light 'em up." Tony put out the plate. Now they were just south of the Station.

Dispatch brought Tony back to reality. "Your vehicle is 10-35. It's a Newton stolen." Dispatch gave a vehicle description. "All units Clear the air for a felony traffic stop. All units go to tac two."

Tony took a breath, held it, and let it out slowly as he had been taught in the Academy. Mickey had already lit them up; otherwise, they'd wait for two more units to get into position. The truck pulled to the side of the street and came to a stop. Mickey pulled in behind it, off-setting the car. Within two minutes, two marked units were on either side of Mickey's car, including Yolis' unit.

Mickey stood behind the driver's door, mic in his left hand, Glock in his right. Tony was at the passenger door, Glock aimed at the truck. Backup was at the ready.

Mickey keyed the mic. "Driver, put your hands on the steering wheel. Passenger, put your hands on the dash. I want you to listen carefully so you don't get hurt. Driver, with your left hand, throw the keys out the window. Do it NOW!"

The driver complied.

"Now driver, exit the car. Keep your hands where we can see them. Any sudden move may get you hurt. If you don't do exactly as you're told, we will release the dog."

Tony played his recording of the barking Shepherd.

"Using your left hand, driver, open the door and get out of the truck. I want to see both hands. If I don't, we release the dog." Tony again played the barking-dog recording.

The driver stepped out of the truck. "Now, slowly, with your left hand, lift up your shirt and slowly turn all the way around." Again, the driver complied. The tall, thin Mexican appeared to be unarmed. "Facing away from me at all times, back up toward the sound of my voice." The driver did as he was told. Slowly, facing away from the officers, he began backing up toward Mickey's voice. He was less than fifteen feet from Mickey when he suddenly turned and bolted in a southeasterly direction.

Yolis yelled, "I got him." She jumped into her unit and went after Speedy Gonzales. Tony and Mickey stayed with the stolen and the passenger.

The secondary unit took off to assist Yolis. Mickey put it out but didn't get to finish. Yolis caught up with Not-So-Speedy Gonzales on the northwest corner of Florence Avenue and Miles Avenue. They had him in custody within two minutes of his attempt to flee. Now they could add resisting arrest to the GTA and whatever contraband they found in the truck.

The passenger followed directions to a tee. When they had him on the ground, just before Tony slapped the cuffs on him, he said in very broken English, 'No dog, no dog.'

"No dog," Tony assured him.

"Where's the dog? Where's the dog?"

Tony stood him up. "He's home sleeping."

Mickey searched the truck but didn't need a detective's badge to know that there had to be contraband in the stolen vehicle. He guessed gun and drugs. He was wrong. He found no gun. He found enough grass to nail the driver with the added charge of possession for sales. Mickey had Tony search the truck again to make sure he didn't miss anything. He had Tony take pictures of the contraband, exactly where it was found.

One of the assisting officers filled out the CHP 180.

Yolis was dragging her collar by the arm. He was yelling that the handcuffs were too tight. "The cell you're going to be in for a couple of years is going to be too tight." Then she said something to him in Spanish. When she finished, he glared at her and spit on the ground.

Tony walked over to the trunk of her unit where Yolis had the suspect bent over and was searching him. "What the hell did you say to him that pissed him off?"

"I told him that his asshole was tight right now but after a couple of weeks in the pen, it would be nice and loose." She smiled.

In classic police terms, an arrest like this, is usually simple and straight forward. The police report can be a cut and paste. Some officers made it just that. This case, because it involved five officers, different officers making the arrest, an attempted-resisting arrest, contraband in the stolen truck, and a passenger who might or might not be chargeable depending on how bright the idiot was, was known as a "cluster fuck" in police parlance. Among other things, all the officers would have to read the report and agree on its substance.

This night, for Mickey, Yolis and Tony had just begun. It was back to the Station to book and question their prisoners, book the evidence, and, if time permitted and things were quiet, begin their report. The remaining officers would wait for HP Tow to come for the stolen truck. "Tony, mark that truck a hold for prints, please."

Between Mickey, Yolis, and Tony, they managed to get the evidence booked before dispatch put out a call of a possible attempted suicide in the Maywood Strip. Four units raced to the scene; among the units rushing code were Mickey, Tony, and Yolis.

They arrived at the scene within four minutes of the call. There was one unit already on scene. Mickey and Tony approached the officer. "Frank," Mickey asked, "what have we got?"

"Three nights ago, this guy's baby mama was killed in a gang shooting in Bell Gardens. She got caught up in the crossfire. Neither Fernando nor his wife were bangers. They were both hard-working second-generation Americans who were trying to get by. He worked two jobs.

"Dispatch talked with him briefly by phone. He's drunk and threatening to kill himself. He says if we enter the house, he'll do himself."

"Where's the baby?"

"The baby's in Bell Gardens with the wife's mother."

"Anybody else in the house?"

"According to what he told dispatch, he's alone."

"What's his weapon of choice?"

"A kitchen knife."

"Any guns in the house?"

"We don't know."

"How many entrances?"

"Two. Front and back."

"Do we know where he is in the house?"

"No. I wanted to wait for more units before I started sneaking around."

"Good call."

"How's his English?" Mickey lit a cigarette.

"According to dispatch, better than hers."

"Do you know his phone number?"

Frank flipped open his notepad. He read the number to Mickey who punched it in his cell phone. "Take Tony and case the house. Be careful. See if you can narrow down his whereabouts in the house.

Also, see if there is a loose screen and open window, a point of entry other than the front or back door."

Mickey walked as few feet to where Yolis was talking to a few neighbors. "Got anything?"

"Just that he is a well-liked, hardworking family man who lost it after his wife was killed."

"Okay, let's see if we can get a couple of volunteers and a couple of cadets up here for crowd control. I don't want any distractions and, although I doubt we'll get much of a crowd, I'd rather err on the side of caution. Get on that, please. Use your cell. I want this frequency clear. Yellow-tape off the area so no one but our guys have access. I want no interference. I want an ambulance at the ready around the corner."

Mickey called dispatch on his cell. He was granted permission to clear the channel for the Maywood Strip team exclusively. All other units and all other radio traffic was directed to tac two. He then asked dispatch for any updates. There were none. "I'm going to attempt contact."

Mickey dialed the phone number Frank gave him. The phone rang twelve times. No one answered.

Mickey waited exactly two minutes He called again. After the third ring, contact. "What?"

"Fernando," this is Officer Mickey Cassidy, my friend. "I want to help you."

"Then bring my wife back."

"You know if I could, I would in a heartbeat. But what you're doing isn't going to help. What's your baby's name?"

"Fernando Junior."

"Listen, it's bad enough little Fernando has no mom. Do you want him to be without a dad, too? I'll help you get through this. I'll do whatever it takes. You're not alone. Let me help."

"You can't help. It's too late."

"It's not too late. Think about the baby. How old is Fernando?"

"Eight months."

"I bet he is handsome, huh?"

"I appreciate your help but it's better this way. My wife's mother will raise Fernando."

"No. No. No. Fernando, hang in here with me for a minute. Stay with me, buddy."

Tony and Frank returned from checking out the house. Frank whispered to Mickey. "Both front and back doors are locked. The windows and screens are secured. We couldn't find a point of entry. He is seated on the living-room couch. He has a bottle of something or another on the cocktail table that he's drinking from. The living room is in the northwest corner of the house. A small light is on behind the couch. That gives you a good view. Last thing. It's not a knife he's holding. He's got a gun. It looks like a .38."

"Shit." That was a game changer. "Fernando, I'd like to come in and talk with you. What do you think about that?"

"You know," Fernando began, his speech a bit slurred. "I always appreciated the police. I actually wanted to become one. I don't know what happened. But it's too late, mister...mister... What did you say your name was?"

"Officer Cassidy, Fernando. Officer Mickey Cassidy."

"My wife and I worked hard to get what little we have. We didn't break any laws. We respected our country, the USA. We fly the Flag on our porch. We keep the house and the lawn clean. We don't have loud parties. We're Americans. We love God. We go to church. Tell me, why did something like this happen to us? Why?"

Mickey swallowed. "Fernando, I wish I could tell you. I can't tell you. But listen, my friend, this is not the time for this. Your baby needs you. Try it my way. Let me come in the house. Let's talk. I'll let you buy me a drink, buddy."

"I can't live with this pain. It hurts so badly. It hurts."

"I can't imagine what you're going through. I can help you through it. Trust me, Fernando, this is not something you want to do." Mickey was sweating and it was a cool evening. "Think about the baby, Fernando. He needs you." Mickey lit a cigarette. He took two quick hits. He inhaled deeply then blew the smoke toward the heavens.

"I was hoping he would be the first one in our family to go to college. Maybe Rio Hondo Academy. Maybe become a police officer. I would dream that he graduated the Academy; that his mom and I watched him at the graduation ceremony. We watched him. He was so proud. We were so proud. He'd give back to this great country in a small way.

"I'm sorry, Fernando."

Mickey heard one shot. "Take down the door," he screamed. "Get in the house now." His hand was shaking. He got dispatch on the portable. "Get that ambulance here code 3. I think he shot himself."

Depending on how many bodies the coroner had to deal with, it could take him a couple of hours to make the trip to the Maywood Strip. The original units had work to do at the scene. They were not free to leave.

Mickey was standing behind his unit. He was trying to be invisible. Tony stood next to him. The tears streamed down his face. He balled up his right fist and suddenly slammed it on the trunk lid. Mickey hit it with such force, he put a dent in it. The side of his hand immediately swelled. He shook his hand. "Damn, damn, damn! Why is it the good die so young?"

The team at the suicide scene finally made it back to the Station at 0430 hours. They had to piece together the suicide report, which was remarkably straight forward. Notifications were more difficult, but that was not going to be the job of the original officers who arrived on scene. Mickey, Tony, and Yolis still had the stolen truck report to complete. They would be working overtime this morning.

Wednesday afternoon, Tony received a call from his attorney that Corrections' offer was solidified. It was signed, sealed, and would be delivered to him within three days. He expected that, by the end of next week, he would no longer be a FLACOE employee.

Yolis, Mickey, and Tony sat down for dinner in Tony's dining room. It was a working dinner. Yolis did the cooking; Mickey and Tony tried to assist. It didn't work out too well. Yolis finally told them to get the hell out of her kitchen and go play with LT in the backyard.

They exited the house gladly, followed by LT and the Frisbee he held between his teeth. Mickey and Tony worked up more of a sweat throwing the Frisbee than LT did chasing it. They were having fun, working up an appetite, and getting negative thoughts out of their mind. When Yolis finally called them for dinner, they were more than ready to eat.

LT was fed first, then the feast began. "This is probably the only time you'll see a Mexican fix wop food. This will be the best lasagna you ever tasted."

Tony uncorked a bottle of red wine. Mickey spooned out the lasagna. Yolis passed the garlic bread. "It's too bad Tammy had to fly down to Florida to check out your house. We'll have to save her some dinner."

They ate and talked. "Are you two really serious about making the move?"

Tony spoke first. "I need a change. It'll be good for me." Tony bit into the lasagna and chased it with a sip of red wine. "Damn—brains, beauty, and a cook and a half. Great lasagna, angel. Out of this world."

"Delicious, Yolis. Tony is one lucky guy."

"I'll second that. Here's the deal. I have another week, give or take, with Corrections. I've got a friend who works property management. He has a young family that wants to lease my place for a year, furnished. He'll then decide whether or not he wants to buy it. His payments will more than cover my monthly mortgage. That puts a few more bucks in my pocket, plus my FLACOE pension won't be taxed in Florida. If you can get me in with a department, and if you can help get my gorgeous cook into a department, we'll be on top of the world."

Mickey helped himself to more garlic bread. "He looked at Yolis. "Are you sure you want to do this?"

"Dead certain. Tony and I have discussed it. We can always come back. We're both welcome back. The only thing left to do is for me to put in my papers."

"Here's a thought. Do you guys have a timeframe?"

Tony responded first. "I'm free to leave any time."

Yolis said, "I've already spoken with the ACOP. He knows I'm considering a move. I just need to let him know when I'm out of Dodge."

Mickey said, "We have a thirty-day window. If we can coordinate this, we can caravan to Florida."

Tony looked at Yolis. She nodded and passed the lasagna platter to Tony. "That should work, Mickey. That should work well."

"And until you two find a place, you're welcome to stay with us. The only thing I ask in return is that once a week Yolis cook us all lasagna and garlic bread."

"Done."

Mickey raised his wine glass. "Here's to new beginnings."

"To new beginnings."

"To new beginnings."

"I'm going to go outside to have a quick smoke. I'll leave you two alone. Is that safe?" Mickey walked out before with Yolis or Tony could answer.

Tony hated packing. But what had to be, had to be. He took his time packing his school office belongings. Numerous times, Tony stopped to savor memories. It was time to move on.

Yolanda was at Tony's house when he arrived home from JFK. She and LT greeted Tony at the door. Lieutenant was a gentleman and allowed Yolanda to hug and kiss Tony before he did. "How was your last school day?"

"Bittersweet. They threw me a going-away lunch, complete with cake that said, 'THANKS FOR EVERYTHING, Tony. Best of luck in your new life.' Paula said a couple of nice words which I thought she might choke on. I shed a genuine tear or two."

They walked to the dining room. "Now you have to let it go."

"I know. I will."

"I know you and your letting go will be like handcuffing a gorilla. I made you a drink. Dinner will be ready in about an hour. Any ideas what we can do to kill an hour?"

Tony had ideas. They took their ideas to the bedroom. They were able to kill forty-five minutes. On their backs, holding hands, savoring the moment, Tony asked, "Are you excited about Florida?"

"Very. I'm most excited about being with you."

"Me too. I feel like I'm twenty-two."

"You're not?"

"Funny. A rental truck can haul the trailer with the Vette behind it. Since we're buying new furniture in Florida, we really don't have that much to pack. Now that I'm off, I can start my packing."

"I gave notice to my manager and to the Department so we're good to go in two weeks. This is going to be fun."

Early Monday morning, Tony went to JFK to pick up the last of his belongings. After making certain he left nothing behind in his office, he met Mickey for breakfast.

Mickey was outside the coffee shop smoking a cigarette when Tony arrived. Tony stood next to Mickey while he finished his smoke. They walked into the Three Meals Coffee Shop together and seated themselves.

Both men were smiling. Tony spoke first. "Why the shit-eating grin?"

"I guess now that decisions have been cemented, I feel better. The house in Florida is ours. The house here is in escrow. Most of our stuff is packed. We're ready." Mickey ordered coffee when the waitress came to their table.

"Me, too, please."

"Are you and Yolanda ready to go?"

"You gotta be kidding. We're working on it, but we have a way to go. We're excited, too; nervous, but excited. I guess the biggest unknown is signing on with a department once we get there."

"I told you, partner, don't sweat the small stuff. Florida is looking for cops. You two are a shoe in." The waitress brought their coffee.

The Department's going-away party was held in the banquet room of the Furious Flame Restaurant in Whittier. Instead of having three individual parties, they threw one big bash for Yolanda, Mickey, and Tony. Neighboring departments took over HP Police Department duties so the Department could enjoy the night—and enjoy they were doing.

A huge blue banner read: "DON'T GO AWAY MAD, JUST GO AWAY!" Another banner read, "BEWARE OF ALLIGATORS!" A third banner read, "FLORIDA IS A SMOKE-FREE STATE!" Of course, one banner was created for each of the retirees.

Those who were scheduled to work later that night, were restricted to soft drinks, tea, or coffee. The three celebrants were off duty, so it was not a liquor-free zone for them.

Mickey and Tammy danced for a minute then walked outside to the pleasant weather so Mickey could enjoy a cigarette. Tony and Yolanda danced close.

There was enough food to feed all the inmates at Twin Towers jail twice. One cake wasn't enough. They ordered individual cakes. Not only were many HP dignitaries in attendance, but police personnel from adjoining departments made appearances. The trio was popular and that was made obvious by those who made it a point to show their presence.

Just before midnight, the band suddenly stopped playing. A uniformed officer wearing Bell Garden patches approached the stage. He took the mic in hand and yelled, "You guys were told an hour ago to knock the noise down to a low roar. Now you're going to get cited, and we're impounding your shit. Since you have nothing better to do, go enjoy a beer!"

The Bell Gardens officer walked to the end of the stage. "Mickey, if you can stop smoking long enough to get your ass up front, get your ass up front!"

Mickey followed directions. The officer looked at a stagehand. "If we can lift the curtain, please." As the curtain came up, three covered easels were on display. One was marked with an M, another with a Y, and the third with a T. "I know that Mickey passed all the tests at Rio Hondo to make it to our Department. I know this because I helped him cheat to pass his tests. While I sat on one side of Mickey to help him cheat, Mario Buerro sat on the other side and helped him.

"I say that to say this. Do not blame me for what is about to be uncovered. Sketch artist Buerro is responsible for these; blame him.

"Mickey, if you haven't figured it out yet, the covering with the M belongs to you. Please walk over to it and stand next to it but keep your damn hands off it." Mickey walked over to it.

"Drum roll, please. Mickey, go ahead and uncover it."

Mickey tore the paper off the 42 x 34-inch Mario Buerro painting. It was a Ford Crown Victoria police car in all its splendor. On the door were the words "HOLLOW POINT POLICE." Instead of the words "TO PROTECT AND SERVE" on the rear quarter panel, Mario painted, "TO SMOKE AND SMOKE AND SMOKE."

"Mickey, from all of us, this is something for you to remember us by. We used to have an expression in our close circle of Departments. We had, obviously, to change that expression. That expression used to be: 'We all step on our dick once in a while.' Mickey stepped on his dick so often, we thought about changing his name to Richard.

"In all seriousness, Mick, you're one hell of a cop and one hell of a guy. Enjoy the east, enjoy Florida, see if you can get your first felony arrest. Stay away from the alligators and be safe, buddy. You're going to be missed."

The crowd burst into a combination of laughter and applause.

Mickey walked up to the stage. Still laughing, he grabbed the mic. "First of all, Mario, I have to ask, 'How the hell can you paint such a beautiful picture of a Crown Vic, better than when it came off the assembly line, when you can't draw a damn sketch that helps us catch a suspect?'" Mickey took a long taste of the cold Corona in his left hand, as everyone laughed.

"Next, to all you Keystone cops out there, it's high time you left police work and volunteered for crossing-guard duty. It's about as far as you can walk at one clip. For the brass who are here, you guys really know the score; and you lost. Police work isn't sitting behind your desk in a suit and tie playing with yourself while you look at porn on the taxpayer-paid computer.

"And finally..." Mickey took another hit off the Corona. "And finally, to those Sergeants who red-lined every goddamned report I turned in, screw you and that red fucking pencil you're in love with. It's probably as skinny as your dick!"

He took another drink from the Corona. Then he lit a cigarette. "The sign says no smoking. Somebody in here with balls, go ahead, arrest me.

"Seriously guys...and gals. You're going to really be missed. You taught me, you trained me, you busted my balls. I love you all for it. Be safe and when you're bored, think about me and that cigarette I'm smoking in the unit."

One Door Closes; Another Door Opens

One of HP's finest took the mic out of Mickey's hand. Carlos Grande was the youngest detective on the force. He was tall, dark, and as solid as a telephone pole. He had an ear-to-ear grin, was as affable as a cop could be, and as tough as starving pit bulls when pissed off. He was well liked by his fellow officers. "It's now time to move on to the better looking of our department. That would be none other than Ms. Yolis.

"When Yolis first joined our department, I have to admit that I felt she couldn't handle the job. After all, how the hell could a woman her size handle an unruly suspect my size; not possible. Wrong! Wrong! Wrong!

"Three days on the force and a call comes out of a grab-and-run strong-arm robbery of a gold chain on Pacific Boulevard north of Saturn. When I arrived on scene, not three minutes after dispatch put out the call, Yolis has this screaming Adam Henry on the concrete and in handcuffs. The dude's horsepower came back at 5'11" and 185.

"I snapped a picture with my cell phone. It's hanging up in the detective bureau for more than one reason. First, it'll teach me to be open minded. Second, it's proof positive that if you want something badly enough, and you work your ass off for it—although Yolis' ass is still there—you'll probably get it.

"I got the courage up to ask Yolis how she made the collar. Her explanation was that she observed the guy running through the crowd of people on the Boulevard. He was running northbound. She pulled her car to the curb, put out the foot pursuit, and the chase was on. What Adam Henry didn't know was that Yolis was a half-marathon runner. It didn't take her long to close the gap. When she was right behind him, she pushed him and over he went.

When he hit the ground, she got on top of him and tried to cuff the bastard. Of course, he resisted. Yolis reached between his legs and squeezed. He still resisted. She grabbed his balls and squeezed. He still resisted. She put her taser between his legs; he complied." (Laughter.)

"Yolis, center stage, please."

Yolis was beet red, maybe a bit redder. She walked to center stage. Carlos gave her a hug. He looked to his audience. When he located Tony who had a shot of Seagram's in his hand, Carlos asked, "Is it okay if I hug her, Tony? I don't want to fuck with the Italians. Somewhere in your background you might be connected." Everybody laughed, including Tony and Yolis.

"In honor of the service Yolis has given our Department, in honor of Yolis' move to hurricane country, and because we all love her and are jealous of her love for Tony, Yolis, please unveil the Department's going away gift to one of our finest."

Yolis shook her head. "I'm more afraid of this than I am of a gangbanger holding an AK-47." She pulled the brown paper covering off the painting. She thought she'd pee her panties laughing, except that she wasn't wearing any. The painting clearly and vividly depicted Yolis, in uniform, on top of Tony. For reasons left to your imagination, she was attempting to put handcuffs on Tony who was not in uniform and was on his back. Tony's head and face were between Yolis' legs which were spread to either side of Tony's chest. The caption read: "TO EAT AND ENJOY." On the top right side of the painting was LT barking, his tail wagging, and his tongue hanging out.

When the cops stopped laughing, when color returned to Yolis' face, she said, "Isn't this obscenity covered in 311 of the California Penal Code?"

She took the mic from Carlos. "I want to sincerely thank our resident sketch artist Mario for his many talents. Hopefully, you were able to get a hard-on while painting this, although from what I hear without one hundred milligrams of Viagra, that's a problem for you." The half-plastered crew was hysterical.

"I want you all to know how much you will be missed. Some of you covered for me. Most of you helped me through probation. One of you glued a penis and a pair of balls to my locker. That must have been Benny 'cause I hear he has no balls!

"I could not have worked with a better, more professional team who probably have more testosterone between them then the Marines down in Camp Pendleton. So, for Mario and the rest of you who dreamed of getting in these panties," she reached into her pocket. "A very little something to remember me by. I wore these all day." She held up a pair of tiny, pink panties. She tossed them into the audience and all hell broke loose on the floor as every guy in the place jockeyed for those pink beauties. To make certain the Department never forgot Yolis and her service to the community of Hollow Point, in the crotch of those worn pink panties, in black permanent marker, Yolis wrote, "IN AN EMERGENCY CALL 911. MAKE A COP COME!"

Tony knew what was coming. He had to be good natured to accept the razzing, but a buzz wouldn't hurt. He got himself another shot of Seagram's and 7 to chase it. No, he felt he was ready for anything. He wasn't.

Yolis walked on stage and took command of the mic. "Less popular in the male chauvinistic department than females, are reserves. Most reserves don't know shit. Tony knows less." She looked at him and smiled. "He can't even drive anything that doesn't have training wheels on it. And if it had training wheels, he'd still need an FTO to tell him when to turn left, when to turn right, and when the hell to stop for a red light. To help Tony learn to drive, we bought him a tricycle." One of the cops rolled a red tricycle with training wheels onto the stage. "Notice the sticker on the back. It reads 'STUDENT DRIVER. KEEP BACK THREE MILES!'

"Next, we chipped in and bought Tony a traffic light. You'll notice that, instead of red and green, it reads GO, STOP, and YIELD. And finally, to remind Tony that there are other vehicles on the road," Yolis walked over and pulled the paper covering off Tony's painting. "We have a reminder of what happens when you don't yield to oncoming traffic." The picture was of a fire truck t-boning a Crown Victoria black-and-white.

The cops in the audience could not stop laughing; neither could Tony. He walked on stage and took the mic out of Yolis' hand. "Now you know why we don't like females wearing a badge. They screw with you constantly, but you never get laid. And as far as the rest of you are concerned, as a reserve I probably put in more time working twice a week then most of you did working four times a week and overtime. I never saw so many alleys, dead-end streets, back parking lots, and driveways where you can hide a marked unit to avoid work. One of these days the Department's going to get smart and put trackers in the unit, then you're all fucked. And finally, and it hurts to say this, except I have enough liquor in me that I can probably blow a point three. You guys..." Tony walked over and put his arm tightly around Yolis. "...You guys and gals are the greatest.

"My life has become meaningful because you allowed me to work your streets. If you think about it, without police out there to keep the peace, there wouldn't be any streets. I say this with all sincerity, you are the greatest. I have never known better—I have never worked with better. Thanks for giving me the opportunity to work the streets of HP.

"Finally, I'm hopeful of getting a full-time position in Florida. I will be thinking about all of you every day. I'm going to take my trike with me and show it to my FTO in Florida. I'm also going to take Mario's painting with me in case they have fire trucks where we're working. And by the way, Mario, you make a better artist than you do a cop. Give up your day job. Thanks, guys!"

Tony and Yolis were no sooner off the stage than Sergeant Heard walked up to the stage and grabbed the mic. "I hate to interrupt such a joyous occasion, but I just got a call from the Lieutenant. It seems that one of HP's finest, another gangbanger slash dealer has dealt his last drugs and fired his last bullet. One Juan "Crazy Eyes" Perez was found tied to the railroad tracks at Clarendon and Miles. There was a dog collar and a leash tied around his neck. The conductor blew his whistle and Crazy Eyes blew his lunch. A team of detectives is scouring the area searching for body parts."

There was a thunderous applause from every cop in the audience. "If anyone has any idea of the significance of the leash and collar, please let the detective division in on it."

Tony felt a twinge of guilt. On his guilt scale, it registered at 2.0. He walked over to the bar and downed another shot. He no longer felt ANY guilt. From across the room, he caught Mickey's eye. Mickey shrugged. He caught Yolis' eye. Yolis shrugged. Tony wondered what Cleveland Archer would think if he only knew. Then Tony swallowed hard. He muttered to himself, "Fuck Cleveland Archer. Fuck the ACLU."

Thirty days later, August 13th, the caravan to Florida originated in front of Tony's leased house. Mickey and Tammy were in their truck towing a full U-Haul. Yolis and Tony were in their rental truck pulling a second U-Haul. Behind the U-Haul was Tony's Pace Car.

On the back seat, with his head out the window, was LT. He had a cardboard sign tied loosely around his neck. The sign read, FLORIDA OR BUST. The Lieutenant was all smiles.

ABOUT THE AUTHOR

Stuart Cannold was born in Brooklyn in 1946. He grew up on the streets of New York and New Jersey and created his own chaos early on and damn near didn't graduate high school. At age 28, Stu started to turn his life around with the help of some amazing people who refused to throw in Stu's cards.

Stu earned a BA from Franconia College in New Hampshire. While attending Franconia College, Stu, a journalism major, spent a semester as an intern for a southern California newspaper. Although he turned down an offer to work for the newspaper, he returned to California years later and made it his home. He went on to earn a Master's degree in education, attending Oakland University, which was then affiliated with Michigan State.

He earned his administrative credential from Pepperdine University and his Doctorate in Educational Administration from United States International University in San Diego. He graduated from the Cerro Coso Police Academy in 1996.

Stu taught classes for many years for the University of Redlands and Phoenix University. He spent 33-plus years as a teacher and school administrator in Detroit and California.

Stu and his wife Jo, who reside in southern Arizona (and love it), collect classic cars. Three of their vehicles are in the Riverside Resort and Casino's car museum in Laughlin, Nevada. As you might have guessed, one of those cars is a 1930 Ford Model A police car. Another is an authentic 1978 Harley Davidson Police Motorcycle with Sidecar, and the third is a 1957 Ford Thunderbird E-Code with overdrive, a rare bird, and a Gold Medallion winner in the 2019 Thunderbird Concours in Flagstaff.

Stu and Jo own a Camaro B4C CHP car that was featured on page one of Stu's first book, *Blueline of Life and Death.* Their 1974 Cadillac Miller-Meteor Criterion ambulance is a rolling memorial for September 11, 2001. **WE MUST NEVER FORGET.**

Stu is terrified of heights. Second to publishing a novel, Stu wants to overcome his fear of heights and jump out of a plane. Years ago, Stu attempted this feat in California but chickened out. Stu doesn't know the meaning of the word quit and one day promises to make a second attempt at skydiving, this time with a jumpmaster.

Stu and Jo share their house with Princess and LT (or Lieutenant), two Norwegian Elkhounds. It's actually their house. Princess and LT rent space to Jo and Stu.

Years ago, a female friend gave Stu a piece of advice that he swallowed and digested: You never fail until you quit trying. That message is part of this book. From an unhappy kid growing up on the streets of New York and New Jersey to a young adult battling the "elements" in California, Stu's skin fits today. He and Jo couldn't be happier; life is great. Stu is ***Happy, Joyous, and Free.***

ALSO BY STUART CANNOLD

BLUELINE of LIFE & DEATH SERIES

When an officer leaves the station, they have no idea whether they will live through their shift or not. Dangers that were not that prevalent years ago are now everywhere and threaten an officer every day they go to work. While the majority of an officer's time is spent on mediocre calls, they never know if one of those calls will escalate into a life-and-death situation.

- Blueline of Life and Death
- Blueline of Life and Death, Chasing the Money
- Blueline of Life and Death, A Leg Up

The trilogy is available on Amazon or through Stu's website at **5TomPublishing.com**

Made in the USA
Middletown, DE
17 June 2024

55905895R00219